CAMBION'S LAW

ERIN FULMER

CITY OWL
PRESS

This book is a work of fiction. Names, characters, places, and incidents either are products of the author's imagination or are used fictitiously. Any resemblance to actual events or locales or persons, living or dead, is entirely coincidental and not intended by the author.

CAMBION'S LAW
Cambion, Book 1

CITY OWL PRESS
www.cityowlpress.com

Cover Design by MiblArt. All stock photos licensed appropriately.

Edited by Heather McCorkle

For information on subsidiary rights, please contact the publisher at info@cityowlpress.com.

Print Edition ISBN: 978-1-64898-113-5

Digital Edition ISBN: 978-1-64898-112-8

Printed in the United States of America

To Jake, who believed I could do it.

RUN, DEVIL, RUN

I STOLE A GLANCE AT THE TWO HUMANS WAITING WITH ME AT THE COFFEE KIOSK and stifled a groan. If I had my way, I'd make PDAs before six a.m. a first-degree misdemeanor.

Quite a hill to die on, huh? Of course, I'd have to leave the D.A.'s office and run for Congress first, but the pithy single-platform campaign slogans wrote themselves: *Elect Lillian Knight and Make Singles Jogging Safe Again. Stop Criminal Canoodling. Think of the children—and have mercy on the celibate-by-choice cambion lurking uncomfortably behind you in the coffee line.*

Alas, even a half-demon like me didn't have that kind of power. And my powers of glaring didn't stop the middle-aged couple in the cafe's outdoor waiting area from mooning over each other.

I wrapped my arms around myself and set my jaw. This early on a dreary weekday morning, I should have had the park to myself, free from lovestruck tourists and their sloppy, tantalizing energy. And yet, here stood these two grown adults in their puffy jackets, snuggling together like teenagers and harshing the living hell out of my happy place.

Maybe I didn't need a caffeine fix before my run. Never mind the biting Pacific gusts blowing off the choppy gray waves of the strait, the thick fog blanketing the rust-orange span of the Golden Gate Bridge, or the gritty haze that clouded my brain after another sleepless night.

I could live with all of that. San Francisco's fog couldn't rival the Pennsylvania winters I'd grown up with, even after eight years of acclimation. Insomnia and I had an intimate, long-term relationship. And the cold didn't get under my demon-tough skin like the two walking heart-eye emojis in front of me.

I licked my lips and slapped my change on the counter. Oblivious to my jonesing, the lovebirds entwined their hands and leaned into each other, a bulwark of two against the chill. I turned away, but their mutual desire thrummed in the air around me like a pair of plucked guitar strings tuned to one another. Its sweetness settled, thick and cloying, at the back of my throat.

Damn my succubus senses. They didn't help anything, and they never knew when to quit.

The synesthetic song of the human couple's desiderata—the energy of their deep-seated needs and desires—didn't hold any secrets simple human perception would have missed. Still, their two-part harmony tugged at me. I'd have given a limb, maybe two, to turn it off at will, but no one was buying. Swallowing hard, I grasped at straws: stocks, sports, anything unsexy and boring. *The Giants had done well this season, right?*

No good. The desiderata behind me hummed all the louder, a tangible vibration running up my spine like a live wire. I risked another peek over my shoulder and winced. The man had bent toward the woman, the breeze ruffling his salt-and-pepper hair. She tilted her head up, lips parted, face aglow, ready for his kiss.

"Screw this," I muttered, and broke into a run.

The barista's call floated after me. "Quad cappuccino for Lily?"

I didn't stop. Bye bye, six hard-earned dollars I paid for the abandoned drink. Too bad, so sad for my wallet, but it wasn't worth the cost to my peace of mind and my succubus sobriety.

The rhythm of my sneakers on the hard-packed earth of the upper trail beat out a staccato counterpoint to the hiss of the surf and the blood pounding in my ears. About halfway into the grove of cypress and eucalyptus that lined the trail, I hit my stride. The trees blurred into a gray-green smear on either side of me, and the siren call of human desiderata faded away.

And then I tripped over something heavy and dense that lay across the trail and went sprawling face-first into the dirt.

The wind knocked out of me, I lay still for a few seconds, tonguing my split and swelling lip. It leaked a coppery tang tainted with bitter earth into my mouth. My palms stung where I'd flung them out to catch my fall.

I rolled over and the gray sky wheeled above me in a dizzy lurch. Damn it, had I hit my head? A concussion would make this a real banner week. I could heal faster than humans did, but to recover from a serious injury, I would need more than strong coffee. I would have to break a vow I'd made to myself and take kether—human life force, the fuel my powers depended on, transferred by touch and emotional connection from their bodies to mine.

I spat grit and blood, craning my neck around for a glimpse of what had tripped me. A long, pale, haphazard bulk stretched across the trail.

My vision swam, and I squinted. "What the hell?"

I'd run this trail plenty in the dark and never fallen once. I could run it in my sleep, if I managed to sleep at all. The city kept the park well-maintained, but a branch must have come down in the night. Blinking, I propped myself up on my elbows.

Not a tree branch or wayward roots: legs. I'd tripped over a pair of bare legs. They belonged to a body that lay motionless on its back beside me, torso concealed in the underbrush.

I gasped and scrambled crablike away from it, heedless of the sand and gravel grinding into my torn palms. Pushing myself into a crouch, I balanced on the balls of my feet and forced my breath to slow.

It wasn't a corpse, surely—a body, yes, but sleeping or drunk. Lots of homeless people slept in the city parks around here. I had no reason to freak out; just check on them and get back to my run.

My heart begged to differ. It hammered in my chest. I stood, knees wobbly from a rush of adrenaline. The person lying on the trail had shapely, feminine calves. The bare feet had clean, uncalloused soles, its toes slightly turned out, manicured nails painted a soft, sparkling, opalescent pink. The legs wore fashionably faded denim cut-offs.

"Hey, are you okay?" I stepped closer and pushed aside the thick brush with numb fingers. Then I froze, a heavy, prickling coldness expanding from my core.

A grotesque parody of a woman's face stared up at the colorless sky, filmed-over yellow eyes with their snake-like slits of pupils shadowed by the heavy, leonine ridge of her brow. Her bloodless lips stretched over pointed teeth in a gaping, rictus smile. In the bleak light of morning, dark traceries of blue-black veins stood out in stark contrast to the wax-paper skin of her temples.

The thing lying on the trail wasn't human but a succubus. And she was definitely, thoroughly, irrefutably dead.

My professional detachment sidled back in at last, cataloging objective details while the rest of me stood petrified. It transformed the scene before me into a body of evidence, not a body that once breathed and dreamed and spoke.

A crater gaped in the center of her ribcage, leaving it a blackened, corroded mess of flesh and bone. Something—acid, fire, or worse—had eaten away at her, outward from the heart, until her chest cavity collapsed into itself. Blackened shreds of silky lavender fabric clung to the ragged edges of the wound, the remains of a skimpy halter top. Deep within her ruined torso, tarnished metal glinted.

Bile rose, burning and sour in my throat. I reeled back from the body with my hands pressed to my mouth. Even my detachment had its limits. I rubbed my palms on my thighs, paced up the trail away from her and back down. I could just leave. Let the next wave of hapless morning joggers deal with it—that couple back at the Coffee Hut, with any luck.

But no, I had to do the right thing. I had to call it in.

I reached for the work phone tucked snug in my sports armband, then hesitated. Death had wiped away the camouflaging glamour that would have let the dead succubus walk unrecognized among mortals. Calling the police would violate the ultimate taboo of demon culture by letting a human see the true face of a cubine, as demons preferred to call themselves.

Secrecy and survival went hand and hand for us. And while the dead woman had passed beyond such concerns, I had no such luxury. The cops would have a lot of questions, the kind I didn't want asked anywhere near me. They might call in the Feds. The Feds might call in Special Forces. And as the witness who found the body, I would have to face them all.

I turned back toward the corpse and knelt by her side. My attorney training scolded me not to touch the body, that it would contaminate the scene, but a deeper training won out.

We must never let them see us as we are. The soft, resonant voice of my mentor echoed in my memory. I steeled myself with a long, unsteady breath and closed her staring eyes. Her cold lids yielded, powder-dry under my trembling fingers like a dead butterfly's fragile wing. Rigor mortis must not have set in, or perhaps it had dissipated already.

With her golden eyes hidden, she looked a fraction less alien. I shuddered and drew back, wiping slick palms on my legging-clad thighs. Still, my phone slipped in my sweaty hand. Who could I call?

Well, I knew at least one person who'd know what to do about a dead demon. But I'd have to unblock his number first.

I shook my head. I couldn't do it. Instead, I dialed Daniela Rios's number by muscle memory. Hopefully, she hadn't changed it.

The line rang four times before she picked up. "Lily? That you?"

At the note of surprise in her sleepy, slurred voice, I almost lost it. I cradled the phone close to my ear. "Hi, Danny."

"Hi, Sugarbean," she said. "It's been a minute."

"Yeah, sorry to call so early. Did I wake you?"

"Nah." Liar. A rustle and a soft grunt, and then her words came clearer, as if she'd sat upright in bed. "How are you?"

"I'm…" I swallowed hard, switched the phone to my other ear. "I don't know what to do."

A pause. "Are you okay? What happened?"

"I found a body." The words tumbled out in a rush.

"You what—?" Her sharp intake of breath gusted over the line. "A body? Seriously? Where?"

"At Crissy Field. I was jogging and it—she—I think she was murdered, Danny."

"*Murdered?*" She made an inarticulate sound, something between a snort and a curse. "You need to call the police. That goes double for a homicide."

"But you're—"

"I'm an assistant medical examiner." A muffled thump punctuated her words. "*Mierda.* Dropped a boot. Lil, it's not the M.E.'s job to secure a crime scene and you know it. Call the cops."

"I can't," I whispered. "The victim isn't human. You're the only one I can trust not to freak out." Danny was one of three people in the world who knew my secret. I thought it should scare her more, but it never had. She'd always treated me like a person.

When she spoke again, her words came slow and deliberate. "What do you mean she's not human?"

"I mean that I'm standing here staring at a fucking dead demon in the middle of Presidio Park, and the cops are gonna go ballistic."

Another silence fell, heavy on the line. Then, in a changed voice, Danny said, "Holy shit!"

"Yeah, you can say that again."

"Holy *shit*," Danny said, obliging me, and I had to chuckle, like she probably intended. Then she added, "Stay put. I'm on my way. But Lil?"

I exhaled. My legs buckled, and I sat down hard on a handy slab of rock at the side of the trail. "Yeah?"

"I'm sorry. You still have to call it in."

"I know," I said. "Thanks, Danny."

"You got it, Sugarbean," Danny said. "Don't do anything rash before I get there, please. And don't touch anything."

Cheeks hot, I closed the hand that had shut the corpse's eyes, as if hiding an invisible stain. "I won't. Who do you take me for?"

But the line had gone dead. She'd hung up. With a sigh and a shiver, I hugged my arms around my knees and pulled them to my chest. Just me and a nameless dead succubus hanging out together on a frigid San Francisco morning. What a way to start off a grim Wednesday in an already shitty week.

"What are you doing out here?" I asked her still form. "Why, of all the jogging trails in all the world, did you have to die on mine?"

Before today, I hadn't run into any others of my kind in San Francisco. In fact, I only knew one other cubine. But I'd put eight years and a continent between us when I moved out to the West Coast to go to law school. For a while, I'd convinced myself that I'd left the legacy of my own cambion's blood behind with him.

I sighed and took out my phone again.

Guess I couldn't run from my demons forever.

2

FRANKINCENSE AND GRR

THE SFPD PRIDED THEMSELVES IN THEIR QUICK RESPONSE TIME, BUT DANNY still beat them—with coffee, no less. She handed it off to me, careful not to brush my bare fingers with hers.

I cupped the warm drink in both hands. "Thank you." It sounded inadequate, but it was all I could manage.

She shot me an unreadable look. Behind her shuttered expression, her desiderata swelled, a synesthetic wave of sea-salt dissonance and bitter cold. However, heavy footsteps from downslope forestalled whatever she had planned to say.

I slumped. The calvary had arrived with impeccable timing. Puffing a bit from the climb, Detective Edwin Huang glanced from me to Danny and raised an eyebrow. "You sure got here quick, Rios."

I sipped the coffee that Danny had brought me and stayed quiet. I'd worked with Huang before. He was one of the good ones, but too observant for my comfort at the moment.

"I was in the neighborhood." Danny gave him her blandest smile, pulling on a pair of fuchsia exam gloves. Not a bland person, Danny, with her pink spiky hair, combat boots, and Bowie t-shirt peeking out from her half-zipped uniform jacket. She gave it her all, but the smile came off as a faintly feral grimace.

I winced, but Huang didn't question her further. He turned back to me. "And you discovered the body, Miss Knight? Hell of a thing, D.A. as witness. How did that happen?"

I gulped my mouthful of coffee too fast. It scalded my throat, and I coughed. "Jogging," I choked out finally, eyes watering.

Danny squeezed my shoulder and moved past me to the body. "You found her like this?"

"Mostly," I mumbled. "I literally tripped over her."

"Can't have been here long." Hands jammed into the pocket of her field jacket, she skirted the corpse. The energy of whatever emotion had briefly seized her ebbed away, replaced by neat angles, round numbers, and the scent of fresh laundry. "This trail gets busy. Whoever did this must have dumped her overnight."

Huang frowned. "Dumped?"

"Clean feet," I said. Huang eyed me, and I made a face. "Sorry. I know, I'm just a witness here. Shutting up now."

The detective ignored this, joining Danny at the corpse's feet. "Maybe they took her shoes."

"It's possible." Danny squinted at the ground. "Not a lot of footprints here."

"The ground's pretty hard through this section," he said. "Would prints even show up?"

"I see a pair of trainers, size six or seven." She glanced my way, lips quirked. "That'll be you, Lil. Looks like you trampled around quite a bit, didn't you?"

"Sorry," I said, flushing. "I wasn't thinking too clearly. No coffee, faceplant, corpse…bad morning."

"Not accusing you of anything. Just observing." Danny shook her head, mischief sparkling for a moment like firecrackers. "Cops and lawyers, man. So quick to get defensive. Don't look like that, I'm only teasing."

"What about this wound?" Huang bent over the dead woman. "That's some nasty corrosion."

The image already lingered in my mind's eye, but I forced myself to look again. Yep, still nasty. I swallowed hard. "Any idea what caused it?"

"Nada." Danny crouched by the body's side and ran gloved fingers around the edges of the crater in the demon's chest. "Some kind of metallic residue here, though. I'll get a sample. Lab might give us something useful."

I leaned in and hazarded a glance at the powdery blue-green stuff dusting her fingers. As I did, the migraine that had hovered like the threat of a storm over my left temple since my fall exploded into a full-on throb. My stomach churned. "Fuck."

Danny glanced up at me, brow creased. Her desiderata surged, warm cinnamon and summer twilight. "Whoa there. You okay?"

"A little woozy." I took a step back, swayed, groped for my trusty trailside rock and sank down on it.

"Get her out of here." Huang's quick headshake dismissed my civilian weakness, and he headed back down the trail. His voice floated up to us, directing the uniforms to set up a perimeter.

Danny abandoned her examination of the body and came to my side. "What's going on, Sugarbean?" she asked, voice dropping low.

"You may not need to send that stuff to the lab." I shuddered and scratched at my arms through the thin fabric of my jogging shirt, where a deep, burning itch had started up. Hives. Just what I needed.

Her eyes widened. "Why not? Do you know what it is?"

"Not for sure, but I can guess." I dropped my head to my knees. "I think that's silver."

"Silver?" she said. "Aren't you allergic?"

"Yeah, I just get a headache and a bad rash. But for a full-blooded demon…" I sucked in a harsh, jagged breath. That was one hell of a rash. "Your gloves. Can you—?"

"Yikes. Sorry! Bagging now." A hasty snap and crinkle. "Do you think that's the cause of death?"

"Seems likely." The world had slowed its spin enough to make focusing tolerable. I straightened, mustering a smile for Danny's benefit. "We're not easy to kill. Short of beheading or immolation, silver is about the only way to do it."

"Good to know." She pressed her lips together, and that sea-salt chill saturated her desiderata again. My reassurance hadn't convinced her. "The hard to kill part, at least. But then, dead demons don't come along every day, do they?"

"No," I said. "There aren't that many of us around to begin with. You could almost say we're an endangered species."

Danny pulled on a fresh pair of gloves, frowning, and headed back to the corpse. She peered into the wound. "Hello. What's this?"

She reached down to fish around inside the dead woman's torso. I flinched and tipped my head back. Above me, the thick fog of early morning had begun to lift, curling into ragged shreds. Shit. I needed to get home, take a shower, and get to court on time for trial. I had an asshole to cross-examine today, and Judge Wong hated tardy lawyers.

"*Dios mio,*" Danny said. Her sudden sharp tone drew my attention. "She's falling apart."

"What are you talking about?"

She pulled her arm back with painstaking slowness. Between her thumb and forefinger, she held a small, glinting piece of metal: a tarnished silver cross that swung on a slim chain. Dust sifted off it in a small cloud. "Is this normal? Look."

With her other hand, she squeezed the dead woman's pinkie. At the pressure, the bloodless flesh and painted nail crumbled away. A fine, pale sand spilled down onto the eucalyptus leaves carpeting the trail.

I stared. "What in the fresh hell?"

"It doesn't make sense," Danny said. "There's no decomp. No lividity. She's fresh. But the level of desiccation is nothing I've ever seen. Like she's made of ash." She stepped back from the body, face ashen under her deep tan as she turned to me. "We may not even be able to move her."

"She's turning to dust. Ariel said…" I broke off. "Never mind. I thought that was a myth."

Danny wiped her hand on her jacket, a mechanical movement. Her desiderata had gone gray as the curling fog, and her grim expression matched it. "Doesn't look like a myth to me."

I shook my head and climbed to my feet. Would this happen to me, someday? Would I crumble into ash and blow away on the wind? "I have to go. When Huang freaks out, remind him he knows where to find me."

"Wait. Lily—" She hurried after me up the trail. "Call me later? Better yet, come have a drink. After this morning, you probably need one."

My steps slowed, and I glanced at her over my shoulder. Her eyes shone, her forehead creased, and her desiderata bloomed with a confusing rush of bright hope and bubbling concern. We'd been friends a long time, and despite my recent distance, she'd never once given up on me. Not even when she found out my deepest, darkest secret.

Not even when it almost killed her.

"I don't know." I pushed the words past the lump in my throat. "I'm swamped. It's a trial week."

"Trial week, schmial week. Isn't it always? You work too hard." Hands on hips, she warmed to our old argument. "You can meet Berry. You'll like her, and she'd love to meet you."

So the new girlfriend had stuck around. Why did that surprise me? Danny's tone had changed when she'd said her name. Her obvious happiness sparked a sharp ache in my chest. "I'll think about it," I conceded.

"We both know that means you won't." She smiled anyway, but the light in her desiderata dimmed. "We'll be at Ladybird's, in case you change your mind."

"Okay," I said. "Bye, Danny."

"Bye," she said softly behind me as I turned away and—no, I didn't run. I *jogged*, like I had come here to do. But guilt cramped my gut, and I struggled to draw a full breath as I picked up speed.

I had my reasons for avoiding the bar scene that had nothing to do with Danny. Too many pitfalls awaited me at Ladybird's, too many walking temptations. Too much unmet desire swirled in the air. I couldn't chance one taste, one slip, one unguarded moment of skin on skin.

My heart thumped painfully at the thought, and I pushed my pace to its limit, chasing a runner's high that would take the edge off this morning's memories and keep my more dangerous urges in check.

But no amount of human endorphins would change the fact that one stray touch could wash all my hard-earned self-control away.

NINE HOURS LATER, I stood in the hall of my downtown San Francisco apartment building, rummaging through my purse for my house keys. After court adjourned for the day, I'd stayed late at the office to tackle the backlog of files stacked on my desk. My workload had almost distracted me enough to forget the dead face of the Crissy Field succubus. By the time I'd halved the file stack, neither wild horses nor indefatigable lesbians could drag me through the drunken masses of a crowded pub. *Sorry, Danny.*

Tonight, I wanted nothing more exciting than a quick microwave dinner followed by drowsing on the couch to the soft repartee of one of my favorite classic films. A day like today called for something with a Hepburn and a romantic ending. *Sabrina* sounded good. I couldn't take off to Paris and learn to view the world through rose-colored glasses, but through Audrey's starry-eyed gaze, I could at least imagine it.

A vaguely musty odor always lingered in the common passageway of my converted Victorian building like the ghost of old milk and boiled vegetables. This evening, though, hints of smoke and spice elevated the usual reek and triggered an unwelcome wave of nostalgia: the smell of frankincense, leather and lace, and warm golden eyes, smiling at me...

I shook my head. My college student neighbors across the hall must have decided to cover up their weeknight weed by burning frankincense instead of patchouli this time. Funny how a single whiff of that aroma could bring back events over a decade old, as if they happened yesterday. I bit the inside of my cheek and pushed aside a nagging sense of déjà vu. My fingers closed around the cold metal teeth of my keys at last, my grip a little too tight for comfort.

The lock required a special touch, another quirk of living in an older building. Most nights, it didn't give me any trouble. Tonight, though, my hands shook with fatigue and the beginnings of a migraine. I had to fight and fumble with the lock, jiggling the key until the tumblers clicked.

The scent of frankincense followed me inside, hanging thicker in here. My scalp prickled, a sour note of unease jangling in the back of my mind, but the haze of the migraine overrode it. I tossed my keys on the kitchen bar without bothering to turn on the light.

"Delilah! Here, kitty, kitty." The fluffy gray cat usually greeted me when I came in, a transparent excuse to beg for food, full bowl or no. But I'd stayed at the office later than normal. She'd likely given up on me and curled up in the bedroom to sleep.

"Delilah, where are you? Are you hungry?"

"Hello, Lillian." The melodious male voice came from behind me, out of the darkness of my tiny living room, and my stomach dropped like a stone.

A tall, broad-shouldered figure sat in the big chair, silhouetted against the dim ambient glow of the city night filtering through the front window. Two sets of luminous eyes, one cat-green, one golden, blinked back at me. To my credit, I did not swear or scream, but all the hairs on the back of my neck stood on end. I groped for the light switch.

Delilah trilled and unfolded from the chair's arm. She stretched, untroubled by my fear.

"Don't be alarmed." Amusement resonated in the musical voice. Its bone-deep familiarity tugged at my core. "I come in peace."

3

JUST INCUBUS THINGS

My shaking fingers finally found the light switch. The lamps above the kitchen island illuminated the apartment's front room, and the blond demon lounging in my overstuffed easy chair inclined his head in greeting.

His pupils contracted to slits at the sudden flood of light, accentuating his yellow irises. His eyes had no visible whites, like a snake's. He didn't bother with a cubine glamour to hide those irises from me, as he would from a human or an unknown demon.

I sagged against the wall, heart racing. "Ariel." My voice trembled despite myself. "How did you get in here?"

My former mentor and sometime lover smirked at me, smug as the cat who'd caught the creamed canary. "Oh, you know... Magic. Sorcery. Just incubus things."

His slight, unidentifiable accent shivered along my spine, and I steeled myself. "What is that, a Twitter hashtag?" Great. I hadn't missed the pleasure of this old guessing game. Had Ariel adopted a human meme for protective coloring, amusement, or pure vain fear of appearing obsolete? "What are you doing on the West Coast?"

"Obvious enough." He flashed me one of his hundred-watt smiles. "I came to see you."

I backed up until I hit a barstool, then sat balanced on its edge. Delilah jumped down from the arm of his—no, *my* chair—and waltzed over to me, twining around my ankles.

"Traitor," I muttered at her, but I toed off my black pump and ruffled her fur with my foot. "When normal people visit," I told Ariel, "they knock. In daylight. And wait for an invitation! You should try it sometime. Better yet, you should have stayed in New York."

"I'm sorry I startled you." Laughter lurked behind his glib apology. "For what it's worth, I didn't think you'd want to invite me."

The lying bastard wasn't sorry one bit. "Whatever makes you think that?" I folded my arms and glowered at him.

"You never answered my texts," he said.

"Oh, right. I guess I kinda, sorta blocked your number, didn't I?" At his moue of exaggerated hurt, I sighed. "Some people might take that as a hint."

"Exactly," he said, like he'd won a point. "You left me no choice."

I ground my teeth. "Ariel, I'm exhausted and I have the mother of all headaches. It's been a long, ugly day, and I don't have the patience for your riddles. The sooner you tell me what you want, the sooner I can tell you 'no' and go to bed."

"Hrm." Ariel unfolded himself from the chair in one fluid movement. Then he blurred toward me, demon-quick.

"Fuck!" I leaped to my feet, startling Delilah. She shot under the coffee table, where she eyed me balefully. As if was all *my* fault.

Ariel loomed over me, looking me up and down. "Headache, eh? Get those often?"

"Jerk. I hate it when you do that." I shifted under his scrutiny. "I get migraines off and on. Why?"

"When did you last feed?" He leaned closer, nostrils flared.

Weirdo. I leaned away, ignoring the heated flutter that stirred in my belly at his sudden proximity. "Um, lunch was a while ago... Why are you looking at me like that?"

"I didn't mean lunch."

Oh. That. I ducked my head. "I don't feed. Not—I'm clean."

"Clean? Lilith's tits, woman! Are you telling me you haven't—How long has it been?"

"Years. Four years, to be exact."

"Four *years*?" He groped behind him for the other barstool and sank onto it, his pupils dilated until only a thin ring of gold remained, like Delilah's when something spooked her. "No wonder you look like death warmed over!"

"Gee, thanks." I rolled my eyes at his exaggerated horror, relaxing a fraction now that he'd put some distance between us. "And here I was so proud of myself for staying on the straight and narrow."

"Proud!" He ran a hand through his blond curls. The familiar gesture tightened the growing knot in my chest. "You're doing this on purpose. Lillian—why?"

"You know why," I said. "It's wrong. I don't want to hurt anyone else."

"So dramatic. It doesn't have to be like that."

"Yeah, it does." I'd tried to find another way, and that had ended in my worst disaster yet. "It's all right, it's better this way. I'm not an addict who goes from lover to lover, looking for my next fix."

My barb didn't land. "We're talking about basic sustenance here!" Jumping to his feet, he paced the room, restless as an agitated big cat in a small enclosure. "That's like calling a human an addict for craving water or sleep. You can't be addicted to something you need."

"I don't need it," I said. "I'm only half-succubus."

"Honey, right now you're only half-alive!"

"I feel fine." I scowled.

"Do you?" He stopped in front of me. "You mentioned headaches. Having trouble sleeping? Nasty dreams you can't shake?"

I avoided his gaze. "I work in a high-stress profession."

"Right. What about joint pain? Ever feel faint for no reason? Nauseated? Fatigued?" He caught my hand, stilling it. "Tremors, Lillian?"

I pulled away, tucking my hand behind my back. "What are you now, my doctor?"

"No," he said. "Your doctor can't help you with this. But I can."

He was right, damn him. A series of doctors had made noises at me about fibromyalgia, depression, and hormones, but none of the human cures they prescribed made a dent in my symptoms. "I don't want your help."

"You stubborn, foolish, irritating woman." He glared down his aquiline nose at me, long fingers sketching an elaborate gesture of frustration. "You and your thrice-damned principles. You're practically killing yourself. And for what? The moral high ground? Your precious humans wouldn't care about that if they found out what you are."

"I'm half-human, too." I matched his biting tone. "I can't look at my own kind as prey."

"But you see your other kind as evil."

"I'm just trying to do the right thing." I swallowed hard to quell the ache in my throat and rose, forcing him to step back. "Why are you here? Did you really break into my apartment to argue moral philosophy with me?"

And why today, of all days, the first day I'd considered calling him in years? I didn't need his guidance or his rescue. Not anymore.

Yet here he stood, hard features softening as a half-smile played around his mouth. "Ah, now, I resent that. You'll find that nothing's broken."

"Not yet," I snapped. "But I can't vouch for that pretty face of yours if you don't get to the point."

Could I make good on the threat? I'd let my self-defense practice fall by the wayside after I moved out here. I couldn't train full out in a martial arts studio packed with humans when one accidental touch could blow up my whole life.

But Ariel didn't call my bluff. He sat back down on the other barstool, expression grave. "Look, I wouldn't have come if it wasn't serious. I'm not fool enough to believe you'd be happy to see me."

A harsh laugh shuddered out of me. "Hey, you were right for once."

"Haters gonna hate." He tossed the quip off in an absent, mechanical way, and I shivered. Someone had killed a succubus, and now Ariel sat at my kitchen counter, with…could that be worry creasing his maddeningly beautiful face? Whatever crisis had brought him out here must have really gotten to him. And he didn't spook easily.

Cold dread coiled at the base of my spine. "Okay. Tell me."

"I came to ask for your help."

I gaped at him. Of all the things he might have said, I hadn't expected that. "What are you talking about?"

He raked his hand through his hair again, mussing the boyish curls into a wild halo while retaining a distracting level of attractiveness. I looked away. How, after so many years, did he still have this effect on me?

"Something bad is happening here." He pieced the words together slowly, like a witness who'd seen something they didn't want to remember. "Cubine women—succubi—are disappearing. Not a word to anyone, not a suitcase packed. Just gone."

A chill slithered up through my core and raised the small hairs on the back of my neck. "What? How do you know this?"

"An old friend called me for help," he said. "I came as soon as I could."

I should have told him about the dead succubus from this morning, but I didn't trust him not to jump to conclusions. "That doesn't answer my question."

"Honestly?" He lowered his voice, smooth words caressing me. "I was concerned about you. This city isn't safe for us, not anymore."

"I'll be fine," I said, jaw set against his powers of persuasion. "I'm not going anywhere."

"I didn't think you would." He cocked his head. "But you're at the D.A.'s office, aren't you? Surely you can look into it."

I stiffened. How did he know where I worked? "That's right, but I'm a prosecutor. I don't investigate crimes. That's a job for the police."

He shook his head, solemn and regretful. "The police can't help us. This is demon business, Lily."

"And that makes it mine?" His distress rubbed off on me, although his emotional energy didn't bleed unconsciously into the air like human desiderata. The image of the dead succubus's face rose in my mind unbidden, and I sighed, giving in. "All right, I'll see what I can do."

"No." A sharp edge crept into the single word. "I'll tell you what you can do."

"Oh, this ought to be good…"

Ariel ignored this. "Come with me." Now he spoke in a soft, urgent undertone, as if sharing a secret. "I want you to meet someone. Her name is Nepenthe, and she's the…sister of one of the girls who's gone missing. It took some convincing, but she agreed to talk with you. I gave my word you'd come."

"Tonight?" I crossed my arms over my chest, lifting my chin. "No way! The only place I'm going tonight is bed. I told you, I'm not feeling well."

"I heard you," Ariel said. "And I told you I can help you."

With one light-speed stride, he towered over me. He took up most of my personal space. Hell, he took up most of the air in the room.

"Whoa." I reared away from him, my nostrils full of the heavy aroma of frankincense. Why a demon should smell precisely like Christmas was beyond me.

"Hold still," Ariel ordered, and for the first time that night, he put real power behind his words.

My mind went blank and a languid heaviness suffused my limbs. Heat flared in my belly. I stilled, trapped like a fly in the amber of his eyes as he bent toward me.

He made a soft, low sound in the back of his throat. Then he put his two hands on either side of my face and kissed me. His fingers stroked my temples and his mouth urged mine to open to him. A wave of liquid warmth flowed over me, filling me from head to toe with pleasure.

The kiss didn't stop. It went on forever, and I melted into it, weak-kneed and unresisting. The past became present, the way he used to touch me in our glory days together, before—

Red and blue lights flashed in my memory, passing over a slack face and empty eyes. My stomach lurched. I shuddered.

"No," I slurred into his mouth. "Get away!"

Ariel released me and stepped back. Now he looked much more like the Ariel I remembered because he looked excessively pleased with himself.

I gasped and swayed in place. Then I aimed a swing at him. "What the ever-living hell, Ariel? That was not okay!"

He dodged my punch adroitly, balanced with inhuman grace on the balls of his feet. His smug grin never faltered. "Come, now. That's no way to thank a demon for a favor. Notice anything different?"

"I... What?" About to launch into a litany of all the boundaries he had crossed, I broke off, blinking.

"Well?" Ariel smirked.

"What did you..." My headache had evaporated. My knees had lost their customary stiff ache and the pain from walking in heels all day had faded from the bones of my feet. His kiss had swept the cobwebs in my brain away. "You bastard," I whispered, dropping back into my seat. "You gave me kether."

Kether: the life energy on which all cubines fed in acts of intimacy with humans. It quickened my heart and lightened my limbs. If I took a step, I might float on air. My veins hummed with power, with potential.

He had given me a shot of it straight to the core of me. He hadn't even asked first. I clenched and unclenched my fists, surprised at the strength of my grip. My breath came fast, my head swimming. "This can't be happening!"

"Believe me, it is," he said softly. "Now do you see?"

"But—how?" Demons craved kether, but they—we—could not create it. I grasped my head between my hands, massaging where his fingers had pressed into my skin. My migraine had evaporated, but the euphoria of sudden painlessness gave me no comfort. "You fed recently, didn't you? You have to take to give. Whose life did you give me, Ariel?"

"I took no life," he protested. "Only energy, not enough to harm, and with consent."

"Like you have any concept of what that means," I sneered. "You didn't ask for consent before you pulled a glamour on me and kissed me."

"I had a point to prove." He showed no trace of repentance.

"You planned this, didn't you?" I jabbed at his chest, and my finger didn't tremble anymore. I gritted my teeth, blood pounding in my ears. If I screamed in his face, he'd take it as a win, but if I didn't, he won too. I opted for murderous calm. "So you seduced some defenseless human, got a nice fix on, then came in here and hyped me up on stolen kether so you can persuade me to do your bidding. 'Just incubus things,' am I right?"

"Not even a little." His indignant pout did nothing to hide his self-satisfaction. "Lighten up a bit. Stop punishing yourself. I didn't do this for me. I did it for *them*."

The succubi who'd gone missing. That shot hit home, but I did my best not to show it. "Oh yes," I said sarcastically. "I'm sure all of your acts are motivated purely by altruism and generosity."

"News flash, honey. Not everything in this world is as black and white as you think it is."

"Yeah, well, it's not as morally gray as you seem to think, either."

"Would it be morally gray to help a woman who has reason to fear for her safety, then?"

I sagged. "Does it have to be tonight?" I didn't owe him any favors in return for one I never asked for. But a succubus lay dead by silver in Danny's morgue. I'd do it for her and the nagging knot of guilt haunting the back of my throat, but not for him.

"Yes, it has to be tonight. We demons don't trust easy. If you stand Nepenthe up tonight, it'll take me months to convince her to meet with you again." He looked grim. "And by then it might be too late."

"Fine." I grabbed my keys from the counter. "Let's go."

"That's my girl," he crowed.

"I'm not your girl." Screw owing him. "You're going to owe me big for this one."

He shrugged. "Price of doing business. Here, you'll want this where we're going."

With a flourish, he produced something that sparkled in the kitchen lamplight: a half-face mask of the kind I'd expect at a Mardi Gras celebration, crowned with black feathers and encrusted with clear stones that sparkled like real diamonds. Painted half-black and half-white: a harlequin's face.

I took it gingerly, frowning first at it, then at him. "Is this a joke?"

"No." He produced a gold and black mask for himself and put it on. His tawny eyes glowed out of it, more alien than ever. They flashed when he smiled.

"Ariel," I said. "Where are you taking me?"

"Why, a masquerade, of course," he said, and offered me his arm.

Oh, hell no. Head held high, I brushed past him to the door.

4

MASQUERADE

I SHOULD HAVE KNOWN BETTER THAN TO TRUST A DEMON.

The little club in San Francisco's SOMA district didn't look like much from the street. But the rush of human desire from within struck me like a bolt of lightning, and Ariel's gift of kether roared to life in my veins. I stopped short, halfway up the dim, claustrophobic stairs.

"What is this place?" The blood pounded in my ears in time with the muffled throb of darkwave electronica filtering into the stairwell.

"I told you," Ariel said behind me, "it's Masquerade Night at the Black Cat Club. Now move. You're a goddamn great fire hazard, blocking the stairs like this."

"Ariel," I hissed. "You brought me to a sex club!"

"More of a goth club, darlin', but there's some overlap, I'll grant you." Placing a hand on the small of my back, he shoved me gently but inexorably forward.

I dug in my heels. "I see people in leather chaps and gimp masks."

"No surprise there. They also have a famous burlesque show here every Wednesday night."

"But tonight's Wednesday!"

Masked faces turned toward us. We'd reached the top of the stairs, and I flushed under my own mask. In my black pencil skirt and royal blue work blouse, I stuck out like a boring thumb. I was overdressed as far as skin showing, under-dressed as far as…everything else.

"So it is. What did you expect? We're not here to meet an abstinence demon." Ariel shuddered theatrically. "Thank the Mother for that."

"There's no such thing as an abstinence demon," I said. "And you're missing the point."

"What point? You're the one who chose to live in a city that throws an annual fetish block party and invites the normies to join in." He inhaled the liquor, sweat, and pheromones soaking the air like a connoisseur absorbing the bouquet of a fine Chianti. "I should have moved here ages ago."

Oh God, he was getting ideas. The full-force din of the club hit us, and I raised my voice. "The point is, you wouldn't bring a dry drunk to a party with an open bar."

"Or lead a starving lioness into a herd of fat gazelles? It all depends on your goals, my dear." Ariel's eyeshine glowed eerily beneath his mask. "It's a meat market like any other bar night. The patrons here are just more honest about it."

We wove our way through the throngs of club-goers gathered in the main room, and I cast a furtive look around. Ariel had taken a bold risk, flashing his demon eyes like that for nothing but dramatic effect. Still, the surrounding humans moved aside to let us through without a second glance.

"There's a reason I don't go out much," I grumbled, but I followed his lead to a less crowded corner near the bar proper.

He leaned down to speak directly in my ear. "A twelve-stepper can have a fine time in a bar with a mineral water and some good company," he said. "But since you're not actually an addict *of any kind*, I suggest you order yourself a drink while I hunt down our friend Nepenthe. It'll do you good. You're wound tighter than an eight-day clock, love."

I turned, ready to tell him where to stuff his unsolicited opinions and archaic idioms, but he had already slipped away into the crowd. His mask glinted at me from halfway across the club, and he waved at me, smirking.

Well, then. I sighed, weighing the temptation of leaving Ariel to solve his own damn problems against my own sense of responsibility. Not to mention the likelihood that he'd show up again unannounced in my living room to demand an explanation.

Humans swirled around me, pressed cheek to jowl, fumbling for connection in their simple, primal ways. The ease with which they sought and offered touch transfixed me and an aching knot of envy tightened under my breastbone.

Then a woman in a crop-top, miniskirt, and fuzzy knee-high pink boots jostled past me toward the dance floor, dragging another girl in a leather bodice behind her. I jumped back just in time to avoid the brush of her bare skin against mine. Their desiderata flooded through me, magnetic and candy-sweet.

The borrowed kether in me thrummed in answer. It stirred a restless hunger in my core. Drawing a long, shaky breath, I turned away toward the bar—and froze.

A slim, dark-haired man leaned his elbows on the bar top a few feet away from me, facing out toward the dance floor, lips quirked in a bemused half-smile. The force and depth of his desiderata snatched the air from my lungs.

In contrast to the rest of the humans here, he wore a white collared shirt and slacks. He had unbuttoned his suit jacket and loosened his tie, his only apparent concession to the exhibitionist atmosphere. The tailored fit of his suit didn't match his cheap white plastic mask, the generic domino kind they'd offered at the door to the unmasked and unwary, which left his high cheekbones and sharp, clean-shaven jawline showing.

Like me, he didn't quite fit in. But his desiderata sang to me with a deep, dark siren call, a craving for control and the loss of it. Deeper still, it keened an unconscious yearning for a rare brand of intimacy which exposed all, offered all...and took all.

The mingled energies of the club dropped to a dull roar, my awareness and all my senses brought to bear by that steady gravity. Ariel's kiss had woken my predatory instincts, but this man presented another experience entirely. Like chasing a quad espresso with a line of cocaine, or so I imagined. Not that I had done anything like that, though some of my law school classmates probably had.

Why did it sound like such a good idea now?

Keeping him in my periphery, I craned my neck to catch a glimpse of myself in the antique mirror behind the bar and raised unsteady fingers to my parted lips.

Since when did I have lips like that—full, rosy, shining, and unchapped? And my hair! Usually a flat, dull brown I had to wrestle into submission on court mornings, it fell in waves of glossy dark curls that skimmed my shoulders. My marsh-gray eyes had deepened to a dramatic green, visible even in the shadow of my harlequin mask. What the mask didn't hide of my face practically bloomed with health.

Ariel hadn't given me any time to freshen my makeup, but I couldn't have achieved this effect if I spent a year's salary on spa treatments. The alchemy of Ariel's kiss and the presence of a worthy quarry had triggered my demon instincts and granted me an automatic glow-up.

"Can I get you something, miss?"

I started. My heightened charms had netted me a bearded young bartender with an eager smile. He hastened to prepare the Whiskey Sour I ordered, ignoring the people on either side of me who clamored for his attention. When I smiled my thanks, he blushed and almost dropped the bottle in the middle of his pour.

He was adorable. I smiled wider, and the power of Ariel's kether gift coiled warm and ready in my belly.

No. The bartender was a tempting morsel, but not the real prize. I accepted the glass and took care not to brush his fingers with mine. With great hotness came great responsibility, or something like that. And taking out the bartender with an unintentional kether pull did not rate high on my to-do list at the moment.

The man in the suit, however…

The bartender waved off my cash, and I winced. I would have paid him if he let me, but arguing would only call attention to his oversight and I didn't have time for that right now. A good tip would have to suffice. I tucked it under an empty glass on the bar.

The suited man had locked his gaze with mine, his expression intent and curious. A shiver prickled down my spine—anticipation, or just nerves? It carried a warning from the parts of me that knew better, that screamed at me to walk away.

I'd made this mistake before. It would end as it always did: poorly. And yet...

Ah, screw it. The better angels of my nature could go straight to hell. I sipped my whiskey with as much nonchalance as I could muster, slipped past a noisy mob of humans waiting for their drinks, and squeezed into the small space at the bar next to Bespoke Suit.

He shifted a fraction to make room for me and arched an eyebrow, wary interest wafting from him. Under it beat the steadfast hum of his desire, heady and intoxicating.

I mirrored his casual pose, my back to the bar, elbows propped so that my left sleeve brushed his arm. "Come here often?"

He laughed, a short, surprised sound. "First time. Am I that obvious?"

"I'm just glad I'm not the only one." I relaxed a fraction at his laugh and the answering giddy buzz spreading through my body.

His wry grin brought a sparkle to his gray-blue eyes. "I'll admit, it's not what I expected. I came here to meet a friend, not for…all this. What about you?"

"Dragged from self-imposed isolation. My friends think I need to get out more." As soon as the words left my mouth, I cringed. Ugh. What guy wouldn't love an asocial shut-in who didn't know how to relax? I hadn't done this in so long, and it showed.

He tilted his head, his desiderata flickering like leaf-dappled sunlight. "Ah, so naturally you came out to the burlesque masquerade. Interesting choice."

I shook my head, perversely compelled to clarify instead of taking credit. "Not my choice."

He blinked, brows crinkling, on the verge of a reply, but the music booming through the speakers cut off and the house lights went down. The sudden hush made us both turn. A spotlight came up on the darkened stage, and I let out a soft gasp.

The woman standing unmasked on the stage wore her shining black hair in a chin-length bob. Her short, fringed black gown conjured visions of jazz halls and speakeasies, gin and sin, while her bangs and kohl-darkened eyes evinced Cleopatra as played by Elizabeth Taylor. But her extraordinary beauty outshone all else, brighter even than the spotlight flooding over her. It tugged at my human blood with a palpable magnetism and sent a jolt of recognition through my demon senses.

I'd expected the burlesque show to feature a drag queen or a belly dancer. I didn't expect another succubus.

Beside me, the man in the bespoke suit stared with rapt attention at the stage. His enthralled expression stirred another primal impulse in me: an animal instinct to claim and to protect.

Then the music started, slow and sinuous, and I forgot him altogether, for the succubus on stage had begun to dance.

How could any of the humans in the room witness such inhuman fluidity and grace, yet still believe she was one of them? But the power of her Presence overrode any other consideration for them and me. I couldn't take my eyes off her, and I *knew* the true nature of the trick she had pulled.

Demons didn't only read human emotions. We could manipulate them, too, and affect their perceptions through energetic projection. We could use our Presence to frighten, to persuade, to calm or command, to seduce, and at times, to go unseen.

Penelope's Presence on stage didn't evade attention, but rather commanded it. Her movements weren't nakedly sexual, but her sensuality carried an undeniable, inexorable charge. She drew me toward her alongside the rest of the human crowd that swayed in unison under her spell. Heat pooled in my core, stronger and smokier than the whiskey in my half-full glass.

Time halted, stumbled. It flowed molasses-thick, molasses-slow and sweet. Only she moved free within it. Even the light seemed to coalesce around her, rippling like molten gold.

I couldn't say how long she danced. When at last the music stopped, a murmur rose from the previously dead-silent crowd, as if we all had woken from a shared dream.

"She's incredible, isn't she?"

The rough edge in my companion's voice brought me back to myself and cut me to the quick. He didn't desire me, not anymore. His desiderata had flowed away from me, his attention trained with laser intensity on the woman posed kneeling on the stage.

I slammed my empty glass down on the bar, too hard. It shattered, but he didn't turn around.

My face heated, and I dropped my head. *Ridiculous*. I didn't know him at all. I hadn't even asked his name. I had no real claim on him, base instincts notwithstanding. But still, my breath came fast and noisy, sullen red spots suffusing my vision.

"Be careful," I said, low-voiced. "You don't know what she is."

He started and frowned at me. "What do you mean by that?"

My glance skated to the stage. The succubus bowed, graceful and gracious, to the admirers who reached out their arms to her in worship and yearning. Her eyes swept across the crowd, searching, seeking, hunting —*for him.*

I bristled, gut clenching. His rich, silky desiderata vibrated like a bass line under all the other human emotions in the room. Did she sense it as well?

"Never mind." Cowardice, perhaps, but I couldn't bring myself to betray the cardinal rule of demonkind. "She's just not what she seems."

His face didn't change, but his eyes hardened, and his desiderata surged, lashing out at me in a sudden icy, whip-sharp shock. The sting of it rocked me back on my heels.

"Thanks for the warning," he said. "But I think I'll take my chances."

Before I could say another word, he strode toward the stage. And as his desiderata slipped away from me, the truth slipped in. It congealed in my throat and tingled in my chest. I crumpled into myself, grasping the bar for balance.

She hadn't been hunting him. I had.

I'd pulled a glamour as tailored to him as that gorgeous suit. I'd laid foundation for a Claim. In less than five minutes, I'd decided to make him mine. And when his interest turned elsewhere, I'd nearly betrayed one of my own kind to keep him beside me. So what did that make me?

I swallowed hard and dug my nails into my palms. *Who's the monster now?*

"What's wrong, Lily?" a smooth voice said close to my ear.

I jumped and glared around at my tormenter. "Damn it, Ariel! Could you be any creepier?"

"Probably," he said. "I'm always working to improve on my strengths. Could you be any jumpier? You look as if you've seen a ghost."

"It's nothing. I just don't like crowds. Where's this Nepenthe person you wanted me to meet?"

In answer, he jerked his head toward the stage.

My stomach lurched. *Of course.* If I hadn't thoroughly distracted myself by leaping into the jaws of temptation, I would have guessed it already.

Nepenthe, the succubus I'd come to see. Nepenthe, the succubus who had just held a club full of humans captive with a power I would never allow myself to wield. She stepped down from the stage with the courtly assistance of the tall, well-dressed man in the simple white eye mask—my would-be prey. They greeted each other with a kiss and a lover's embrace. I turned my face away.

By the time I looked back, they were heading toward us, her hand tucked in the crook of his elbow as he smiled down at her. The surrounding humans still yearned toward her, but the crowd parted as for royalty and left a clear path for their approach.

Ariel met them halfway, pecking Nepenthe's cheek and shaking her companion's hand before leading them back to where I stood frozen with dismay.

"Penelope, my dear," Ariel said, "this is Lily Knight. She's the attorney I wanted you to meet."

Penelope? But the succubus nodded to me. He'd introduced her by her human alias. I gathered my scattered wits about me. "Hello."

"Thank you for coming." She had a low, throaty voice and, like Ariel, a touch of an accent I couldn't pinpoint. Inclining her head to the man whose arm she held, she added, "This is my friend, Sebastian."

"A pleasure," he said, and held out his hand.

I hesitated. Skin to skin contact with a human held risks for both of us, especially considering our encounter a few minutes ago. His desiderata turned spiky and he quirked a brow, but dropped his hand with a half-shrug.

"Shall we go somewhere a little more private?" Ariel suggested.

Nepenthe—or Penelope, as I had to remember to call her so long as Sebastian stood by, his keen, ice-blue eyes fixed on us—shot a quick glance around the club. "Upstairs," she said. "There's a VIP lounge."

We followed her up to the club's second level, where a bouncer unhooked a velvet rope for us without asking our names. On the dance floor, the DJ started a new set of thumping industrial bass, the reverberating beat only slightly muted up here.

Penelope selected a table against the wall, tucking herself in a corner seat. "Sebastian," she said softly. "Would you mind getting me a gin and tonic, please?"

"Of course. Anyone else want anything?"

I shook my head, and Ariel waved him off. When he had headed toward the bar, Penelope turned to me. "Did Ariel tell you why I need your help?"

"A little. He said some…some of your people have gone missing. Is that right?"

"Yes," she said. "But that's not the only thing."

I raised an eyebrow, waiting for her to go on, but her gaze darted across the balcony and she licked her lips, a gesture more nervous than predatory. I frowned. "What is it?"

"You said 'your people.' But you're one of us, aren't you?"

"I'm half." As if it mattered. "I'm a cambion. Why?"

She leaned forward, speaking in an urgent undertone. As if even in this deserted corner, she worried someone would overhear.

"Because someone is hunting us," she said. "And they're going to kill me next."

5

HELL OF A HASHTAG

PENELOPE'S BLUNT WORDS KNOCKED THE AIR OUT OF MY LUNGS. I SAT BACK IN my chair. "You think someone's trying to kill you? Why?"

"Because," she said. "I'm the only one left."

"What do you mean, the only one?" I glanced at Ariel to gauge his reaction, but his face had gone stony and still under his mask. I couldn't read the shadows there.

"There were four of us. Astarte, Salome, Lais, and me. We stuck together, you know? It's not like the old days. We looked out for each other. We had to." Her breath hitched, her husky voice cracking. "It wasn't enough. They're gone. Vanished one by one, like smoke in the wind."

Or like dust, crumbling at the touch of a finger. I cleared my throat. "Maybe they left town?"

"They wouldn't do that, not without telling me. We were friends."

It sounded odd, a succubus with friends. Cubines were traditionally solitary creatures, apex predators who stalked our own ranges and pursued our own hunts. "What do you think happened to them?"

"They're dead." She spoke with quiet, matter-of-fact conviction. "They have to be dead."

After this morning, I was inclined to agree with her. "I'm so sorry,

Penelope. I'm an attorney, not an investigator. I'll do what I can, but I may not be much help."

"But…" Penelope fell silent. Only her eyes still spoke.

I followed her gaze to where Sebastian wove his way toward us, drinks in hand, mask dangling on its elastic around his neck. He looked around the table, frowning.

"Everything all right here?" He placed the gin and tonic in front of Penelope. She snatched it up and gulped it like water, earning a quirked eyebrow and a frisson of concern from Sebastian as he folded his long limbs into the chair next to her.

"Just discussing politics," Ariel said. "Lily stepped in where angels fear to tread."

I eyed him. What lay behind that easy smile? He hadn't spoken at all since we'd sat down—unlike him, but his tone now betrayed nothing beyond his typical smooth-tongued charm. "My mistake." I stood. "Excuse me. I need to visit the ladies' room."

In the relatively peaceful sanctuary of the women's bathroom, I stared at my masked reflection, unseeing, until Nepenthe's face appeared over my shoulder.

I pretended to examine my makeup. "Tell me who is hunting you."

"There's a man." She joined me at the mirror. "A stranger, but he comes here sometimes. I saw him with Salome and with Astarte before she disappeared. They were dancers, too, you see."

"Surely that wasn't out of the ordinary, seeing them with strange men?"

"No," she said. "But this one…I'm telling you, there was something wrong with him. I felt it. *You* know."

We had to take care what we said, even in here. I raised an eyebrow at her. "Lots of men have something wrong with them."

"This one was different," she insisted. "Listen. They were…strong women. They would have fought off a stranger's attack easily. It had to be someone they knew, someone who could get close to them on purpose and persuade them to let down their guard."

"I think you're making a big leap, there." I pressed my lips together, blotting lipstick I hadn't bothered to apply.

"You don't believe me, do you?" She faced me, speaking in a low, fierce tone. "Why won't you help me? Someone is coming after your own kind! Not just my people. *Our* people!"

I took a step back, hands raised. "It's not that I don't believe you. I just can't do anything about it."

"You could at least try," she muttered. "I'm sorry, I don't mean to be rude. But..." She cocked a knee, baring a fishnet-stockinged thigh, and drew a small wallet from her garter. "Here."

She held something out to me—a 2 by 3 inch headshot of a stunning blond woman with piercing blue-green eyes.

I squinted at it. "Is this one of your friends?"

"It's Astarte—Astrid Jones. That was her stage name." She meant the modern name, the human name. "She was the last one, before me."

I took it. The woman in the picture didn't look familiar. But she also looked human. The dead succubus from this morning had light hair, too. Ash and dishwater, though, not this spun gold. My mouth went dry and a chill sifted through me. "When did you see her last?"

"Last Wednesday," Penelope said. "She was here for the show. I haven't heard from her since."

I tried again. "Penelope, I definitely think this is a police matter."

"Do you know how many other succubi have any connection with law enforcement?" At my headshake, she said, "None, Lily. There are no others. You're the only one I can trust to ask the right questions."

I sighed. "Okay."

Her head came up, her eyes suddenly alive with hope. "Okay, what?"

"I'll see what I can do. Run some database checks, maybe call in a few favors. And here—" I rummaged for my business cards and handed her one. "In case you need to get in touch with me."

She stared at me. Then she threw her arms around my neck. I stiffened before I remembered that my touch couldn't hurt her. She had more control than I did, too—no kether pull. "Thank you," she said. "Truly, thank you so much."

I extricated myself as politely as I could. "Can I keep this?" I held up the picture of Astrid Jones.

She nodded. Clumsy in the face of her gratitude, I fumbled the photograph into my purse. "We should go back out there. Our friends will wonder what's keeping us."

She followed me out of the restroom and straight into the arms of the devil himself.

Okay, not really the devil, and in fact, we collided head on with a bone-shaking thump. But he wore the right costume: horned mask, red robe, scarlet fedora. He took me by the shoulders with both hands as if to steady me, but behind his gold and red mask, his intense, feverish stare fixed on Penelope.

His desiderata flared and shuddered around him, an eerie light that pushed the edge of the visible spectrum, an ultraviolet hum. She recoiled, her face bloodless, a protective glamour blurring the air around her until she half-faded into the shadows of the wall. The man in the devil mask gripped my arm hard, his fingers flexed with bruising strength.

"Take your hands off me," I snapped, grabbing at his wrists...and reeled at the touch of his skin on mine. Like a dizzy fall into unseen fathoms or the sick suction of phlebotomy. Bitter, rank kether flowed into the gap, at once magnetic and nauseating.

We broke apart. He stumbled backwards and I doubled over, retching.

"What *are* you?" he snarled.

"What are *you*?" Half-choking, I threw the words back at him.

Then, from behind me, came a voice laced with Penelope's Presence. Unlike her stage Presence earlier, it didn't attract anything. It aimed to protect, to threaten, to instill dread.

"Walk away." At her command, my legs strained to move against my will despite my wobbly knees. But she hadn't meant the compulsion for me. "Walk away from her now and don't look back."

His footsteps receded, slowly at first, then quickly, pounding down the stairs toward the main room. I straightened, eyes streaming and stomach threatening to turn itself inside out. Penelope panted beside me while Sebastian and Ariel hurried our way.

"Who was that?" I rasped.

"That was him," Penelope said, her voice grim and empty now of Presence, her eyes wide and wild. "That was the man I told you about." She ran to meet Sebastian, dragging him with her toward a door in the back of the room marked with a green-glowing exit sign. "We have to go," she told him, then glanced back at me. "Lily, you have to leave. Now."

I swayed in place. Mildew spots danced in my vision. How much of the red-robed man's twisted kether had I drawn from that brief touch? Involuntary kether pulls intensified with emotional connection, but he'd taken mine and replaced it with energy that scoured my veins and belly like acid.

Ariel came to my side, slipping an arm around my waist. "You're all right, Lily." His soft voice soothed and steadied me as he steered me toward the exit. "Easy does it. I've got you."

And when he stopped me in the stairwell and kissed me full of sweeter kether, I didn't care to protest.

By the time the club's back stairs spit us out into the foggy chill of the autumn night, I had gotten some of my fight back.

"Get away from me." I belatedly shrugged off Ariel's supporting arm and breathed in deep, sobbing gulps. The empty alley echoed with the slam of the door. Penelope and Sebastian had disappeared. We'd taken our time in the stairwell. The fresh salt of ocean air mingled in my nostrils with the stench of petrochemical exhaust and the city's filth, but I didn't care. My lungs needed the oxygen.

Ariel frowned, but he released me. "What happened back there, Lily? What did she say to you?"

"It's not what she said." I sucked in another sharp breath. "It was that man. Penelope was right. There's something wrong with him."

"Wrong how?"

I shook my head. "I don't know. She said he was hanging around the other girls before they disappeared. Hunting them, maybe. But with kether like that, I don't know how he'd get close enough to them." Shuddering, I wrapped my arms around myself. The cold had started to seep in, a symptom of the tainted draw.

"Let me take you home," he said. "I'll get us a cab."

"No!" I backed away from him. "You've done enough tonight. I never wanted to come here, and now..."

"Now what?" he inquired mildly. "Now you have to care about her, don't you?" His elaborate mask didn't hide his radiating triumph.

My fists itched to pummel that smug look off his face. Gritting my teeth, I dug my nails into my palms. "This was all just one big manipulation, wasn't it? Pushing kether on me. Showing me what real succubi do. Making me care. It's all just your way of pulling me back in."

"So it's working, then?"

"Fuck you, Ariel."

"Really? Because that can be arranged."

"*Damn* you," I growled, and adrenaline roared in my ears. I flexed my hands, shifting my weight to the balls of my feet. One more quip from him, and I—

"I hear that's already been taken care of."

My sucker punch connected and snapped his head back. Either he'd underestimated the speed of my recovery, or he'd gifted me a pity punch. He pressed a hand to his mouth, his mask askew. His fingers came away bloody, and a heady rush of power warmed me at the sight.

Then he laughed, his demon eyes flashing at me. "Feel better? Sometimes it helps to hit something, doesn't it?"

"It helps to hit *you*." I rubbed my bruised knuckles, glaring at him.

"I live to serve," he drawled. "Now can I call us a cab?"

"I'll get my own, thanks." But I paced back to him after a few steps toward the cross street. "Ariel?"

He stood still in the alley, head dropped. His long black coat swept around him like hulking black wings. "Yeah?"

"You must have a theory," I said. "About who's doing this."

"Isn't it obvious?" He didn't raise his head. "It's Tonepah Valley all over again. Humans can't stand knowing they're not at the top of the food chain. If they can't find a way to use us, they hunt us. Hunt or be hunted, just like it always was."

I drew a sharp breath. The warm buzz of besting him drained out of me, leaving me cold and hollow.

A nuclear accident had turned the Tonepah Valley military base into a no man's land, a vast exclusion zone in the wilderness of the Nevada desert surrounded by high electric fences, radiation warning signs, and a whole lot of nasty rumors. According to Ariel, the U.S. government had once imprisoned demons there.

He called it an act of genocide that put the "human" in "inhumanity." He always did have a way with words.

"Not all humans are like that," I said. *Danny, for instance.*

"You're killing me, Lily. Your answer to Tonepah is 'not all humans?' That's a hell of a hashtag."

His mood had darkened, and it was no use talking to him when he got like this. "I've got to go." I cleared my throat, stepping back. "I'll see if I can find anything out. How can I reach you if I do?"

"You could," he said, "unblock my number. But failing that, don't worry. I'll find you."

At the mouth of the alley, I glanced back at him, a motionless silhouette in the half-shadow of the orange sodium lights. His shoulders hunched slightly forward, the posture of a watchful hawk perched on a telephone wire.

I sighed, shivered, and turned the corner, leaving the club's back door and the brooding incubus behind me.

HEAD DOWN, I hurried away from the Black Cat Club. Humans in varying degrees of sobriety, dressed for conventional nightlife at the SOMA district's mainstream bars, gave me a generous berth and more than a few sideways glances. That didn't surprise me, given my professional suit, gaudy harlequin mask, and definitely-not-restful bitch face.

I had to stick to speed-walking over the uneven sidewalk or risk falling ass over teakettle in front of God and everyone, but I wanted to run until my lungs ached and the frigid night air cleared my mind of Ariel's honeyed kisses, Sebastian's ice-blue eyes, Penelope's stark fear and her desperate gratitude.

Someone is hunting us...

My pace slackened as I reached a better-lighted block closer to Market Street. I dug out my phone, my numb fingers fumbling over the touchscreen.

Danny picked up on my second try, a cheerful clamor of bar noise behind her shout of, "Hello?"

"It's me." I clutched my phone to my ear and checked nearby doorways and alleys for listeners. More streetlamps here just meant deeper shadows in the places the light couldn't reach.

"Lil?" Danny said. "I can hardly hear you. Are you actually coming out? Did Hell freeze over? Is the moon blue?"

"No. Well, yes. I went out. I am out. Something weird happened tonight—"

"What? Sheesh, it's pandemonium in here. Hang on." After a moment, the racket on the other end of the call dropped off. "Did you say you went out? You sound upset."

"I'm fine. I—Oh, hell. I might as well say it. I fell off the wagon."

"You fell off the—Lily! Are you drunk?"

"No. I don't know. Maybe a little." It wasn't the alcohol, but the disorienting mixture of kether swirling in my blood. The clean stuff Ariel had given me in the stairwell had diluted the stranger's tainted contribution, but my head still spun and my heart raced painfully. Regular alcohol never gave me much of a buzz no matter how many drinks I downed, but if humans went through this whenever they drank, why did they even bother?

"You keep giving me three contradictory answers to every question," Danny said. "What's going on with you?"

I hesitated. I'd already strayed too close to outing one of my kind tonight, and I had to tread carefully. Ariel wouldn't take kindly to me sharing his identity with a human.

"Are you still there? Talk to me, Sugarbean."

"I think I might have a lead on our Jane Doe."

"What? The one from today? Hold up! You're out playing detective and you didn't invite me?"

"Not exactly," I said. "I wasn't looking for clues. This one found me. Danny, I don't want to be alone right now. Can I come meet you?"

"Of course. I'm at Ladybird's, like we talked about." Danny sounded taken aback. "Are you sure you're okay?"

That made the third time today she'd asked me that. "No," I mumbled. "I'm not."

"What happened?"

"I met someone." A faint scuffling sound echoed behind me. I whirled to survey the sidewalk, the empty street, the shadows.

"You *what?*"

Movement flickered where shreds of fog curled at the edge of the streetlight's glow. Fabric rippled, and an indistinct shape faded into the gloom.

"Someone's hunting demons," I said. "And I think they're following me."

"Lily—"

"I have to go." I ended the call, scanning recessed doors and alleyways for another glimpse of whomever—or whatever—lurked there. Was it watching me? My skin crawled.

"Who's there?" My voice echoed back to me from the dark bulwarks of the high-rise buildings on either side of the street.

All lay still. I retraced my steps toward the last cross-street, thumb poised over the emergency call option on my phone screen. When I drew even with the streetlight, someone burst from the cover of a nearby doorway, feet pounding away from me around the corner. Scarlet robes fluttered, and the figure glanced over its shoulder.

Horns curved from its forehead in silhouette.

"Hey!" I gave chase, high heels be damned, and the devil took off running. "*Wait.*"

My demon Presence resonated in the word, made it a command, and he stumbled, his steps dragging to a halt. I grasped him roughly by the shoulder and spun him to face me.

He twisted out of my hands more easily than I expected. "Get away from me!" Bars of blue and orange neon light from a nearby pawn shop's iron-barred window illuminated his snarl. Under his grotesque mask, the whites of his eyes showed like a cornered animal's.

"I'd be happy to." I advanced on him, forcing him back a step. "Just as soon as you tell me why you were following me."

6

TICKET TO THE TOUGH LOVE TRAIN

THE MAN IN THE DEVIL MASK SHOOK HIS HEAD, A QUICK, JERKY MOTION. HIS desiderata drew around him in a rank and sweaty shroud. "I wasn't following you. You came after me!"

"Don't lie to me." My Presence pulsed again, and he cowered away from it.

"You're one of them." He dragged at a chain around his neck. A crucifix glinted there. "The power of—"

"Shut up." Had the devil really just tried to exorcise me? I stepped toward him again, and he flinched. "That doesn't work. It only pisses us off."

"Depart, seducer! Unclean spirit, begone!" He waved the little cross in my face.

I eyed it, wary. Silver? I couldn't tell in the shifting neon half-light, but the image of Danny pulling a cross from a corpse's chest flashed through my mind, and I drew back. Best to err on the side of caution. "Strong words, coming from a man dressed as Satan himself," I said. "One might even call them fighting words. Also, untrue. I showered this morning."

"Stay away!" His eyes darted and he shuffled his feet. Not about to let him make a break for it, I grabbed for his upper arm, careful to avoid the bare skin of his wrist and hand.

Still, it was a mistake. He turned and lunged at me.

I dodged too slow. His tackle slammed me to the concrete. The bone-juddering crunch shuddered through my spine and knocked the breath out of me. My kether reserves kept the pain at bay, but he still had me pinned before I could recover.

Damn, he was fast, strong, and solid-built. I struggled to dislodge him, but he used his weight advantage to keep me down and clawed at my face.

My mask! I snapped my teeth at him, biting air. He tore at the paper mâché and his fingers on my face delivered another jolt of his revolting kether.

I gasped and bucked my hips. He braced himself with one arm, and I promptly pulled it out from under him. He toppled and I threw myself sideways, away from him.

But he still had a grip on my mask, and he took it with him. Its elastic band ripped painfully through my hair and the cold air stung my now-exposed cheeks.

"Fuck *off!*" I dove on him, driving my knee into his groin. He grunted and went limp. I sprang backward, but his hand closed around my ankle and pulled me back down, hard. It hurt more this time. His sick kether had side effects I didn't expect.

However, he'd recovered far faster than he should have, and he didn't make the same mistake this time. He straddled my chest and his hands closed around my throat, his disorienting energetic push and pull taking hold of me again. Spots of black swirled in my vision and my heart thumped in my ears.

Lady Gaga saved me. Danny's ringtone blared from my pocket with a fanfare of absurd triumph. My opponent's grip loosened on my throat, and I took the opening. Flipping him off me, I landed in a half-crouch on the balls of my feet.

He crab-crawled away from me and rose, panting hard. We eyed each other narrowly, both a little unsteady: a draw.

He'd seen my face. He had made me, all right, but two could play that game.

"You're one too," I said, breathless. "One of us. One of *me*. You're a cambion, aren't you?"

His desiderata shrank from me. "I don't know what you're talking about."

"I'm kicking myself that I didn't see it before." I circled toward him as he sidled away. "You go both ways, just like me. You can draw kether and you can give it. And such kether! My God, and here I thought I had the corner on half-demon self-loathing. You've got me beat by a mile!"

"You're lying," he said.

"I don't think so." I smiled without humor. "I can't wait to tell Ariel about this. Next to you, I look positively well-adjusted."

"You can't tell anyone!"

Discordance flared through his desiderata, sharp and twitchy as static. I leaned my shoulder against the wall of the pawn shop to hide the wobble in my knees. My phone's tinny rendition of "Born This Way" concluded and immediately restarted as Danny called again.

"I've got to take this. My friend works for the police." Not precisely true, but she did work *with* them, so close enough. "She'll turn this city upside down looking for me if I don't check in. And if you hurt me, she'll tear you a new one." Closer, or at least I liked to think so.

"I don't want to hurt you," he said, sullen-toned. "You attacked me!"

I inclined my head, granting him the point despite his belligerent tone. I chose not to remind him that he'd tried to banish me like some B-movie priest. "Okay, then. Tell me why you were stalking me in there." My phone bleated Gaga's last lines and fell silent abruptly. I palmed it into my purse. Maybe he wouldn't notice.

"I'm not stalking you. I was looking for *her.*" His eyes shone overbright, his words running together. He was putting her on a pedestal like some eldritch goddess, not the scared, grieving small-stage performer I'd just met.

I studied my nails. "Her who?"

"You were with her. She protected you. I thought you'd know where she went."

I frowned. I didn't need Penelope's protection. If anything, she needed my protection—from him. "I don't think that's any of your business. What are you, her number one fan? I didn't know exotic dancers had groupies."

"Don't call her that," he said hotly. "And you've got it all wrong. I just wanted to talk to her. To warn her."

"Buddy." I stared at him. My phone started ringing again. "You know she was afraid of *you*, right?"

"But—"

"That's a no. Got it." I rolled my eyes and accepted Danny's call mid-refrain. "Danny, I'm *fine*."

"No," Danny proclaimed in my ear. "This is not fine and that was *not* okay. You tell me a murderer is following you right before hanging up, and then you don't answer your phone? Are you kidding me?"

"It's not a murderer." I glowered at the devil, who edged farther away from me. "It's just an idiot."

"Well, I'm glad you're alive," she said, but she didn't sound mollified. "You almost gave me a heart attack. Where are you?"

I squinted at the street sign on the corner. "Tenth and Howard?"

"We're coming to pick you up." Her tone left no room for argument. "You better not be dead when I get there, or swear to God I'll—"

"Kill me?"

"That's not funny, Lil."

"I think it's—Hey! Get back here, you!"

I directed this at the man dressed as the devil, too late. He took off running again with inhuman speed. I sighed as his flapping red robes disappeared in the direction of Market Street. The skin-to-skin contact with him had drained me again, leaving me feeling all-too-human and vaguely ill, but he'd tapped into his cambion's strength without a problem. He must have gotten his second wind directly from me.

"You're welcome," I yelled after him. "Asshole!"

"Stop shouting," Danny groused in my ear. "What's going on over there?"

"Nothing," I said. "I just lost my idiot."

"You're having a hell of a night, aren't you?"

I grimaced. "You could say that." My quick inventory revealed that my skirt had torn where I'd skidded across the sidewalk. I'd have bruises, too, but those would fade quickly enough. The black and white harlequin mask Ariel had given me lay in the gutter, feathers oily and bedraggled, false jewels tarnished. I picked it up, turning it over in my hands. A jagged fracture split it between the eyes.

"Be there in ten," Danny said. "Try not to do anything stupid." The "anything *else*" went unspoken.

I dropped the mask back into the gutter. It had served its purpose, a beautiful illusion. But I couldn't salvage it, and I wouldn't wear it again.

"No promises," I said, and sank down on the curb to wait.

"BUT I CAN'T GO home with you guys," I protested. "You're on a date!"

"Shut up," Danny said, briskly releasing the clutch.

Upon arriving for curbside cambion pickup, Danny had taken one look at my face, wrapped me up in her big leather biker jacket, and bundled me into the back of her girlfriend's Volkswagen Rabbit. They had arrived in seven minutes, not the promised ten. Danny must have played fast and loose with speed limits on the way over.

That made it twice today that she'd rescued me. I shifted in my seat, chewing a broken nail, a souvenir of my dance with the devil.

Berry turned around in the passenger seat. "It's okay, I promise." She had a gorgeous smile, light brown eyes that matched her curly brown hair, and a constellation of freckles across the bridge of her nose. I could see why Danny liked her.

"You are being way too nice," I said.

"I tell her that all the time." Danny grinned at her partner. "It's useless. She can't help herself."

At Danny's apartment, Berry disappeared into the master bedroom and shut the door. Danny padded around and brought me pajamas, blankets, pillows, and a cup of chamomile tea. Once I seemed unlikely to make a break for it or have a nervous breakdown, she curled up in the papasan chair she'd hung onto since med school. "Okay," she said. "What really happened tonight?"

I dug in my purse for the small photo that Penelope had given me. All the things I couldn't tell her weighed on the tip of my tongue. "Could this be our Jane Doe?"

She took the picture, frowning. Then her eyes widened. "I'd have to check the file, but this could be her. Where did you get this?"

"Let's call it an anonymous tip."

"So you're not going to tell me." Her tone flattened, her desiderata ebbing in resignation.

"I can't." Catching her narrow glance, I added, "Some secrets aren't mine to tell, Dan."

"Sure, but this picture doesn't help me ID her."

"I can give you a name," I said. "Astrid Jones. She's—she *was* a succubus."

She whistled. "So your anonymous tipster…"

"Knew her, yes." I hoped this wouldn't end in more trouble for Penelope. "Astrid's been missing about a week. Does that help?"

"Well, it's something. I'll run her through the databases." Danny shot me another hard glance. "What else aren't you telling me? Didn't you say you met someone? They weren't the one who put those marks on your neck, were they?"

I flushed, pulling the blankets up around my chin. "No, that was someone else. The idiot I tangled with."

"Hmm… But didn't you say you fell off the wagon?"

"It wasn't like that," I said. "Nothing happened, except… I almost lost control. I pulled a glamour on a human. I tried to stake a claim."

She raised an eyebrow. "Did they fall for it?"

"Maybe. For a second." I rubbed my temples. In fact, he hadn't exactly acted like a man enchanted—or not with me, at least. It didn't make me feel any better. The only thing worse than realizing you'd acted like a lust-addled succubus was realizing that you had failed as a lust-*addling* succubus.

Maybe he had resisted my charms because *she* had already claimed him. From what I recalled of Ariel's lessons on cubine claims, they amounted to a few vague rules he'd probably cribbed from a bad soft-core S&M novel.

"But you made your interest known," Danny said. "That's progress. What's his name?"

I groaned, diving under the pillow she'd given me.

"Lillian Knight! You met the man of your dreams and didn't even bother to get his name?"

"It's Sebastian," I said into the pillow. "And he's not the man of my dreams. He belongs to someone else."

"Are you sure? You did meet him at the kinky burlesque. Maybe they have an open relationship."

"You're incorrigible." I yanked the pillow from my face to scowl at her. "No, I didn't ask about the terms of their relationship. But I don't think it matters after what I did."

"But you didn't do anything," Danny said.

I couldn't explain the real problem without telling her how I'd almost outed Penelope. "Can't you see I'm trying to wallow in inconsolable angst here?" I grumbled.

"Oh, Lil, you're being too hard on yourself. I'm proud of you for putting yourself out there."

"Why? He didn't even like me!" His anger at my warning still stung, fresh as when it first seared through me. The bad kether I'd drawn from the red-clad man hadn't helped, but the lingering nausea didn't trouble me as much as the way Sebastian's desiderata had frozen over before he walked away.

Danny sighed. "My point is, Sugarbean—and I say this with all the love in the world—this isn't super-extra-special snowflake cambion angst material. This is normal life stuff. So you got rejected? Ouch. It happens. Cry over it, get over it, and then get back on the horse."

"Wow," I said. "When did I buy a ticket for the tough love train? That's easy for you to say!"

"Yep. Know why? Lots of practice."

"Practice telling me to get over things?"

"Practice getting rejected." Danny extracted herself from the depths of the papasan and blew me a kiss. "Get some sleep, honey. It'll be better in the morning, I promise."

"Thanks, Dan." My eyes prickled with unexpected tears. "You're the best."

"I know. Night, Lil."

"Night," I mumbled, huddling down into the blanket as she switched off the light and headed to her nice warm bed with her nice warm Berry. Suddenly, I couldn't ignore that everyone had someone except me. Nothing had changed, but my loneliness hadn't bothered me until I saw someone I wanted and couldn't have.

Or had everything changed when Ariel kissed me in my living room, reminding me of all that I denied myself?

Alone now, safely tucked into Danny's couch, the past flooded back in vivid flashes, decade-old memories I preferred to keep locked away: black lace and red satin, slick leather and warm skin, my arm linked with Ariel's as his exquisite voice murmured in my ear, pointing out my next target.

With the delicious ache of kether and desire humming under my skin, it became all too easy to crave the ecstasy of the Exchange, everything I'd done my best to leave behind.

"Damn you, Ariel," I whispered.

Danny had hit the nail on the head when she implied I had little experience with rejection. When I embraced my demon side, a huntress at the top of her game, I never got turned down. Back then, Ariel and I had spent countless nights at places like the club we'd visited tonight.

Twenty-one-year-old Lily had none of the qualms I had at thirty-one. She held the world in the palm of her hand.

Dressed to the nines, I would sail into the midst of the New York City nightlife herd on Ariel's arm. We'd stalk the crowds until Ariel had picked out my lucky victim *du jour*. I would close on the chosen one like a homing missile, and they would fall for me in no time at all. In the space of an evening, an hour, mere minutes, I would take my human lover home, or they would take me home, and I would feed from them.

To mitigate the strength of a pull fueled by emotional connection, I never let them get too close and never fed from anyone more than once, for their safety and my own. My prey would have the night of their lives, and they would never know that they felt lightheaded and fatigued because a succubus had stolen their life force. Their kether regenerated quickly, the original renewable resource. Meanwhile, my glamours and Presence kept them unsuspecting of anything out of the ordinary, convinced that they had no reason to feel afraid.

Afterward, I would go to Ariel and he would feed, too. He called it another lesson, said it benefited me to understand both sides of the Exchange, how good it felt to surrender my kether. I let myself lose control with him the way I resisted with my human partners but it always left me dizzy, exhausted, and craving our next hunt, eager for the following night when we'd do it all again.

I didn't understand the risks for them or me back then, not like I did now.

If I believed Penelope's theory and Ariel's grim worldview, someone had turned the tables on the cubine population of San Francisco. Hunter had become hunted. The age-old ritual of Exchange between demons and humans had acquired a new level of danger.

And now I couldn't think of anything else.

I WAS sixteen when I found out that I was different; not human, a monster. Sixteen when I found out about my father—the real one, not the one who seemed to hate me more and more each year, but the one I'd never met, my demon sire.

The man I called my father taught comparative religion at a private university. He liked to invite his favorite students for dinner—we were all part of one big family, he would tell them. The year I turned sixteen, his chosen proxy son was a boy named Ben. A man, actually; tall and lanky at eighteen, he had a ready smile, a quick mind, and rich brown eyes he couldn't keep off me.

It was a warm Pennsylvania summer night, heavy and humid as a lover's embrace, and the fireflies danced twinkling down the hill where the creek ran past our house. Ben had followed me out into the shadows of the porch. I watched him out of the corner of my eyes, all my senses heightened and my heart beating like a drum in my ears.

It was his desiderata singing to me, but I didn't understand it at the time. And when he put his hands on me and kissed me, clumsy with hunger, driven by the cubine glamour that in my ignorance I couldn't control, I took everything he had to give and left him nothing at all.

My father found me there, sick, stumbling, and crying hysterically over Ben's unconscious body. He looked at me as if he'd never seen me before. It was dark on the porch but every detail of his expression etched itself into my mind, the way his face twisted with disgust and fear and fury. He knew. He must have suspected before, and this was the confirmation he'd needed to condemn me.

"I want her out of this house," he told my mother, and she obeyed him.

She always obeyed him, except for the one time she hadn't, the original disobedience that had resulted in my existence.

She confessed her sins to me in my childhood bedroom over a half-packed suitcase, her voice soft and toneless, her drowned violet eyes pleading with me for some kind of absolution. But I had nothing like that to give her. I could barely comprehend the words. It sounded like delusion, like a fantasy, and all I had in me was rage.

What did she expect? If I believed her, then forgiveness was never in my nature. What does a demon know about absolution, anyway?

Ben never woke up, and my parents sent me away to a religious correctional school upstate, where Ariel found me and got me out. He showed me how to survive as a demon, how to control the kether pulls, how to live free and unnoticed among humankind.

When no one else thought I deserved salvation, Ariel saved me in the only way he knew how.

He saved me by making me more like him.

7

YOU ALWAYS HURT THE ONE YOU LOVE

"You always hurt the one you love." I met the gaze of each juror in the box in turn, taking the measure of their desires.

Their hunger and impatience hung heavy in the air. They didn't care about my classic pop culture references, no matter how apt. Most of them had never heard of the Mills Brothers. They just wanted lunch.

So did I. This day had gone on too long already. I'd woken before dawn, my neck cricked from sleeping on Danny's couch despite a surfeit of pillows, and raced home to prepare for court. Waves of nausea and vertigo had dogged me all morning, souvenirs of my dance with the devil.

Time to change gears and wrap this up. I allowed a hint of disdain to enter my voice, spooling it out to them like a baited line. "Defense counsel used his closing statement to tell you that the defendant loves his wife. I won't dispute that assertion. I'm here to say that what the defendant did to Gina Altamont had nothing to do with love. And you are here to evaluate the evidence—not of what he felt or didn't feel, but what he did."

A few of them shifted in their seats, their gazes skating away from mine. Their individual emotional flavors mingled into a harsh mélange, the bitter wine of discontent.

It wasn't quite what I wanted, but it was a start. I had to take that discomfort and nurture it, distill it until it matured into a stronger medicine: anger. Until they wanted the same thing that I wanted.

"Justice," I said. "That's why we're here today."

I lifted my exhibit with the crime scene photographs and balanced it on the rail, confronting them with the devastation that Dr. Richard Altamont had wrought on his wife's face and body. "This is what the defendant did to the woman he vowed to love and cherish. But this was not love. This was a brutal, bloody beating. And it wasn't the first time. He broke her down over a period of seven long and painful years. He made her believe she deserved this."

I took a breath, letting the words sink in as I replaced the exhibit on its easel. I flicked a glance toward the distinguished man sitting beside his attorney at the defense table, his face an impassive mask. Clean-cut and well-educated, a respected professional in his mid-forties with glasses and graying hair, he didn't fit most people's stereotype of a low-class, ignorant wife-beater. If I could get the jurors to reexamine their assumptions, it would bring me halfway home.

Turning away from him, I faced the gallery. Gina sat in the third row on the left, her head in her hands. Her court-appointed advocate touched her shoulder and Gina looked up, revealing the ragged scar from the glass that had sliced her cheek open. "Intimate violence is the worst form of betrayal," I said. "It leaves lasting scars."

Now you have to care about her, don't you? Ariel's words from yesterday mocked me. He had manipulated me last night just as I now manipulated these twelve humans, for a good cause. He had reeled me in and made me care. He hadn't even needed a Presence to do it. He used his superhuman insight into my desires to cast the perfect hook—a woman who needed my protection.

I faltered, my well-rehearsed arguments scattering. Did the ends justify the means?

The judge cleared his throat. "Counsel. Will that be all?"

Black motes danced at the edge of my vision. I reached for the edge of the prosecution table to steady myself. "I apologize, Your Honor. I just need a moment."

"Proceed," he said, stern. He wanted his lunch, too.

Behind me, the jury whispered. I shut my eyes and took a breath, gathering the shreds of my composure. Restless images from my early-morning dreams flitted across the backs of my eyelids. Twisted masks with eyes that never quite saw me. A figure glimpsed in reflections and peripheries, a shadow with no face and tattered wings. Tendrils of darkness wrapped around my limbs, slowing my steps, dragging me down—

"Ms. Knight." Judge Wong's impatience lashed out at me, whiplike, and I pulled myself back to the present with a start.

It was my last chance to make them care. "Mrs. Altamont deserves justice." I opened my eyes and groped for the next words, momentum building with each phrase. "She deserves the justice that only you can provide. She deserves your compassion. She deserves your protection. She deserves to see you do the right thing by finding the Defendant guilty of all charges, up to and including attempted murder."

"A life without fear is the very least of what Mrs. Altamont deserves." I spoke not only for the jury, but for the woman in the gallery with her scarred face and silent, shuddering sobs. "And you have the power to give it to her."

I gave the jury one more long, challenging look before I pivoted to Judge Wong. "Your honor, the prosecution rests."

"Thank you, counsel." The judge peered over the wire tops of his reading glasses at the jurors gathering their belongings in anticipation of release. "The court will adjourn for lunch, with jury instructions to begin promptly at one thirty."

Judge Wong vanished into chambers without further ceremony. The bailiff opened the jury box and its contents filed out, twelve glum faces. No one ever looked forward to jury instructions.

I sank into my chair and drew another long, shaking breath, sorting my notes and exhibits back into my battered accordion file with the rest of the case documents.

"Are you feeling all right, Ms. Knight?"

Opposing counsel loomed over me, too close for comfort.

I called him "counsel" out loud and "McSkeezy" in my head, so it took me a moment to remember his actual name. "I'm fine, Mr. Bayer."

"Sure about that? You choked up there, and you never choke."

"I didn't choke." I swept my files into my briefcase.

"No need to get testy," he said. "I have to say, it's a relief to see you crack. Maybe you're human after all, eh?"

I stared at him. "What do you mean by that?"

"Nothing, Lily, nothing. I can call you Lily, right?" His desiderata washed over me, oily and thick as his slicked-back hair, and I flinched. He didn't notice. "What do you say to drinks after this circus is over? Put it all behind us, get to know each other better?"

Did he really just ask me on a date? I stood, closing my briefcase with a snap. "I don't think that's a good idea."

"Don't be like that. We don't have to be enemies just because we're on different sides." His smile had become a leer. He'd positioned himself so that he blocked my exit. His crude-oil desiderata shimmered and oozed toward me.

"Step aside, please, counsel."

He didn't move. I contemplated providing him with a live demonstration of aggravated assault. Satisfying, yes, but beyond the obvious downsides, it required physical contact. I didn't need any more of his greasy energy crawling over my skin. Plus, an accidental kether pull could cause a stir, to put it lightly. In my current state, I couldn't trust my self-control.

Instead, I used my Presence.

Not a major Presence designed to enthrall a room full of humans, like the one Penelope had employed last night on the stage of the Black Cat Club, but one tailored to my target, projecting my distaste and aggression for him alone. No one else would see it. As for him, his own mind would determine what exactly he saw, built from whatever vile fears and hatreds he harbored deep within his wormy little soul.

Bayer blanched and retreated, his backside hitting the defense table. The bailiff lounging at the little desk to my right glanced up from his phone.

"What—" Bayer sputtered, as I stepped delicately around him.

"Best not to think about it too much," I advised him, and left him to it.

I'd taken a big risk, but he'd sound crazed saying that he'd seen a demon in the middle of a crowded courtroom when no one else had seen anything out of the ordinary.

At least, I hoped so.

Outside the courtroom, the hallway leading to the elevators swarmed with jurors, attorneys, and clerks. The roar of voices and unfiltered clash of emotions hit me like a ton of bricks.

"Hell." I flattened myself against the wall as the throng pushed past me. That projection had taken more out of me than I thought. No way I could handle an elevator stuffed with mortals right now. I'd have to take the stairs.

I fought my way toward the stairwell against the tide of humanity surging toward the elevators. I needed open air. I needed to breathe. I needed a drink.

I needed—

No. For the hundredth or so time in the last sixteen hours, I cursed Ariel's name. He'd only given me a few tiny tastes of second-hand kether and now I couldn't get my mind off it. Even McSkeezy's unsavory offer had tempted me. For one brief moment, I'd imagined taking him off to some seedy hotel and...

Gross. Talk about junk food cravings. His shallow, uncomplicated desire wouldn't have dulled the edge of my real hunger. It would only whet my appetite for something more. Something deep and dark and pure, like what I'd sensed within Sebastian of the Bespoke Suit.

Well, forget him. He was filet mignon and lobster, too rich for my blood. Nepenthe could keep him.

In the blessedly empty stairwell, I leaned against the cool cement wall and pulled out my phone to call Danny. She always made me feel more human when the demon got restless under my skin. The phone buzzed when I turned it on, heralding a series of texts from her:

Danny: *911. Call me when you get out of court.*

Danny: *I've got another one.*

I frowned down at the display. "Another what?" I hit the "call" button and pushed off the wall, my heels echoing as I made my way downstairs.

My first call didn't go through: no signal. I tried again when I reached the courthouse lobby, but got her voicemail.

"Damn it, Danny. Pick up!" I dialed a third time and pushed my way through the main doors, sucking in a welcome lungful of crisp fall air. The ring tone sounded twice, interrupted by the soft beeping of call waiting. Danny must have called back on her lab phone.

"Danny! Finally. What is it?"

A pause lengthened on the other end of the line, followed by a quick indrawn breath and a man's voice, low and rough with emotion. "Is this Lily Knight?"

My steps slowed, and I frowned at the unknown number on my screen before pressing it back to my ear. "Lily speaking. Who's this?"

"Lily, thank God." The speaker seemed to gather himself. "This is Sebastian Ritter. We met last night at the Black Cat Club."

"Sebastian." I swallowed, my mouth suddenly dry. "I remember. How did you get this number?"

"I need to talk to you. Penelope—" His voice broke on the name. Background noise crackled behind him—a two-way radio, or maybe a P.A. system. "Something's happened."

Ice crept down my spine. "Where are you? Why are you calling me?"

"They arrested me," he said. "I need your help."

"You're calling me from *jail*," I said, disbelief flattening my tone. "Sebastian, I'm not that kind of lawyer." The man had a fortune. Surely he had enough money to hire a private defense attorney. Hell, he probably had one on retainer. So why spend one of his jail calls on me?

"You have to tell them that I'm innocent." He sounded plaintive, desperate, like a man about to break, on the verge of begging.

In another context, I would have appreciated that more.

"I don't understand what you're asking me to do. Innocent of *what*?"

"Lily, I didn't kill her," he said, and I almost dropped my phone. "You have to believe me."

"No." Cold expanded outward from my chest. It left me dizzy and numb, unable to draw a full breath. "No, I don't."

He started to say something else, but I stabbed at the touchscreen until it hung up on him. My knees wobbled, and I staggered to a pillar, leaning against it until I could breathe again.

Another one, Danny's message had said. She'd meant another demon corpse.

Penelope was right.

"You didn't have to come all the way down here," Danny said.

"Yes, I did." I shoved my hands deep into my coat pockets, not looking at her but at the observation window. Blinds covered the other side. I shivered. "Do you know what happened to her? What killed her?"

She stared at me for a long moment, her expression undecipherable, her desiderata swirling with conflict. "Same as the other one, silver. But..."

"But what?" I demanded, when she didn't seem inclined to continue.

"This time we have a murder weapon."

Foreboding crawled over my skin. "What weapon? Why are you looking at me that way?"

"Sorry. It's just..." She looked down at her hands in their blue nitrate gloves. "It was a stake," she said to her hands. "A silver stake through her heart."

"A stake?" I gaped at her. "What, like in *Dracula*? That's—"

She shrugged, still not meeting my eyes. "Weird. I know."

"It's absurd. We're not vampires. Vampires are a myth."

"*I* know that," she said. "But I don't think everyone is capable of those fine distinctions."

"It's not a—never mind." I jumped up, pacing the length of the room. "Is that how you knew she was a demon? The silver?"

"That and her eyes," Danny said. "We check them as part of our initial exam. I might have mistaken it for jaundice, but..." She grimaced. "It's hard to miss the pupils."

"*Shit.*" I stopped short. "Did anyone else see them? The CSIs?"

She shrugged again. "If so, they didn't put it in their notes. Maybe her eyes looked different when they bagged her at the scene. The other body—Astrid—she started to look less and less human over time. If it's the same decay process..."

Her theory made sense, that a demon's glamour would decay along with her body. I would have expected an all-or-nothing transformation at the time of death, but Danny had said Astrid looked more "normal" when she arrived at the morgue. I started pacing again. "Show me, please."

She placed herself between me and the window, arms crossed, so that I had to meet her eyes. "You don't need to do this."

"I'm *fine*," I said. "You don't have to protect me. I'm not made of glass. I need to know."

She sighed and nodded once before she turned away, using her key card to open the inner door. I stepped closer to the window, waiting. Inside the room, she raised the blinds, her lips a tight line.

A sheeted form lay on the single table in the center of the room. I set my jaw. I would stay objective, no matter what.

At the morgue table, Danny paused, inhaling. Then she drew back the sheet, and I stifled a cry.

Unlike the body of Astrid Jones, the woman on the table still looked mostly human. Her short brunette bob fell back from her high cheekbones, revealing closed kohl-smudged eyes under disheveled bangs. Her vibrant, singular beauty had already begun to fade, leaving her skin gray and stretched taut over the planes of her face. Death had aged her decades in mere hours.

They're going to kill me next, she'd said.

I turned from the window, away from the still, dead face. I couldn't breathe. My vision blurred with tears, I groped for the nearest chair and fell into it. Behind me, the door to the inner room opened, and a moment later, Danny's hand dropped on my suited shoulder, careful as always not to touch my skin.

"Lily," she said, voice gentle. "You knew this one, didn't you?"

"I literally just talked to her." Numb, I shook my head. "Last night. She gave me that picture. She was scared…"

Danny sucked in a breath. "*She* was your anonymous tipster?"

Unable to speak, I nodded. She had asked for my help and then someone killed her.

"I'm so sorry," Danny said. "Would you like to know her name?"

I found my voice at last.

"Her name was Penelope," I said. "She danced like an angel, and she didn't deserve to die like this."

"Who was she to you, Lil?"

"Nobody," I said. "A stranger." The only other succubus I'd ever met. An artist with her Presence. She walked that grimy stage like a queen, and never let them see how she feared for her life.

I should have talked to Penelope more in the short hour I'd known her. I should have asked her so many things. How she lived, where she'd come from. How she handled knowing that her life and survival depended on human kether, on people who would hate and fear us if we showed our real faces.

How she'd met Sebastian Ritter. Whether she loved him.

But I couldn't ask Penelope any more questions. Now, only the terrible kind of questions mattered, like why Sebastian Ritter killed her. And why he'd thought he could get away with it by calling *me*.

8

THE KILLER IN HIM

After an interminable afternoon at the courthouse, I dumped my stack of exhibits, valise, and coat into the controlled chaos of my desk and stalked into my boss's office without bothering to knock.

D.A. Basra frowned up at me over the rims of her glasses. "Knight? Aren't you supposed to be in trial today?"

"Quick verdict," I said. "We lost on count one, but we got him on count two." The jury hadn't bought that Altamont had intended to kill his wife, but they couldn't deny the evidence of corporal injury. He'd serve some time, at least. On a day like today, I'd take it as a win.

"Good work." Basra's desiderata, hard to read at the best of times, rippled with complex shades. The light of her attention prismed as if through cracked glass. I'd already slipped her mind.

I cleared my throat and stood up taller, gathering myself. The shreds of kether in my veins hummed into readiness, stretching like Delilah after a nap. Who had Ariel turned me into with his cajoling kisses? I hadn't used a Presence in years, and now I prepared to resort to it for the second time in one day.

What had happened to the unassuming Lily Knight who tried to stay under the radar, play fair with humans, and keep to the straight and narrow?

The painful truth solidified into a knot under my breastbone. I'd worn that self like a mask and discarded it as easily as the feathered Mardi Gras confection I'd left in the gutter last night. My whole life was a series of masks, while my real self, demon Lily, waited beneath them for her moment to mess everything up. And now I didn't have the choice of playing fair, not if I wanted to keep the promise I'd made to poor, beautiful, dead Penelope.

"Make me lead on the Ritter case," I said, and put all my power behind it. I deserved this. I could handle it, and Basra could trust me—

"Of course. You've earned it." She rummaged through the files stacked on her desk. Her workspace had scarcely less chaos than my own, littered with multiple coffee cups and the remains of a half-eaten working lunch. "We just got this one. I'm surprised you heard already."

"Everyone's talking about it." Guilt gnawed at the pit of my belly—I'd only gotten my promotion to felony grade prosecutions last year—and I mercilessly pushed it down.

"Then you know the media will be all over us." She came up with a slim folder and a stern look, the glasses slipping down her nose. "Cross your Ts and dot your Is on this one. Defendant is a tech wunderkind and his father's a senator. It has to be ironclad if we're going to make this stick."

Well. I shouldn't have expected glazed eyes and hypnotized acquiescence from Fatima Basra. "A senator...Wait. He's James Ritter's son?"

"That's right," Basra said patiently, holding out the folder.

"Ritter of Ritter Security?"

Basra fixed me with another stern look. "The very same. I thought you wanted this case, Knight."

"I did! I do." I took the file gingerly, held it between my fingers like the explosive device it was. I had asked for it, but I hadn't anticipated a media bomb that could blow my career sky-high if I made a wrong move. I'd never run a murder case, much less a high-profile one. What had I gotten myself into?

"Everything all right? You're looking a little pale."

For a brief moment, I hesitated. I should tell her, right now. I should tell her that I met him last night, mere hours before…whatever had happened. I should tell her I'd met the victim. I should tell her…

But anything I told her would lead to more questions, ones I couldn't answer without giving away too much of my own secret.

"No," I said. "No, it won't be a problem. Thank you."

"Don't let me down, Knight."

"Yes, ma'am," I said, and fled, holding the file close to my chest.

BACK AT MY OWN DESK, fingers clumsy and numb with the aftermath of kether use, I shuffled through the file labeled *People v. Ritter* and found the scanned California driver's license. She stared up at me from the photo, short dark bob, limpid brown eyes, a smile to break your heart. The license listed her name as Penelope St. Cyr.

The report didn't mention any demonic characteristics in its description of Penelope's corpse. They didn't understand the significance of the silver. It also meant the investigation would proceed, at least for now.

My stomach knotted as I read through the initial report. Danny had shielded me from the worst details of Penelope's death. She hadn't told me that they'd found the body naked in the bed of the hotel's luxurious Presidential Suite. She hadn't told me that whoever killed Penelope had driven a sharpened silver stake through the demon woman's chest with such force that it pierced the mattress beneath. She hadn't told me that Penelope had died slowly, struggling, like a butterfly impaled on a pin.

The police had found Sebastian—my Sebastian—*Penelope's* Sebastian—Sebastian of the Bespoke Suit in the room with her, covered in her blood, lost in some sort of fugue state. His shadowed, blue-gray eyes stared back at me from the booking photo, haunted with an expression I couldn't name.

And I'd thought I had a bad picker because he was taken. No, I had thrown myself at a stone-cold killer. Nausea rose in my throat, sour and stinging, and I choked it back down.

God help me, I had *wanted* him. I had wanted to taste his desire for myself, its darkness and its depth. Deep enough to fall into and never rise again.

How had I failed to sense the killer in him? Had Ariel's shot of kether undone me so thoroughly that I couldn't see past my own compulsion to hunt, to claim, to feed?

I closed the folder and buried my head in my hands. A sequence of events had begun to take shape in my mind, and I didn't like it at all.

I had warned Sebastian Ritter about Penelope. I told him that she wasn't what she seemed. A few hours later, he'd murdered her, and now he wanted to see me. He thought I was on his side, somehow.

What if this was my fault?

If I'd given her away, where had he gotten the stake? That didn't add up. No one just happened to carry something like that to a romantic rendezvous. How would one get their hands on a silver stake, to begin with? A niche item, certainly. Custom-made, perhaps.

No, that stake meant something. It meant premeditation. It meant preparation. It meant cold calculation. And it meant the killer had known Penelope's secret, and her greatest weakness. They had known what to use and where to strike.

I shivered. Had Sebastian planned this all along? Did he have the weapon on him when I spoke to him? Had he sought out Penelope that night with the intent of murdering her?

I dropped my hands from my face and stood, taking a long, slow breath.

I had failed to save Penelope's life. I couldn't change that. But Fatima Basra had handed me the opportunity to bring her killer to justice. If I played my cards right, I could still put this monster away for life. I could still avenge her death.

Sebastian Ritter had asked for me. Well, he'd get me, all right.

Time for me to face the monster down.

DEFENDANTS AWAITED arraignment in custody for one of two reasons. First, because they were too poor to put up bail, like most people. Second, because they faced charges of a capital crime with no set bail amount, like Sebastian Ritter. Either way, in the hours leading up to their initial bail hearing, we literally kept the defendant in Limbo.

That's what we called the underworld of gray concrete beneath the courthouse. Long, shadowy, echoing tunnels connected it to the main jail across the street. Early each morning, corrections shuffled the day's unlucky winners in their blue and orange jumpsuits through the tunnel to the holding cells below the halls of judgment. When the bailiff finally read the defendant's name off the list, they would lead him up to the surface and lock him in the courtroom's cage. There, he would face his fate and his accuser, i.e., me.

Limbo was normally the province of public defenders, cops, and criminals: the damned and the damned-adjacent. D.A.s didn't go down there if we could help it. But twelve hours after Penelope St. Cyr's death, I descended into Limbo via a public elevator redolent of urine and despair. The fluorescent light above my head spit and flickered in an uneven rhythm that sparked an answering throb in my temples.

The elevator car thumped, shuddered, and considered its options for a long moment before the doors opened and it disgorged me into the underworld. I squared my shoulders with a sigh and stepped out, the too-loud tap of my heels on the dirty linoleum echoing in the empty tunnels.

A uniformed officer directed me down a dreary corridor to an even drearier block of interrogation rooms. He stopped in front of a room with a wide observation window screened by closed blinds. I shivered, remembering the window I'd stood before earlier that day in the morgue.

The officer rapped on the door, and Greg Greyson opened it, looking harassed. I liked Greg, even though we sat at opposite sides of the table. You couldn't really call a D.A. and a defense attorney *friends*, but you might call us professional frenemies. His integrity made a good antidote to Joe 'McSkeezy' Bayer's sleaze.

"Hey, Knight," Greyson said. "I've been trying to convince my client not to talk to you. This is highly irregular."

"Don't I know it." I gave him a wry grin. "And *you* know it's Mr. Ritter's 6th Amendment right to waive."

Greyson sighed, gloomy with resignation. "He's not in his right mind. I'll challenge any statement you get out of this."

"Let's not get ahead of ourselves. He asked for this meeting, didn't he?" I craned my neck to catch a glimpse of the man seated at the interrogation table, but saw only the top of a dark-haired head over Greyson's broad shoulder.

"Against vehement advice of counsel, yes."

I could only imagine. I caught the officer's eye. He shrugged, half-smirking, as if to say *You two fight it out.*

"Sounds like a knowing and intelligent waiver to me," I said.

"I'm telling you, my client's mental state is compromised."

"Come on, Greg. Stop stonewalling." I took a step forward, my posture challenging him to move aside. "We can argue it out in front of the judge for as long as you like—later."

"Can't wait." His sarcasm held a real spark of humor. Nice that he didn't entirely hate me, either. After a moment, he stepped back from the doorway, and I strode past him into the room where Sebastian Ritter sat.

In his orange jail scrubs, with his shoulders slumped and his head bowed, Ritter barely resembled the confident, well-dressed man I'd met last night. His hair flopped damply over his pale forehead. His eyes had drifted shut as if he'd fallen asleep in his chair. He looked wrecked.

"Mr. Ritter," I said loudly.

He started at my voice, raising his eyes to meet mine.

Those eyes—I faltered. The shadows under them had sapped them of their vibrancy, leaving them gray and desolate. The energy that had drawn me to him last night still tugged at my hunger, but faintly now, the whisper of a memory. Over it lay a thick fog of confusion, fear, and the aftermath of shock, mingled with a thick, choking bitterness.

Guilt—or grief?

"Thank you for coming." Each word seemed drawn from him with an effort, but he still managed to evoke the gravity of a CEO welcoming me to a board meeting.

"I'm not doing you any favors, Ritter." His composure irritated me. I wanted to shake him.

He shook his head. "I'm not asking for any." His gaze skated to Greyson. "Go away, Greg," he said.

"Wait," I said. "Mr. Ritter, do you understand that by sending him out, you're waiving your right to counsel for this interview?"

"Yes." Impatience spiked through the fog cloaking his desiderata. The handcuffs curtailed his dismissive gesture.

"I want to be very clear about this." Irritation with his nonchalance sharpened my words. "I'm not your friend, and I'm not here to help you. It's my job to prosecute you for a charge of first degree murder. Do you understand that?"

He dropped his head. "I understand."

I turned to Greyson with a raised eyebrow. "He seems pretty lucid to me."

"You're making a big mistake, Seb." Greyson didn't sound hopeful.

"You've done your due diligence." Despite his obvious exhaustion, Ritter's tone resonated with authority. "Out. Now."

"Fine." Anger flared behind Greyson's professional calm, but he stepped outside without further objection. I shot him a half-smile of sympathy. Ritter had placed him in an unenviable position. Sure, Greyson would get paid either way, but damage control for a recalcitrant and well-known client with money to burn didn't make for a good day in this business. If Ritter got convicted because of his own poor choices, his lawyer's reputation would take a hit, whether justified or not.

"I'll be right outside." The officer reached over and opened the blinds. "You can turn on the intercom whenever you like," he told me.

"No," Sebastian said, quiet and forceful. "No intercom."

His voice affected certain parts of me in ways that I did *not* want to think about just then. In handcuffs and prison orange, his face puffy and shadowed with fatigue, he still spoke as if he owned the room.

No. The man was a killer. I had to pull myself the fuck together.

The door banged shut, and Sebastian turned his attention back to me. "Ms. Knight. I didn't think you'd come."

"Yeah, well," I said. "I probably shouldn't have. Your lawyer was right, you know. This was a mistake, for both of us. But mostly for you."

"You're angry." Momentary surprise flashed through the static of his weariness.

Something in me snapped. I took a stride toward him and slammed my palms down on the table. Leaning forward, I got right up in his face. He flinched. *Good.*

"You're damn right, I'm angry," I snarled. "Why'd you do it, Ritter? Why did you kill her?"

The blood drained from his cheeks, leaving him gray and haggard. "That's just it." Despair flattened his words. "I didn't do it."

"Oh, sure." I didn't hold back my sarcasm. "If I had a nickel for every perp who tried that line, I could pay off my bar loans and retire early."

"Please," he said. For a moment, his control slipped, and his voice went ragged. "You have to listen to me."

I straightened, taken aback. His desiderata rang true. He believed what he'd said, and part of me wanted to believe it, too. I shoved that part ruthlessly back. "You keep saying that. I don't *have* to do anything."

"You're right." He exhaled, meeting my gaze. "But you could at least hear me out before you decide."

I hesitated. I didn't owe him that, either.

But I did owe it to Penelope to find out the truth. "Okay, fine." I yanked the chair out and flung myself into it, glaring at him. "I've read the report, Ritter. You were the only one in that suite with her. The only one who could have done it. How do you explain that?"

Confusion and fear roiled within him. "I can't."

"There's a reason we always suspect the boyfriend first, you know." *You only hurt the one you love.* Bile rose in my throat, and I choked it down. "But let's say I entertain your theory. If you didn't do it, who did?"

"I don't know. She was alive when we...when I..." His Adam's apple jerked as he swallowed. "I fell asleep. I don't know for how long. And when I woke up..." He faltered, a wave of emotion swelling in him. Horror, sorrow, helplessness, and with it a stab of discordance.

I frowned. "Are you lying to me, Mr. Ritter?"

"I swear I'm not." The words burst out clipped and harsh. Anger rose in him again, anger and desperation. "I don't know how to make you believe me. But I did...not...kill her."

"You didn't answer my question."

He made a sound in his throat, a near-growl of fury and frustration. The handcuffs clinked against the table as he lifted his wrists from the table, reaching toward me.

Why did I let him touch me? My demon reflexes should have kicked in, moved faster than his eye could follow, away from him. But perhaps the demon in me didn't want to move away.

Behind me, the door banged open. Two uniformed officers rushed in, with Greyson close at their heels. The uniforms grabbed Ritter and pulled him backwards as Greyson sputtered something about excessive force.

I sat frozen in the midst of the hubbub. In that brief moment of contact, when his fingers had brushed mine—

No kether in that touch, no desire. Its energy stirred far beneath his surface and ebbed away before it reached me. And yet a shock of connection had flashed between us. A powerful imprint of emotion that did not belong to me flooded my veins and with it flowed a series of images, a sudden sensory overload that my mind struggled to process.

His memory. It had to be.

He had opened his eyes to find her like that: blood bubbling from her lips, panic in her slitted, golden eyes, her demon eyes. Her hands had clutched at his, at the hilt of the stake protruding from her chest as she gasped for breath, trying to speak. Her life's blood had soaked the sheets, sluicing her skin. His hands had slipped, trembling, as he tried to pull the silver from her body, the light fading from her eyes as he held her in his arms.

"Oh, my God," I whispered.

He hadn't killed her.

He'd seen her true face, and he'd tried to save her.

The cops had Ritter in a chokehold. He didn't resist them. He gasped for air, but his gaze sought mine.

"That's enough," I snapped. "Let him go."

The officers dropped Ritter back down into the chair without ceremony. They stood close behind him, one at each shoulder. Ritter sucked in a breath, eyes fluttering closed. His lips moved.

His voice emerged hoarse and uneven, barely more than a whisper. But I heard him perfectly.

"I thought so," Sebastian Ritter said.

9

BLOOD IN THE WATER

AT MY FIRST STEP INTO THE D.A.'s PRESS BRIEFING ROOM, BRIGHT WHITE flashbulbs popped like a lightning storm. I controlled my flinch, afterimages blooming in my vision, the whir and click of camera shutters echoing in my ears.

A low buzz of excited conversation intensified among the reporters clustered in the aisles and huddled in folding chairs. In the center aisle, the local TV networks had set up shop for a live primetime broadcast, floating booms and the flat black eyes of their steady-cams all aimed directly at me.

I wet my lips and glanced sidelong at Basra. She jerked her head at me, urging me toward the waiting microphone.

She'd made me the lead prosecutor on the case. Now, at my first press conference, framed by flags and seals, the trappings of justice, I would have to step up to the podium and announce charges against an innocent man.

I didn't have a choice. I couldn't explain why I believed he didn't do it. I'd never experienced anything like what had happened when Sebastian touched me. The images had played out behind my eyes with the clarity of memory, stronger and more coherent than the dreamlike, synesthetic desiderata-impressions that marked my typical human interactions. I couldn't shake that vision, the sharp emotion of Penelope's last moments as seen through her lover's eyes. And I couldn't shake those three soft words he'd said to me.

I thought so.

I hadn't wanted to ask what he meant by that. He'd known Penelope's secret, and I had a growing suspicion he knew mine, too.

But how? In that moment when his fingers brushed mine, had he felt something, too? I needed to talk to Ariel, ask him what it meant, if other demons had experienced moments of clairvoyance.

Crap. Ariel. My chest tightened, my stomach dropping. He didn't know. I'd have to tell him about Penelope. I'd have to tell him I'd failed to save her.

But first, I had to get through this.

The hum of conversation swelled. The pack of journalists fixed their gazes on me, their mingled desiderata sharkskin-rough and hungry for scandal. They smelled blood in the water, chummed by earlier unconfirmed reports of a high profile arrest at the Ritz.

They wanted me to throw them a bone. And like the jury this morning, I could play on their desires for my own ends.

I drew a long breath and took my place at the podium. The murmurs dropped to a rustling whisper.

"Thank you for coming." I cleared my throat. "I'm Assistant D.A. Lily Knight. As you may have heard, around four this morning, officers responded to a 911 emergency call at San Francisco's Ritz Carlton Hotel. A single victim was pronounced dead at the scene. That victim has now been identified as Penelope St. Cyr, a San Francisco resident and nightclub entertainer." Her still face floated in my mind, and I hurried on. "S.F.P.D. has determined Ms. St. Cyr's death to be a probable homicide and detained a suspect at the scene. I can now confirm the identity of the suspect."

I paused for effect. My audience waited, hushed. The rumors had already circulated, but they needed to hear it from me, the D.A.'s official mouthpiece. "As of this evening, Sebastian Ritter has been charged with one count of first-degree murder and is being held without bail pending his arraignment, which will take place tomorrow morning at the main courthouse."

The silence broke and their shouted questions crashed over me like a wave.

"One at a time, please." My voice cut through the current of noise and they quieted, though not without some grumbling. Trying not to lay my Presence on too thick, I pointed to a blond woman in the first row of seats. "You, in the front."

"Thanks, Ms. Knight. Can you confirm whether Mr. Ritter and the victim had a sexual relationship?"

My cheeks heated. "Because the investigation is ongoing, I can't comment on the details of the case."

"Was she a prostitute?"

"What? No!" Two minutes into my prime time debut and I had lost control of the narrative. "I mean, I can't discuss—"

"Is it true that Mr. Ritter and the victim engaged in S&M activities before her death?"

Where had they gotten that sordid little tidbit? "I'm sorry, but I can't discuss the particulars of an ongoing investigation."

"Why are you covering up evidence that Penelope St Cyr wasn't human?" This question came from a man the back of the room.

I stiffened. "Who said that?"

The questioner stood and the cameras panned toward him. "Tobias Kaine, independent journalist." He had a square jaw, a piercing gaze under dark-rimmed glasses, and broad, muscled build that filled out his khaki blazer and blue jeans well. "You might have heard of me. I have a podcast called *The Truth*."

"*The Truth*? You must be joking." I forced a laugh, but the joke was on me, thanks to whoever let a crackpot conspiracist who thought he had a smoking gun into my press conference. "Who gave this guy a press pass?"

The staff exchanged glances, brows furrowed. A uniformed officer moved toward Kaine, but he held up a hand and the officer stopped. I frowned.

"You didn't answer my question," Tobias Kaine said.

I gritted my teeth. "I don't entertain nonsense, Mr. Kaine."

"You know it's not nonsense, Ms. Knight. What about the others?"

Did he mean the other missing succubi? How the hell did he know so much? "That's enough." I caught the uniformed officer's eye. "Get him out of here already."

Finally, the officer advanced on my heckler. Kaine held up his hands. "Don't bother. I was just leaving." He raised a small camera and took a snap of me standing bewildered at the podium. Then he walked out. The slam of the press room door echoed like a gunshot in the dead quiet he left behind.

Then the rest of the shark tank shook itself out of its daze and the shouting began all over again.

"What did he mean, not human?"

"Is there a cover up?"

"What others?"

Basra made a cutting gesture, her expression grim, and I almost wept with relief. "That's all for tonight, folks," I said over the din. "The D.A.'s office has no further comments at this time."

I left the podium, head held high, and swept out of the room, Basra at my heels. As soon as the door slammed behind me, I leaned against the wall of the dingy hallway that led to the elevators and tipped my head back, trying to catch my breath.

Basra's hand fell on my shoulder and I couldn't help it this time. I flinched away from her touch, even though my suit jacket would protect her from any energy pull.

"Tough crowd," she said. "You handled it well."

I scrubbed clammy palms over my face, eyes burning with tears I refused to shed. "You've got to be kidding. They ate me alive out there." My Presence-fueled command from earlier must have addled her so thoroughly that she couldn't see how badly I'd failed.

"Sometimes it's like that," Basra said. "They hear what they want to hear, and they want to hear whatever makes the best story."

"Yeah, well, they'll have a hell of a story now."

"You mean Mr. Kaine? He used you to put himself in the spotlight." She paused, giving me a long, searching look. "Do you know what he was talking about?"

I shook my head, an automatic lie. Maybe I should have shared my suspicions about the corpse from yesterday, but then I'd have to explain my theory. I didn't have a good pretext for making a connection between the two victims. "I'll ask Detective Huang to look into it."

"Tomorrow," she said firmly. "Go home, Lily. Get some rest."

"Yes, boss." I pushed myself away from the wall. But I'd lied to her again. I couldn't go home, not yet.

First, I had to give an incubus some very bad news.

THE ADDRESS ARIEL had given me for our meeting led me to a dark and narrow alley behind the San Francisco Museum of Modern Art and a series of doors that resembled an industrial warehouse more than an art storage facility. One door about midway down the row had a length of black satin ribbon tied around it, like the ribbon of Ariel's mask from the previous evening.

"Hello?" I called, pushing the heavy door open. "Anyone here?"

"Come in." His voice echoed through the darkened space beyond, velvet and hollow.

I stepped inside, then stopped short with a sharp indrawn breath.

A bound woman hung suspended in the center of the room, illuminated by a stark column of light. The rope flamed vivid scarlet against her bare skin, which gleamed with a fine sheen of sweat despite the chill in the room and the goosebumps standing out on her smooth limbs. Desire sifted from her body in motes of gold dust, slow like honey, shimmering in the stage lighting that blazed down from above. Her lids half-dropped over glazed eyes, her swollen lips parted, she swung gently in a nonexistent breeze, tawny hair falling about her in a spill of balayage waves. She looked peaceful, though the bands dug into her chest and hips at the pressure points.

Ariel stood at the spotlight's edge, his face half in shadow, his blond curls gleaming like a halo. "Welcome to my parlor," he said, and his voice held a dangerous smile of triumph. "You always did have perfect timing, Lily fair."

"What is this?" My experience told me the tension would leave divots on her perfect skin, lines of braided bruises. It might even bleed. Ariel never did learn to rig with kindness, even after centuries of practice.

"What does it look like? I brought you a present." Ariel reached up to the suspension line, spinning his subject toward us. He dipped his head to kiss her, and the bound woman moaned into his mouth.

The soft, needy sound woke a fire deep inside my core. "Stop it," I said, my own mouth dry.

"Why?" He smirked. "It's just you and me here. You don't have to pretend that you don't like it."

Just Ariel and me and Ariel's apparently very willing captive, spinning in a wash of light. He looped a coil of rope around my wrist, lassoing me, and drew me closer. The fibers scraped my skin, waking memories that waited just beneath the surface.

"You remember how it used to be." Ariel echoed my thoughts. "It could be like that again, if you wanted it." He stroked one finger down my cheek, feather-light, but enough to send a soft pulse of kether through me.

Once upon a time, we would have chosen her together. Once upon a time, I would have bent to kiss her before letting him sip her kether from my lips like the wine of salvation.

"No." Even if he had picked her up as a willing one-night stand at a bar, this was going too far. "I didn't meet you here for more of your games. Unbind her, Ariel. Let her go. I need to talk to you."

"This was her desire. Would you deny her that?"

I shook my head. "She's in thrall. She can't consent like that."

"On the contrary, I didn't force anything on her. She asked for this. But if this one's not to your liking, I can get you another." He cocked his head. "What flavor would you prefer? A man perhaps, like Nepenthe's plaything? You do like them tall, dark, and slender, don't you?"

"Nepenthe," I said, my tongue stumbling over the name. It broke through the haze of need his hypnotic words had woken in me. Right, I came here for a reason, not to negotiate—whatever Ariel wanted to negotiate. I grasped the rope around my wrist and tugged him away from the suspended woman and into the shadows, speaking under my breath so she wouldn't overhear. "Ariel, something happened."

"I'm aware." All the playfulness drained from his tone, and his elusive accent emerged to clip the words with stark clarity. "I saw your press conference."

"You did?"

"Seven hells, Lillian." Annoyance cracked his smooth facade. "I watch TV, you know. I may be old, but I'm not a Luddite."

"But then—" Behind his shoulder, his rope partner stirred and whimpered softly, surfacing from her trance.

"Be right there, love," he called and she stilled, eyes fluttering shut.

I clenched my jaw against the heat stirring in my belly. "You knew she was dead, but you still felt it was the right time to partake in a little light bondage?"

"Hush." He dropped his voice again, for my ears only. "We all grieve in different ways. Pray keep your judgment to yourself, and spit it out. What do you want from me?"

"I need to ask you about last night. And…about her." I cleared my throat. "About Penelope."

"You can use her real name." The edge in his tone caught me up short. "Nepenthe. That human name was just a lie. Call her by her real name, Lillian."

The order cracked through me like a bullwhip, demanding obedience. It set my teeth on edge, but now wasn't the time to challenge him on semantics. "Nepenthe," I repeated. "How did you know her?"

He didn't answer at first, his expression unreadable in the dim half-light. "We went back a long time," he said at last.

"How long?" I frowned. "Ariel, how old *was* she?"

"A succubus never tells," he said. "Or an incubus, for that matter. She was old enough to know…"

Again, I waited, but he seemed lost in thought or memory. "What did she know?" I kept my tone gentler this time.

"Nothing. Never mind," he said. "She was old enough to remember how it used to be for us. That's all."

"How it used to be?" I suddenly wished I knew more about my father's kind, about our history. Getting a straight answer from Ariel was proving even harder than expected. "When? Like…before Tonepah?"

"Sure." He chuckled, a dry, mirthless noise. "Before Tonepah. You could say that." He fell silent, brooding gaze turned away from me, then stepped back into the circle of light to his waiting partner.

Agile fingers busy over the woman's bonds, he released the weight-bearing knots one by one and eased her body down to rest on the floor. She drew her knees up to her chest and leaned her head back against his legs, eyes fluttering closed. He dropped a hand to stroke her hair, his expression shuttered and absent. Together, they glowed like the figures in a pre-Raphaelite painting, while I stood in the dark, a mere observer, a tourist in the world to which I'd once belonged.

"The police think they know who did it," I said into his silence. "But they're wrong."

His head snapped around at that. With a quick squeeze of his partner's shoulder, he left her in the light, and I faltered before his demon-quick approach, like a mouse beneath a hawk's swift shadow.

On an urgent undertone, he said, "Who?"

"The man we met last night," I said. "Nepenthe's friend, Sebastian. They found him with her…" I couldn't bring myself to say 'with her body'. Not to Ariel, not just then. Not the way he was looking at me.

"But you don't think he killed her," Ariel said. "Why?"

"That's one of the things I wanted to ask you about," I said. "I talked to him just a little while ago, and he…well, he touched me, and I think I saw into his head, somehow. Into his memory. I saw her die through his eyes, and I know he didn't do it." It sounded silly when I tried to put it into words. "Is that even possible? Can a demon read a human mind, Ariel? Can we pull a memory from their skin like kether?"

"Anything is possible," he said. "It would certainly be unusual. Are you sure that what you saw was real?"

"Maybe not. But it felt real."

"I don't doubt that. But this man, Sebastian… You wanted him, didn't you, Lily?" He went on before I could answer. "I saw you, last night, the way you watched him. You tried to stake a claim."

My cheeks heated. "I didn't," I said. "It…I couldn't."

"Of course, silly Lily. He'd already been claimed."

"I don't see what that has to do with anything."

"You want him to be innocent, don't you, love? So maybe you saw what you wanted to see."

I set my jaw, stubborn now. "No, that's not it. I know what I saw."

"And what was that?"

"Her face," I said. "Her golden eyes. A silver stake. Her blood—God, so much blood. And his hands. He was trying to save her."

"A moment in time," Ariel said. "But what happened before that? Did you see that, too? Did he see anything, anyone else?"

I shook my head. "It was just a flash. A moment, like you said. But I felt him, too. His fear, his grief. No guilt. He couldn't have killed her."

"Not all murderers feel guilt, Lily. Or maybe he killed her in—what do you lawyers call it? The heat of the moment?"

"No," I said again. "I don't buy it. He's not like that."

"And you know him so well? Whose side are you on, anyway?"

I glared at him. Everyone kept asking me that, and I didn't know how to answer. "That's not fair."

"No," Ariel said, but he'd relaxed a fraction, and now he relented. "It's not fair that she's dead, and it's not fair of me to lay that on you. I'm sorry, Lillian. I'm not thinking straight, either." He sighed. "If your Sebastian didn't do this, who did?"

"He's not my Sebastian," I said. "And I don't know who murdered Nepenthe. But I'm going to try to find out. I promise you that."

With a fractional shake of his head, he returned to his rope partner and bent over her, whispering in her ear. When he looked back at me, the harsh shadows pooled in the angles of his face, leaving it haggard, weary. Old. "You do that, Lily," he said. "Let me know when you find the bastard, will you? I'd like to have a little chat with him myself."

10

THE LEAST WRONG THING

I SHOULD HAVE GONE STRAIGHT HOME AFTER I LEFT ARIEL. I MEANT TO GO home. I couldn't stay and watch him play with his food, no matter how willing she might seem. But the burn of his latest kether gift fizzed under my skin, electricity searching for a grounding point. And I only trusted one person in the world to ground me when I got like this.

I took a rideshare into the Castro to Ladybird's Bar and slipped through its mellow crowd and pink neon lighting to the outdoor patio. A few of the patrons in the jungle-like backyard garden shot me curious glances, but I managed to pick my way mostly unnoticed through the patio's shoals of odd statuary and rainbow-painted skull shrines. Unnoticed, at least, until Danny stood up from a table in the back corner, spread her arms, and shouted my name.

"You came!" She advanced on me, holding out her hands, and almost grabbed mine before I tucked them behind my back. "Oops, sorry. Forgot."

I frowned at her. "You're drunk."

"You better believe it." She threw a careless arm around my shoulders and steered me back to the table. This close, her desiderata washed over me with a pang that seized me by the throat and took my breath away. "Come, sit. Drink with me. Tell me what you've done with my hermitlike friend. Is this two nights in a row you've gone out? Are you sure you're not a pod person?"

"At this point, I can't guarantee it." I pulled away and took a seat. "Danny, where's Berry?"

Danny's brows drew together, her grin turning wry. She looked more rumpled than usual, her eyes overbright and her shrug too casual. The ache of her desiderata intensified into a searing mouthful of ash and Angostura bitters. "She went home."

"You two had a fight, didn't you?"

"It wasn't a fight, more of a disagreement." Danny downed the last of her beer. "Don't worry about us. We'll be fine."

But I did worry, because her energy had shifted, now a broken mirror jagged with guilt and self-recrimination. It reflected my own face back to me, and my heart contracted. "It was about me," I said. "You fought about me."

"Lily, no. I hate it when you do that." The mirror's shards flared into a fountain of sparks, her anger flashing out at me before it subsided. "Let me have my secrets."

"Sorry." I could have bitten my tongue. We had an unwritten pact, Danny and I. We didn't talk about certain things. I usually did better at pretending that I couldn't read her any more than a normal human could. "Want to hear about my disaster of an evening instead?"

"Oh, lord," she said. "Please do. Distract me."

She ordered us drinks and I launched into an account of my evening, with a dramatic reenactment of my interview with Sebastian and my subsequent catastrophe of a press conference.

At my tale's conclusion, Danny sat back with a low whistle. "Tell me if I've got this right. You're a material witness in this case. But instead of fessing up, you demanded first chair, flirted with the primary suspect, and had a Spidey-sense vision of the murder that convinced you the suspect is innocent."

"Hey," I said. "I don't appreciate that! I didn't flirt with him. I interviewed him, *with* a 6th amendment waiver."

She waved that away. "Sure, whatever, but I'm not finished. Now you have exonerating information you can't explain to the cops, you're supposed to arraign this Sebastian cat tomorrow, and you have zero admissible evidence to back up your alternate theory."

"Sounds about right."

"If we keep quiet about Penelope being a succubus, the wrong guy might go to jail. And if we don't keep it quiet, whoever did it for real will probably get away with it anyway, because it'll end up in an X-file somewhere while the powers that be pretend it never happened."

"That's the long and short of it, yep."

"So what are you going to do?"

"Umm.... Quit my job and go into business as a private investigator?"

She snorted. "Not if you want to pay our rent in this city."

"Then I'm out of ideas." I turned the glass in my hand, leaving overlapping rings of condensation on the sticky frosted glass of the table.

We both fell silent. I abandoned the rest of my beer and slumped in my chair, closing my eyes. It didn't help. The memory that didn't belong to me still haunted the darkness behind my eyelids. Nepenthe's lovely face gazed up at Sebastian, emotion welling in her golden eyes before the light faded out of them, something that ran deeper and softer than pain.

Ariel had taught me that demons didn't possess their own souls and we didn't have the same range of emotions as humans. That's why we craved human lust and desire, the energy we lacked within ourselves. But even if that were true, did that mean we couldn't love?

I thought I could, but then, I had never fully proved that to myself.

And besides, I was still half-human.

"Danny, I need a favor," I said. "Can you send me a copy of your autopsy report?"

For a long moment, she didn't answer. In the pause, music murmured over the patio's speakers, a woman's plaintive voice and acoustic guitar. It mingled with soft laughter from across the courtyard.

"Berry thinks I shouldn't get involved," Danny said, finally. "She says I'm over-invested."

I straightened, eyes snapping open. "How much does she know?"

"Don't freak out. I didn't tell her about you." The words she didn't say hung in the air between us.

"But you're over-involved?"

"She worries too much," Danny said. "I'll send you the file tomorrow morning."

"And the pictures? The ones that show her eyes?"

Danny met my gaze. "Don't worry," she said, voice soft. "I didn't think those were necessary."

"You do have them, though?"

She nodded, looking conflicted. "Lily…"

"Can you send them to me? Just me? Separately."

"Why?" she said, an edge coming into her voice. "What are you going to do?"

"I don't know yet." I stood. "I need to figure out what the right thing to do is. Or maybe just the least wrong thing."

"Wait." Danny rose too. "Be careful. You could lose your job."

"I'm aware, but I need all the ammunition I can get my hands on, just in case."

She stepped toward me too quickly, swayed, and almost fell. I reached out and caught her by her bomber-jacketed arm, steadying her. "Whoa there. Let's get you home."

"You don't have to babysit me," she said, mulish.

"Now you sound like me." I hooked her elbow in mine and tucked my bare hand in my pocket, out of danger. "Come on, it'll be nice not to pretend I'm not the disaster for once."

She grumbled a protest, but let me guide her out of the bar and down the street. We walked the three blocks to her Dolores Park apartment in companionable silence. But when we reached her door, she stopped suddenly and faced me.

"Lily, I—"

"Please don't." I reared back from her desiderata, the way it reached out to envelop me, feather-soft and cinnamon-sweet. "I can't. It's not safe."

"That's bullshit and you know it's bullshit."

I shook my head. "I know things are rough right now with Berry, but she seems amazing. Don't mess that up on my account." I needed Danny to stay my friend, uncomplicated, uncompromised. "You don't—it's not *real*, Danny. You're drunk, and I'm a monster. I don't want to hurt you." Didn't want to hold her in thrall, didn't want to wonder whether she cared for me because of *me* or because of the power I exerted over her.

Even though I already did.

"You're wrong." Danny looked up at me with her eyes dark and her desiderata aflame, bittersweet and wild. "You're not—what you said. But you're still deciding what *I* want."

"It's better this way," I whispered. "I promise it's better."

"Just forget it." She turned away, fire fading to fitful blue embers, its split-second flare extinguished in a split second. "It never happened."

"It never happened," I agreed, and waited for her door to shut behind her before I let myself take a full breath. But the taste of cinnamon still lingered on my tongue for a long while afterwards.

TEN YEARS AGO, when I told Ariel I planned to move across the country for law school, he had raged and sulked. Then he refused to speak to me for weeks, disappearing from the apartment we shared in NYC and all his accustomed haunts. When he finally reappeared, shortly before my move out west, he kept me at arm's length. His distance hurt and confused me, but it also came as a relief.

I didn't think he would let me go. I'd expected him to try to follow me.

I still didn't know why he hadn't. But he had his own life, one he'd never shared with me even back when we spent most of our time together.

He let me go, and I'd made my own way. I packed my lace and satin and leather into storage. At first I sought the Exchange on my own terms, but in a way I could live with. I flirted in regular bars with regular men, tasting without drinking too deeply. I wore gloves in all seasons and told my law school classmates I suffered from circulation problems. Paresthesia, Danny called it, when I told her that lie for the first time.

But not long after my law school graduation, she found out the truth. Her apt comment yesterday evening about practicing getting rejected hadn't only referred to my own inexperience, but to the time I rejected her.

I had never pulled tainted kether before that night, not like that. Not the kind that boiled through me with gut-wrenching violence like a bad trip. Cubines feed off a human's essence, and some humans have rot deep in their cores, spoiled and sickening as old milk at best, or disorienting and damaging as heroin laced with PCP at worst.

I didn't know what happened that night, exactly, but when I came back to myself, the man I'd gone home with wouldn't wake up.

The EMTs said he'd had an aneurysm or a stroke. I didn't stay to find out because deep down I knew the truth. He had died because I took too much of his kether.

I fled, dazed and stumbling. I was half out of my mind with fear and delirious with fever. That's how Danny found me when she got home from her shift at the hospital: lying half-dressed and prone on the blessedly cool tile in our shared bathroom, moaning some disjointed lunacy about how I thought I could fly if the room would just stop spinning.

When she placed her hand on my cheek, a flash of her kether jumped from her skin to mine. It revived me enough, and I flung myself across the room with inhuman speed, bowling her over in the process.

"I'm sorry," she'd said, sitting up. She looked drawn and ashy, frightened of me. "I didn't mean —"

"It's okay," I told her in a weary voice. "It's me. My fault. Don't try to stand," I added, as she started to get to her feet.

She swayed and grabbed for the edge of the sink. "Whoa. Head rush." She frowned at me. "How did you know?"

"Just a hunch." My own legs less than steady, I slid back down to the floor, facing her.

"That was really weird," she said. "Wait, are you okay? What happened? Did you pass out in here?"

"Something like that." It amazed me how much my mind had cleared with just one touch.

"The way you moved." She frowned. "So fast. I could have sworn..."

"You shouldn't have touched me," I said.

"I wasn't hitting on you, Lily." Her tone sharpened. "I was trying to help you. You know that, right?"

But she must have wanted me, at least a little, or her kether wouldn't have hovered at the surface like that, waiting for our skin to touch. "It's not that."

"Okay," she'd said, still sounding pissed off. "I'll take your word for it."

And I could have let it go at that: the moment, the friendship, the first human I'd ever allowed myself to get close to for more than one night. But selfishly, I didn't want to lose her. The prospect of lying yet again exhausted me.

I lifted my chin and met her eyes. Her confusion and hurt showed as clearly in her face as they did in her desiderata. I liked that about Danny. She came with zero pretensions, with nothing held back. So different from myself.

"It's not that I don't want you to touch me because you like women," I said softly. "I don't want you to touch me because I'm a demon."

She stared at me. "You're not serious."

I tipped my head back against the door. My heart pounded, adrenaline bubbling up through my exhaustion. "Dead serious."

"Okay." She sat down slowly at the edge of the tub. "What the hell does that mean?"

So I told her. I let her see me. And she looked and didn't run away. Even now, I couldn't say why I took that leap and trusted her. I couldn't say why she believed me. But her friendship, not her kether, saved my life that night.

Since then, she'd taken care never to touch my bare skin, but she hadn't stopped saving me.

Still, the question haunted me. Did she care for *me*, or had the demon inside me clouded her judgment and fooled her into thinking I was someone worth saving?

11

A DEMON'S DUE

AFTER COMING HOME FROM DANNY'S, I STAYED UP PAST MIDNIGHT TO DRAFT the complaint against Sebastian Ritter. I put on *Breakfast at Tiffany's* in the background, but even Holly Golightly, the original hot mess, could do nothing to comfort me.

When I finally lay down to catch a few hours' rest, I barely slept a wink. I tossed and turned until Delilah, usually a faithful sleeping companion, jumped off the bed with a huff of disgust and padded out into the shadows of the living room. Left alone, I lay staring into the darkness with burning eyes, pulse racing at every creak and crack as the old Victorian settled in the night's chill, every upstairs neighbor's footstep shuddering across the ceiling.

Maybe Ariel's keyless entry trick last night had disturbed me more than I wanted to admit. As if the thought of Penelope's body slowly crumbling into dust in Danny's morgue and charging an innocent man with murder wasn't enough.

I finally drifted off just before dawn, but my dreams didn't improve matters. I wandered lost in a nightmare house of mirrors and webs of scarlet rope through a masked crowd whose eyes never quite saw me, pursued by a figure I glimpsed only in reflections and peripheries. It had no face and shadows spread out behind it like great, tattered, batlike wings. Quickening my steps, I tried to run, but tendrils of darkness wrapped around my limbs, dragging me back and downward until I fell flailing into an eternity of empty air, a void without light or bottom.

Out of that endless fall, I awoke with a start, my sheets soaked in sweat. My heart pounded in my throat as I blinked open eyes still gritty with fatigue. The gray, foggy light of morning had begun to filter through from the front room. I squinted at the green display on the clock beside the bed and groaned. 6 AM had come too soon and I had come no closer to figuring out the least wrong course of action, let alone the right one.

Three hours later, I set my jaw and threaded my way through the lawyers crowded in front of the railing that set the pit apart from the gallery's public seating. Greg Grayson nodded to me from where he stood in solemn consultation with his team by the defense-side table and I nodded back.

Then the knot of huddled lawyers shifted, and I locked eyes with Sebastian Ritter. His desiderata hit me with an electric jolt, a last-ditch plea, a prayer, an invitation. It was all I could do to stay rooted in the spot, to keep myself from going to him and answering his need.

He sat quiet and still as the currents of the courthouse eddied and flowed around him, at the center of the chaos, yet set apart from it. The privilege of his station may not have saved him from a murder charge, but it had afforded him some benefits not typically available to accused criminals. Usually, the accused sat in the holding area in the basement until the bailiff called down and the deputy brought them out into the "cage"— the barred holding cell that dominated the left side of the room.

Not so for Sebastian, who got to sit at the table. No cage or chains for him; they'd let him trade his jumpsuit for an impeccable dove-gray business suit, crisp white shirt, and navy tie. It made for an inoffensive but arresting look. *No pun intended.* He'd also had a shave, but the bruise-like shadows under his eyes suggested he'd slept about as well as I had, if at all.

I tore my gaze from his. To hide my confusion, I set my valise down with a thump at the prosecutor's table and pulled out my laptop. I barely had time to regain my composure before the door to the judge's chambers swung open. The bailiff raised his voice to be heard over the clamor of the crowd.

"Please remain seated and come to order. Court is now in session. The Honorable Judge Mariah Nichols presiding."

Judge Nichols took her seat, and I faced the bench. "Calling the matter of *People v. Ritter*," she said. "Let the record reflect that the defendant is present with retained counsel for arraignment. Are the People ready?"

It took me a moment to realize she'd spoken to me. "Uh, yes, Your Honor. Lillian Knight for the People."

"Thank you, Ms. Knight. Mr. Greyson, the defendant has retained you in this matter, is that correct?"

"Yes, your Honor."

"Let us proceed," Judge Nichols said. "Sebastian Ritter, you are charged with violation of Penal Code 187, homicide in the first degree..."

As she droned on, reading Sebastian the complaint I had drafted, I couldn't help but steal another glance at him. The blood had drained from his face as he listened, leaving it gray and drawn. A pang of regret cramped my stomach. I'd accused an innocent man of murder, and I had no way to stop it. Even if I came clean about my reasoning, no one would believe me.

"A copy of the complaint has been provided to Mr. Greyson. Mr. Ritter, do you understand the charges that have been brought against you?"

Sebastian's Adam's apple jerked as he swallowed. "Yes." The hoarse, strained syllable made my chest tighten. I faced forward, steeling myself against my traitor heart.

"This is a capital case, so you have the right to be represented by an attorney at all stages of these proceedings. You have the right to a speedy and public trial and to have your case tried before a jury of your peers. You have the right to produce witnesses on your behalf and to confront the witnesses against you. Do you understand your rights as I have read them to you today?"

"I do."

"Would you like to enter a plea at this time?"

Greg Greyson stood. "Your Honor, my client pleads not guilty to all charges. I'd like to formally apply for a bail determination to be set today as well."

"So entered and noted. Do the People have any objection?"

Silence reigned in the courtroom. I dragged my attention away from

Sebastian's bloodless face and back to the judge, who cleared her throat loudly. "Ms. Knight?"

"Sorry, Your Honor. If I could have just one moment—" Flustered, I shuffled through my papers.

The pages trembled under my fingers like leaves in a stiff breeze off the Pacific, the words sliding and blurring. Basra wanted me to request denial of bail, given the crime and the resources at Sebastian's disposal. But the image of Penelope's face and pleading eyes haunted my memory. She had cared for Sebastian. She wouldn't want him taking the blame like this.

I stole another glance at him. He stared straight ahead. His face gave nothing away, as if graven in stone, but his desiderata echoed with the hollow resignation of a long fall into the dark.

Basra would have my hide. She might even fire me. But in that moment, I knew what I had to do.

"Your Honor," I said, "At this time, the People formally request that the charges against Sebastian Ritter be dismissed without prejudice."

In the wake of my words, chaos broke out in the courtroom. The reporters in the gallery all began gabbling at once, excitedly, into their phones and to each other. The judge and Greg Grayson both stared at me as if I'd grown a second head. But I didn't care, because Sebastian looked up and locked his gaze with mine. Warmth flooded through me at the sparkle there, bright as sun on the Bay breaking through the morning fog. With a visible shudder of an exhalation, he lifted an eyebrow, lips quirked as if about to speak.

But the rap of the gavel cut through the noise and his eyes slid away toward the judge.

"Order, please!" Judge Nichols cleared her throat. "Let the record reflect that all charges against Sebastian Ritter in this matter are dismissed without prejudice on the request of the people. Mr. Ritter, you are free to go."

The clamor rose again. In my hand, my phone began to buzz with a call from the office. The press surged toward the railing, shouting my name, demanding answers.

"Ms. Knight, why did your office drop the charges?"

"Has the D.A.'s office learned new information?"

"Who really killed Penelope St. Cyr?"

I stood, frozen, for a moment. Sebastian's lawyers had converged on him again. Their suit jacketed backs hid him from view.

"No comment," I muttered. "No comment." Then, grabbing my valise, I made a break for it out the courtroom's side door and hurried down the empty hallway to the elevators.

I STABBED at the elevator buttons blindly until the door closed. Struggling to catch my breath, I tipped my head back against the smooth metal wall. The elevator dropped and my stomach sank with it—and most likely, so did my career.

What had I done? I could lose my job. I'd ruined everything, and for what? Sebastian didn't care about me. He didn't need me. His team of expensive lawyers would probably have gotten him acquitted anyway.

My phone buzzed again and I switched it off. Then the elevator doors scraped open and I stepped out to find myself face to face with Ariel.

Thrown off balance, I stumbled, reaching out to steady myself against his chest. Under my hands, he was warm, and solid, and the last person who would judge me for following my heart.

"Whoa there, Lily fair." He caught me by the shoulders. "Everything all right?"

I leaned into his familiar bulk for a moment, drinking him in, *not* drinking him. I had missed touch. No, I'd missed uncomplicated touch: touch without fear of harm or being harmed, without the drama and heightened responsibility of a possible kether drain, just simple physical contact with another being. "What are you doing here?"

"Looking for you." His hands had dropped to my waist, pulling me closer like it was the most natural thing in the world. "You seem glad to see me for once," he murmured into my ear. "Bad morning?"

"Something like that. How did you know where to find me?"

He shrugged without letting go. "Educated guess."

"I *am* glad to see you," I admitted.

Passersby stared at us, some of them my colleagues. I extricated myself from his arms regretfully and stood on my own two feet, which already hurt like hell. I'd worn what Danny called my "badass female of the species" shoes today: three-inch stilettos with pointed toes and shiny patent leather the color of cabernet, or heart's blood. Shoes meant for intimidation and a confidence boost, not comfort.

Danny once said she didn't understand why comfort and confidence couldn't exist in the same shoe. I told her it was a lawyer thing. She snorted and said that it was a *femme* thing, the conflation of beauty and pain, and that the power granted by masochism was overrated compared to its price. I'd maintained that if it didn't hurt, I probably wasn't trying hard enough.

I'd tried to do the right thing today, but hurting didn't mean I'd tried hard enough. It didn't work both ways.

Ariel steered me toward a quiet corner, away from the madding crowd. "Talk to me, Lily. You're pale as milk. What happened?"

"Not here," I said softly. "I'll tell you, but not here."

"How mysterious and dramatic of you. I like it. Lead on, Mata Hari."

I pulled him across Van Ness to the emerald lawn of the War Memorial Opera House. There, in the shadow of two grand theaters, set apart from the bustle of the Civic Center, an octagon of polished stone reflected the gray of the sky. An actual memorial hadn't stood in this space until a few years back, after decades of political infighting blocked its installation. Most of the city's residents forgot that it existed.

That made it perfect, in my opinion. It meant that this early in the day, the courtyard would remain empty, other than a small mob of irreverent pigeons and two demons looking for answers.

Pulling my coat around me against the chilly morning wind, I ran my fingers over the letters engraved in the stone, a poem about the lost, about lives cut short.

They say: We leave you our deaths. Give them their meaning.

We have died: remember us.

A shadow fell across the stone's limpid surface, Ariel's silhouette merging with mine as he peered over my shoulder.

"*They are heard in the still houses...*" In his resonant tones, the poet's blank verse took on the music of a Psalm. "Bit of wishful thinking, isn't it?"

"I like it."

He scoffed. "Such a deeply human sentiment. Always trying to strike a bargain with death."

"I dropped the charges against Sebastian." I didn't turn around. But I felt him tense behind me like a spring coiling.

"Did you," he said. "And why is that, I wonder?"

"There were pictures," I said, guilt twisting in my belly. "They showed her real face. We couldn't prosecute. If those got out—"

"So the DA won't press charges because she's a demon." He slumped, the tension abruptly draining out of his tall frame. "I told you so."

"It's not like that." I shivered, more from the icy scorn in his voice than the wind this time. "It was my decision. He's innocent, Ariel, and they're not closing the investigation."

"Nonsense. They're not closing it…*yet*. They can't close it, *yet*. They need plausible deniability. They'll let the case go cold, let the news cycle move on. Then they'll pack her away in a box and never think of her again." His voice dropped to a low and dangerous register. "Lily, did you tell them what she was?"

"No! I didn't tell them anything. And I can still—"

"Don't." He spun on his heel, pacing away from me down the length of the lawn, his long black coat flaring out behind him in the wind like a cape. The pigeons scattered before him and rose in a flurry of beating wings.

I didn't go after him. I stood still, miserable, surrounded by the names of the dead.

They have a silence that speaks for them at night…

Who would speak for Nepenthe? Who would remember her? Only me, and Sebastian Ritter, and the blond demon currently kicking at the flawless sod and cursing fluently under his breath. Or so I guessed from the twist of his lips and the storm in his expression.

After a few minutes, he stalked back to me, still thunderous of brow. "So that's it," he said. "It's over."

"I'm sorry," I said.

"Sorry?" He spat the word like an expletive. "Don't be *sorry*, Lily. You know what sorry means? Pathetic. Pitiful. I never want to hear you say that you're *sorry* again!"

"I'm—I don't know what else to tell you."

"Tell me," he said, "that you tried. Tell me you cared. Tell me you did everything you could. Lie to me if you have to! After all, I am a demon. It's my due."

"I cared! I care. And I won't lie to you." I took a long breath, forced myself to look him in the eyes. Their false blue had shrunk to a narrow ring around the true amber beneath. "You were right, okay? You were right about everything. There's no justice in the legal system for Nepenthe. Hell, even humans have to be pretty lucky to get real justice there. There's nothing more I can do—as a prosecutor."

"What are you saying?"

What *was* I saying? "I have the file," I said. "I have the evidence, the forensic reports. I have a witness. I even have a suspect."

He frowned. "Do you? I thought your Sebastian was innocent as a lamb and harmless as a dove."

"Not him," I said. "Someone else." An inappropriate laugh bubbled up in my chest. I swallowed it down. "The devil himself."

"You lost me there."

"You saw him that night." I shuddered as the memory of his desiderata crawled across my skin. "The one who ran into me at the club. And then again—later. He was looking for Nepenthe. They knew each other. She was scared of him."

"She never said anything to me about him." Ariel looked skeptical.

"You must remember. He wore a red devil costume, horns and all. "

Ariel made a face. "So tacky. So obvious. So very cliche." But he seemed intrigued despite himself. "Do you know who he is?"

"No idea," I said. "But I'd know his kether anywhere. Like sucking swamp water." I hesitated. I didn't know *who*, but I might know *what*. "Ariel, there's something else."

"What is it, darling? Speak the words trippingly on the tongue, and for the love of Lilith, stop beating around the bush, burning or otherwise."

"He pulled from me." I ignored Ariel's literary and theological flight of fancy. "I think he was another cambion."

Ariel's normally mobile face went still at that, gray and graven as the stone monument. "You think, but you're not sure?"

"No, I'm not sure. I've never met another cambion before. But I've never felt a two-way pull like that. It was awful. Like coming and going at the same time, and not knowing which was which."

"I bet," Ariel murmured. "Well, well, well. That *is* interesting. Very interesting, indeed."

"So you think it's a lead worth following up?"

"I think it's the best one we've got." As he said it, his gaze slipped past me, fixed on something in the middle distance. Clearly, his interest had already begun to flag.

Wait, when had Ariel and I become a we *again?* There hadn't been a *we* between us for a long time. I didn't know how I felt about that, except sarcastic. "I'm so glad you approve."

"I do. Good luck." He dropped a kiss on top of my head, again absently, patted my shoulder, and was gone. "We're all counting on you," came floating back to me across the square.

"Who's we?" I grumbled to no one, and turned to head the other way.

Only then did I see what must have spooked him. A dark, unmarked car with tinted windows had pulled up to the curb on the Van Ness side of the courtyard and sat idling there. It looked fancy, though I didn't know cars. As I stared, the uniformed driver got out, rounded the car, and opened the rear passenger side door. He gazed straight at me, as if he expected something.

Well, either I was about to be recruited for the CIA or I was about to be kidnapped by someone filthy rich. I took a wary few steps toward the car and then stopped short as the vehicle's passenger unfolded his long legs from the back seat and held out his hand to me.

"Good morning, Ms. Knight," said Sebastian Ritter. "Can we talk?"

12

APPEARANCE OF IMPROPRIETY

GREYSON MUST HAVE BROUGHT SEBASTIAN A CHANGE OF CLOTHES FOR HIS arraignment, because for a man lately in custody for murder, he looked remarkably good. Recently shaved and neatly coiffed, he wore a perfectly-fitted dove gray suit and polished wingtip shoes. *Good enough to eat.*

No, Lily. Stop it.

I couldn't take the hand he offered me, so I shoved my own hands deep into my coat pockets. I didn't need the chivalry, and I certainly didn't need the temptation of his skin against mine. He kept his arm outstretched for a moment, then shrugged and gestured me toward the car instead.

If this was a kidnapping, it was an incredibly polite one. Not to mention an elegant one. The rich, dark leather upholstery of the car's interior enveloped me as I slid into the back seat, which warmed beneath me. Faint classical music filtered through the speakers, and a touch screen installed in the back of the driver's seat offered high-speed internet, streaming media, and a stock ticker.

Beside me, Sebastian tapped commands into his touchscreen, and a tinted window rose with a soft hum to shut our cabin away from the driver. The vehicle pulled away from the curb.

"I don't mean to be so clandestine," he said, with a sheepish glance in my direction. "I'm afraid there's something of a media frenzy nipping at my heels."

"Mr. Ritter, I really shouldn't be here. Not without your lawyer present."

"Why?" He frowned. "You dropped the charges. We're just two private citizens having a conversation."

"I've already put my job on the line for you and there's this thing called appearance of impropriety that I'm technically supposed to avoid."

He let out that short, startled laugh I remembered from the night I'd met him. Two days ago, an age ago. "Impropriety? So what, we need a chaperone?"

"Something like that."

"I promise not to do anything improper. How's that?"

He wasn't the one flirting with an ethical dilemma, but I let it go for now. "I'll consider it a waiver. Where are we going?"

"For a drive." A soft pulse of satisfaction at my acquiescence briefly soothed the underlying turmoil in his desiderata. "And then, I thought we might have breakfast. If that's not too improper."

"It's pushing it. Is your driver discreet?"

"He's the best money can pay for."

Must be nice. While I was a lawyer, I wasn't exactly a high earning one yet, especially with San Francisco's living expenses factored in. "I didn't even know people bothered with chauffeurs anymore."

"I usually don't." He leaned back in his seat, eyes fluttering closed, the first outward betrayal of fatigue cracking through his smooth manner and light tone. "I prefer to drive myself, except when I'm being picked up from county jail after twenty-four hours of hell."

I eyed him. "Because that happens often?"

"I admit it was a novel experience," he said. "Not one I care to repeat."

"It's not supposed to be a five-star resort. Why am I here?"

"I told you, I wanted to talk." He turned to look at me, cheek against the headrest. "And now we're talking." He waved a hand, vaguely. "See? I got what I wanted. I'm very good at getting what I want, you know."

Was he making a pass at me? I sampled his desiderata cautiously, wary of reading my own desire into his words. As with the previous evening, stress and grief clouded his energy, making it hard to read. But this morning, a deeper emotion stirred beneath his surface, crackling like a live wire I didn't dare touch.

The vulnerability and danger of it tantalized me. Brush that current once, and I might not be able to let go. I pulled my awareness back from him, folding my hands in my lap to keep them from reaching out.

So the guy was a little punch-drunk. I could hardly blame him for that. I pressed on anyway. "What are we talking about?"

His sleepy relaxation vanishing, he sat up straight. "I wanted to tell you what really happened. With Penelope."

What really *happened? Shit. Maybe this was a confession, after all.* "I'm not your lawyer, Mr. Ritter."

"I know that." His irritation flashed out at me, then subsided. "I wanted to talk to you because I think you're the only one who will understand."

I shifted, uncomfortable at the intensity in his gaze. "I don't know what you mean by that."

"Yes, you do." He leaned forward, speaking in a low, urgent tone. "I recognized it in the club, or thought I did...but then I thought that I was wrong. And then, last night, I touched you and I knew I wasn't. You're one of them, aren't you?"

The question sent a cold rush of adrenaline through my blood. "One of what?"

"You're like her. Like Penelope. You're a—"

"Cambion."

He frowned. "What?"

"A cambion, that's what I am." I grinned horribly at him. "Half-woman, half-beast, half-breed, all evil. How did you know?"

"There's only one other woman who ever made me feel the way you do, Ms. Knight, and she's dead." His answering half-smile twisted with pain. "I do appreciate your trying to warn me about her, but I'm afraid it came a little late."

"You knew," I breathed. "How?"

"She was always honest with me about her intentions."

Well, that stung more than it should have. "And you didn't mind? What are you, some kind of demon fetishist?"

"That's not fair," he said. "I'd never met anyone like her before. What she offered me was unique and I was more than happy to give her what she needed in return."

"You gave her kether, and she gave you sex." I didn't bother to hide my disgust, and I wasn't sure which side of the exchange I was more disgusted with. Was he a victim, or a john? Did it matter? I expected better from him.

Then I shook my head at myself. I barely knew the guy. It was a little early for expectations.

"It wasn't like that," he said. "You make it sound cheap and exploitative."

"You're telling me it wasn't?"

"Just because sex was involved doesn't mean that we didn't respect each other."

I raised an eyebrow.

"She was a person to me, Ms. Knight, but she was a person with needs. So was I." There was that pained half-smile again, making it hard not to believe his version of things, no matter how much I disliked it. "Our needs happened to fit together...very well."

So he had been her kether-donor, and she had been his...what? The word concubine came to mind. I had heard of such arrangements before. It all seemed so unsavory to me, though. He thought of himself as a willing participant, but I'd experienced the power she could exert in a public space. In private, her focused Presence must have been extraordinary. And for her part, a succubus who did not feed could become a true monster, or simply wither away into a pale shadow of herself. How was that choice or consent, for either party?

"A relationship of convenience, then." I tried to defer my rush to judgment. "Of mutual need."

"As I understand it," he said, "that is the usual nature of such exchanges. A kind of symbiosis between human and demon."

Symbiosis, huh? That was a new way to spin a predator-prey relationship, even if I wasn't entirely sure which one was which in this particular situation. "I'll take your word for it."

He looked surprised. "You don't approve?"

I couldn't answer that question. "I just don't understand what this has to do with her death."

"All right," he said. "You do know how it works, don't you? The Exchange?"

I stared at him, my senses sharpening, hunter's instinct at the ready. Was he going to ask me to engage in the Exchange with him? Here, now? Had Nepenthe really gotten him that addicted to the pleasure only one of our kind could provide? "I'm familiar, yes."

"Then you know what happens to a human when a succubus feeds from him, don't you?"

Oh. Of course. I should have known. Or perhaps I had known, deep down, but hadn't wanted to think about it. "That's why you didn't wake up," I said. "You were drained. Unconscious."

"The price I paid. We took each other to our limits." His breath caught, and he swallowed hard. "We didn't know it was the last time, but we always played like it might be."

"A dangerous game."

"But worth the risk. I never regretted it, before..." He faltered, fell silent.

His story made a lot more sense now, except for one thing. A kether drain wasn't like normal sleep. It sent the human body into hibernation until their kether had sufficiently regenerated to sustain consciousness. Even the cops pounding on the door shouldn't have roused him. "So what woke you up?"

"I don't know. I thought..." He hesitated. "This may sound silly, but I thought I heard her calling me." His voice broke then, just for a moment, before he regained control. "When I opened my eyes, she was holding my hand."

She woke him? Unbidden, the memory of Ariel's lips on mine rose in my mind, how the power of kether had flowed into me at the touch, rejuvenating my weary body.

As her life's blood had flowed out of her, Nepenthe had used her last remaining kether reserves to wake her lover, passing it back from her body to his. But why? To ask for help? To protect him, perhaps?

Or...just to say goodbye?

"Was that all you wanted to tell me?" I kept my voice gentle, mindful of Sebastian's sorrow. His grief shimmered through the warm cocoon of the cabin, thickening the air and distorting the sound system's soft, cheerful concerto into a plaintive requiem.

"No," he said. "There's one more thing. The most important thing."

"I'm listening."

"When she woke me up," he said, "she tried to speak. But she couldn't, not very well." He dragged his palms over his face, his expression haunted. I saw it with him, the memory he'd shared with me: her desperate eyes, blood bubbling from her lips as her throat worked.

"Sebastian," I said, even more gently. I hadn't meant to use his given name; it just slipped out. "What did she say?"

He raised his eyes to mine. "She said, 'Tell Lily it's a—'"

INTO DUST

NEPENTHE HAD WOKEN SEBASTIAN RITTER FROM KETHER-DRAIN TO GIVE HIM A message for *me?* Cold washed outward from my core. "Tell me it's a *what?*"

"I don't know. That was it. She started coughing, and then…" He bowed his head, shoulders shaking with suppressed grief.

"I'm very sorry for your loss, Mr. Ritter," I said, and immediately wished I hadn't. It sounded so inadequate, so formal. Pathetic, just like Ariel had said. *I never want to hear you say that you're sorry again.*

"Thank you." The words emerged muffled and thick.

Tell me you cared. Ariel's words raked me.

"I'll find out who did this," I said. "I'm going to make them pay." It still didn't seem like enough. Moved by impulse more than thought—and not my better instincts—I reached out and dared to squeeze his shoulder lightly through the fine gray wool of his suit.

It should have been safe enough to touch him that way. Any kind of physical barrier between our skin would dampen the kether exchange. But then, without lifting his head, he reached up with his left hand and covered my fingers with his own.

I gasped out loud as the contact jolted through me. It wasn't like the first time, like last night. This time, he wasn't reliving Penelope's death, empty of all emotion but that singular memory. Today, his small gesture of unearned intimacy carried the full weight of his kether, still heavy with grief but rich with yearning. I could taste the ghost of connection he'd found with her, the connection he wanted back again. I could drink from the heady, oceanic roar of his need behind it.

I snatched my hand away, breathing hard. His head had jerked up, his lips parted and his eyes glittering as we stared at each other in silence.

"That was stupid," I said, when I could speak again. "*Fuck*, that was stupid."

"Fuck is right," he said in fervent tones, leaning toward me. "Do you—"

His desire pulled on me, every fiber of my being straining toward him like a compass to her pole. "No!"

He paled at the vehemence in my denial. "Oh, God, I'm sorry," he said. "You don't even know me, and here I am—I shouldn't have assumed."

"Don't be." His mortification had dampened the force of that magnetic need, and I could almost think straight again, enough to reassure him. "It's not that. It's my fault. You're grieving. You're vulnerable. And I should know better."

"Then I should too." He sat back again, but his fingers flexed on the thighs of his slacks. "Maybe we should call it a mutual folly, and leave it at that."

"Maybe." I had to stop thinking about his thighs. That way madness lay, among other things. "Maybe you should take me back to my office now, before anything else mutual happens that we're both going to regret later."

He looked like he wanted to say something else. Then he sighed. "You're probably right."

"I am right." I smoothed my skirt down over my knees, even though it hadn't ridden up. We hadn't *done* anything. But I wouldn't have known it from the afterglow suffusing my limbs, leaving them light as a feather and flush with easy strength.

I could walk on air. I could lift a bus. I could leap a tall building in a single bound. And that was from just one chaste—well, mostly chaste— touch. I had to get out of there before I ravished him.

"I can't help noticing you didn't change our destination," I said.

He gave me a sidelong, apologetic smile that didn't help my self-control one bit. "I don't know the address."

"Oh." He could have taken me back to the courthouse, but I wasn't going to call him on it. "Bryant and 8th Street."

"Got it." He bent toward the touchscreen, tapping in the command, while I examined the long, lean lines of his back and tried not to feel jealous of a glorified tablet. After a minute, the car executed a neat U-turn, heading back downtown. We'd gone a fair way out from Civic Center, the Pacific ocean a waxing blue crescent at the edge of the GPS display.

"Just where were you taking me, out of curiosity?"

"Cliff House serves a good breakfast."

"Cliff House?" I laughed in disbelief. "You call that a discreet location? It's crawling with tourists and social media addicts trolling for the perfect picture."

He looked sheepish. "I reserved the lounge."

"You're kidding."

"No. Too much?"

"The whole lounge?"

"Yes."

"They don't even take reservations!"

"Now you tell me." But his gratification at my reaction flickered in his quick half-smile.

"Awfully confident of you to reserve it first and then invite me. Not that you did invite me," I added. "More like kidnapped me."

"Awfully confident of you to think I reserved it for you," he said. "Maybe I really just wanted an iconic ocean view while I enjoyed my first meal as a free man."

"Funny. You don't strike me as the sentimental type."

"You say that now, but you haven't heard my feelings on clam chowder."

I laughed, for real this time. *Damn.* Rich, delicious, and he had to be low-key funny too? I was in real trouble, and he was a complication I didn't need right now.

The car rolled to a smooth stop, none too soon. But when the driver held the door open for me, I didn't want to get out.

"Seb—I mean, Mr. Ritter—"

"It's all right," he said. "I think we're past last names at this point, don't you?"

"Sebastian." But I had to stop there. I'd forgotten whatever I'd meant to say.

"Lily," he said, as if savoring the sound of it. "Here." He took out his wallet, extracted a card, scribbled something on the back, and handed it to me. We both took studious care not to brush our fingertips.

I looked at it, then back at him. "What's this?"

"My number," he said. "Call me if you need anything. I want to help."

Puzzled, I slipped it into my pocket. "Help…?"

"You said you'd find whoever did this to Penelope." His expression turned serious again, his energy grim and focused. "Money's no object, Lily. Make them pay."

Wordless, I nodded, and forced myself up and out of the car. From the interior, Sebastian gave me a quick wave. The driver shut the door and got in. The car slid smoothly and almost silently away from the curb. I watched it go. It was definitely a Rolls Royce.

Well, then.

IN A DAZE, kether-high, and more than half-besotted, I floated into the lobby of the city building and up the stairs. Had that really just happened? Had Sebastian Ritter, senator's son, tech wonder boy, and local millionaire, really just handed me his card with his personal number scribbled on the back?

And had he really just offered to bankroll an off-the-books investigation I had no business volunteering to pursue?

Still walking on air—I had to check to make sure my feet actually touched the ground—I entered the office, and the hush that fell brought me back down to Earth despite the kether buzzing in my veins. No one said anything, but the younger DAs exchanged glances as I passed their cubicles and ducked their heads when I tried to make eye contact.

Then Basra stepped out into my path. "Lily. My office. Now."

"Give me a minute." My Presence surfaced without my conscious bidding this time, and she moved aside, frowning. I strode past her to my own office door and stopped short.

Tobias Kaine lounged at my desk, hands behind his head, legs crossed with ankle resting on one denim-clad knee like he owned the place. He straightened up with a grin.

"What the hell is this?" I craned my neck, scanning the cubicles behind me for signs that the junior DAs had decided to play a prank on me, but everyone stared at their computer screens with assiduous focus.

"Nice to see you again, Ms. Knight. Your office manager said I could wait for you in here."

Usually our admin staff had better sense. I scowled. "She shouldn't have done that. You need to leave."

"Not before we have a chat." He stood, rounding the desk toward me, and extended a black-gloved hand. "You might want to shut the door."

I held my ground, folding my arms. "I'm not going to talk to you. Get out."

"No." His grin faded, and his green eyes hardened. He dropped his voice lower. "Not until you tell me what you're hiding."

Ice-cold fingers of dread crept along my spine and my heart thudded in my chest. Wordless, I closed the door and pulled the blinds shut with a snap. Then I turned to face Kaine.

Something in my expression made him fall back a step. I seized the opening and moved around him to put the desk between us.

"Let's assume I knew what you mean by that." My even voice belied the roil of my stomach. "What's your angle, Kaine?"

"I'm a journalist. I want the truth."

"The Truth. Ha! That's the name of your blog, right?"

"It's a podcast," he said. "So you remember me, then?"

"The so-called reporter who spouted groundless conspiracies and supernatural nonsense at me just last night? Yes, I remember."

"It's not groundless." A feverish spark kindled in his eyes and he leaned forward. "You know it as well as I do. Demons are real."

The cold solidified, a knotted weight at my core. "Now you've lost me. What are you saying?"

"I'm saying Penelope wasn't human. She was a demon. She shouldn't have died like that. She would have been strong, stronger than any man—"

"You knew her." I stared at him, and he flushed, a slow mottled flow of color that crept up his neck and over his face. "Didn't you?"

"Just through my work," he muttered. "She was a source, that's all."

"Interesting." I had him running scared now. "When did you last see her?"

His eyes slid away from mine. "That's none of your business."

"Actually, it is very much my business." I stood. "If you don't have any useful information to share, then this conversation is over, and I'll get a warrant for your notes."

"You don't want to do that." He bared his teeth at me in a parody of a smile.

"And why not?"

He put both hands on the desk, leaning toward me. "Because I can prove you met with the victim that night."

I sat down, slowly and carefully. "What did you just say?"

"You heard me. I have pictures of you with Penelope. With Ritter, too. What were you doing at the Black Cat Club, Ms. Knight?"

"No comment."

"I see, so it's like that. You know, I think your employers will be very interested in my information. Wouldn't you agree?"

I caught a whiff of his desiderata for the first time, vindictive pleasure mingled with heavy cologne and—what? It carried a fetid undertone of rot, of dank cellars and black mold, and it did not make for a charming combination. I sat back, breathing through my mouth as surreptitiously as I could. "You're extorting me."

"I wouldn't say that. I'm doing you a favor, Ms. Knight. A favor for a favor."

I considered my options. I didn't like any of them. I could overpower him, thanks to Sebastian's kether, but that would only make things worse. I could call security, but it wouldn't help.

"Right," I said. "Extortion. Get to the point and tell me what you want already."

"Now we're in business." He rubbed his hands together. "If you don't want me to publish what I have on you, you're going to have to give me something better."

I didn't like where this was going. "Like what?"

"I want the inside scoop," he said. "Something good. Something juicy. Something that will resonate with my audience."

"I can't comment on an active—"

"My story isn't about your investigation," Kaine said. "It's about Lily Knight, the only known demon prosecutor. I want an exclusive."

Adrenaline hit me like a punch to the solar plexus, sending my heart skittering in my chest. Spots swam in my vision and I gripped the arms of my chair.

How the hell did he know about me? "You're wrong." My voice sounded strange, far away, like it belonged to someone else. "You have no proof."

Kaine had his hands buried in his jacket pockets. "You deny you are a demon?"

"I wouldn't dignify the allegation with a response."

"I thought you'd say something like that." Kaine grinned his shark's smile. "What if I could prove it?"

"You can't," I said, breathless. "No one would believe you."

"Really," Kaine said. He withdrew his hand from his pocket and extended something to me.

It glinted in the fluorescent office lighting, and I recoiled. "Where did you get that?"

He held a silver stake in his gloved hand. Its business end looked sharp enough to pierce skin. "Go ahead," he said. "Take it. Prove I'm wrong."

I shook my head and shoved my hands deep in my own pockets. "Why are you doing this?"

"I think the public deserves to know." He shrugged, pocketing the weapon. "Think about it. You have twenty-four hours or I go forward with the pictures. It's not a bad exclusive in itself and it will certainly raise a lot of questions. Like how you knew the victim and whether you had a reason to want her dead."

"I have some questions too," I said, grim. "How did you get these alleged pictures? Where were you late Wednesday night?"

He sputtered. "I don't have to answer you, hellion! Just tell me whether we have a deal."

I stood up, and smiled when he jumped. "No deal." Letting a subtle menace seep into my Presence, I advanced on him with slow, deliberate steps.

"What are you doing?" Eyes wide, he retreated out of arm's reach until his back almost hit the wall.

"Get out, Mr. Kaine," I said, and reached around him to open the door for him.

He actually flinched, flinging the door open himself and hurrying to the elevators like a man with the devil nipping at his heels. When he glanced over his shoulder at me, I smiled fiercely back at him. He blanched and turned away, pounding on the elevator's down arrow with the heel of his palm.

His fear gratified me, though it didn't do much to staunch my creeping existential dread. But with Sebastian's kether still running euphoric in my veins, I could almost convince myself that everything would be okay.

No. This was bad, kether-high notwithstanding. I could lose my job. I could lose everything.

I slumped in the doorway. What chance did I have that Tobias Kaine was bluffing? Why did he know so much about Penelope?

And why had he acted so squirrelly when I'd asked him about his whereabouts?

I'd let Sebastian off the hook, and now with Kaine's threats, I stood poised to take the fall. I needed to do something, find a new lead. I needed a likely suspect. Above all, I needed to discover who really killed Penelope St. Cyr and bring them to justice, like I'd promised.

I had to go looking for any clues SFPD had missed.

And for that, I needed Ariel.

SMALL DEATHS

"BUT THIS IS MY MURDER," I TOLD THE COP BLOCKING MY PATH AT THE elevator doors on the top floor of the Ritz.

I hadn't chosen the exact right turn of phrase there, because he just gave me a deeply suspicious look. I took a breath and started over.

"Officer, my name is Lillian Knight, and I'm the deputy district attorney working the case. I really just need to have a look at the crime scene. It's important."

"Sorry, ma'am," he said. "My orders were to keep the crime scene locked down. No looky-loos. We've had a lot of journalists poking around, so unless you have official clearance, you just get right back on that elevator."

"But that's what I'm telling you." I rummaged for my wallet and flashed him my bar card. "Look, I *am* official! This is my case."

The officer eyed me with obvious skepticism. "That may well be, ma'am, but you're not on the list."

"Oh, please," I said, losing my grip on my temper. "It's not the Battery Club!"

Behind me, the elevator doors slid open, and the familiar scent of frankincense wafted out. "Whoa, whoa," the cop said, as Ariel simply stepped around us. "Stop right there, sir. Do you have authorization to be on this floor?"

"Apologies." The badge Ariel flashed said "SFPD," but that wasn't his real trick. The air rippled with his energy as he pulled at the officer's perceptions and motivations, reshaping them like taffy.

"Go ahead, sir," the cop said instantly.

"Ah, Ms. Knight." Ariel turned to me. "I see you beat me here. Has this officer been giving you trouble?"

I frowned at him. Just what was he playing at? "I was just explaining to him that I needed to have a look at the crime scene before they release it."

"Of course. She's with me," Ariel said.

The officer stepped aside without a word.

"Thank you," I said, half to the cop, half to Ariel, as he hurried me along the hallway towards the hotel room door garlanded with telltale yellow tape. This was a terrible idea, but thanks to Tobias Kaine, I didn't have a choice.

At the door, the incubus produced a room key and nonchalantly slid it in the reader. When the light flashed green, he swept aside the police tape with a gallant gesture.

I reached for the door handle, then hesitated. "I wish I'd thought to bring gloves."

Ariel grinned. "Ask, and you shall receive, my dear." He reached in his left pocket and drew out a black nitrate pair.

I eyed them, then him. I'd never get used to how he pulled things out of the air like that. "Really?"

"No glove, no love. Go on. They're unused, I promise."

"Eugh." I hadn't even thought of the reasons an incubus might carry gloves until just now. I accepted the gloves gingerly. They did look clean, at least. I slipped them on, then opened the door with a quick, nervous glance over my shoulder.

The cop on guard was staring at the elevator, expression wooden, guarding those doors as if his life depended on it.

Ariel sighed. "Lily. Come *on!*"

With a start, I stepped forward into the darkened foyer. Ariel replaced the tape with care. I had to admit, I admired his attention to detail. The door shut behind us, leaving us standing together in the room where Penelope St. Cyr had died.

"How did you get an access key?" I hissed at him.

"My native charm," he said, next to my ear. "Don't worry, that cop just forgot we were ever here. Now, where's that light switch...ah."

The soft light in the entryway did little to illuminate the rest of the suite. I wrapped my arms around myself, shivering. The air conditioning had been running in here, chilling it to icebox levels. I hung back, but Ariel moved further into the room.

"Tell me why we're here again?" Despite his studied nonchalance, the high set of his shoulders betrayed his discomfort.

"You know why," I said. "We have to investigate what the cops won't know to look for."

A long moment passed before the light came on at the other side of the suite's lounge area. Ariel stood silhouetted in the doorway of the bedroom, his head dropped, chin on his chest. I blinked at what had to be an afterimage, a trick of the light: twin shadows stretching over his head, unfolding and flexing, like a memory of wings.

I blinked again, and it was just Ariel, tall and broad-shouldered, head haloed with golden curls, his body a little hunched as if against an icy blast of wind. The glow from the suite's bedroom lamp spilled out around him into the lounge, revealing the yellow evidence markers decorating the floor and the surfaces of the expensive furniture.

I'd stared at the crime scene photographs and evidence log long enough that I could reconstruct what each marker represented. Here, an expensive suit jacket had hung over the back of the leather couch. There, a pair of strappy black Jimmy Choos had lain discarded in the middle of the carpet, as if kicked off between the sitting area and the bedroom door. On the wet bar, an abandoned, half-full bottle of champagne had bathed in a bowl of water that had once held ice. Beside it, two glass flutes had stood, one with blood-red lipstick on the rim.

It was exactly what I would expect to find the day after a lovers' rendezvous. Not the day after a murder.

All of that was gone now, of course. The glasses and bottle had gone to forensics for analysis, while the shoes and jacket had gone into an SFPD locker. Nothing to see here.

With a sense of sick apprehension, I followed Ariel to the door of the bedroom. He moved to make room for me as I came up behind him, and we both stood side by side in silence, looking at the place where Nepenthe had breathed her last.

Her blood had gone everywhere. It soaked the bedsheets, stained the carpet in scuffs and smears, tacky and almost black now, over twenty-four hours after it had been spilled.

I had forgotten to breathe. I sucked in air, and almost gagged at the smell. Death, sex, fear, and under it all, faint undertones of sandalwood and jasmine: a succubus's scent.

"My God." My choked imprecation emerged as half-whisper, half-sob.

"God had nothing to do with this." A palpable bitterness sharpened Ariel's tone.

I glanced at him sidelong. What did he believe in, if anything? We had never talked about that but the edge to his words told me he would have something to say if I asked him.

I didn't. "I wouldn't be so sure of that," I said instead. Grabbing the file out of my shoulder bag, I thrust the loose paper on top at him. "Look."

Ariel took the page I'd printed from Tobias Kaine's website between two disdainful fingers, as he might hold a dead toad. "What's this?"

"I think it might be an advertisement for the murder weapon." I'd found the merchandise site with a simple browser search after Tobias left my office. It hawked an all-silver arsenal, with a prominent splash page for silver stakes of various sizes and weights. "Have you heard of a podcast called The Truth?"

"Not until last night." He made a dismissive noise, something between a huff and a grunt, as he handed the paper back to me. "Kaine knows nothing. He's a child playing make-believe, and these are just toys. Renaissance Faire stuff."

"Maybe," I said. "But do you think all of them are? Hundreds of thousands of people go to that website every day. How inconceivable is it that just one armchair vigilante took this ad as a call to battle against the forces of hell?"

"Hmm." A dubious rumble.

"Someone like Kaine…he probably believes it's his God-given right to kill demons. No, not just a right. A *duty*." I swallowed, hard. "You said it yourself. They are hunting us. And Nepenthe…she wasn't the first. There were at least two victims before her."

The blood drained from his face, leaving it white as marble. I could say this much for Ariel, he might have been the most obnoxious creature on the planet sometimes, but he was not a stupid one.

"Oh, no." He spoke with quiet resignation, shock without surprise. "Astarte and Salome. How do you know?"

"They were in the morgue database as Jane Does. Cold cases, now."

Ariel shook his head like a boxer shaking off a hit. I sympathized. Every new fact in this case was like a punch to the gut, and the hits kept coming. "And you say Ritter didn't see anything useful?"

"Not from what I saw in that memory flash, or whatever." I didn't want to talk about that. It seemed private now, a confidence exchanged between Sebastian and me. "It all happened so fast. I don't think he had a chance to look for an intruder."

Hoping to change the subject, I cast a look around the room. The file had described signs of a struggle, but little remained in the wake of evidence collection. A few shards left behind by the CSIs still glinted in the thick pile of the carpet, where the lamp by the bed had fallen to the ground and shattered. Had Nepenthe fought back, or had she knocked it over in her death throes?

"The security footage outside showed that no one entered or exited the room after Ritter used his key card at 2:15 AM," I said. "He swore no one else was with them, and the cameras confirmed that. The murderer must have gotten in somehow before they did. He must have planned it that way."

Ariel looked unsettled. "You think the killer was here, lying in wait?"

"Nothing else makes sense." I shuddered at the thought of the two lovers, wrapped up in one another, never noticing that death was with them, watching. "Maybe out there." I gestured to the French doors that opened onto the balcony. Heavy blackout curtains shrouded them, designed to keep out the city lights and morning sunshine alike.

"I suppose it's possible." Ariel crossed to the doors, moving fastidiously around the stains in the carpet, and pulled the curtains apart in one dramatic movement. Arms spread, he brooded, staring out into the night.

After a minute, I joined him, skirting the worst of the bloodstains as he had.

The Ritz's penthouse suite did offer an incredible view. Beneath us, the city lay spread out in strings of lights that sloped sharply down to the surrounding shores, an island of jewels bounded by the utter darkness of the ocean beyond. To the north and east, the bridge lights stretched like delicate spiderwebs across the water to the far shores of Richmond and the Marin Headlands. But it was the balcony itself, not the view, that interested me.

I bent to examine the sliding glass door. "It doesn't look like they even dusted for prints."

Ariel scowled. "So they were lazy. They didn't check because they thought they had their killer."

I tried the door with a light hand. It slid open almost noiselessly, as smooth as if it were oiled. Ariel and I stared at each other, then at the darkened balcony. Cold air wafted in, but it wasn't just the added chill that raised goosebumps on my forearms.

"Maybe our loving couple went out to enjoy some fresh air?" Ariel suggested, after a pregnant pause.

"Maybe the CSIs went out and forgot to lock it?" I wasn't convinced, and I didn't think he was, either.

I flipped the switch for the outdoor light and stepped out onto the balcony. About five feet deep and running the width of the suite bedroom, it had a wrought iron railing, with two small chairs and a table arranged to my right, away from the door.

"The killer could have waited out here for them to come back to the room," I said. "If they never opened the blinds, they wouldn't have noticed anything different."

"Seems like a big risk." Ariel walked to the railing, frowning down upon the city. "What if they decided to come outside for a nightcap? Or what if they decided to go at it while looking down at the city of free love, and pulled back the curtains?"

I glared at him, not liking the mental image of Sebastian and doomed Penelope in the throes of a debauched Exchange. "Not everyone thinks like you, Ariel."

"A pity. The world might be a better place if they did. It might have saved Nepenthe's life, for one thing." He fell silent, staring off across the city. A dense fog was rolling in from the ocean, and the lights of the Golden Gate Bridge winked out beneath its shroud, one by one.

I didn't remember him being so broody back in the day. He had changed. Or maybe contemplating the fate of his kind had changed him. "You don't know that," I said. "The killer must have known what Nepenthe was. He targeted her and armed himself to kill a demon that night."

"That's not a comfortable thought, is it?" Ariel started pacing again, restive as a caged animal, even if that animal was a sleek and well-fed predator. "We're talking about cold-blooded, premeditated murder. It had to be someone who had studied and planned for this. Trained for it, even. Someone strong, fast, and smart."

"Or someone who has been close to one of us. Trusted." My mouth twisted with grim irony. "Maybe even someone who has been prey, and didn't like it. Maybe they even knew her."

"That's the other thing that bothers me," Ariel said. "She had just drawn kether, right? And I get the feeling that this guy is no lightweight."

"He's not," I said.

Ariel's side-eye told me he hadn't missed the implications. He really didn't miss much. "Of course not," he said. "He wouldn't be, if a succubus like Nepenthe chose him as her thrall. You saw her on stage that night. She was a master, at the height of her power. She could have had anyone she wanted."

My cheeks heated. "What are you getting at?"

"Just this: a succubus who has just fed to satiation is no easy target. We're predators. We're stronger than humans. We're built that way, for the sake of survival."

Tobias Kaine had said the same thing. Uneasy, I chose to address his argument instead of his conclusion. "I thought you didn't like it when I called demons predators."

"I don't," he said. "But it's because of the way you say it, all judgmental and superior because you don't hunt. I've got no illusions about what we are. I just don't think we're evil for doing it."

"But feeding on a human can kill them!"

"Is a cat evil because it kills a mouse? No, it's just doing what is in its nature. And cubines don't have to kill. In fact, we usually don't, because killing doesn't help us."

"Then we're what?" I said. "Parasites? Vampire bats, taking what we need from the cattle and leaving our victims weakened but alive, the better to feed off the following night?"

"Vampires are a myth."

"Yeah, but I bet the myth came from people who'd run across unscrupulous cubines."

"It's possible, I'll grant you. But myths, like history, are written by the victors. What stories do you think the mice tell about the cats? Or for that matter, what do the cattle think about the humans you love so much, and their unending appetite for steak and hamburgers?" His beautiful voice dripped with disdain. "This is nature, Lil. Red in tooth and claw. It's not a morality play. We all gotta eat. At least we give our prey pleasure rather than cruelty in the act."

A kind parasite was still a parasite. But I didn't argue the point. "Maybe he knew about the Exchange, too. Maybe he knew that after draining Sebastian's kether, Nepenthe would be as good as alone…"

"Or," Ariel said, turning from his examination of the iron working of the balcony railing, "maybe the murderer is another demon."

I didn't like that thought one bit. "We have met the enemy, and it is us," I said softly. "But why? Why would a demon kill another demon?"

"Why does anyone kill anyone, Lil? We're not so different from humans, you know. Most of our reasons would be the same reasons human kill each other. Jealousy is one that comes to mind, in this case."

"But he said he had never met another succubus."

"That he knew of! We're sneaky beasts, as I'm sure you're aware. If this Ritter guy was as delicious as you'd have me believe, perhaps he was a commodity in high demand. Maybe another cubine wanted a taste of that sweet premium kether."

His mocking tone irritated me. "You're just speculating. We don't know —What is it?"

Ariel had stopped his restless pacing short with a sharp exclamation. "Mother of monsters," he swore. "*Look.*"

Swooping down like a hawk to its prey, he reached back behind one of the deck chairs and pulled something out of the darkness.

Undone ribbons hung from the thing he held, twirling and tangling in the stiff breeze that rose up out of the canyon of the high-rise hotel. In the ambient light, it looked almost black, like a face made of shadow. But the unmistakable shape of two short horns curved off its forehead, and I caught my breath at the familiar silhouette. "But that's—"

The mask of the devil. The mask of a cambion…

"It's his," Ariel said. "It's him, isn't it? The man you saw in the club?"

"It sure looks like it." I moved closer to him. "Let me see that."

But before I could say anything else, he stilled beside me. "Shh," he hissed, and then I heard it too: the sound of voices from inside, and then the thump of someone opening the hotel room door.

We stared at each other, wide-eyed.

"Damn it," I mouthed. "What now?"

The voices had stopped to chat in the room's lounge area. I couldn't distinguish the words, but the tone sounded official—and concerned. Had they noticed the room lights we'd left on? Or would they figure the last investigatory team had left them that way?

Ariel stepped toward me and spoke in an urgent whisper. "Kiss me."

"What?!"

"*Kiss me.*"

"Mmph!"

He had the decency not to pull a Presence on me this time, but he did physically pull me with him into the corner of the balcony, where the half-opened curtain would just barely conceal us from anyone casually glancing out. We were still screwed if they came right up to the window, though.

Ariel's kiss this time did not carry with it the warm and gentle gift of kether of two nights ago. His mouth pressed hard and hungry over mine. He had wrapped one hand around the back of my head to keep me still, while his other arm snaked around me, holding me flush against his body. An unexpected rush of heat bloomed in my belly, rising to meet his obvious arousal.

The kiss broke off as abruptly as it had begun, and I opened my eyes to meet his. They shone amber-green in the near-darkness, pupils blown by desire, desperation…and fear? If only I could read him. "What are you doing?" I said, breathless.

"Please, Lily," he murmured against my lips. "I need you to trust me on this."

"But—"

He cupped my face in his hands, holding my gaze. "We can't let them catch us here. I can get us out, but I need kether--a lot of it, now."

"I don't understand."

"You may be half-demon, but you're half-human too. Human enough." His eyes blazed brighter as he spoke, seeming to absorb all the light on that dim little balcony. "Do you trust me, Lily?"

I took a long, shaky breath, my pulse speeding up. My stomach dropped, a falling sensation like the moment on an airplane when the plane leaps into the air, the push of gravity before the Earth lets go.

From behind the glass door, slow footsteps approached. Whoever was out there was coming into the bedroom. It sounded like several someones.

"I trust you," I whispered, not sure it was true. But I didn't have time to think about it before his mouth covered mine, his long-fingered, clever hands running the length of my body. His energy flowed over me, too, as he touched me. Seeking, pulling, drawing my desire closer and closer to the surface with a curious, heady sensation, like the draw of blood through a needle. He reached between our bodies, the sound of his zipper echoing to my heightened senses, his other hand pulling up my skirt. Then he drew back a fraction, his gaze seeking mine once more.

"Let me in, Lily. It's the only way I can get us out of here." Barely vocalized, the words brushed over my skin, a caress of air.

I nodded once, my eyes half-closing despite myself, dazed with want but agonizingly aware both of his closeness and of the voices on the other side of the glass.

He lifted me onto him as easily as if I weighed nothing at all, entering my body in one sharp thrust, and his energy invaded mine. His presence stirred in the corners of my mind, ran through my blood like fire and wine, lodging deep in my core as he began to feed in earnest. A sweet, dizzy pleasure took hold of my limbs and my mind, and I would have actually fallen if he wasn't holding me tight. The pleasure rose swiftly to its peak.

Darkness swirled in my vision. "Sorry, Lil," Ariel said into my mouth. "Hold on." He was taking more, taking everything, and I struggled against him, starting to panic. The shadows grew above us, around us, stretching and unfolding, great black pinions that flexed against the sky.

The shadows flowed into my thoughts now and my consciousness had begun to slip. I floated, weightless, my ears thundering as with the beat of giant wings.

But surely I imagined that. And then darkness rushed up and swallowed me.

AFTER THE FALL

I DREAMED OF FLIGHT.

Exhilarating at the rush of cold air across my face, I leaned into the wind, stretched my wide wingspan, and soared. Others circled around me as I flew, bright beings with shining wings. They caught the light of the rising sun and refracted it, each feather a crystalline facet, so that it almost hurt to look. Our cries spilled joy into the wind as we wheeled and dipped, and the whole earth lay new beneath us, wild and untouched in its splendor.

As I flew I heard my name. "Lillian!"

I turned in the air and somersaulted a few times, just because I could, delighting in my abilities. I couldn't see where the voice came from. Insistent, it called again, and my irritation grew. Who had any right to call me out of my joyous dance?

"Lillian, come back!"

I refused. I ignored it. I flew higher still in rebellion. I caught a thermal, circling closer and closer to the sun, its brilliance spilling off me in beams of sparkling light. But the wind up here blew stronger, much stronger. It seized me, yanking me off track. It buffeted me until I fell, out of control and spinning toward the earth.

"Lil, wake up!"

In a world where I had no wings, someone was shaking me. "No," I muttered, curling away from them. "Go away. I was flying…"

"Please, love. You have to wake up. You're scaring me."

I tried to place the voice. It was male, low and melodious with the hint of an accent, and it woke in me a confusing mixture of annoyance and arousal. I knew that voice. But somehow I wasn't used to hearing it sound so worried.

"Leave me 'lone," I grumbled. "Want to sleep."

Now that I wasn't dreaming anymore, my whole body hurt. I ached like I'd been hit by a Mac truck that had backed up over me a few extra times to try to finish the job, somehow without actually crushing any necessary bones or organs.

My head hurt like the end of days. I must be sick. Maybe I had the flu. I buried my face in the pillow and groaned.

"Looks like she's finally coming around," said another voice, this one a lighter, bemused baritone. I knew this one, too, although it made no sense to hear it in this context, i.e. no context whatsoever.

"I'd stand back if I were you," warned the other. "I really don't know what state she'll be in when she fully wakes. She was pretty far gone."

"You mean this isn't normal?"

"Who knows what normal is for her? I don't work with many cambions. In fact, she's the only one."

"Interesting," murmured the baritone. Soft footsteps moved toward the bed. His proximity tugged at me, stirring a deep and primal hunger.

"You might want to stay back."

"She doesn't look dangerous to me," said the baritone, and then his hand lightly brushed the hair from my forehead, his fingers warm and gentle and full of—

The touch shot through me like lightning. I lunged toward him, my lips twisting into a hungry snarl. But my weakened limbs failed me, the sheets tangling around them. My pounce fell short as my quarry jumped away.

I fell back to the bed, catching myself on all fours. The light in the room burned my eyes even through the mats of tangled hair that curtained my face. Sore, confused, ashamed, and so very, very hungry, I wanted to cry.

But the sound that rose from my throat was nothing like a sob. A low, eerie, keening growl bled out of my aching bones into the room, a predator's wail of ageless yearning. It didn't seem like the kind of sound that should belong to me.

"Wow," said the baritone, from considerably farther away.

"I told you, she's regressed a bit. Gone feral, as it were."

"That seems like more than 'a bit,'" the baritone said, stern.

"There's a reason why I wanted to restrain her first, especially if you wanted to touch her like that. It would have been a lot safer."

"Not for her." The baritone voice circled a little closer again, and I turned my head, seeking him like a flower seeking sunlight. "In this state, she could have injured herself. Even if she didn't, the trauma of waking bound would be considerable. What did you say happened to leave her like this?"

"She was kether-drained. A human might not have survived it. A succubus might not have either, for that matter. A cambion, however..."

I swung my head back and forth as each voice spoke. So familiar. They had names once. No, they still had names, but I didn't know them. I knew no names at all. I would not have known my own name except that the first voice had called me by it.

Lillian. Lily. Lil.

"I see," said the baritone. He didn't sound pleased. I tracked his voice again, trying to focus on him despite the pounding agony digging its way into the space around my eyeballs. The room still blurred with stinging light, the two tall, indistinct figures silhouetted against it.

I had a tongue behind my lips. A clumsy one, too big for my mouth as I forced it to shape sounds into words. "P...puhlease..."

One of the figures stepped forward, but the other put out an arm to pull him back. "Wait. I'm telling you, it's not safe."

"You can't just leave her like this! She needs help!"

"Neeeed..." I stretched one hand out for the one who wanted to come to me, but lost my balance, falling forward onto the soft mattress. I struggled to rise again, weaker than ever, and lifted my head like a baby animal, blindly seeking what I craved. The keening wail escaped me again, this time broken by despair.

"Christ, man. How can you just stand there?" The baritone's fury laced his desiderata, his heart beating loud in his chest, strong with his desire to help, to hold, to *claim*.

He wanted me…

The other figure moved toward me. I flinched from his hand when he reached for my shoulder.

"Shh, shh, Lily," he crooned. "I'm going to help you. We're going to give you what you need, but I'm going to need you to do something for me first."

He slid his arms beneath me, lifting me. I hissed, part aggression, part fear, and part from pain at the pressure against my tender skin.

"Listen to me." The low rumble troubled my aching head. "You're very ill, and this man here can help you. But for his safety, and yours, I'm going to have to restrain you, ok? Otherwise, one of you could get hurt. Do you understand?"

The meaning of the words filtered in slowly. If I did what he said, I would get what I wanted, what I needed. If I didn't do what he said, I'd get hurt. I glanced from him to the other with a little questioning whine.

"It's okay." A wave of unease rolled off the baritone as he said it, but then his resolve strengthened. "You can do what he says. I will help you, I promise."

The restraints were stiff leather that fit close around my wrists, but the inside was lined with lambskin. They didn't cut into my skin when he drew my arms back and secured them above my head, leaving me helpless. I drew my knees up to my chest and squinted against the light.

"You'll still need to be careful," the one who bound me said. "Remember, you must remain in control. Don't let her take too much at once, or she could break free and really hurt you. Kether is transferred only by skin-to-skin contact, so if you feel her pull too much, break contact immediately."

"I know." The baritone didn't let him finish before he approached again. "I'll be careful."

Even though I had sprung at him the first time, he exuded no fear now. His heartbeat steady as a drum, his self-possession comforting as gravity. I couldn't help straining toward him, and the short chain connecting my restraints to the headboard clinked and thunked as they pulled taut.

"Easy," he said, voice soft, as if soothing a wild creature. The mattress moved as he sat down, near me but not so much that I could touch him.

"You can go now, I think." His tone changed when he spoke to the other man in the room, becoming austere and chilly.

"I'll be right outside." The door closed quietly, leaving me alone with the man on the bed and his steady drumbeat heart.

I whimpered. In this close proximity, his desiderata and my need almost choked me. "Please..." I whispered.

"God, you really are in rough shape." He leaned toward me, his breath warm on my skin, his scent filling my nostrils, soap and light aftershave with a hint of masculine musk. "How did this happen? Who did this to you?"

"Aaa—" But the name on the tip of my swollen tongue escaped me.

"It's okay," he said again. As before, his hand touched my forehead, brushing aside the tangle of hair that veiled my face and clouded my vision further. I turned my head toward his touch, half-sightless still, and my cheek pressed into his palm. He caught his breath, a quick, sharp, startled sound.

With the touch came a tiny measure of clarity, a slight abatement of the hungry need that gripped me. I took a breath of my own, one that hurt a little less. Then I whined again, bereft and unable to stop myself, as he removed his hand.

"It's not right," he said. "I could do almost anything and I don't think you'd object."

I shook my head. Almost wasn't right. I would let him do anything for one more touch.

"Okay, then. Let's just do this." He swung his legs up on the bed beside me and wrapped me up in his arms.

I let out a soft cry of relief as his skin brushed mine. He was fully clothed, so most of the contact came from his palms splayed across my bare stomach and his lips against my hair. His arousal filled my awareness, hard evidence against my back and in the energy that flowed steadily from his body to mine at each point of contact. It was a mere trickle, nowhere near what could have passed between us in a full Exchange, and nothing that would slow him down at all. For me, though, in that moment, it was enough.

It was enough that after a little while, lying there curled up with him holding me, I began to have real thoughts again. I greeted them with regret, because being held without thinking was comfortable and comforting and my actual thoughts were neither of those things. They had inconvenient questions like: where was I? How did I get here? Whose bed was this?

Why was I wearing so few clothes?

My breath caught ragged in my throat. Someone had partially undressed me while I slept. I wore only my underwear, my thin camisole shell, and my collared, wine-colored work blouse unbuttoned over it. The camisole had ridden up, exposing my midriff. At least I hadn't lost too much time, since I vaguely remembered putting on the same blouse this morning before court.

Had that been only this morning? And with that question, the events of the last forty-eight hours seeped inexorably back into my mind.

I remembered the crumbling body in the park, Ariel's eyes, gold behind a silver mask, and Penelope, begging me to save her. I remembered the devil, his robes blood-red, his energy sick and slimy-thick as sewage. I remembered Danny's call, Penelope's body, Sebastian Ritter's fingers brushing mine and filling my mind with the moment of her death. I remembered following Ariel into the room where she died. And then...

What had happened then? It all smeared and blurred together in my mind after the hotel door had opened. Something had happened with Ariel. Ariel and a red mask and wings that blotted out the sky. I couldn't remember how, but Ariel had saved me, had saved us from a very awkward and dangerous position. Had he brought me here?

But where was here?

I stirred, and the arms that held me close released me instantly.

The arms that...wait a minute. Turning my head, I stared at the man who had just risked his life to pull me back from the brink of becoming a real monster.

"Hey, there," he said in a soft voice. He had moved to sit at the edge of the bed, just out of my reach again. "Welcome back, Lily."

"Hi. I...*you?*"

Sebastian Ritter gave one of his short, startled laughs. "Indeed. I take it that means you remember me."

How could I forget him? "Of course I remember you. But..." I shook my head, trying to clear it. "What time is it?"

"About ten in the morning."

"Last night…" I frowned. Was that last night? "It's Saturday, right?"

Ultraviolet concern flared in his desiderata. "It's Monday, Lily."

"Monday!" I tried to lever myself into a sitting position, but the cuffs around my wrists hampered my movement and my muscles trembled with weakness. I sank back to the mattress, panting. "Shit. I'm missing work."

"It's okay." He reached out to me, but drew his hand back as I surged up toward it. "It's just one day. You can call in sick. What's the last thing you remember?"

"Ariel…" I almost had it, but the memory slipped away again. "Where am I?"

I glanced around at my surroundings, expecting a hospital room, perhaps, or a psych ward. But whatever I expected, this large, high-ceilinged, white-painted bedroom wasn't it. The hardwood floors glowed with sunlight from a huge west-facing bay window lined with thin white curtains that fluttered in a gentle breeze. The furnishings said money, but they didn't scream it. They spoke of quality, nothing ostentatious.

Sebastian cleared his throat. "Actually, you're in my house. In my bed, as it happens."

"Oh," I said in a small voice. "Did we…?"

"No, we did not." The force of his denial took me aback, and my surprise must have shown on my face because he softened his tone. "You were unconscious. I would never…I'm sorry. I don't fully understand what you've been through, but I know you must be frightened and disoriented. I'll explain as best I can, but first—you are feeling more yourself now, aren't you?"

"Yeah," I mumbled, flushing and dropping my eyes. Sebastian Ritter had seen me like *that*. He'd witnessed me begging, feral and desperate as an animal in heat. "Um, I don't know how to thank you. That must have been pretty weird for you, just now."

"It's fine," he said. "I was happy to help. It was touch and go there for a bit. I wasn't sure if you'd wake up at all. I think even your incubus friend worried about that."

I frowned. "My incubus…Ariel?"

"He stepped out a little while ago." He rose. "Want me to call him back in?"

"No! No, please. Not right now. I just—I need a minute."

"Should I go?"

"No." My chest tightened and I drew a short, panicked breath. "Can you…would you mind staying?"

He sat back down immediately. "No, Lily. I don't mind. I'll stay as long as you want me to."

"Thank you." I had no idea why he was being so kind to me. After all, he barely knew me. For that matter, I couldn't say why I found his presence so comforting, why I wanted him to stay, why I trusted him to begin with. Maybe it was that steady drumbeat of quiet confidence, the leash that kept his underlying intensity in check. Maybe it was how obvious he made it that he'd cared for Nepenthe. Maybe it was that he hadn't taken advantage of an out-of-control succubus who would have literally begged for it, even though he wanted me, even though nothing and no one would have stopped him, least of all me.

I peeked up at him through my tangled hair to find him eying the cuffs that held me in place.

"I'd like to take these off," he said, gruff-voiced. "Seems to me you're back in your right mind. What do you think?"

"You're not worried that I'll attack you again?"

"It's a risk I'm willing to take. As a rule, I prefer not to have ladies chained up in my bed unless it's been properly negotiated first." He had already started unhooking the chain.

"I was ok with it at the time."

"Sure you were." Anger prickled through his desiderata, but it didn't turn toward me. "I think it's safe to say you were also in an altered state of consciousness at the time."

He unfastened the chain, coiling it in his hands. I lowered my bound arms, rolling my shoulders as much as I could to try to release the lingering soreness.

"Better?" he said, watching me.

"Yeah."

"The cuffs next. Give me your hands."

Wordless, I offered them to him, palms up. Holding my wrists gently, he produced a key from his pocket and unlocked one, then the other. I shivered at his touch and the gentle flow of his kether, his desire more muted now. Then, as the cuffs fell away, a more violent shudder racked my body. Teeth chattering, I groped for the bedclothes, pulling them up around me and huddling inside as I shook. But neither the blankets nor the sunlight could take the edge off the chill that seized me, as if rising from the marrow of my bones.

"You ok?" Alarm flickered through his desiderata like St. Elmo's fire.

"C-c-cold," I managed, between the racking chills.

"Hang on." He moved away from me, crossing the room with long-legged strides. No expensive suit for him today. Instead, he wore jeans that fit him admirably and a plain but fitted black t-shirt. His feet were bare, sinewy and graceful as the rest of him.

I tore my eyes away. Guilt prickled through me, chiding me for my over-intimate, voyeuristic appraisal.

He disappeared through the far door, and I wrapped myself tighter into my cocoon of sheets. If only I could get warm. Sebastian reemerged moments later with an armful of what looked like a cloud and turned out to be the softest, fluffiest white robe ever made when he tucked it around my shoulders.

I unwound myself from my nest long enough to encase myself in the cloud, and then burrowed back under the covers. "I'm s-sorry," I said through chattering teeth. "I d-d-don't know why it hit me like this."

"At a guess, it's a delayed shock reaction to physical and mental trauma. I've seen it before in people who have just come out of an…intense experience." He came back to sit beside me on the bed once more. "Is there anything I can do to help?"

I hesitated to ask for what would help the most. Instead, I edged closer to him on the bed, curling myself around him where he sat, his body heat warming me more than the blankets and the robe between us. Without the risk of the kether pull, I sought the comfort of physical closeness for more than sustenance.

After a minute or so, his hand dropped to lightly stroke my hair. I craned my neck to find him looking down at me with an odd expression on his face.

"Still not entirely yourself, are you?"

Heat washed over my exposed skin. My shivers had begun to subside as soon as he touched me.

"I'm sorry," I said again, pulling back. He caught my hand, another pulse of his kether passing from his skin to mine. Suddenly no longer cold, I went still.

"I don't mind," he said. "It's just that the Ms. Knight I met last week was a very different person than the one I'm getting to know now."

"Yeah, well, I'm full of surprises." My guard had snapped up at the mention of my professional persona. There was nothing professional about what had happened here, was happening, or could happen if I didn't pull myself together. I reclaimed my hand and sat up, pulling the robe closer around me, not for warmth but for modesty this time.

"Don't get me wrong," he said. "As surprises go, this one has been... not unpleasant."

"Ha! That's one way to put it."

"Sorry, I'm bad at this. I'm trying to say that despite everything else, I'm glad to get to know you better, Lily."

"Me too." I sighed. "It's not that I don't want to get to know you. Not that I don't want you to...know me. I just don't know why I let Ariel—"

I broke off as the memory finally blossomed into awareness. Mother of monsters. How had I forgotten what Ariel and I had done on the balcony at the Ritz Carlton, mere moments away from likely discovery by the police, while Nepenthe's blood still soaked the room inside?

What in heaven and the seven hells had I been thinking?

I hadn't thought. That was the problem. It had felt so good, I had said yes. It had been the first time in such a long time that I had let anyone touch me like that. My body had mostly made that decision for me. My body knew him, even after all these years. But then that strange sensation had overwhelmed me as he took my kether, like floating above myself, free from the confines of gravity, dissociated from the act of the Exchange. And that inexplicable final vision kept haunting me, defying logic and all attempts to dismiss it, that memory of massive, not-quite-corporeal wings the color of night unfurling from Ariel's broad shoulders.

Had we *flown* out of there?

Impossible. I squeezed my eyes shut, shaking my head, but I still could not shake the unreasonable conviction that we had done exactly that.

Whatever had happened, I certainly had a lot of questions for a certain incubus of my acquaintance.

16

THE DRUG OF FORGETTING

Sebastian's voice broke into my scattered thoughts. "Are you all right?"

"Fine," I muttered. "I think I need a shower." I needed to wash Ariel's touch from my skin. How could I let him take advantage of me like that?

"Of course. You probably need food, too. You must be hungry."

"Only ravenous, but thanks to you, no longer rabid." I gave him a faint smile, scooting to the end of the bed to perform a tentative test of my legs. They wobbled.

"Whoa, let me help you." He came to my side in an instant, steadying me as I swayed on my feet.

"I'm *fine*." But at his stern look, I sighed and accepted his proffered arm.

"Trust me," he said. "This is way easier than picking you up off the floor."

"I don't understand why you're being so nice to me," I said, as we made our slow way to the door.

"Do I have to have a reason?"

"No," I conceded. "But you barely know me. In my experience, people don't do nice things for no reason."

"Hmm," he said. "It sounds like you just don't have much experience with people being kind to you."

He wasn't entirely correct. Case in point, Danny giving hot tea and good advice to an adult cambion with teenage problems. "It's not a kind world," I said instead. Not for my kind, at least.

A large, airy landing waited on the other side of the door. Ariel was nowhere to be seen. Only the faint, telltale scent of frankincense lingered to mark his presence.

"Huh, that's funny," Sebastian said. "I wonder where your friend went."

"Who knows. And he's not my friend." I said it as much to remind myself as to correct Sebastian. "He comes and goes as he pleases. Like a cat."

"Yeah," Sebastian said. "A cat who walks through walls without tripping state of the art security systems. I noticed that last night."

"Last night..." I hesitated. "Was I with him?"

He shot me an indecipherable look. "In a sense. Here's the bathroom. You'll find the facilities through that door. And may I suggest a bath instead of a shower? I don't want you staggering around on those colt-like legs of yours and knocking yourself out again, after I only just got you up and about."

"Good call. That would just be asking for a lawsuit," I deadpanned.

His laugh warmed me. He *was* kind. It hadn't been that good of a joke.

The enormous bathroom featured royal blue and white marble everything, with a bathtub I could probably swim laps in. Another door to the right concealed the toilet and sink. I puttered around in there until the sound of water running in the room outside gave me pause. I hadn't expected him to draw my bath for me.

Then I glimpsed myself in the big mirror with its dark wood frame and winced. God, I looked monstrous, my eyes like bruises in a ghost-pale face, framed by wild masses of snarled hair.

At least I knew he wasn't just being nice to me because I was pretty.

When I emerged, Sebastian was fussing about with towels and toiletries, laying them out neatly on the wide lip of the half-full, steaming tub.

"What do you mean, in a sense?" I demanded.

"What?"

"You said I was with Ariel, in a sense. What does that mean, exactly?"

"Oh. Yes." Sebastian busied himself with an array of soaps and washcloths, his precise arrangement fascinating me. Without turning around, he said, "He greeted me from my own stairs with you limp in his arms." He tested the water, still without looking at me. "At first, I thought you must be dead."

Like Penelope. He didn't have to say it. "That sounds like Ariel. He's very dramatic. Melodramatic, even."

"It was quite an entrance. Very Gothic romance." Sebastian straightened from the tub. "Not exactly what one expects to see in one's own castle, so to speak, and I'm more of a Modernist, myself."

"I'm surprised you let us stay, after that."

"I didn't do it for him." Sebastian moved toward the door. "He's lucky I didn't shoot him or call the police. Fortunately, I recognized you."

"He let himself in?"

"I have no idea how." Annoyance and a sense of injured pride spiked through his desiderata. He must put a lot of stock in his fancy security system. He'd probably designed it himself.

"Strange," I said. "It's just like Ariel to show up unannounced, but not at all like him to trust a human."

"I don't think he had a choice. As he explained it to me, I was the haven of last resort for saving you."

Ariel had a lot to answer for. No wonder he had made himself scarce. "I'm very much in your debt."

"You don't owe me anything." Fiercely serious, his statement brooked no contradiction. He gestured to the now-full tub. "Your bath. I'll leave you to it."

"Thank you, Sebastian."

"That I will accept," he said. "I'll be right next door. Try not to drown. And if you must slip and fall, try to make a lot of noise."

His tone had lightened, but I caught the reassurance layered under it. As the door shut, I had to admit that the reassurance had worked. His steady energy gave me a sense of safety I'd never felt with anyone, even Danny.

I hoped my trust in him would not be my undoing.

I hoped his kindness would not turn out to be his biggest mistake.

THE BATH LEFT me feeling substantially more human. Almost standard levels, even if that was only half. Sebastian's kether buzzed beneath my skin. He had dulled my demon hunger, even if he hadn't sated it. In its stead the pangs of everyday mortal hunger made themselves known.

I didn't want to dress myself again in the clothes I had worn for the last three days as I lay in kether-drought. I bundled them up in my damp towel. Maybe Sebastian would let me use his laundry room. After a lengthy and painful struggle to tame the knots in my hair, I wrapped myself back up in the fluffy white robe he'd given me and ventured out onto the landing.

Something smelled delicious out there. I dithered for a moment at the top of the curving staircase, but I couldn't resist for long. My stomach growled, and I padded down on bare feet, following the rich scent of bacon frying. It made it easier to find the kitchen, despite the house's intimidating size. How had they even fit this place into the crowded parcels of San Francisco's streets?

Who knew if I was even still within the city limits. Ariel could have taken me anywhere.

After wandering through at least three living rooms, I rounded a corner and found myself in the kitchen doorway. Sebastian stood at the stove, his narrow back to me, scrambling eggs in a cast-iron pan. A plate of bacon sat to his right on a shining dark granite countertop, and a carton of eggs lay open beside it. He was whistling to himself, a familiar tune that I couldn't quite name.

"First you try to kidnap me off to Cliff House, now this," I said. "It's like you're obsessed with feeding me breakfast."

He broke off his tune at the sound of my voice. "I didn't know what you liked so I made some of everything." He waved his spatula at a plate of what must have been an entire package of bacon and a pat of hash browns frying on the back burner.

"I have no objections." I slid into one of the bar stools at the counter. "Still no Ariel?"

"I checked the house again but I haven't seen hide or hair of him. I think he took off." Sebastian methodically assembled a plate with generous helpings of eggs, potatoes, bacon, and fruit. His long-limbed economy of movement couldn't match Ariel's poetry in motion, but it mesmerized me. And he *was* about to feed me, after all.

He shot me an odd look. "What is it?"

"You cook for yourself? I wouldn't have guessed you were this domestic."

"I'm a man of many talents," he said, straight-faced.

Had he intended that double entendre? His desiderata radiated amusement and pride shot through with a little uncertainty as he placed the heaping plate in front of me, along with a tall glass filled to the brim with orange juice.

"Jesus, this looks amazing."

"You're welcome." He grinned. "Can I take those to the laundry for you?"

I glanced down at the bundle of clothes I'd carried in with me, cheeks heating at the thought of him sorting through my used underthings. "No, thank you. It's just... I don't have anything to wear."

"Hence my offer of laundry."

"That's okay. I'll do it later. Um...did you undress me?"

He shook his head. "Your friend Ariel took charge of all that. He made it clear that my role was primarily that of a battery cell."

"Ugh, I'm sorry. 'My friend Ariel' can be a real dick sometimes."

"I'm getting that." Sebastian frowned. "Let me ask you something. Just how well do you know this Ariel?"

"I've known him for a long time." I avoided his gaze. "He was my... mentor, of a sort. But we've been out of touch until this week. Why?"

"Just curious." Sebastian leaned his elbows on the other side of the counter, frowning as he pushed a napkin around on the slippery granite. "I'd never seen him before until the other night. The night Penelope..."

I stared at him. "You think Ariel...No. Ariel came to me for help that night. He was afraid for her, and for the others."

"Others?"

"Other succubi," I said. "Other victims. Ariel comes off as kind of a jerk, and he doesn't really care for humans, but he does care. He said she was in danger and he wanted to protect her."

Sebastian's frown deepened. "She never mentioned anything to me about being in danger."

"Of course she didn't. She was a demon." At his questioning look, I went on, "You asked me how much I know about Ariel. Well, let me ask you this. How much did you know about Penelope, outside of the time you spent together?"

"That's not fair." But the pained note in his voice told me I had struck a chord.

Fair or not, I pressed on. All's fair in love—and murder. "I heard what you told the police. She was a very private person, and that worked for you. Isn't that what you said?"

His posture stiffened. I had him on the defensive. "Yes. But..."

"So what did you really know about her? Did you know her fears? Her dreams? Her secret hopes? Did you even know who her friends were, or where she lived?"

"No," he said, expression stricken. "She never told me any of that."

"And you never asked." I laid down my fork, bitter triumph driving my words. "You were satisfied with knowing just her body, and the pleasure she gave you. I bet you didn't even know her real name."

"Her real name?" He looked blank. "Penelope wasn't—?"

"Nepenthe." He didn't deserve the naked anger in my voice, but just then I didn't care. "Her name was Nepenthe."

Chastened, he tried it out. "Nepenthe."

"It's a succubus name, an ancient name. They all have them, the full-blooded demons. The secret names they use among themselves."

"I didn't know that."

"Yeah, well." I lifted my fork again, picking at my eggs, appetite lost. "You wouldn't. Don't worry, that's not your fault. I told you, it's a demon thing." *We're solitary beasts.* Ariel's words.

"It means 'forgetting'," Sebastian said.

"What?"

"Her name. It's from Homer. Nepenthe, the drug of forgetfulness. 'That which chases away sorrow...'"

I suddenly regretted my harsh cross-examination. My heart contracted at the grief in his bleak tone, his draught against it lost forever. If only I could offer him some panacea, words that would allay his pain...

But there were none. Not for humans, and not for demons. Only time could dull the knife's edge of loss. For today, distraction would have to serve in its stead. "Now that, I didn't know. Homer, you said? So, you're a student of the classics, as well as an excellent short-order cook."

His short laugh still sounded a bit shaky, but it was something. "My parents had old-fashioned ideas about education, and Mother was an ambassador. I went to secondary school in England for a few years. They still teach Greek and Latin there."

"Your mom was an ambassador? That's not in any of your bios." I paused. "Not that I read your bios or anything. Or searched your name on the internet."

He raised an eyebrow at that. "Of course not. Yes, she was a force to be reckoned with. I spent most of my childhood traveling with her while my father stayed in Washington. I burned with envy for all my classmates who got to stay in one spot with friends they'd known since kindergarten."

"Sounds pretty lonely."

"You're not wrong. It didn't help that I was the world's biggest nerd at the time."

"At the time?" I deadpanned.

"*Touché.*" The laugh sounded more real this time, if a bit self-deprecating. "I like to think that now, I'm at least a nerd made good."

"Yeah, you're a real underachiever." I glanced around at the beautiful kitchen surrounding us—everything of the highest quality, everything in its proper place. "But is it any less lonely?"

He stared at me for several seconds. Then he passed a hand through his hair, dislodging a few strands that fell out of place over his forehead. The slight rumpling of his carefully groomed exterior made him look far younger and a bit lost, but somehow even more attractive. "Jesus, Lily," he said. "You really know how to go right for the jugular."

"Wrong monster." I flashed him a winning smile. "I'm a demon, not a vampire. But they didn't make me a district attorney for nothing." If I still was one after last week.

"And after I took you in and nursed you back to health, too. Not to mention making you breakfast."

"That might get you out of answering the question."

"I'll take the fifth, if it's all the same to you."

"We're not supposed to use that against you," I said. "But you know, juries always read into it anyway."

"Hmm." Amusement sparked in his eyes again as he picked up the gauntlet I had thrown down. "And what about you, Ms. Lily Knight? What are your...oh, let's see, how did you put it? What are 'your fears, your dreams, your secret hopes'?"

I couldn't knock the man for being a bad listener. Or a slow learner. I shifted in my seat, uncomfortable all of a sudden. "Hey, wait a minute! That's not how this works."

"Isn't it?" He seemed pleased with himself. "The prosecutor falls apart on the stand, huh?"

"That question was vague and ambiguous." Now he'd challenged me, and I didn't like it much. "Besides, I barely know you. Maybe you don't get to learn those things yet."

"I'd like to know you better." His striking light eyes caught mine and held them. I looked away first. "All right, objection sustained. I should have been a lawyer," he teased.

"Ha! No, you made the smarter choice. Tech pays way better, if your fortunes are any indication."

He waved this off. "I'm not going to let your base flattery throw me off track."

"Ooh," I said. "You're better at this than I thought you'd be."

"Base flattery. Didn't I just say that? All right, damn it. I'll rephrase my question. Where did you grow up?"

"Eastern Pennsylvania." That seemed safe enough. "A small town north of Philly."

"Aha, a transplant. What brought you west, young padawan?"

"You really are a nerd."

"Guilty as charged. Answer the question, Lily. What brought you so far from home?"

"Escape," I said softly.

"A hit, a very palpable hit. I should stop before you actually do hit me, I think." He took my raised eyebrow as a green light. "What were you escaping?"

I looked up from a careful study of my own hands. "My family. Myself, I think."

"And did you succeed?"

"I think, maybe…I succeeded better than was really good for me."

"What an interesting thing to say."

Indeed, I hadn't really known the answer until it came out of my mouth. "You *are* good at this."

"I may have an unfair advantage in this situation. You are on my turf, after all. Barefoot in my kitchen and wearing nothing but the robe I lent you."

Despite his joking tone and my own better angels, my succubus senses tingled. The hum of his desiderata had deepened as he spoke. The smooth gray-blue of his eyes gave nothing away, but I knew better.

My hunter's instinct surged again to the forefront of my mind. I was still hungry for him, after all. All the delicious breakfast in the world couldn't take the edge off that. "And you like that, don't you?" His eyes narrowed, holding my gaze. "I already confessed my predilections in the interrogation room and. I see no point in hiding it. I couldn't anyway, not from you."

"No." I slipped from my stool, padding around the bar toward him. To his credit, he held his ground as I slipped into his personal space, until only inches of space separated our bodies.

"Lily…" His voice roughened, half-question, half-invitation.

"Have a care, Sebastian." I pitched the words low and quiet, resonating with a minor Presence designed to prickle his senses with a warning of danger. "You offer temptation that's hard to ignore. Harder now that I've tasted you."

His pupils dilated, but not with fear. "Harder for both of us, I think." He did step back from me then, though his desiderata strained toward me. His control in the face of my powers was like none I had ever encountered. The challenge made me want him more, even as it frightened me.

But if he could resist me, I could control myself too. I could bide my time.

No. I was a person. I was more than my drives, more than my nature, more than the starved monster I had embodied earlier. And he was more than simply prey, more than a kether "battery." He was a person, too, one who had seen the monster and not run from me, one I liked more than I wanted to and more than I found reasonable for someone I had known less than a week.

"I should go," I said, breaking the pause that had stretched between us as we locked gazes. "I'll get my things, call a cab. I've imposed on you enough today."

"Perhaps that would be best." He hid his disappointment well, but not quite well enough to keep it from my demon senses. "But don't call a cab. I'd be happy to drive you."

"You don't have to do that."

"Yes, I do," he said. "Let me show you why."

Puzzled, I followed him out of the kitchen to the expansive front room, where he pulled aside a corner of the filmy white curtains that covered the wide bay windows. His house was set back from the street a fair bit, with tall cypresses and manicured hedges screening it from passersby. But a white van with a blue logo and satellite equipment on top lurked just outside the hedge.

"A news van? Really? What do they want?"

"They've been out there for days, hounding me. Needless to say, since this weekend's news cycle, they'd jump on the chance to get some shots of the beautiful young D.A. who dismissed the charges against me as she attempts to depart my home by taxi." He let the curtain fall, then noticed my expression. "What is it?"

"You said a story hit the news yesterday." Foreboding trickled down my spine like ice water. "What kind of story?"

"You don't know?" He shook his head. "I guess you really were out for a while."

"Since Friday night," I said. "*What story?*"

"There are photographs of us," he said. "You and me, and you and Penelope, from that night. They're investigating *you*, Lily. They think you might have something to do with her death."

So Tobias Kaine hadn't been bluffing, after all, and I'd slept right through his blackmail deadline. I sank down on a leather couch, which probably cost more than my school loans and enveloped me in a comfort I couldn't enjoy "But why would they think I..."

"Oh. Yes." Sebastian's mouth quirked, but his bitterness hung acrid in the air. "That's because of me, I'm afraid."

"They think I killed her out of jealousy? But that makes no sense! I barely knew you. I barely *know* you!"

"That's not all," he said. "They have crime scene photographs and in the photos, she…Well, she doesn't look human." Brusque, he turned away. "My car is in the garage and it has tinted windows. Impose on me a little more for both our sakes, and let me drive you home."

Frozen in panic, I didn't move. "The crime scene photographs," I whispered. "They couldn't have leaked them. They weren't even in the official file."

He wheeled around, face darkening. "What did you say?"

"No one else had those photographs," I said. "No one, except me."

17

ANALOG DEMON

"I don't understand." Kneeling on the thick-carpeted floor of Sebastian's palatial bedroom, I sat back on my heels. "It's all here. The file, the pictures. Nothing is missing." I exhaled. I hadn't forgotten my bag on the balcony of the Ritz like I'd feared. Ariel must have delivered it when he delivered me and left it leaning against the wall by the bed where I'd woken in kether-drought.

"You had the file with you this whole time?" Sebastian stood in the doorway, arms folded, his expression unreadable.

"I took it with me when I left work Friday. I was going to work from home, read over it and see if I could find anything…" I trailed off. "What is it?"

"You don't know where you were the last few days," he said. "You blacked out. But how do you know you were unconscious that whole time?"

"I don't know. I—wait. You think I did this?"

He shrugged. "As you pointed out earlier, we don't actually know each other that well."

Adrenaline surged through me. What if I *had* done it? What if I'd gone on some kind of kether-withdrawal bender? Where had Ariel and I been before he brought me here? I didn't know anything at all. I grabbed my phone from the bag's front pocket, scrambling to my feet. "I need to call Danny." I looked down at the black, unresponsive screen. Dead. "Never mind. I need to charge my phone."

"This is a problem I can solve." Still somber, he opened a drawer in the nightstand and handed me the correct charger on the first try. No surprise there. The man knew his technology.

Power needs taken care of, unable to call my lifeline for the time being, I sank onto the bed. "So what else are they saying about us?"

"Trust me. You don't want to know." Sebastian walked across to the window, frowning out at a spectacular panorama of steep tree-lined slopes dropping to the flat blue expanse of the Bay in the middle distance. Ariel hadn't taken me out of the city after all. At a guess, he'd taken me no farther than Pacific Heights. San Francisco's most tony neighborhood, famous for its extravagant mansions and nosebleed-graded streets, seemed to fit Sebastian's profile.

"Maybe not," I said. "But I need to know. I can handle it."

Blue skies out there, thunderclouds in here. His desiderata roiled with frustration and rage. "Some right-wing outlet got a hold of it first and framed the conversation. It only gets uglier from here, Lily."

"What right-wing outlet? You can't protect me from this. I know how people are."

In answer, he turned and clapped his hands. "Media," he said.

I stared at him in confusion, then jumped when panels in the near wall slid apart with a soft hum, revealing a gigantic flat-screen television. "Wow," I said.

Sebastian ignored my oh-so-intelligent commentary, addressing the wall. "Network. Channel 10."

The screen sprang to life. "...broadcasting live from the famous San Francisco hotel where the woman was found dead under unusual circumstances Wednesday night. Sebastian Ritter, the son of a prominent U.S. Senator and the CEO of multi-million dollar tech startup Ritter Security Industries was arrested at the scene, but authorities released him and dropped all charges as of Friday morning. The district attorney's office had no comment when we reached out to them. However, yesterday these frightening pictures of the victim were made public via an anonymous source."

The newscaster looked fake-concerned. Probably salivating for the big reveal. "The images we are about to show are graphic and not appropriate for children or other sensitive viewers."

Almost before she finished speaking, the pictures began to flash across the screen. Nepenthe's sightless yellow eyes stared out at us in high definition.

"Oh, my God," I said. "Those are them. Those are the pictures Danny gave me."

The camera switched back to the announcer, young, blond, pretty, and merciless. Then the shot widened to show the person standing next to her, a tall man with a broad, stubbly jaw and a light of fanaticism in his bright green eyes.

I leaped to my feet. "That bastard!"

Sebastian shot me a disapproving glance. "You know this clown?"

"I wish I didn't. He came into my office on Friday and tried to blackmail me."

The news announcer went on in perky tones, "I'm here now with host of a podcast called The Truth, Tobias Kaine. Mr. Kaine, how did you happen to come by these pictures?"

"As you know, Marcie, we journalists are ethically bound to protect our sources." Tobias got even more self-important with a camera pointed in his face. I wouldn't have thought it possible. "But I can tell you that the leak came from a person with knowledge of the case…"

"Hang on. Mute," Sebastian said, and Tobias Kaine went silent. "He tried to *blackmail* you?"

"He sure did! And he knows what I am. I don't know how he knows, but he does." A sudden thought struck me like a bolt from the blue. "You don't think *Tobias*…Oh my gods and little monsters."

Sebastian raised an eyebrow at the curse I'd stolen from Ariel, but let it pass. "What is it?"

"Tobias was in my office," I said slowly. "When you dropped me off that morning, he was waiting for me. The file was in there. Maybe he made copies."

"There's only one problem with that," Sebastian said, looking thoughtful. "Those were high quality images. You wouldn't get a resolution like that from a copier. Or a scan, for that matter."

"Okay, fine," I said, with unreasonable irritation. "What about the cloud? That gets hacked all the time."

"Please don't tell me you uploaded those pictures to the cloud, Lily."

"I don't think so?" His expression of disbelieving horror had made me nervous. "Does it put them in the cloud automatically?"

"Good lord," he said. "Your cyber hygiene needs some serious work."

Cyber hygiene? What the hell was that? I was pretty sure he'd just insulted me, and I didn't even know what the insult meant. "I don't know, okay? I'm just an analog demon in this digital world. The point is, he got the pictures somehow."

He looked doubtful. But before he could respond, my phone came back to life with a veritable chorus of chirping notifications.

"You're in demand, it seems," he observed dryly.

"Shit." I had eight new voicemail messages and twenty texts. Most of them were from Danny. I'd promised to meet her again at Ladybird's after my little field trip with Ariel, but of course I had never made it.

I could read her emotional journey in the tone of her texts.

First, irritated that I was late: *STOP WORKING.* Then, resigned and more than a little pissed: *I just wish you'd told me you didn't intend to make it out tonight.* Then worried. *Lil, where are you? Are you okay?*

When I still hadn't responded, the texts became progressively more frantic.

I went to your place and you didn't answer the door.

You BETTER not have been home.

Where the hell are you?

OMG, you better not be holed up with that rich guy, what's his butt. Bazleton or whatever.

Wait, you better be holed up with him. The only way this could be considered acceptable is if you are FINALLY GETTING LAID.

I swear to GOD, Lil, if you don't text me back in the next twenty-four hours I will report you to the SFPD as a missing person.

Then, mid-afternoon on Sunday, she'd changed her tune again.

What the hell is going on? Have you seen the news?

Where did they get those pictures? This is bad.

This is really, really bad. Call me, please.

Three of the voicemail messages were from Danny as well. Four of them were from the office. *Double shit with a side of fucking hell.* I didn't feel ready to listen to those yet.

The most recent message was from an unknown number. No content. Just a crackling thump, like someone slamming down a rotary telephone. Did anyone even have those anymore?

"Something wrong?" Sebastian inquired.

I looked up from the phone, flushing when I found his intense focus trained on me. "The police might be looking for me. I need to call my friend. Would you mind...?"

"Of course." He headed out before I finished speaking, shutting the door behind him with a soft click.

The news had moved on to some other story, still in silence.

"Media off?" I said in a tentative voice. Nothing happened. The system probably had voice recognition and only obeyed Sebastian. For all I knew, it was one of those smart TVs that spied on your conversations. It wouldn't do any good, but I turned my back on the screen before I called Danny.

She picked up on the first ring.

"You ASSHOLE," she greeted me.

"Love you too, Dan. I'm okay."

"I've been worried sick!"

"I know. I'm sorry."

"What the hell happened? Where were you?"

"I was ill. And my phone died." I didn't like lying to Danny, even a lie of omission, but I wasn't ready to talk about Ariel, Sebastian, and my descent into feral hunger yet.

"Since Friday night?"

"About then, yeah."

"You couldn't have called?"

"It came on really fast." Not a lie, either. "I only just started to feel human again this morning."

"Is that a joke?" she said, sounding suspicious.

"No, I'm dead serious."

"Where are you? At home?"

"No." I cast a quick glance over my shoulder at the door. "I crashed with a friend."

"What friend?" Now she sounded really suspicious. "Lily, *I'm* your friend."

"You make it sound like you're my *only* friend."

"Well…"

"Shut up." I lowered my voice in case of eavesdropping. "Danny, I'm at Sebastian's house." I winced as the whooping sound she made nearly blew my eardrum out. "Jeez. Quiet down, or he'll hear you."

"You're shitting me! You spent the night with Richie McHottiepants?"

"Yes. I mean, no. Not like *that!* He's been taking care of me while I was sick, that's all."

"Uh huh. Sure he has. How did this happen?"

"I have no idea. It just did." Still not a lie. I got some satisfaction out of that.

"Okay, sure," she said. "I'll let that go for now, but only if you give me the juicy details. What's he like?"

"He's odd, but nice. No…that's not right. He's not nice, but he is kind."

"So, not your usual type."

"Feeling a bit attacked here, Dan."

"No, not at all. I like it. You deserve to have someone kind but not nice."

"I told you, it's not like that. I didn't—I don't *have* him." Except for breakfast. "I don't even know him. We didn't do anything." Much.

"Shh," she said. "You're ruining the moment."

"Fine," I said. "Let's talk about something else. What the hell is going on with this news story?"

"I was going to ask you that." Her tone went abruptly serious. "Yeah, I have no idea. The pictures of you in the club are bad enough, but the crime scene pictures—you didn't leak those?"

First Sebastian, now Danny believed I might sink that low? I tried not to think about Sebastian's idea that I'd released the photos in some kind of feral succubus fugue state. "I did not. I would *never*—"

"Whoa, lady. Don't get your panties in a twist. I didn't think you would, it's just that only you and I had them, you know? And I know *I* didn't…"

I let out a breath. I hadn't known until that moment, but some part of me had feared that Danny had leaked the photos. "Of course not."

"So then who? Basra?"

"She didn't have copies. I think Tobias stole them from me somehow. I just don't know how."

"What are you going to do?"

I sighed, curling my toes in the soft throw rug at the foot of Sebastian's bed. "I don't know if there's anything to do. It's out there now. I can't put the demon back in the bottle."

"But the police investigation…"

"This fucked it all up," I said, voice dull. "Even if they can find the real culprit, they'll never get a conviction thanks to my involvement. Unless they decide I look good for it."

"But you have an alibi," Danny said. "Me."

"I hope that's enough. Listen. Friday night, before I got sick, I got a lead."

"Got a lead? What is this, a bad detective story?"

"I found a clue," I said, impatient, and ignored her snort. "To the real killer's identity."

"What do you mean, a clue?"

The ribbons had twirled, hanging from Ariel's hand, red as blood. "The killer wore a mask. He left it at the crime scene. It probably has his DNA on it…" I crouched by my bag, searching its pockets. "Damn it! It's not here."

"What are you talking about? Lily, are you carrying around physical evidence? The chain of custody—"

"Doesn't matter anymore. We can't take this case to court."

"I wish you'd tell me what was going on, in a way that makes *sense*."

"I will, Dan. I promise." I straightened up. "I have to go. I have to find Ariel."

"Ariel? What does he have to do with this? Is he in town? Lily—"

"I said I'll tell you later." Cutting off her protest, I ended the call before she could ask more questions, but I couldn't escape the ones racing through my own mind.

How had I neglected to tell Danny about Ariel's reappearance? I told her everything, but somehow that little fact had slipped between the cracks.

Where had Ariel gotten off to? And where had I been between Friday evening on the balcony of the Ritz, and Monday morning in Sebastian's light-drenched bedroom?

And finally, the question I wasn't sure I wanted to answer.

What had I done?

NOT A DIAMOND RING

I SLIPPED OUT OF SEBASTIAN'S BEDROOM DOOR TO THE LANDING AND LEANED over the polished wooden banister. Dressed in his robe with my hair still wrapped in a towel, surrounded by that big, fancy, echoing house, I felt like Eliza Doolittle in *My Fair Lady*. I could have danced all night on his kether, but ultimately, I didn't belong.

But then, I was no Audrey, and Sebastian, thank goodness, was no Rex Harrison.

I had worried earlier that he would stick around to eavesdrop on my call, but he'd made himself scarce. He hadn't gone far, though. His presence tingled in the periphery of my awareness.

From somewhere below, his voice floated up to me, his words indistinct but his warm tone unmistakable. A door shut, and then he came into view, crossing the hall to the foot of the stairs.

"There you are." He held a brown paper shopping bag in one hand, not the kind from the grocery store, but department-store style, with corded handles.

I eyed it, and him, with suspicion. "Was someone at the door?"

"Not to worry," he said. "Just a delivery. A trusted courier. No reporters."

"What's that?" I descended the stairs at a cautious pace, wary of the way his gaze followed me.

"Oh, this?" He glanced down at it as if he'd forgotten what he held, his expression sheepish. "It's for you. I took the liberty of sending out for some fresh things."

"You did *what*?"

He offered the bag to me, his face pinking up slightly with boyish pride at the cleverness of his gift and pleasure in his skill at anticipating my needs. "You said you didn't have anything to wear."

"I wasn't asking you to buy me clothes! Sebastian…"

"At least look at them first."

With unwilling hands, I took the bag from him. It contained several soft packages wrapped in neat white tissue. I set it on the stairs and lifted out the top package. His focus on me made my fingers clumsy as I tried to unwrap it without ripping the delicate tissue. Under it, I found a collared, button-down silk blouse in midnight blue. Simple, sleek, and yet obviously expensive.

"No," I said. "I can't accept this. It's too much."

"It's just a shirt," Sebastian said. "It's not a diamond ring, Lily."

I shook my head. Setting the shirt aside, I picked up the smallest package, then dropped it back into the bag with haste when a peek inside revealed demure blue lace and soft cotton. "And *underwear!*"

"You'd prefer to go without?"

My face heating, I avoided his eyes. The next package, bulkier this time, proved less embarrassing. Black jeans, almost certainly designer if their supple denim was any indication, although I didn't recognize the brand. "There are no tags."

"No, that would be tacky. You don't like the clothes?"

Face still averted, I folded the jeans back into the bag. "You can't just give me things. I can't—I don't—"

"Then don't," he said. "You can go home in your dirty clothes if you want. Or the robe. I really don't care. I just thought…" He trailed off, the pleased excitement in his desiderata curdling into hurt.

Well, crap. He really did care, a lot. "I'm sorry. That's not—I barely know you."

"You said that before, and I'm not sure it's true anymore."

"But—"

"There's no *quid pro quo* here. I have more money than I have ways of spending it, and I like solving problems with it when I can."

Had he solved problems like this for Nepenthe too? Bought her beautiful things? I made a wry face. "I guess I'm not used to gifts that don't come with strings attached. I don't know what to say."

"A simple thank you would suffice."

"Oh," I said in a small voice. "Um. Thank you, I'll try them on."

"Better, and you're very welcome." His return flash of a smile warmed me more than the words. I fled back upstairs, bag in hand, to change.

The buttery silk of the shirt slid over my skin like a caress, its mother of pearl buttons gleaming with subtle iridescence. The skinny jeans hugged my curves like a lover. Everything fit as if tailored for me, including the lingerie. Even alone, I couldn't stop blushing.

At the bottom of the bag, I found a shoe box with a pair of low-heeled black ankle boots with decorative buckles. I picked them up, fingering the velvety brushed suede. They were my size.

He didn't miss a single detail, did he? Each item was simple, even minimalist in its lines, but infused with an understated yet undeniable sensuality.

Too sensual. Too sexy. It was too much, as I'd told him, but somehow, also just right. Wearing them, I felt different. Not unlike myself, exactly, but I wouldn't have picked these items out on my own. He'd nailed what would have been my style if I gave this much of a damn. Myself, upgraded. Lily 2.0.

Deep in thought, I collected my purse from the bedroom and tucked my bundle of discarded clothes into the empty shopping bag. Then I went to rejoin Sebastian.

His eyes lit up when he saw me, and his desiderata sparkled like a Christmas tree. "So? What's the verdict?"

I smiled and ducked my head in a half-nod, suddenly shy. "You have good taste."

"I'll say." His appreciative look spoke volumes more. "Ready?"

I nodded again, not trusting myself to speak.

"Then your chariot awaits. This way to the garage."

He shepherded me down the hall and through the far door, where another set of stairs descended into a cavernous garage. I couldn't hold back a soft exclamation. No wonder he liked to drive. The glacier blue two-seater parked nearest to us looked like something from a James Bond movie.

"Not you today, I don't think," Sebastian said, catching me staring. He patted the roadster's hood in apology as he headed past it to the second vehicle. Equally shiny, but less attention-grabbing, the black BMW sedan had tinted windows, as promised. On the other side of it sat a black and chrome beast that might have been a Lamborghini.

Sebastian went around the BMW and opened the passenger door. I remembered myself belatedly, closed my mouth, and slipped past him to sink into the soft leather of the seat.

"Holy car fetish, Batman," I said as he folded his long legs into the driver's side. "Wait! *Are* you Batman? Because I feel like that would explain a lot."

"I was thinking of getting a license plate holder that said 'Bruce Wayne is my co-pilot,'" he said, straight-faced, and I laughed outright. "What? Too much?"

"You think?"

He grinned and shrugged, letting out the clutch. The garage spit us out onto a back street, with no news vans in sight. I relayed my address to the GPS at his prompting, and we sped precipitously down the hill toward Van Ness and my real life.

I rode in silence, thinking about what I needed to do next. I needed to get home, feed the cat, call my boss and eat crow, then find out how the hell Tobias had gotten a hold of those pictures. I also needed to search for an incubus who could be anywhere and a masked murderer whose identity I had no way of knowing.

I sighed. I'd lost the only clue I had when Ariel drained me.

"Are you okay, Lily?"

"Yeah." I mustered a smile for him. "It's just—this week has been a lot."

"I'd say that's an understatement." The muscle above his jaw twitched as a sleeper wave of grief surged up between us. Our flirtation had distracted him for a while, but that loss still ebbed and flowed beneath his surface like the dull roar of a distant ocean.

Damn it, I hadn't meant to bring it up again. "Nepenthe deserves justice," I said. "I just don't know how to get it for her. But I'll try."

"I know you will." But his expression remained bleak. The car turned and slowed, pulling up to the curb beside my shabby building. "Well, we're here," he said, unnecessarily.

Just as before, I found myself balking at leaving his car. I fumbled for the right words, finally settling on the viciously inadequate. "Thank you, Sebastian, for everything." For his kether, for his kindness, for keeping me safe and sane.

"Should I walk you up?"

I shook my head, opening the passenger door. I didn't trust myself and I'd taken enough from him already. "Better not. I'll be fine."

He frowned, but didn't argue. "Don't be a stranger, Lily Knight. You have my card."

I'd almost forgotten about that, but when I dug my hand into my jacket pocket, there it was, smooth as the silk of the shirt I now wore. I clutched it like a talisman. "I do."

The car sat idling by the curb as I went up the steps. When I looked over my shoulder, the opaque windows hid him from sight, but my skin still tingled with the acute awareness of his gaze on me.

TWO TO TANGO

SOMEONE HAD PROPPED THE STREET DOOR OPEN WITH A BRICK, AS THEY OFTEN did during daylight hours. Grateful that they had saved me the awkwardness of hunting in my messenger bag for my keys while Sebastian watched, I slipped inside.

I climbed the dark and dingy stairwell with reluctant steps. It seemed even darker and dingier after the high, airy ceilings and graceful winding stairs of Sebastian's house. When I finally reached my apartment door, I stood still for a moment, transfixed by a sense of *deja vu* before I shook it off and dug around in my bag for my keys.

I couldn't find them.

"Shit," I muttered, and checked all the pockets again. "Shit, shit, *shit*. You've got to be kidding me." Frantic now, I sank to my knees and upended the bag, shaking its contents onto the musty carpet of the hallway. Nothing. Well, a lot of receipts, pens, stray cough drops, and other detritus. But no keys.

The soft click of the lock pierced my haze of panic like a shot. My head jerked up as the door swung open, a shadow falling over me. Someone loomed above me, my lost set of keys jingling in his hand. I scrambled to my feet.

"Looking for these?" Ariel inquired.

I launched myself at him with an inarticulate cry of rage. I got one good punch in, connecting with his shapely jaw. But when I went for another, he captured my wrist in an inexorable grasp and spun me around, pinning my arms to my sides.

"You bastard!" I struggled against his grip in a fruitless effort to free myself. The heavy, sweet scent of frankincense clogged my nostrils and tickled the back of my throat. "How *could* you?"

"How could I what? I saved you, Lillian."

His breath blew hot on my neck, but I shivered. "You drained me! And left me in a stranger's bed!" My fists clenched, the pain of my nails digging hard into my palms a welcome distraction from the heavy allure of his Presence. I should never have trusted him, never given him the chance to beguile me in the first place. He'd delivered me to Sebastian's bed like a gift, like I was his to give. He may as well have placed a bow on me. What gave him the *right*?

"You would have rather the cops discovered us at an active crime scene? Your boss would not have been pleased. And I hardly think that your Sebastian qualifies as a stranger."

"He's not *my* Sebastian!"

"Isn't he?" Ariel sounded amused. "Your Claim is all over him. Signed, sealed, and delivered."

I stilled, frowning. "What are you talking about?"

"You work fast, my dear. I'm quite impressed."

"I didn't *do* anything." I renewed my struggles. His arm around my waist was like a band of steel. "I could have—he might have—anything could have happened!"

"Maybe." Ariel grunted as I managed to jab an elbow back into his ribs. "I doubt it. You don't seem all that worse for wear. Quite the opposite, in fact. You look stunning, Lily fair. His kether suits you." He renewed his hold, pressing himself hard against my back.

He's enjoying this. With that thought came clarity, and my self-defense training kicked in.

"Get off me, asshole." With a snarl of frustration, I ground the blocky heel of my boot into his instep, forcing him to shift his balance to the other leg. My next elbow jab slammed right into his sternum.

He cursed, the breath knocked out of him, and his hold loosened. I got enough distance to pivot toward him, aiming a snap kick at his crotch. But he'd recovered too quickly. He caught my knee and threw me to the ground in one powerful, fluid motion.

I landed hard on my back. He danced away, out of range of the sweeping kick meant to take his legs out from under him.

"My, my, you *are* feeling better," he purred. "Take more than the recommended daily allowance, did you? How is dear Sebastian this morning? Still standing, I hope."

"He's fine." I rolled up onto my feet, circling him. "No thanks to you."

He eyed my clenched fists, rubbing his jaw, but his eyes flamed bright. "Really? The way I see it, you owe me. I gave you both a gift by bringing you there. You should have seen how he looked at you, Lillian, while you lay there helpless. Demon-thrall is a beautiful thing, I always say—"

"Damn you!" I charged him, swinging wildly for his wide, mocking mouth, and he lunged at me.

His tackle took me back to the floor with him on top of me. Inexorably, he forced my arms up above my head, one hand pinning both my wrists, his weight heavy on my midsection. Try as I might to shift my hips up and dislodge him, I couldn't gain traction. He laughed, bending toward me.

"Careful," he said, lips inches from my own. "I could do it all over again if I wanted to. You tasted so good, my sweet. I'd forgotten how good you were."

I turned my head aside, a sick sense of helplessness slackening my limbs. He had me. His control far exceeded mine, and his touch exerted no real kether-draw. But it warned of a ready polarity, balanced in his favor. Should he open the channel, all my strength would flow to him.

No. I couldn't let his Presence sap the will from me. "Stop it."

The words came out in a breathy whisper despite my best efforts. We'd danced this tango too many times, him over me. I could play the role of his naïve mentee in my sleep, as my dreams attested. The choreography had etched itself into my bones, and I fell into step like it was second nature.

But the tune had sounded different then. His weight pressing down on me had lit a fire in my belly, not churned it with sick self-loathing like it did now.

"No," he said. "Not until you do. Stop fighting me, Lily fair. We're on the same side, you and I."

I bit the inside of my cheek, grounding myself with the tang of copper heavy on my tongue, and forced myself to step wrong. "I'm on my own side. Let me up!"

His smile faded, but he held me still for a long moment, his eyes burning into mine.

I set my jaw, pulse thundering in my ears, and stared him down. "I mean it, Ariel. Enough."

"Takes two. You're the one who picked this little spat, remember?" But he finally released me, rising to stand above me as I scrambled away from him.

I rubbed my wrists to bring the circulation back, not looking at him. First the manacles this morning, then his iron grip. If not for my cambion healing factor, I didn't doubt I would have bruises. "What are you doing in my house?"

"I thought I should feed your cat," he said.

"Delilah?" I glanced around. The little gray cat crouched on the top of my easy chair, watching us. Now that the conflict in the room seemed resolved, she blinked at me and relaxed into a Sphinx-like pose, laying her chin on her outstretched paws.

"I didn't know when you'd be done with Mr. Ritter, after all." Ariel smirked. "Seemed cruel to leave her here on her own. I've been keeping her company."

"So, you just made yourself at home?" Still wary, I put the kitchen bar between us. My hands shook, and I hid them behind my back.

"I knew you'd want to find me." He slid into a barstool, leaned his elbows on the bar. "You must have a lot of questions, so ask them already."

"Okay." I crossed my arms. The gentle whisper of the blue silk shirt across my skin comforted me like Sebastian's touch. "Where did you take me after the hotel balcony?"

He looked surprised. "Back here, of course. I put you to bed. I thought you'd recover more quickly, you see. When you didn't, I got worried."

"So you took me to Sebastian? Why him?"

"I found his card in your pocket," Ariel said. He added, sly, "And I tasted him in you. It was a good bet. No, not a bet at all, really. A well-informed choice, shall we say?"

Ugh. I shuddered. Of course Ariel could taste my most recent kether draw, but I didn't have to like it. "I could have really hurt him." *And he could have hurt me.*

"Ritter's smart and this wasn't his first rodeo. Remember, he knew Nepenthe. She claimed him first, before he was yours."

"I know that." I bridled at his pointed words. They hit home with an unexpectedly deep sting. Jealousy was an inopportune and unseemly emotion for a succubus, or even just a cambion. Especially jealousy of a dead woman.

"He interests me," Ariel said, his tone thoughtful. "Not many humans seek our kind out willfully and knowingly. Fewer still come back for a second round."

"You stay away from him," I spat.

He held his hands up in mock surrender. "Whoa there, mama bear! Have no fear. I couldn't sway him if I wanted to. I'm not his type. Even more relevant, he's not mine."

"And your type is what?" I had to challenge that. "Not willful and knowing?"

"That's low, Lily. No, I've always preferred women and they're always willing."

I raised an eyebrow. "Always?"

"I told you, I have a code now. Consenting partners only."

"Oh, now you have a code? Sure, okay." I rolled my eyes, but chose a different tack. I didn't need him to regale me with any tales of his latest conquests. "Ariel, I need to ask you something else. Something important."

"Hit me." He held up a hand. "*Not* literally."

"Ha, ha. Do you have the mask?"

"What mask?" Brow furrowed, he seemed nonplussed by my sudden change of topics.

"The devil mask. Remember? You found it on the balcony, right before…"

"Oh! Right. I'm afraid I left it where I found it. I had more pressing concerns in mind."

"Damn it." I paced the scarce three steps across my kitchen and back again. "Maybe the police…"

"Is it really so important to have the thing in hand?" Despite his languid tone, he tracked my restless movement closely. "Doesn't its very presence on that balcony tell us all we need to know? The man in the devil costume was there, at the scene. He must have done it. He killed her, Lillian."

"It's evidence, you jerk. There could be DNA on it, like hair fibers and fingerprints. Something I could bring to the lab." I glared at him, frustrated with his unconcerned attitude. "I need to know who the devil *is*. Don't you want to know? Then we can do something about it. Stop him from coming after anyone else."

"You mean kill him," Ariel said calmly.

"No! I mean arrest him. Put him away for good."

"That's not going to happen, and there won't be any charges. Your office won't prosecute. And if you're right—if he's a cambion..." He bowed his head, his expression sorrowful. "It's like I said that night. No humans involved."

"There has to be something. The feds..."

His eyes blazed, amber, fierce, inhuman. "You think that's a better justice for one of our own? No. I've been there. I've seen it. There are worse things than death at their hands, Lillian. Far worse things."

"What's your solution, then? Vigilante justice? Become a law unto ourselves?"

"I'd call it self-policing."

"No." Emphatic, I shook my head. "It's not right. Our kind are people, too, and people deserve due process and a fair trial. We can't just take the law into our own hands like that. We can't play God."

"And why not?" Ariel leaned forward, his voice low and urgent, angelic features dark with memories of horrors unimaginable. "They'll experiment on him if they don't shoot him outright. Silver bullet to the heart or a lifetime of scientific torture. Laid out on a table, cut open, still alive, in agony, screaming... They want specimens. They want to know what we are, how we tick, what we look like from the inside. How to hurt us better. How to destroy us once and for all." He heaved a shaking breath. "Don't you see? Tonepah wasn't enough for them. It will never be enough."

I recoiled from his visceral words, the terror and revulsion written plain on his face. Clearly, the unknown traumas of his past still haunted his present, reliving itself behind his burning amber eyes.

Unknown, but now I had some idea. Enough to guess, at least. And I didn't like my guesses much. "Okay." I sighed. "No feds."

"All right." He sounded somewhat mollified. Still on edge, though, like a cat with hackles raised.

"So how do we find him?"

Ariel's long, clever fingers traced patterns on the bar-top. "Are you sure you want to find him?"

"I'm sure. I'll figure out what to do with him afterward, if I can find him at all." I grimaced. "I have no earthly idea where to start. I never saw his face but he saw mine."

"I have an idea." Ariel grinned, sudden and sharp. "But you're not going to like it."

"No," I said. "Absolutely not, I won't do it!"

Ariel shrugged. "Fine. You don't have to do anything you don't want to do. I'm just saying, if you want to find your devil, you need to be willing to make sacrifices. That's how this kind of thing goes."

"And I'd be sacrificing what? My dignity? My privacy? My principles?"

"You're overreacting. Besides, there are worse things you could sacrifice."

"I've worked hard to pass as human, to stay invisible. You want me to throw that all away? It could end my fucking *career*, Ariel!"

"And maybe start your *fucking* career." He smirked, then leaped backwards as I rounded on him, teeth bared. "Whoa, Lillian. I'm just kidding. Lighten up, would you? I don't *want* you to do anything, least of all lose something so important to you. I'm just brainstorming here."

"Well, keep brainstorming because I am *not* going to make myself demon-hunter bait. Not like that."

"All right," he said, in a tone of eminent reason. "If you really feel that strongly about it, we'll just have to find another way to flush the killer out."

I started pacing again. "Yes. But how?"

"How indeed?" He laced his hands behind his head and stared up at the ceiling with the barstool tipped precariously back on two legs, apparently deep in thought. I could tell that he was mocking me.

"I hate you," I muttered.

He righted himself with a crash, transforming a flash of affronted pride into a brilliant grin. "Come on, you love me. Take it back."

"I will not." Hands on hips, unable to hold back my fury any longer, I let him have it. "I had a good life, Ariel. I was building something here. I was clean and sober—" He snorted at that and started to speak, but I steamrolled over him. "No, you listen to me. You know what? You weren't in that life and I liked it that way. I was better off without you. I was doing just fine."

"Lily fair—"

"Then here you come, feeding me stolen kether and stolen kisses and lines about black and white and gray and nature red in tooth in claw, and it's all bullshit. And I know it's bullshit but I eat it up anyway, because it's you and it's me. But Ariel, there is no you and me anymore."

"Lillian, we—"

"No! There is no 'we.' Maybe there was once. Maybe I loved you then, but I don't anymore, and if I could take back what happened on that balcony, I would take it back in one heartbeat, I swear to *God* I would." My voice broke on the last words and I turned away from him, blinking back traitorous tears.

"Lily, I'm sorry. I had no idea you felt that way. Your desiderata—"

"*Don't.* It's not the same thing, and you know it."

"I'm not sure I do." His soft step sounded behind me, and he laid a tentative hand on my shoulder.

I flinched away. "Don't touch me." Dashing the wetness from my face as I put my back against the counter, I faced him again, crossing my arms in front of me. "Leave me alone."

"I'm sorry," he said again. "I want to fix this. I care about you, Lily. Tell me how to fix it."

"I told you," I said stubbornly. "There is no 'this.' There's nothing to fix."

He bowed his head. "I'm sorry you feel that way. I never intended—"

"Oh, please," I said. "Spare me the dishonest self-flagellation and get the hell out of my house."

His head jerked up at that, his eyes wide with surprise and hurt. "What?"

"You heard me," I said. "I think you should leave. And give me my damn keys."

Still looking dumbfounded, he reached in his pocket and dropped the keys into my outstretched palm.

"As you wish, Lillian." He turned and strode out of the apartment without another word. I followed him and slammed the door behind him, locking it and throwing the deadbolt with vicious energy.

Only then did I let myself cry. I collapsed onto my old, shabby couch and buried my face in the pillows, sobbing. After a while, I felt Delilah's cold nose on my face and her rough tongue as she licked the salt away.

"Thanks, kitty." I sniffled, stroking her warm, silky fur. "Your person's a hot mess, isn't she?"

Delilah chirruped at me, purring, and I sighed. She didn't care whether I was a demon or a human. As long as I kept the premium wet food and the treats coming, I could be a Vulcan for all she cared.

I sniffed again and sat up. It was time to call my boss and figure out how much trouble I was in. And whether I could afford to keep Delilah in the lifestyle to which she was accustomed, or if I was about to be out of a job.

YOU WOULDN'T LIKE ME WHEN I'M HUNGRY

BASRA HADN'T SAID MUCH WHEN I GAVE HER MY EXCUSES AND APOLOGIES. IN her dispassionate voice, she'd told me to take the rest of the day off and meet with her first thing in the morning. She didn't mention the pictures or the Ritter case. It made me more nervous, not less. I hadn't slept a wink.

I thought I'd come in early, but when I walked into the DA's office at seven thirty on Tuesday morning, most of my cohorts had already arrived. They stood around in little knots, staring at me as if they thought I couldn't see them, whispering among themselves.

I pretended not to notice, but I gave the whisperers a wide berth as I charted my path to my office. I had to meet with Basra in less than an hour, and I did not anticipate pleasantries. Apparently, neither did the rest of the unit. How had they all gotten wind of it?

I almost made it to my door before one of the junior prosecutors detached from one of the huddles and fell in step with me. "Hey, Knight," he said in sympathetic tones. "How are you holding up?"

"Can it, Jimenez." I kept my gaze fixed ahead of me.

"For what it's worth, I don't believe you leaked those pictures. Or the other stuff they're saying." He hesitated. "You didn't, did you?"

"Of course not," I snapped. "What do you mean, other stuff?"

He looked uncomfortable. "It's nothing, just stupid rumors. Don't listen to them."

I turned to glare at him. "If you aren't going to tell me…"

"All right, in here." He ducked into my office ahead of me, shutting the door behind us.

Of course everyone else had turned to look. I closed the blinds with an overenthusiastic crack. "Okay, spill it. What are they saying about me?"

"They say you're one of *them*," he said on an undertone. "Like her. A— you know."

My knees had gone to water. I sat down firmly in my chair before I fell down. "A hooker?" My tone dripped with acid.

"No," Jimenez said, still not looking at me. "Not a hooker. One of those…things. You're not, are you? I feel like I'd know if you were."

"You wouldn't," I said coldly. "But no, I'm not a *thing*. I'm a person."

"I knew it." His desiderata flashed with genuine relief. "Thank God for that, anyway."

"Penelope Jones was a person, too," I said.

The relief vanished with a nearly-audible pop. "But she—but you— what are you saying?"

I leaned back in my chair, suddenly weary to my bones. "I'm saying you should get out of my office before you get a reputation for hanging out with *things*. And before I get hungry. You wouldn't like me when I'm hungry."

He flinched back from my toothy, mirthless smile as if he really thought I might eat him for breakfast, and fled without another word.

I groaned and sunk my face in my hands. *Great going, Knight.* I'd just intimidated my coworker, all but confirmed the worst rumors about my identity, and was probably about to get fired. And it wasn't even 8 AM.

A knock on my half-open door startled me. I raised my head to find Julie, the office manager, peeking around the door-frame.

"Sorry to disturb you, Lily, but there's someone downstairs to see you."

I mustered my composure with an effort. "To see me? I don't have any appointments." An alarming thought occurred to me. "It's not Tobias Kaine again, is it?"

She shook her head. "It's a woman. She says she needs to speak with you immediately about a case. She won't talk to anyone else."

"Fantastic." The woman downstairs was probably a habitual tipster who had somehow fixated on me from all the television coverage. We got a lot of those. Just what I needed on this morning in particular. "I'm supposed to have a meeting with Basra in twenty minutes. I don't have time for this. Can you take a message? Tell her to come back later?"

"I can try." She glanced over her shoulder, eyes widening. "Um, never mind. She's here. She just came up the elevator."

"Are you kidding me?" Annoyed, I rose, rounding the desk to peer over Julie's shoulder. "Not again. This office has the worst security." Then, catching my first glimpse of my visitor, I fell silent.

She stood by the elevators, her posture irresolute, her darting sideways glances betraying a furtive anxiety. She wore a vintage-style emerald dress, with masses of shining strawberry-blond hair tumbling in artful waves past her shoulders. Tall, statuesque, she drew every eye in the office with her presence.

No. With her Presence. The charismatic aura rolling off her invited deference and even worship with a force of superhuman magnetism. I doubted that anyone else had noticed the nervous tics behind that regal cloak of power.

The woman who had come to see me was almost certainly another succubus. And beneath her glamor and daunting Presence, this succubus was afraid.

"Stay here." Leaving the office manager staring from the door of my office, I strode toward my visitor.

She noted my approach, gathering herself up with a quick inhalation. "Hello. I am looking for—"

"Assistant D.A. Lillian Knight." On an undertone, I added, "You shouldn't be here. Come with me."

Aware of the curious gazes on us, I ushered her into an empty conference room and shut the door. She didn't sit. Instead, she came toward me, reaching out her hands. Her voice carried a slight accent, perhaps Eastern European. "Ms. Knight, thank you for seeing me."

"You didn't give me much choice." I stepped back to put space between us.

She moved too quickly for my eye to follow, and before I could hide my hands behind my back, she had caught hold of them. Her skin hummed with power, testing and tugging at my energetic boundaries. I snatched my hands away.

"So it is true." She inclined her head, lips a little parted, as if tasting my scent on the air. "You are half the race of Lilith. A hybrid. Interesting. You keep this secret?"

The small hairs on my neck stood on end, and I moved to put the table between us. "Not anymore, it seems. What is this about?"

"My name is Theodora." The succubus's eyes flashed, the same vibrant green as her dress. "Penelope Jones was my sister. And I think I know why she was murdered."

"You're Nepenthe's sister?" I considered the woman standing before me in a new light. To me, she looked nothing like the succubus I'd met in the Black Cat Club, other than her powerfully sensual Presence. But perhaps biology didn't enter into it. Perhaps sisterhood meant something different among my father's kind.

Theodora looked surprised. "You knew her name. You knew her?"

"We weren't friends," I said. "I mean, we'd met, that's all. I'm very sorry for your loss, Ms. Jones."

"That's not my name," Theodora said. She pulled out a chair from the conference table and sat, her movements deliberate.

"Sorry. Of course, it wouldn't be."

"It's all right." Theodora sighed, looking down at her hands folded tightly in her lap. "My sister and I weren't close," she said in a soft voice. "Not at the end. We'd had a disagreement, you see."

I followed her lead and took a seat, mirroring her posture, legs crossed, body inclined forward. An old prosecutor's trick, mirroring. Gain the witness's trust, and they'd tell you almost anything you wanted to know. "What did you disagree about?"

"Nepenthe had a different way of doing things." Theodora seemed to choose her words with care. "She believed that the old ways of the Hunt and the Exchange were wrong. I thought her ideas were dangerous."

"How so?"

"She thought we should be honest with our human...partners." It sounded like she had almost said *prey*. "She said that the Exchange became even more powerful if we did not resort to deceit or coercion. That it wasn't right unless the mortal knew and understood all that our Claim entails."

"And what does it entail?"

She shot me a glance, startled and a bit disdainful. "You do not know?"

"I'm just a half-breed," I said, heavily sardonic. "As it turns out, I don't know much."

"I did not mean to offend." A little frown creased her otherwise perfect, unlined forehead.

"Don't worry about me. I'm fine. Tell me about the Claim. What does it mean?"

"Why, their souls, of course."

"*What?*" She'd said it in such a matter-of-fact tone, I thought I'd heard her wrong. I hoped I'd heard her wrong. "Did you say *souls*?"

"Yes, souls. This is foundational," she said, impatient now. "You should have been taught—no matter. When we stake a Claim, we bind their mortal essence to us. Their kether is the bond. Their souls become our own, at least in part. And every time we taste them, the Claim strengthens. It is no small thing."

"I'll say." Ariel had never said anything about souls. I didn't think Ariel even believed in souls. I wasn't sure I believed in souls, either, but then, I was no expert. "That's fucked up."

"Some of us feel the same, but perhaps not for the same reasons. A strong Exchange goes both ways. Many cubines choose to take a little from many, so they are not bound too closely to any one soul. But Nepenthe—she believed otherwise."

"She believed in what? Soul-monogamy?"

"She thought that we should choose to partake deeply, and take more care in whom we chose, whose energy we took into ourselves. And she said that deception and beguilement tainted the Exchange, that we must obtain what she called informed consent."

"Very progressive of her." I was still processing the revelation that we essentially fed on human souls. Tobias Kaine would have a field day with this if he ever found out. "But you disagreed?"

"I thought it would get her killed," Theodora said simply. "And I was right."

"You think she died because she told the truth."

"Yes. For our kind, to be known is death. We learned that lesson in Tonepah Valley." Theodora shook her head, a familiar pain shadowing her beautiful face. "But Nepenthe was an idealist. She found it easy to think the best of humans, and forget the worst."

Nepenthe, the drug of forgetting. And Tonepah again. Always Tonepah, the valley of the shadow of death. "So, who hated her idealism enough to kill her?" I said softly.

"I think it was a man," Theodora said. "I think she loved a human, and he killed her for it."

"You mean Sebastian Ritter?"

She waved a hand. "Whomever. I think he killed her to get his soul back."

"To get his soul...back?" I frowned, confused.

"This is how it works," she said, as if speaking to a child. "Don't you understand? Their kether is our lifeblood. If we die, the kether becomes unbound, and their souls are released. The Claim is broken. They are freed."

"That's *really* fucked up."

"It is what it is," Theodora said. "Most of our Claims belong to us until they die. What they gave of their souls goes on with us."

"So you think he killed her to free himself." And what of the others? Astarte and Salome? "You're Lais, aren't you," I said, and she inclined her head in assent. "She thought you'd disappeared, too. Like the others."

"I saw it coming," she said. "I tried to warn them but they didn't listen to me. They followed her to their doom. I had no choice but to cut off all contact. I had to save myself."

"Wait. You think Seb—I mean, Ritter killed all of them? Why would he do that?"

She shrugged. "How should I know? Maybe they shared his Claim among themselves. Maybe he was a demon-chaser, a fetishist. Maybe he changed his mind after Nepenthe told him the truth about the Exchange."

Her theory of the case tracked my own close enough to give me pause. I knew Sebastian hadn't done it. But maybe Nepenthe had leveled with someone else about her identity, someone with a connection to all three victims. "The Claim," I said. "You said it goes both ways but that's not entirely true. The stronger the Claim on the mortal, the less power other cubines can exert over him, right? But it doesn't work both ways. You...*we* can Claim as many as we wish, for as long as we wish."

"Of course. We are not bound to one source of kether. We can take as much as we can hold, as much as we can use."

"Peachy," I muttered. "A supernatural double standard. Liking us less and less all the time."

"What?"

"Nothing. What about giving? How does that work?"

Theodora looked taken aback. "You mean a kether push? Yes, but it is rare. Not wise to give away one's power. What if they used it against you?"

"What if you could use it to save someone? A person you cared about?"

"You are foolish." Her tone held scorn, but the corners of her green eyes crinkled with wistful sadness. "You are like her, idealistic and romantic. You believe in the power of love."

I had to laugh at that. "I don't think I've ever been accused of being overly romantic before."

"Pfft. It is bullshit, you know. Love is a mortal emotion, a mortal weakness."

"But you said you thought Nepenthe loved Sebastian Ritter?"

Theodora turned away, her mouth twisting in a bitter smile. "I said Nepenthe was weak." She got to her feet, her purse in hand. "I have told you what I know. I've done my part for her. Now I must go."

"Wait," I said. "I'd like to talk again. Learn more about Nepenthe. How can I contact you?"

"I will find you if I want to talk," Theodora said. "But here." She dug in her bag and handed me a scrap of paper with a few words scribbled on it. "If you want to know more about Nepenthe, here is an address."

"Address?" I squinted at it, trying to remember what the file said. "What address?"

"Nepenthe's address," Theodora said. "Nepenthe's home. You go there, you find out more. You don't need me for that."

She swept out, leaving only the scent of jasmine and sandalwood behind her, along with one very confused and troubled cambion.

I looked up at the clock, and swore. Make that one confused and troubled cambion who was also running very late for her own personal firing squad. It was 8:20 am, and far past time for me to face the music.

I turned, steeling myself to perform my walk of shame into Basra's office, and found to my dismay that I didn't have to. The firing squad had saved me the trouble by coming to me. DA Basra stood on the other side of the glass, arms folded, scowling. Even more alarming, she wasn't alone. Behind her stood Detective Huang and Tobias Kaine with a tall, well-dressed, white-haired man. He looked familiar, but I couldn't place him. None of them looked pleased, with the possible exception of Tobias. He had to be positively bursting with glee, though he put on a good disapproving face.

I opened the conference room door and let them in.

21

THE FIRING SQUAD

"I'M GLAD YOU COULD MAKE TIME FOR US TODAY, MS. KNIGHT." BASRA DIDN'T look at me over her glasses as she strode past me, slapping a file down on the table. She didn't look at me at all. "This is Senator James Ritter. He'll be sitting in on our meeting today."

The white-haired man nodded sharply to me. His desiderata crackled like a thunderstorm, and he looked well and truly pissed.

I fell back a step. So that's why he looked familiar. He was Sebastian's father. This day just got better and better.

"Senator Ritter." My voice sounded high and reedy in my ears. I cleared my throat. "Uh, nice to meet you."

"Have a seat, please," Basra said.

I did, but I glared at Tobias as he trailed in behind Sebastian's father. "What is *he* doing here?" I demanded.

"Mr. Kaine is here as an outside consultant. An expert on the paranormal." Basra radiated distaste, though whether for me, Tobias, or the entire situation, I couldn't tell. "At Senator Ritter's insistence."

"And with all due respect, Ma'am, what is the senator doing here? What is this, anyway?" I stared around at their hostile faces. "Are you firing me? You didn't need to convene a quorum for that, you know."

This time Basra did fix me with a brief, dispassionate gaze. "Not at this time. This is a formal disciplinary inquiry. The senator asked to be present because he has a personal stake in the matter."

"I see." I frowned. She had to owe him a major favor to allow him in on a disciplinary meeting.

"We have some questions for you." Huang slid a folder across the table to me. "Are you familiar with these photographs, Ms. Knight?"

I knew what it would contain before I opened it to meet Nepenthe's dead gaze. "Sure," I said. "These are the pictures that your friend Mr. Kaine posted on the internet this weekend. Shouldn't you be asking him about them?"

Huang and Basra exchanged a glance.

"We did ask him," Basra said. "He told us he got them from you."

Of course he did. "But—"

The senator spoke for the first time. "You may have dropped the ridiculous charges against my son, but his good name is still being dragged through the mud because of these pictures. He doesn't deserve to have his reputation sullied in the news media. Did you stop to think about of that, Ms. Knight?"

"I—"

Huang leaned toward me across the table. "The thing I want to know is where you got them from. Those pictures were never in our file. We didn't even know about them."

"Hang on," I said. "I didn't send those pictures to Tobias."

In answer, Huang flipped the folder in front of me open again. Pushing aside the images of Nepenthe's demon face, he held up the single sheet of paper I'd missed underneath them. It was a printed copy of an email addressed to Tobias Kaine. No text, no subject, just two attached images.

The sender's address was my own name.

I stared at it in blank horror. "What is this?"

"Do you deny sending this email, Ms. Knight?" Huang said, relentless.

What could I say? I was half-dead at the time. *My incubus ex-whatever ate my soul. I completely blacked out and I can't remember a thing.* "I don't recall sending anything like that. Not to him and not to anyone."

Huang frowned. "This was only a few days ago. Seems like the kind of thing you'd remember."

"Must have been a hell of a weekend." Tobias smirked like he'd said something clever.

I rallied, stung by his uncanny accuracy and the indecent triumph oozing through his desiderata. "Look, I can't deny that's my email address but I don't know how that email got sent. I would never share confidential information with the media. And I certainly wouldn't share it with someone like him."

"So what are you saying?" Basra raised an eyebrow. "You were hacked?"

"I don't know what happened." I glared daggers at Tobias. "I'm saying that if I wanted to leak crime scene photos, which I did *not*, why on earth would I give them to a slimy conspiracy theorist with no regard for the truth?"

"That's what we're trying to find out," Huang said, without a trace of irony.

"I'll tell you why," Tobias said, his triumph audible now.

They all turned to look at him, and my heart plummeted. "This guy's a liar," I said. "His whole business is telling lies. He shouldn't even be here. Why are you listening to him?"

"We'll be the judge of that," Huang said. "Go on, Mr. Kaine."

Tobias folded his hands in front of him, putting on a solemn face. "The truth is, Ms. Knight sent me those pictures as a payoff. It was *quid pro quo*."

"What?" Basra glanced from him to me, incredulous. "That's quite an accusation. A payoff for what?"

"She wanted me to kill a different story," Tobias said. "A story about her."

"No," I said. "That's not true. He's lying!"

"I'm not lying!" Leaping up from his chair, Tobias pointed at me with a shaking finger. "She's the one who's lying! I know what you are. You're one of *them*." His voice rose, shrill with denunciation. "She's a demon, too. Can't you see it? Are you all blind? Why can't you *see* it?"

A heavy, uncomfortable silence fell. Tobias looked around the table, wild-eyed.

"Wow." I layered a Presence of shocked innocence and disbelief into the word. If there was ever a time to take refuge in my demon powers, this was definitely it. "This is unbelievable. And you thought this guy was a reliable expert? You must not have looked at his website. He's a total crank."

In the ensuing pause, I held my breath. The other three shifted in their chairs, avoiding looking at either of us or each other. Even Basra radiated embarrassment.

"I think we should move on," Huang said, shuffling his papers.

The senator harrumphed. "We don't want to make any baseless accusations here."

Basra pushed her glasses up her nose and finally looked me in the eyes. "Lily, would you like to respond?"

"Thank you, ma'am. I would." I stood, facing Tobias across the table. "The truth is, Tobias *was* planning to write a story about me. He came to me and tried to blackmail me with it on Friday morning. He wanted a scoop to raise his media profile."

"Lies!" Tobias shouted, purple with fury.

I ignored him, working my Presence as hard as I could. It helped that I didn't have to lie. Much. "Like the senator said, the story is baseless, so I refused to give him the information he wanted. I didn't think that he had the smarts for hacking, but—" I shrugged. "Just goes to show, you can't judge a book by its cover."

"Seriously?" Tobias sounded nearly apoplectic. "You believe this bullshit? Come on! Occam's Razor, anyone? Isn't the simpler answer that she sent me the pictures herself?"

Huang eyed him. "I think her claims warrant further investigation."

"Extorting an officer of the court is a crime we would take extremely seriously," Basra said.

The senator rose, tight-lipped. "I'm sorry I wasted your time," he said to Basra. "I'm sure your office can sort this thing out."

She gave him a curt nod and he stalked out. Basra cleared her throat. "There's still the question of the other photographs. I don't understand why you didn't disclose that you had met with both the suspect and the deceased. Or why you requested to work the case when you were a material witness. Care to explain?"

I shook my head. "I'll cooperate with the inquiry. But I'm not answering any more questions in front of Mr. Kaine."

Basra shot a pointed look at Huang. "Get him out of here. Now."

Huang ushered Tobias outside, and Basra turned back to me. "I mean it, Lily. I'm disappointed in you. Between this leak and the other pictures that Tobias published, you showed a serious lapse in judgment, and your actions reflect poorly on you and on this office."

"I'm sorry, ma'am."

"Not to mention the implications for the investigation. They'll have to clear you now."

"Yes, ma'am."

Basra sighed. "Why did you do it? Why didn't you tell me you knew the victim?"

"I wanted to help." I bowed my head. "I didn't know Penelope that well, but she asked me to get involved. I let myself get too close."

"I understand the instinct," she said. "But the end result is the opposite. It damages our credibility."

"What's going to happen to me?"

Her lips twisted, her desiderata murky. "You'll be suspended, of course, pending inquiry. Six weeks paid leave to start. We'll need access to your desktop, laptop, and phone for forensics purposes." She held out her hand. "I'll take your phone now, if you don't mind."

Shit. My phone held more than enough incriminating evidence even without the email they'd shown me—texts with Danny, the crime scene photos she'd texted me outside of standard procedure, and maybe more than that. Sebastian's warning about cyber hygiene echoed in my mind. Could they track my past location with my phone and confirm my ill-considered, unsanctioned visit to the crime scene Friday night?

"Of course," I said, forcing myself to remain calm. "I just need to make a call first."

"Go ahead."

I slipped out the conference room door, my hand deep in my pocket, clutching my phone with sweaty fingers. Guilt gnawed at me for the trust she'd just shown me. Trust I was about to betray.

Once out of sight of the conference room, I ducked into an alcove and glanced from side to side down the hallway. Then I darted for the back stairwell to the street, taking the steps at a precipitous clip.

When I burst out into the cold, gray light of morning, I couldn't quite breathe. A bustling crowd of commuters flowed and eddied down Bryant

Street, so I bowed my head, hurrying along with them. My mind raced, thoughts tumbling over one another in their haste to escape their own conclusions.

I shouldn't have run. I couldn't have stayed. I didn't know what the hell to do next. I had to clear my name and prove I hadn't sent the photos.

I wanted to call Danny, but I'd already mixed her up in this far more than I should have. Would the hammer fall on her next? Would she lose her position at the medical examiner's office? She shouldn't have given me those pictures outside of official channels. I shouldn't have asked for them. I shouldn't have taken the case, shouldn't have gotten involved. Nepenthe was dead, and no number of ethical failures on my part could change that.

In my pocket, beside my phone, my nervous fingers found something else. A card, smooth as silk with embossed letters, a temptation, a talisman. A lifeline.

For this problem, I needed an expert. I needed a man who knew his technology. I pulled out the card and called the number on it.

"Sebastian Ritter speaking." He sounded different on the phone than he had in person, his smooth baritone crisp and impersonal. "Who's this?"

"Sebastian," I said. And then, to my horror, in the middle of the crowded San Francisco sidewalk, I started to cry.

"Lily, is that you?" Sebastian's voice warmed on my name, the note of concern for me only making it harder to keep it together.

"It's me." I tilted my head back and blinked furiously, but the tears kept coming. "I'm in trouble. I screwed up, Sebastian. I can't seem to stop screwing up." Another sob rose in my throat, and I choked it down. "I'm sorry. I shouldn't have called. It's weird and you're probably busy. I should go—"

"I'm glad you called," he said. "And for you, I'm not busy. Where are you?"

"I don't know." I gazed around me in a vague, bewildered hunt for a street sign. "I just left work. They suspended me."

"Why? Because of the pictures?"

"Among other things." A hysterical giggle bubbled up in the wake of my suppressed sobs. "Oh, by the way, I met your dad. He seems nice."

His voice sharpened. "My father was there?"

"He was. Did you know that he knows Tobias Kaine? And my boss, he knows her, too."

"He knows a lot of people," Sebastian said, brusque and remote again. "Is that the reason you called?"

"No." My steps slowed, and a few passersby gave me sidelong, wary looks. I hunched my shoulders and walked on. "They want my phone. They're looking for evidence that I sent those pictures. I don't know what to do. I...Sebastian, I need your help."

"I'll be right there," he said.

The line went dead and I was left alone on the busy downtown street. With a quick glance behind me, I gathered my Presence, a camouflage and a comfort, and let myself blend into the human tide.

22

I PUT A SPELL ON YOU

SEBASTIAN HAD MEANT IT LITERALLY WHEN HE SAID HE'D BE RIGHT THERE. I'D barely made it another two blocks when the rumble of superfluous horsepower overtook me. Belatedly, I released my don't-notice-me Presence. The black Lamborghini roared past, stopped short, reversed without regard for the angry honking of the drivers behind it, and pulled neatly up to the curb in a red zone. Sebastian reached across and opened the door for me. "I didn't see you there at first."

"Hi." I slid into the passenger side, managing a shaky laugh. "You brought the Batmobile."

"I had to. You sent up the bat signal." He navigated us back into traffic with an expert hand and glanced at me, his brow knit with concern. "Are you okay?" Tucked into belted dark jeans, his collared shirt was robin's-egg blue, a few shades lighter than his eyes. He wore no tie, and he had his sleeves half-rolled again. My fingers itched to trace the taut-muscled lines of his forearms.

I shook my head. "I think I'm going to lose my job."

"I'm sure it's not as bad as all that."

"No, it definitely is." The more I thought about it, the worse it got. "They have an email from me to Tobias with those crime scene photos. An email I don't remember sending."

"Oh."

"Oh, yes." I slumped in my seat. "And Tobias tried to tell them…what I am. They didn't believe him, but that could change. Especially if they start digging through my private life."

"They'd fire you for being half-demon?" His desiderata rippled outward like I'd thrown a stone into still water.

I shot him an incredulous look. "If it got out? Of course they would. You can't have a demon prosecuting humans. People would riot."

"But you're half-human. Doesn't that count for anything?"

"Just one drop of poison in a cup of wine makes it a poisoned cup."

He drove in silence for a minute or so before looking back over at me. "You're not poison, Lily."

"Yeah, well," I said. "Tell that to your dad. He'd probably be thrilled to know I'm driving around with you while he's working overtime to preserve your reputation."

"Oh, Lord," Sebastian said. "To preserve his reelection chances is more like it."

"You don't get along with your dad, do you?"

"We've never been that close." Sebastian pressed his lips together, his energy defensive and shut down. "What's this about an email?"

"I don't understand it. Tobias gave them a printed copy. It was sent while I was…" *What? Unconscious? Rabid?* The lost time loomed in my mind. I didn't know if I wanted the answers, but I needed them.

"And you're wondering if maybe you sent it after all?"

"I'm wondering if you can help me find out."

"Easy enough," he said. "Your phone is basically a tracking device that you willingly carry around."

"That's not a comforting thought."

"It shouldn't be." We had reached the heart of the downtown SoMa district, where the Lamborghini growled to a stop at the entrance to a gated garage. Above us, a glittering tower of dark glass and steel soared into the overcast sky. I craned my neck to catch a glimpse of the logo adorning the corner.

"Um," I said. "Your name is on this building."

His mouth twitched upward. "I'm aware."

A uniformed attendant nodded to Sebastian and the gate rose, admitting us to the tower's inner sanctum. We ascended in a series of tight-cornered right turns and pulled up into a reserved space on the top level. Sebastian opened the door for me and guided me to the elevator, where he pressed his finger onto the biometric scanner. The elevator invited him in by name in a sweet-toned, automated feminine voice.

I eyed him as the glass-walled elevator rose floor after floor in swift succession. "You're showing off."

"Maybe a little."

"Are you sure this is a good idea? Should I really be seen with you?"

"Relax," he said. "Enjoy the view."

At his words, filtered daylight washed over us. I turned. The city fell away beneath us, two layers of glass separating us from a vertiginous urban canyon. To the east, the fog had begun to break up into cottony shreds, beams of mid-morning sun glittering on the smooth surface of the Bay.

The speed with which we rose made my stomach flip, and Sebastian's proximity didn't help. I groped for a topic of conversation. "You do enjoy living above it all, don't you?"

"I love this city," he said. "It's at the leading edge of everything. I like to see the boundaries of it. The sea, the shore, the bridges, and the sky."

Danny would say that his industry and his high-rise tower had ruined the skyline, gentrified the streets, and priced out the city's counterculture. "You didn't have to come rescue me," I said to change the subject. "But thank you."

"You're welcome, but you didn't need rescuing." His light gaze caught and held mine. "You needed someone in your corner. You called me, and I'd be a fool not to take you up on it."

I wanted more than someone in my corner. I took a breath to say so. The way his gaze fixed on my parted lips stopped me. He stepped toward me, leaning in. His closeness rang through me like a clarion call, his desiderata pouring over me with the sudden warmth of a summer storm. My eyes fluttered half-closed. He was going to kiss me. He was...

"Stop." Breathless, I turned my head away, gripping his upper arms where his shirt shielded his skin to hold him back. To hold myself back. "What are you doing? What are *we* doing?"

He shook himself as if pulling himself out of a dream. His biceps twitched under my hands, but he didn't push back or fight me, just stilled himself with a visible effort. "I don't know," he said, his voice rough around the edges of the words. "It's like I can't think straight when I'm around you. I can't help myself. I want you, Lily. What are you doing to me?"

"I'm not—" I started. And then fell silent.

The Claim. Ariel had mentioned it again yesterday. What had he said? *Your Claim is all over him. Signed, sealed, and delivered.*

You work fast. I'm impressed.

Demon-thrall is a beautiful thing...

"What is it?"

"Oh, God." I whispered. "I didn't mean to. I didn't think...I'm so sorry."

"Sorry for what?"

"I worked a glamour on you. I put you in my thrall." I stared at him in horror. "Sebastian, I *made* you want me."

His eyes widened, dilated with desire and alarm. He frowned and half-shook his head. "No. That's not possible."

"It is," I said, miserable. "That's how it works. It's what we do. It's what I am." *The better to eat your soul, my dear.*

His throat worked, swallowing, but he bent toward me again.

"Don't," I said. "It's not safe."

"Lily, I—"

The elevator hummed to a stop. The doors whispered open on a gigantic executive office drenched with natural light from floor-to-wall windows. We almost jumped apart. I dropped my hands and Sebastian faced forward, squaring his shoulders.

In front of the windows stood a familiar tall, white-haired man in an impeccable suit. "Seb," he said, and then he recognized me. "What is she doing here?"

"Hi, Dad." Sebastian stepped out of the elevator and turned to face me. His father came to stand beside him. With them next to each other, I could see the resemblance between the older and younger Ritter. They had the same build, the same cheekbones, the same frown. The same easy sense of privilege, as if they owned any room they entered.

I backed away. "Oh, hell no."

"Lily—"

I slammed the heel of my hand onto the button to shut the door. "I thought you said you were on my side."

"Wait," he said. "I didn't—Lily, I can explain!"

I just shook my head. The doors slid closed, hiding his pleading face from view.

Sebastian had said I needed a friend. But how could I trust his offer of friendship, his desire, his kindness? It wasn't real. It couldn't be. It was only my own wanting that had beguiled it out of him. And who knew how long it would stick once I left the room and my pheromones or whatever they were stopped working on him? Who knew where his loyalty would fall then?

No, Sebastian couldn't help me. I had to do this on my own.

I leaned against the rail, shut my eyes, and let the elevator carry me back down to earth.

SEVERAL HOURS LATER, I stood on a grimy sidewalk in the heart of San Francisco's Tenderloin district, staring up at a shabby tenement building wedged between two single room occupancy hotels. Its droopy crown molding and half-hearted Victorian facade haunted it with a ghost of its former grandeur. The peeling paint, barred windows, and sleeping homeless bodies lined up in sad heaps along the foundation told a different story.

No wonder Nepenthe had preferred to meet Sebastian on the top floor of the Ritz.

The October twilight descended early. I glanced over my shoulder. Restless shadows shifted in the corners of my vision, furtive clusters of desperate humanity gathering in stinking doorways and dark corners.

The Tenderloin had a notorious reputation for crime and seediness at any time of day, but particularly after nightfall. San Francisco's least fortunate population of the dispossessed, destitute, and drug addicted tended to concentrate themselves into the narrow rectangle around O'Farrell, Turk, and Polk Streets. The gentrification that had slowly drained the soul from much of the rest of the city hadn't touched this place.

But a different kind of rot had set in here, in this realm of the lost and forgotten, the devalued and unloved. The contrast between it and the rich loneliness of Sebastian's glass tower and light-filled mansion burned sour in the back of my throat.

I tried the building's front door. The iron grating rattled but did not yield—locked. If only Theo had handed me a key along with the scrap of paper that bore the address.

Stepping back, I tilted my head up to assess the fire escape. Could I jump high enough to swing myself up? The ghost of Sebastian's kether, lingering from our contact the previous day, whispered through my veins that I might, if I'd only had the guts to taste him today.

I dug my nails into my palm to ward off the whisper of temptation and pressed the buzzer beside the door. As I did, the inner door swung open, and I flinched as a hunched figure loomed out of the darkness on the other side of the wrought iron grate.

"What do you want, girl?"

"I'm looking for someone." I peered through the grate of the door, trying to see the person's face.

Their energy eddied around me, jagged and wary. Sharp eyes glinted, narrowing. "You a cop? No offense, but you don't look like you live here."

"I'm not a cop," I said. "I'm a friend of Penelope's. Do you know her?"

"Penny?" The person on the other side of the door turned, spat. "Oh honey, you won't find her here. Ain't you heard? She dead."

"I know," I said. "Her sister sent me to see to the place." I took solace in the half-truth.

"Didn't know she had a sister." The gatekeeper glanced down the street to either side before unlatching the barred door from inside. "Come on in real quick and don't loiter. You stick out like a sore thumb."

"Thanks." I stepped into the dingy corridor, shutting the street door behind me with care until I heard the lock click home.

A guttering sodium light at the top of a narrow stairwell revealed my benefactor as a bent old woman with a flinty, wrinkled face. She waved me past her up the stairs. "Her apartments up there. Third floor, second to the left. Have a care, the steps ain't what they were."

"Thank you," I said again, and ascended, testing each step before I put my weight on it.

On the third floor, second to the left, the number 3B hung crookedly from a single nail on Penelope's locked door. My quick search for a key under the mat came up empty. Well, damn. I didn't know why I expected this to be easy. From somewhere down the hall, a deep bass line thumped away over arguing voices. I rattled the door handle a second time. Then I set my shoulder against the old splintery wood and pushed. It creaked but didn't yield.

If I wanted in, I'd have to break in. Inhaling, I took a step back, planted my left foot, and drove my other foot into the door just below the lock with focused force.

The kether-strength roared to life in my veins, like it had lain dormant waiting for a needful moment. The lock splintered away, the door frame cracked like plywood, and the door swung inward with a crash as momentum propelled me over the dark threshold.

"Holy hell," I muttered, my nostrils clogged with the scents of sawdust and sandalwood. If nothing else, the thick, sweet aroma told me that until very recently, a succubus had lived here. I fumbled around for a switch, which lit up the area to my right with a flickering fluorescent ceiling light.

The tiny studio apartment had old, shabby fixtures and overflowed with boxes, racks of clothing, and shelves of odds and ends. An old-fashioned four-poster bed took up most of one side of the room, while the fluorescent lighting illuminated the stained tile floor of a bare-bones kitchen made up of a sink, a few cupboards, and a small refrigerator.

In contrast to the barren kitchen, the rest of the apartment revealed that Nepenthe had been something of a hoarder. Or maybe just sentimental. I picked my way into the living space, brushing my fingers along the rich fabrics crowding the rack. An assortment of photographs pinned to the wall above the bed caught my eye.

Some were recent. One showed her and her "sisters," cheek to cheek in a crowded dressing room in sequined burlesque costumes with a pink boa draped around all their shoulders. But some were much older. Yellowed Polaroids from the Eighties gave way to clippings from a Sixties-style fashion spread and something that looked very much like an ancient black-and-white daguerreotype.

The daguerreotype showed a woman reclining on a couch, dressed as an Egyptian queen, fan and scepter in hand. Well, half-dressed. Bare-breasted and cat-eyed, Nepenthe stared out of the photograph at me with insouciant sensuality. She looked exactly the same.

I reached out to brush its edge with my fingertips, and realized it concealed another photograph under it. Frowning, I pulled the pin that held both pictures from the wall as gently as I could.

The picture under the daguerreotype was much newer. Almost a century newer, I guessed, but also black and white. It showed Nepenthe with eyes shadowed not by kohl, but with fear and fatigue, her cheeks gaunt, her clothing drab and buttoned up to her chin. She stood on hard-packed dirt in front of a cinderblock building. Barbed wire pierced the sky and bounded the edges of the photograph, a prison yard. A tall, beautiful man stood slightly behind her, his arm snaking around her shoulders, his hand splayed over her clavicle, his jaw set in defiance against the photographer, against the world.

I knew that face, knew it almost better than I knew my own.

"Ariel," I whispered.

"Strange that she would keep that photograph," said a meditative voice behind me. "All these years, I thought she wanted to forget what it was like."

I spun to find him lounging in the broken doorway. In the flesh, on the shadowy threshold with his eyes alight, he could have been a ghost, a demon, or an avenging angel.

"This was you," I breathed. "This was you and her at Tonepah."

"That was another life." He advanced on me, plucking the photograph from my unresisting fingers, eyes dull now, haunted by that familiar pain.

"I don't understand."

"Of course not, little Lily. You're far too young to understand what it means to survive like we did. The things we did. The things we saw. We watched the rise of humankind, and we watched our own kind fall."

"But you got through it," I said. "You survived, and so did she." Or she had, until last week.

"Yes, we survived," he said, abruptly harsh. "For what? A diminished existence, living in their shadow, on their good will and their scraps." He tucked the photograph away in his pocket, and his tone changed, smoothed into its customary silk. "Why are you here, Lillian?"

"Investigating," I said. "Looking for what the cops won't find, like you said the other day. But I should ask you the same thing. Why are you here? Did you follow me?"

"I might have," he said. "You should be more careful. It might not always be your friendly neighborhood incubus on your tail."

"You couldn't have just let me know you wanted to come along?"

He shrugged. "I didn't think you'd want the company. You were pretty mad at me yesterday."

He had a point. "I'm sorry," I said. "I shouldn't have said those things to you."

"Why?" His eyes flashed out again. "They were true."

"Still, it wasn't kind," I said. "So, I'm sorry."

"Pfft." He waved a hand, dismissive. "Didn't I tell you never to apologize? That goes double for telling the truth."

"Never apologize for telling the truth? Or never tell it in the first place?"

"What do you think?" He cast his scornful gaze around at our crowded surroundings. "How did you find this place, anyway?"

"I got a tip," I said. "From a succubus called Theo. Do you know her?"

"I know of her, yes." He frowned. "Nepenthe told me she left town."

"Well, apparently she's back, and she had some interesting information to share. Did you know that Nepenthe was preaching the virtues of an honest life to her sister succubi?"

Ariel ducked his head with uncharacteristic modesty. "Actually," he said, "that was because of me."

He couldn't have surprised me more if he'd said he was researching a cure for cancer. "Wait, Nepenthe decided to be honest with her prey because of *you*?"

"It's just a thing I've been working on," he said in a sheepish tone. "Informed consent, improved demon-human relations. Enabling us to no longer live in the shadows."

I tried to integrate this with what I knew of Ariel, the carefree trickster, and mostly failed. "I didn't know you were an activist."

"Oh, little Lily," he said. "I love your innocence sometimes. But right now, you're being just a teensy bit dense. Why do you think you and I became friends, back when you were just a baby demon stretching her wings in the big wide world? Do you really think that was a coincidence?

I've been working for years to try to improve the lives of our people. Training fledglings is only part of that work."

It was like everyone was going out of their way to catch me off guard today. "But... you...why?"

"There you go again, assuming that altruism is just a human trait. I think that's arguable, don't you?"

"I guess I do, when you put it like that." But I still eyed him with suspicion.

"Oh, come on, Lil. When you've been around as long as I have, self-interest gets really old."

"What does that have to do with Nepenthe? You convinced her to live honestly?"

"Something like that. I suggested to her a new way to get her needs met." And then he froze. He reached out to the bedpost as if groping for balance, his knuckles whitening as he gripped it.

"What is it?"

"I can't believe I didn't think of this before. Astarte and Salome were mine as well. My... converts, you could say." He turned to me. His pupils, dilated in panic, glowed like a wild animal's in the dim light of the studio. "Do you think they were killed because of that? Because of me?"

A chill slithered down my spine. "I don't know what I think," I said. "But Theo thought so. There are probably plenty of demons out there who believe that coming clean with their human prey is a radical idea. Some of them might see it as a threat to their very existence."

He raked his hands through his curly blonde hair. Between the mussed curls, the agonized expression, and the luminous eyes, he brought to mind a possessed cherub. "But they haven't come after me. Why haven't they come after me?"

"Maybe they don't know you're behind this whole consent initiative."

"Shit," Ariel said, wild-eyed.

I couldn't help but share his sentiment. At the same time, I wasn't altogether convinced that radical honesty was the key to a better existence. I wasn't about to say that to Ariel, though. He was clearly feeling bad enough already, blaming himself for Nepenthe's death. He'd begun to pace from wall to wall of the tiny apartment.

The limited space curtailed his restless motion, putting me on edge.

Watching him, I remembered a lion I'd seen at the San Francisco Zoo the one and only time I'd visited. The lion had stalked from side to side in his small concrete enclosure, only pausing long enough to shake his mane and roar. The walls had shuddered and my skin crawled in sympathy with the twitch of hyperthesia that rippled along the animal's back.

Ariel did not roar. He didn't say anything at all, but my spine prickled with tension just the same. There was a reason I'd never gone back to the zoo. Creatures like that didn't belong in cages.

"We don't know that's the motive," I said, trying to soothe him and myself.

"It's a damn sight more likely than jealousy or spite," Ariel said. "Do you think Theo…?"

"I don't know." Then I drew a sharp breath as another scrap of glossy paper pinned on Nepenthe's wall drew my attention. "There is something I do know, though."

His head came up. "What's that?"

I plucked the page from the wall and held it up so he could see it. "We really need to find that devil."

The page was a clipping from a local news magazine, a review of the Black Cat's burlesque masquerade. And the picture that went along with it showed Nepenthe arm in arm with a man wearing a red devil's mask.

Ariel raised an eyebrow, face brightening. "We're on for tomorrow night, then? You changed your mind?"

"We're on," I said, grim. "And anyway, it's not like I have all that much to lose."

23

DANCE WITH THE DEVIL

"You're sure you want to do this?" Danny said, for about the umpteenth time.

"No, I'm not sure." Fed up, I banged my closet door shut and flung an armful of dresses onto my bed. "I just think it's the only way."

"And this was Ariel's idea?"

I picked up one of the dresses, a long, slim black number with an asymmetrical skirt, and held it up to my torso. "What do you think of this one?"

Danny tilted her head to one side and made a face. "Too plain. You're deflecting."

I sighed and tossed the dress aside. "Yes, it was Ariel's idea. Happy now?"

"Not really," she said. "From the little you've said about him, your relationship with him was kind of fucked up. And isn't he like, way older than you?"

I almost laughed. "You could say that."

"So why do you listen to him?"

"He may not be especially trustworthy, but he knows about demon stuff." I held up another black dress, this one shorter and a little bit slinky. "How about this?"

"Maybe. Don't you have any dresses that aren't black?"

"Nothing that's appropriate for where I'm going."

"Come on, Lil. It's a burlesque show, not a funeral."

"That's what you think," I grumbled. "Are you sure you want to come to this? It's not really your scene."

"Oh, please," she said. "I wouldn't miss it."

"Miss what? Me humiliating myself?"

"You'll be fine," she said. "I'll be there to support you, cheer you on. Besides, you need someone to keep you out of trouble."

You need someone in your corner. The memory of Sebastian's words irritated me. "I can handle myself. Why does everyone assume I need a babysitter?"

"Don't be an asshole," she said. "I just care about you, that's all."

About to snap back at her, I caught myself and sighed again. "Sorry, Dan. I'm nervous, and it's making me tetchy as hell."

"It's fine, Sugarbean. Stage fright is totally understandable." Her expression turned sly. "Is Sebastian coming?"

"No!" Damn it, she shouldn't have been able to read my mind like that. "I haven't told him about it," I admitted.

She raised her eyebrows. "Don't you think he'd want to be there? Since you guys spent the weekend together and all?"

"I told you, we did *not* spend the weekend together. Or if we did," I amended, "it doesn't count because I was basically dead the whole time. Besides, it's complicated."

"Sure it is." She waved me away. "Go on, try on the dress. Let's see if you can dance in it."

Grateful for the excuse to escape several conversation topics I didn't care to dwell on, I ducked into the bathroom and shimmied my way into the little black dress. Examining myself in the full-length mirror on the back of the door, I dithered over the silhouette. It showed off my figure well enough, but like Danny had pointed out, what really mattered was whether I could move in it. I swiveled my hips in a sinuous motion for the mirror, and then stopped, embarrassed.

Why did I think I could do this?

A loud knock from the other room made me jump. "I'll get it!" Danny called.

"Wait—" But she had already headed down the hall. Muttering a curse, I threw open the bathroom door and padded after her.

"Lily," she said, a note of warning in her voice, just before I rounded the corner and found her standing at the open front door, staring down an incubus. Her outstretched arm blocked his entrance and she was giving him her best stink-eye of the first water.

"Hi," I said. "I'm glad it's just you, I thought you might be a subpoena."

"Hello, Lillian." He carried what looked like a dry-cleaning bag over one shoulder. "Can you tell your friend that I am not a threat, please?"

"It's ok, Dan. He's not a threat or a subpoena, thank goodness. This is Ariel."

"*This* is Ariel?" She looked him up and down, her expression saying plainly that she didn't think much of him.

"You've heard of me," he said, with one of his patented incubus grins.

"Oh, I most certainly have," she said, in a tone that implied '*and nothing good*'. She didn't lower her arm, either. It warmed my heart to see that she seemed immune to Ariel's charms.

"Ariel, this is my friend Danny."

"Daniela Rios to you." She finally moved aside just enough to give Ariel room to squeeze by her. She didn't offer him her hand. She had learned that, at least, from all the time she'd spent with me. Cubines didn't shake hands, not without an ulterior motive.

"Pleased to meet you, Daniela." Ariel walked around her, appraising me with his head to one side. "Is that what you're wearing, Lily fair?"

I smoothed the black dress down over my thighs. "Um, I think so. You don't like it?"

"You look perfectly lovely," he said. "For a cocktail party with the hoi polloi. No, that won't do at all. Here." He held out the garment bag to me with a flourish.

I didn't take it. "What's this?"

"It's your costume for tonight, of course," he said, with a smug smile.

"Oh, fine." I snatched it from him. "I swear to God, if another man buys me clothes this week, I'm going to develop a complex."

Ariel raised an eyebrow. "Usually that's considered a good thing, honey. The clothes, not the complex."

"Wait, who else gave you clothes?" Danny had pricked up her ears.

"Who, indeed," Ariel crowed. "Who could it be but her lovelorn millionaire, the hapless Sebastian? Just what did he give you, my dear? A pearl necklace and some lingerie, I hope?"

"Ooh, yes," Danny chimed in. "Please tell me it was lingerie?"

"Stop encouraging him," I said. "And you, stop encouraging her! In fact, it would be better if you two just didn't talk to each other at all. It's making me break out in hives."

"She's not answering," Danny said to Ariel. "That means it was definitely lingerie."

Ariel glanced from her to me, then threw back his head and laughed. "I like this one. She's funny!"

"And I'm still right here," Danny retorted. "Don't push it."

"Oho, and a little spicy." But he looked at her this time when he spoke. "Or is that salty?"

"Both," Danny said. "Like a jalapeno margarita." She grinned.

Maybe she wasn't completely immune to Ariel, after all. Scowling, I peeled back the plastic of the garment bag to find a slick, shimmery gold material in a snakeskin pattern that whispered through my fingers like water. "Ariel, where did you get this?"

"Secondhand, Lily fair. I hope you don't mind."

I opened the bag further. Where had I seen a dress like this? In a store window? On a billboard? On a...costume rack? Wait a minute. "Is this..."

"From the closet of a dear departed friend. I think she would have wanted you to have it."

I dropped it like it had burned me, backing away. "No," I said. "I can't wear this. I won't."

"You must." Ariel picked it up again, smoothing out the fabric with loving hands, and thrust it at me. "It's perfect, you'll see. Try it on."

Danny was looking between us, confused. "What's going on? Whose dress was it?"

"It belonged to Penelope," I said. "Ariel, how could you?"

"You seem to be forgetting the point of this exercise, Lillian," he said. "The goal is to draw the bastard out. To do that, you need drama. You need bravura. You need to step into her skin. Can you do that?"

With unwilling hands, I took the dress back from him, held it up against my body. It shimmered and flowed, a fitted bodice with a plunging back and a detachable wraparound skirt that would hug my hips and swirl in filmy layers when I spun. The sewn sequins would catch the stage lights and the length would hide any amateurish steps.

"All right," I said. "You win. I'll do my best."

"I knew you would." His benevolent smile warmed me, but I shivered as I turned away. Tonight, I'd wear a dead woman's dress, and play a dead woman's part.

I hoped I would make it through alive.

I CHECKED my makeup one last time in the cramped green room behind the Black Cat's stage, then lingered, staring into the mirror for a long moment. I almost didn't recognize myself. The fringed black bangs of the wig I wore changed the shape of my face, and the eyeliner Danny had helped me apply changed the shape of my eyes. The gold snake-patterned dress fit me like a second skin, with cleavage for days. I just hoped everything would stay where I'd put it, and come off when I wanted it to.

Now for the final touch. The mask hung on the wall beside the mirror, an elaborate confection of gold and black feathers, sequins, beads, and embroidery in what Ariel called "Venetian" style. Nepenthe had not worn a mask on stage, but I had insisted on it, a concession to my desire for anonymity.

Outside, what had started as the sound of individual voices had risen and merged into an ocean of noise. I tried to ignore it. I took the mask from its hook and placed it over my face, pulling the black ribbons tight around and under my black bob wig.

A soft knock on the door came as I finished securing the ribbons with hidden bobby pins.

"Come in." I rose with deliberate care. The mask constrained my peripheral vision and I had to hold my head high to balance the extra weight.

I'd left my feet bare. Dancing in the mask and the dress required plenty of dexterity. I didn't need high heels to compound the challenge. Besides, my only relevant experience was the belly dance classes that Danny used to drag me to under protest on weekday nights back in our grad school days. I'd trained in classical ballet as a kid, but that was about as far from burlesque as opera was from yodeling.

"Hey, it's almost time." Danny poked her head around the door, her eyes going round when she saw me. "Wow. Lily, you look stunning. Weird, but stunning. Like a sexy, snaky alien empress."

"Thanks, I think." I stepped forward, distracted by the soft rustle of sequins in my gown, like a real snake moving through dry leaves. "Do you think this is going to work, Dan? Do you think he'll come?"

"I don't know," she said. "But either way, it'll make a hell of a story."

"That I can never tell anyone who wasn't actually here."

"Too late to back out now, Sugarbean," she said. "Let's get your fabulous self into those wings now."

"Wings?" It said something about the state of my life these days that my mind went to the feathered kind, the dream kind. The shadow kind, bearing me off into an insensate night.

"Wings of the stage, doofus."

"Oh, yeah."

She rolled her eyes. "Come on, I'll help you. Can't let the alien snake empress trip and fall before her big moment."

I wore long black and gold opera gloves that covered my arms to the elbow, but I pulled back from her hands. "Whoa. Careful." Grabbing the shawl I'd brought from the back of my closet, I wrapped it tightly around my bare shoulders and upper arms. "Okay. Now we can go."

She gripped my arm gently above the elbow to guide me down a hallway and upstairs into the darkness of the waiting stage, where she left me with a whispered message of luck I didn't understand in the least. Unlike her, I'd never been a theater kid.

The oceanic noise washed over me from the other side of the curtain, then ebbed like a tide and sank to silence. Lights went up, filtering through the heavy damask, and the master of ceremonies stepped onto the boards.

"Good evening, ladies and gents, birds and beasts, demons and angels of the night." It was Ariel up there, a few feet away from me, working the crowd, strutting his two minutes upon the stage and having the time of his eternal life. "We have a very special guest for your Masquerade tonight. It's her first ever performance as a burlesque girl. So after her debut, you will be able to say with complete sincerity that you have witnessed, with your own eyes, a genuine Original Sin."

Scattered laughter and cheers rang out. I took my place at center stage, just behind the curtain. My heart began to pound in my ears, louder and louder, a bass line that gathered speed as I caught whiffs of the desiderata floating on the air. In a few moments, that swirl of intoxicating, chaotic, unfocused human energy would all focus on me.

"And now, without further ado. She came before Eve and refused to lie before Adam. The one, the only...*Lilith Fair*."

On the cheer that went up, they raised the curtain and the lights blazed over me as I stood stock still in the spotlight, my back to the stage, one arm outstretched overhead, one trailing to the side, head bowed as I waited for my cue.

And then the music started and I began to move. Serpentine and slow, my body followed the beat of desire in the room as much as the rhythm of the music. I switched my trembling human brain off and let the demon in me take the lead. She led me by the hips and shoulders, undulating, my Presence intensifying as I turned to look out over the sea of humanity below me.

At first the stage lights blinded me. Then my hunter's senses sharpened and I could see all of them. Each and every one had tipped their face up to me, enraptured, swaying in unison to the cadence of the music. No, to *my* cadence, my body, my dance. My power caught and held them like souls in amber, forbidden fruit ripe for the plucking.

I owned that room and for a long, exquisite moment, I gloried in it. I let the scarf I'd wrapped around my upper body flutter to the ground and danced for them in earnest. I cupped their yearning hearts in the palm of my hand.

I succumbed to my own spell, more than a little. I'd reached my hands behind my back, pressing them into a reverse prayer position as I performed a hip isolation I didn't know I had the chops for. Revolving in place to give the audience their due, I slid my fingers down my spine to caress my own curves and, almost as an afterthought, unhooked the wraparound skirt.

Then I saw *him*.

The diaphanous fabric rippled down and pooled on the stage to reveal the boned golden corset-body and ruffled train beneath, and I met Sebastian's gaze.

I did not freeze, but I did falter. I hadn't expected to see him standing there by the bar again, this time unmasked, his drink forgotten in one lax hand, his lips parted and eyes hungry. I hadn't expected the song of his desiderata to drown out that of every other soul in the Black Cat Club, a keening descant over the music from the speakers. I hadn't expected him to volunteer as tribute.

Why was he here? I'd run from him without a word and hadn't heard from him since. His father and Tobias had threatened my job, and a relationship with him threatened my self-control. I couldn't trust him, shouldn't want him. That's how this went, wasn't it?

In my heightened state, I couldn't remember why his father's opinion mattered at all. The energy that drew him to me hummed between us and us alone, and as for control, I held the power here.

He moved toward me like a sleepwalker chasing a dream. The crowd parted for him, and now I danced only for him. I stretched my hand toward him and crooked my finger, drew him closer still, advancing to the stairs that led down from the front of the stage.

"No, Lily," a voice hissed somewhere behind me. "Not him. Focus!"

But I didn't stop. I descended the stage stairs step by slow step, the varnished wood cool on my bare feet, and found my Claim waiting for me at the bottom.

The music had faded, but the audience stood silent, still, ensorcelled. One could have heard a pin full of dancing angels drop.

Sebastian's fingers gripped my hips with a force that might have bruised me, but I didn't care. He lifted me up against him and I took his face between my gloved hands. Our mouths crashed together, our tongues tangled, and his kether shot through my body like a high voltage current.

Someone shouted. Someone else shrieked. The spell of silence broke into an agitated hubbub. The audience eddied around us, jostling us. Sebastian's grip shifted, loosening. My feet found the floor and now he clung to me, staggering as the effect of my uncontrolled drain struck him.

Crap. That shouldn't have happened. Riding on the high from the audience, I'd let myself go for a moment. I put my gloved hands over his to steady him as voices washed over me.

"Watch out!"

"Oh my God!"

"He has a gun!"

Wait, what?

I lifted my head, stared down the cold barrel of a 9mm semi-automatic pistol, and looked the devil in the eye.

"Get away from him!" The red-cloaked figure's harsh voice rang out over the mutters and cries of fear from the humans around us. I put Sebastian behind me, shielding him with my body. I could probably take a gunshot. Unless the bullet was silver.

"What are you doing? Lily!" Sebastian grasped the railing of the stairs for balance, reaching out with his free hand to pull me back. I dodged him with ease.

"Stay where you are, Sebastian." I didn't take my eyes off the devil. He wore an identical mask to the one he'd sported one week ago, although it couldn't be the same. Ariel and I had found its twin on the balcony outside the room where Nepenthe had died.

The masked cambion stared back at me, the whites around his irises showing like a spooked animal's. He had a square jaw with a five o'clock shadow and he stank of fear. His desiderata shuddered around him, a writhing miasma of bile and mania. The pistol aimed at my midsection wavered for a moment.

Cambion or not, the devil was scared of me. I didn't know if I should take that as a compliment.

"What's your plan here, buddy?" I kept my voice even, layering it with my Presence, soothing and subduing him as much as I could with just my powers of suggestion. "What do you want?"

"You're a demon." Spittle shone on his lips. "And I'm here to stop you."

THE DEVIL YOU KNOW

"YOU'RE HERE TO STOP ME FROM WHAT? DANCING?" I TOOK A CAUTIOUS STEP toward the masked devil. "You definitely stopped that, so kudos to you. Kind of a drag, to be honest. I was really getting into my groove."

"Shut up!" With a jerky motion, he racked the gun and aimed it at me once more.

I froze. Well, shit. He didn't seem all that susceptible. "You're going to what, shoot up the nightclub for great justice? Go on, let these people go. This isn't about them."

"You hypnotized them, you…you hellmare!"

Hellmare? Really? "Maybe a little." I glanced around me at the cowering, bewildered crowd. "Personally, I think they were doing just fine until you showed up." I didn't see Danny among the rest of them. Maybe she'd slipped out to do something sensible, like call the police.

"What about *him*?"

"Who? Sebastian? He'll be okay. He knows I'm a hellmare. I think he might even like it."

The hand clutching the gun trembled, just a bit. "You're crazy! You're both crazy."

"Hey, I'm not the one holding this club at gunpoint."

This seemed to penetrate his thick skull. "Fine," he said, through gritted teeth. "They go. You stay."

"You hear that?" I raised my voice, added a Presence of command. "Nothing to see here. Get home safe, all of you! Quick and quiet, no stampeding. Call a cab if you've been drinking."

An eerie silence fell as the human crowd flowed out like a riptide, leaving the dance floor cavernous and empty. Just the two of us now.

Make that three. "Sebastian," I said, though I didn't use my Presence this time. "You too. Get out."

"No. I'm not leaving you alone with this lunatic." But his voice wavered and his energy flickered as a candle might in a strong draft. I'd really done a number on him with that kiss.

I felt like a million bucks, and also guilty as sin.

In the periphery of my vision, at the dark edge of the dance floor, something moved. Sebastian had distracted me and my opponent just long enough. A tall blur with golden curls charged at the gunman, head down, trench coat streaming behind him like dark wings.

The devil had seen him too. He swung the pistol around.

Time stretched, slowed, hung glittering in the air with the motes of dust in the stage lights. Ariel's face had gone blank with fear as he tried to change his trajectory at the last minute, diving to one side away from the gun's barrel. Slow, too slow. The cambion in the devil costume had his thumb upon the trigger, squeezing it, squeezing it...

I hurtled toward him faster than both of them, a wordless cry bursting from me. My tackle took the devil to the ground just as the gun went off. The shot battered my eardrums with apocalyptic blast. I saw stars.

No, I didn't. A spotlight had exploded in a shower of sparks and shattered glass. I couldn't see Ariel anywhere. The acrid stink of gunpowder and fear clogged my throat.

My vision cleared. I straddled the gunman's chest, one hand pinning his wrists above his head. He strained against my grasp, to no avail. My kether-fueled strength far outmatched him. I wrenched the weapon away from him and sent it spinning toward the side wall, out of his reach. Teeth bared, he whipped his head from side to side, trying to bite me.

I reared back and punched him in the face with my free hand. My gloved fist crunched through cartilage and paper mâché. He grunted, blood flowing profusely from his nose and split lip.

"Enough," I said. "That's enough, asshole."

He snarled, panting hard, and spat blood and what looked like a tooth. *Yuck.* "You're a monster," he said. He slurred the words, but the slur still came through loud and clear.

"Maybe that's true, but I'm a well-fed monster right at this moment." I squeezed his ribs between my thighs until he gasped. "And you're a murderer."

"What…? I'm not—ah!"

I kept squeezing. "I know you were there that night," I said. "You left something of yours. A red devil mask."

"No." Under the mess of blood and snot, his cheeks paled.

I put my face close to his, but not close enough to risk touching it. "You killed her, didn't you?"

"Uhhh," he whined. "I—I can't—"

"Why did you do it?" I let him suck in a breath before I increased the pressure again. "Was it because you didn't dare live honestly like she did? Or was it because she was stronger than you? Did you fear her like you fear me, little man? Is that why you staked her and left her to die like a bug on a pin?"

"No…" He whimpered and squirmed, his desiderata a paroxysm of impotent terror. *Pathetic.*

"Let's see who you are, shall we?"

"No! Damn you." He renewed his struggles when I reached for his mask, so I hit him in the face again instead. His eyes rolled up in his head and he fell back, stunned.

Thank God for the opera gloves. They had probably taken some of the impact out of my punch, but I had force to spare and I didn't want to touch his skin with my bare hands. I grabbed the devil mask by the nose and shoved it up his forehead.

And stared down into the bruised and bloodied face of Tobias Kaine.

"*You?*" I leaped to my feet, putting space between me and the man I'd just punched into the floorboards. "But if you're the devil, then…holy shit. *You're* a cambion?"

Tobias Kaine moaned. He raised himself up on his elbows, squinting at me through two blackening eyes. "I'm not like you."

"No," I said. "You're worse than me. You stir up hatred against us. You hunt your own kind."

"So do you! Your other kind."

My cheeks tingled with heat, and I gritted my teeth. "I don't hunt."

"You hunted *him*." Tobias jerked his chin at Sebastian.

"Hey," Sebastian said. "I resent that." He looked a little less wobbly but based on the way he'd propped himself against the riser, arms crossed, he was still feeling the effects of my kiss.

"It's not like that," I said.

"Isn't it?" Tobias demanded. "I saw what you did to him up there."

I shot another sideways glance at Sebastian. "I may have gotten a little carried away."

"I'm fine," Sebastian said. "Really."

"That's not the point." Tobias staggered to his feet. "You can't just...*use* people like that. It's not right."

How had I ended up on Ariel's side of this argument? I looked around for the incubus, but he'd disappeared. Typical. Always popping up uninvited, and then never around when I wanted him. "So, me kissing Sebastian is wrong, but you killing Penelope was right?"

"I didn't kill her!" He circled away from me.

"I don't believe you." I circled toward him, cutting off his path to the exit. "Why were you looking for her that night?"

"It's none of your business." Tobias's eyes slid away from me to his left.

Sebastian's voice crackled with alarm. "Lily! The gun!"

Tobias darted sideways, but I had seen it too. I dived after him. The kether in my veins propelled me into him at inhuman speed and he hit the ground hard. He groped for the pistol, but I stomped on his fingers and kicked the gun out of his reach.

Cursing, he leaped back to his feet and away from me. His face twisted with fury and frustration, his eyes wide and wild, the blood still streaming from his nose. He seemed about to speak.

I stepped toward him. But his focus had shifted, fixating somewhere behind me. His face changed and he backpedaled. Then, without another word, he broke for the exit.

I started after him, but a flash of movement cut me off. It emerged from the shadows in pursuit of Tobias, stirring a gust of frankincense-scented air in its wake.

"Ariel?"

The slam of the outer door answered me, followed by a harsh, metallic click that echoed through the room. Heart in my mouth, I turned to find Sebastian standing behind me. In his hand, he held Tobias's gun.

I froze. "Don't!"

"Hm?" With a practiced motion, he released the clip. Just like that, the thing lay in his palm in pieces. I stared, transfixed, as he pulled the slide back.

A bullet dropped out of the chamber and clattered to the floor. It rolled a few feet and lay there glinting. Sebastian bent and picked it up between his thumb and forefinger. He held it up to the light, frowning at it.

I caught my breath. "What is it?"

He looked at me then, almost surprised, as if he'd forgotten my presence. "It's silver."

An icy wave of adrenaline washed over me. It was all I could do not to back away from the tiny, deadly object in Sebastian's hand. I wanted to turn and run, like Tobias had. Instead, with careful steps, I walked over to one of the tables along the side of the dance floor and dropped into a chair. My mask had been pulled askew during the struggle with Tobias. I yanked it off, letting the ribbons trail from my hand to the floor.

"A silver bullet," I said, voice flat. "You're sure." Tobias's shot must have gone wide when I tackled him. If the bullets really were silver like Sebastian said, even a graze would have seriously fucked Ariel up, and he couldn't have chased Tobias out in a supernatural blur of speed.

"I'm not sure, no." He pressed the loader down and snapped the bullet back into the top of the magazine. "Could be aluminum or nickel plating, I suppose. Either way, it's unusual-looking. Most bullets are copper-jacketed."

"You know guns." I wrapped my arms around myself, clenching my teeth to keep them from chattering.

"Occupational hazard of being raised a Ritter. My dad taught me." He came to my side, draping his coat around my shoulders. "Have you ever shot a gun, Lily?" He held out a hand to help me up.

I didn't take it. "No." I didn't need the assist, and he had just held that poison round. "And I don't plan on it. Guns scare me."

"Scaring people is the point." He sighed and dropped his hand to his side. "You should consider it. It seems like you might need to defend yourself."

"I think I did just fine with what I've got." Despite myself, his proximity teased at my demon senses, and I relented. "But I couldn't have without you and what you gave me."

"Really?" He flashed a rueful grin, relaxing a little. "And here I thought I was mostly swooning in the background the whole time."

I flushed. "I'm sorry about that. I really did get caught up in the moment. I didn't mean for it to go so far."

"Are you kidding me? That was glorious. You're magnificent, you know."

"Thank you." Then I glanced down at myself—bare legs, golden corseted body-suit, gold gloves streaked with a cambion's blood—and made a face. "Oh, God. I really need to change."

"Too bad," he said. "You look like a goddess."

"I look like a grindhouse girl."

"Fine, a grindhouse goddess. Patroness of bloody, sexy vengeance." He strode up to the stage, collecting my discarded scarf and skirt. It seemed he had recovered from the kether drain without any lasting ill effects.

"Get dressed," he said. "I'll drive you home."

I rose, accepting the bundle of fabric from him. "I'll just be a minute. We should get out of here before the cops show up." I should have stayed far, far away from this place, from Sebastian, and from anything else that had to do with Penelope's death. I didn't want to explain my presence here to Huang or his cohorts, let alone how I'd emptied the club in less than a minute and disarmed a gunman without breaking a sweat.

"I'll be here," Sebastian said.

Padding barefoot toward the stage door, I glanced over my shoulder and caught him watching me with a bemused expression. "What...?"

"I liked kissing you, Lily Knight."

Face aflame, I ducked out the door and slipped into the green room at the back of the club to collect my things. Just like the front of the club, the back was eerily silent and abandoned. Apparently, I'd sent even the bouncers and bartenders home with my kether-fueled power of command. The thought scared me more than I wanted to admit. And where had Danny gone? Had my Presence swept her up as well?

I stuffed my skirt and shawl into my bag. Not wanting to battle with the corset while Sebastian waited, I pulled my jeans up over it and buttoned Sebastian's coat to hide my decolletage. With my soiled gloves tucked into one pocket, I slipped on my flats and rejoined my ride.

Sebastian jumped to his feet as soon as he saw me. "There you are." His desiderata had lost some of its steady calm. It quivered with adrenaline.

"Something wrong?"

He shook his head. "Just creeping myself out. It's too empty in here. Let's go."

YOU'RE NEXT

IT HAD GROWN LATE, AND THE NIGHT BREATHED THICK AND DAMP WITH A keen, salt-sea breeze. Sebastian offered me his arm as we headed down the dark street. After a moment's hesitation, I stepped into his warm desiderata and took it. We walked on together without saying anything. I didn't trust myself to speak, and he didn't seem inclined to break the silence.

His roadster waited, glowing the same pale blue as his eyes, in the well-lit center of a near-empty parking garage. He slipped the attendant several bills and held the passenger side door open for me. I still hadn't gotten used to his manners, or the casual way he threw money at normal people problems.

He started the car, and I dug around in my purse, frowning.

"Something wrong?" The car made almost no noise, just a soft purr as he accelerated out of the garage.

"Nothing. I just can't find my phone. I think I must have left it at home." I wanted to call Danny and check in on her, but that would have to wait.

"Hmm." He lapsed into silence again for a while. I observed him sidelong, more with demon synesthesia than human vision, sampling the mixed emotions churning under his impassive exterior. I had begun to learn his flavors. Unease, anger, frustration, and yearning shifted like shadows over the surface of still, deep water.

"Do you really think Tobias murdered Penelope?" he said after a few wordless minutes.

So that's what was troubling him. It bothered me too. When Tobias had denied the murder, I hadn't felt the lie in him. But maybe, like full-blood cubines, other cambions would be harder to read. "I don't know," I said. "I thought so, but now I'm not so sure."

"You mentioned he was there that night, at the hotel. How do you know it was him?"

"We found a red devil's mask on the balcony."

"On the balcony," Sebastian said, flat-voiced. "You mean he was out there the whole time? Watching me with Penelope?"

"Somebody was."

"Jesus." In the dim light from the dash, his face took on a haunted cast, a visible shudder running through his body. "And the silver...I didn't know that was a real thing, until I saw your face. Is that—?"

I nodded. "It wasn't the stake itself. It was the stuff it was made from. Silver is...it's like our kryptonite."

Sebastian's lips tightened. "He came prepared to do some damage tonight."

"That or he's just really fucked up and scared."

"Those aren't mutually exclusive." His dry tone belied the turmoil in his desiderata. "And he's what, half-demon? Like you?"

"Not like me." I echoed Tobias's earlier declaration. "Murderer or not, that guy is twisted. His whole brand is stirring up fear of us on the internet."

"Maybe it makes him feel safer. If he's the loudest voice in the room shouting about how much he hates demons, no one will suspect him."

"Well, that's stupid," I said. "Which is probably why you're right."

"I think it's sad. He must really hate himself."

"Yeah, well." I turned away from him, fixing my attention on the lights of the city flowing past us. "Murderer or not, I don't think I have any sympathy to waste on him."

"That's fair." Sebastian turned onto my street and brought the roadster to a soundless stop in front of my building. He didn't say anything else.

After a moment, I glanced over at him to find him watching me in the half-light.

"What?"

"Nothing." He set the parking brake. "Are you sure you're safe to go up alone?"

"Not really." The last time we'd done this, I'd found an incubus lurking unannounced. God knew what I'd find tonight. "The real question is, are you sure you'd be safe going up with me?"

He swiveled around in his seat to face me, and my heart flipped over. "Don't do that, Lily," he said, low and earnest. "You said you're not like Tobias, so don't hate yourself like he does. You're not dangerous."

"How can you say that?" My voice caught on the words. "After what I did to you in there? Come on, Sebastian! You could barely stand up afterwards and that was just one kiss."

"That was one a hell of a kiss," he said, with a faint smile. "To tell you the truth, I don't actually know whether I got lightheaded because you did your succubus—sorry, cambion thing, or because all the blood in my brain rushed south at once."

"Right." I didn't buy his attempt to reassure me, even though his statement had a dramatic effect on my blood flow as well. "Well, I do know. It was a cambion thing, and I don't hate myself. I'm a realist. I could hurt you, Sebastian. It's happened before."

"I'll take my chances. Besides, I don't think walking you up to your door poses any significant risk to my immortal soul."

Damn him, he was stubborn. If only he knew. But I wasn't ready to have that particular conversation with him.

Had Nepenthe told him? If she had held to the principles Theo described, she must have revealed something of the reality of the exchange to him. The real price, the soul bond. But perhaps, like me, she failed to find the nerve.

"Okay." I sighed. "But keep your hands to yourself if you know what's good for you." After everything that had happened that night, I didn't want to climb the dark stairwell at this hour by myself, even with Sebastian's kether still hot in my veins. I'd used a lot of what he gave me to subdue Tobias, and I didn't know how much I had left.

"Touch you at my own peril. I get it." He sounded entirely undeterred.

I fixed him with a quelling glare as he opened the passenger door for me. He grinned and shoved his hands in his pockets, his warm presence following one step behind me while I unlocked the outside door and cautiously scaled the stairs to my apartment.

I had my key ready in my hand this time. But when I pushed it into the lock, it jammed. The door, partially ajar, swung open at my touch.

"What the fuck?" I said loudly.

"Lily, wait." At my back, Sebastian reached for my arm, but I shrugged him off, dodging his touch.

Hadn't he listened to me at all? I marched into the apartment and flipped on the light. Nothing seemed disturbed, other than the now-useless lock on the front door. "You've got to be kidding me."

"Be careful." Sebastian hovered in the doorway. "They could still be here."

"I hope they are," I snarled. "Close the door, would you? The cat will get out. If she didn't already. Delilah!"

Sebastian came inside and shut the door. To my surprise, he didn't argue. Instead, he withdrew the pieces of Tobias's gun from his pocket and reassembled it with quick, methodical motions.

I hid my flinch. My tense awareness of that silver bullet twitched at the base of my spine. He held the gun with the muzzle pointing downward, his finger near but not on the trigger. His desiderata spiked with adrenaline but offered no threat to me. Still, I had to force myself to put my back to him as I moved further into the room.

"They didn't take anything." My work laptop sat on the kitchen table. It should have reassured me, but foreboding slithered in my belly. Why break in and not take the first visible expensive electronic device?

"What's back there? Bedroom?" At my nod, he moved past me toward the darkened hallway.

Relieved to no longer have the gun at my back, I fell in behind him and switched on the hall light. Nothing stirred. We crept along the wall to the half-open bedroom door.

Sebastian nudged it further open with the muzzle of the gun. His tension vibrated through me, visible in the stiff line of his back. The light from the hall pooled at our feet and deepened the shadows it couldn't reach. Keeping my movements deliberate, I reached around Sebastian for the light switch.

The light from the ceiling fixture flooded the room, and I gasped.

"My God." Sebastian swore under his breath.

As in the front room, nothing had been taken or even rearranged, but the intruder had left their mark.

Big, drippy, red letters defaced the wall above the bed. It looked like blood, but the oily tang that hung heavy in the room told me it was only paint. That knowledge didn't make it any less threatening.

I KNOW WHAT YOU ARE, it screamed. And then, below it:

YOU'RE NEXT.

NOWHERE SAFE

"YOU HAVE TO LET ME CALL THE POLICE," SEBASTIAN SAID.

I sat on my bed, cradling Delilah close to my chest. This disastrous night had granted me one scant blessing when I found the fluffy gray cat crouched beneath my bed, watching me with wary green eyes. I'd coaxed her out with a bag of her favorite treats, and now I didn't want to let her go.

I spent all my time in the outside world guarding my true self, my expressions, my desires. Once upon a time, my home, my room, had been the only place I'd let them flow. But now, my sanctuary had been desecrated by hatred. Tears threatened to spill over into the cat's soft fur, and I shook with sobs I still couldn't fully let loose.

"I don't have to let you do any damn thing." My words came out muffled, my face buried deep in Delilah's ruff. She must have sensed my need for comfort, because she tolerated the contact without protest or struggle. She turned her head to lick my hand, purring as if to say, *'There, there. It will be okay'*.

I appreciated it, but it didn't convince me that anything would be okay, ever again.

"This is a crime, Lily!" Exasperation crackled in Sebastian's voice.

"They can help you. They might be able to catch the guy who did this once and for all."

"No," I said. "No cops. They can't help with this."

"There must be evidence that they can find! Fingerprints, maybe?"

"Oh, like they found at the last crime scene in this whole debacle?" I raised my head just enough to glare at him. "Whoever this is, whoever is hunting us, he's smart. He didn't leave any prints in that hotel room. I highly doubt he left any here."

"You don't know that. Shouldn't you at least report it?"

I released Delilah and crossed my arms over my chest, hunching my shoulders. The painted letters on the wall behind me loomed in my mind. "You're awfully pro-cop for someone who was just wrongly arrested last week."

"You're awfully anti-cop for someone who works for the DA's office."

"I'm not sure I do work there anymore." Basra hadn't contacted me since I walked out of the office yesterday. Maybe she figured I needed some time to cool off or maybe she was too busy preparing subpoenas and indictments with my name on them. I'd put my money on the latter.

"Okay," Sebastian said. "No police, but you can't stay here tonight. It's not safe."

"No, it's not." I wasn't safe here. I wasn't sure I was safe anywhere.

"You can stay with me if you like." Sebastian's suggestion sounded tentative, even shy.

I almost laughed. "Thanks, but that's *definitely* not safe. For either of us."

"I don't mean in my bed," he said. "I have nice guest rooms, you know."

"I bet you do, and I said no." I sprang up and started digging through the pile of dresses I'd left on the bed during my fashion show with Danny. "I can stay with a friend. I just need a ride up to the Haight, and I need to find my damn phone so I can call her."

We turned over the room, and then the living room, until it looked like I really had been robbed. Sebastian had even called my number to see if we could hear it ring. No luck. My phone had vanished.

"You can use mine," Sebastian offered. I hadn't let him rifle my dresser drawers, but he'd helped me rummage through my personal possessions without a single disparaging comment. He really was too good to be true. Or maybe spending time around Ariel had acclimated me to expect a certain level of mockery as a given.

I'd saved that dratted incubus from death by silver bullet, and he hadn't even stopped to thank me in his haste to chase down Tobias.

And what would he do if he caught him? I shifted, uneasy. *Had* Tobias vandalized my apartment? The message sure sounded like him. But in all the chaos of the last few days, not to mention my little vacation from consciousness, I still didn't have the piece of the puzzle that would bring the whole picture into focus.

Focus. I tapped Danny's number into Sebastian's sleek, futuristic-looking smartphone. Thank God I had her number memorized, probably the only one I knew by heart. I waited for her to pick up and start cursing at me for scaring her again.

Instead, the number just rang through to voicemail. Of course, I'd called from a strange number. I hoped she was just screening her calls, not asleep already.

"Hi Dan," I said at the beep. "It's me. Something happened at home, so I'm coming over. Call me back at this number when you get this."

With Sebastian's assistance, I wrestled an unhappy Delilah into her carrier, packed an overnight bag, and collected my laptop. No reason to leave it for the next burglar who noticed the broken lock. Standing at the doorway, I took one last look around my apartment and sighed. Tomorrow, I would have to come back and deal with the wall and the door. Tonight, I just wanted to curl up in my pajamas and drink Danny's herbal tea while she teased me about Sebastian and told me that of course everything would turn out okay.

Sebastian insisted on shouldering my bag, and it said something about my mood that I didn't even raise a token objection. I followed him back downstairs with the cat carrier. Inside, Delilah sang the protest song of her people, not caring in the slightest that she was about to be ferried by the most exclusive chauffeur service in the greater Bay Area.

The roadster had no back seat, so I had to sit with her carrier between my feet. I leaned back on the headrest and scrubbed my hands over my face with another heavy sigh.

Sebastian's concern washed over me as he took the driver's seat again. "It's been a hell of a night, hasn't it? I'm so sorry this happened to you, Lily."

"Thank you." I wrapped my arms around myself, staring out the windshield at the night. "It's just...he's been in my house, Sebastian. He's coming after me and I don't know how to stop him."

He patted his pocket where the gun pulled the line of his coat askew. "I know at least one way."

"Are you kidding?" I let out a short laugh. "I told you, I've never shot a gun before in my life and I don't want to."

"I get that," he said. "But if you change your mind, I'd be more than happy to teach you how. To ease my own mind, if nothing else."

I leaned forward, typing Danny's address into the GPS. "I'll think about it."

"I'll take it," he said. We ghosted away from the curb, and Delilah howled again.

I prayed she didn't plan on filing a formal complaint by vomiting, or worse, on the floor of the undoubtedly very expensive car. Otherwise, I was inclined to agree with her opinion. I'd never get used to the smooth, noiseless motion of the vehicle. It made for a disorienting, frictionless sensation, like riding in a spaceship. But maybe that was my demon side, analog and animalistic, balking at humanity's tireless push into the future.

Searching for a topic to distract me from my inner demon's restlessness and my inner human's worries, something else odd occurred to me. "I never asked you why you came tonight."

"And miss your burlesque debut?" He chuckled. "Like I could stay away."

"No. I mean, how did you even know about it?"

He glanced over at me, taken aback. "Lily, you texted me."

"What?" I stared back at him. "I did not!"

"Okay, don't fuck with me. That's not funny."

"I'm not fucking with you." I rolled my shoulders to dislodge the prickling sensation crawling up my spine. "I'm telling you, I didn't text you. Hell, I would have been even more nervous if I knew you'd be watching me."

"You didn't seem that nervous," he said.

"Well, yeah, by the time I saw you, I was…never mind. Let's go back to the text I definitely didn't send you. When was this?"

"Just a few hours ago. You really don't remember? I still have the message on my phone from your mobile number. You can look if you want."

"No, I believe you. It's just…this is really creeping me out."

"Me, too." He made a wry face. "You know, I was relieved to hear from you. I thought you might still be pissed about being ambushed by my dad."

"Your dad got me put on leave. He's working with Tobias! I *was* pissed."

"I know." He shot a glance at me. "And now?"

"Now I'm just scared. I don't have room to be pissed."

"Oh," he said again. "I am sorry about that, by the way. I said that in my text, but…" He shrugged. "You probably didn't get that, either."

"Nope, I did not." I slumped in my seat. "I wish I knew when I'd lost the damn phone."

He raised an eyebrow. "You really think someone stole it just to push us together?"

"It does sound silly, when you put it that way." I frowned. "I wonder… maybe Danny sent that text, now that I think about it. She's a big fan of you, and she's not above pranking me if she thinks it's for my own good."

"It's good to know I have fans, but would she really steal your phone?"

"I don't know, maybe? I hope not. But I'm sure she'll own up to it if I ask her."

We made it to Danny's without any cat-related incidents, other than the incessant mewing. Once again, Sebastian insisted on carrying my bag for me. I hefted Delilah's carrier, struggling to balance it as she paced and yowled within. "Shhh," I told her. "I'll let you out soon, I promise."

But I'd spoken too quickly. Even though it was nearly midnight, all the lights blazed in Danny's street-facing apartment. Before I could even knock on the door, it jerked open to reveal a frazzled-looking Berry. She took one look at me and her face went white, her hands coming up to cover her mouth.

"Lily! You're all right. Thank God." But fear and puzzlement suffused her desiderata, and an answering dread bloomed in my stomach.

"Hi, Berry," I said. "Where's Danny? She's not answering her phone."

Berry wrung her hands. "I know. That's the thing." Her voice trembled. "I thought she was with you."

"What?"

"Danny never came home tonight," Berry said. "She said something happened at the club and she was meeting you at your house. You haven't seen her?"

Sebastian and I exchanged glances. "I saw her at the club," I said, my words slow and heavy. "But that was a while ago and my phone got stolen. You haven't heard from her?"

Berry shook her head, tears welling in her expressive brown eyes.

"I think we should call the police now," Sebastian said.

"It won't do any good." I set Delilah's carrier down and leaned against the doorframe, suddenly weary beyond measure. "She's an adult and they won't do jack until she's been missing more than twenty-four hours. Besides, we have no clear reason to think that something bad happened. Maybe she ran into some friends unexpectedly."

"This isn't like her," Berry said. "You know it's not."

"I know," I said. "You're right. It's not. I'm sorry."

"So what do we do?"

"I don't know." Then I turned to Sebastian. "But I have an idea."

He eyed me. "Why does that worry me?"

"Don't worry," I said. "It's legal, I think. It better be, because it's your technology. I was reading up on it the other day. What you do is super creepy, by the way. It's basically stalker tech."

"We prefer the term 'intelligence gathering,'" he said mildly. "You researched my work? I'm flattered."

"Just doing my due diligence. *Intelligence gathering*," I shot back.

"Judge me later," he said. "Maybe after you're done availing yourself of my services. For now, tell me what you need me to do. I want to help."

"Whoever stole my phone took Danny." I picked up Delilah's carrier again, squaring my shoulders. "If we can find it, we'll find the kidnapper. Sebastian, I want you to track my phone."

✿

AN HOUR OR SO LATER, I ensconced Delilah safely in one of Sebastian's spare bedrooms and reconvened with him in his study. He had a veritable battle station in there, with multiple monitors and what looked like a private server block.

"There you are." He swiveled his chair half-around to face me, his fingers racing across the keyboard as he typed out commands by touch. "I need you. Come here."

I hesitated, flushing. "Need me for what?" His scent and desiderata lay thick between us, threatening to overwhelm my senses. He smelled amazing, almost as good as he'd tasted when I'd kissed him. Given all the time I'd spent in enclosed spaces with him this evening, holding back my kether-hunger would soon become an increasing strain on my self-control. And I had to keep control. Danny's life could depend on it.

He rose and offered the chair to me. "Account information, please."

"Oh." My flush deepened. Of course he meant tech credentials, not some blatant proposition. Conscious of his proximity, I slid past him and into the big cushioned chair, and paused with my hands hovering over the keyboard. Would entering my password mean he had access to my phone's location forever?

But I had gone too far to stop trusting him now. Even though recent events might call my good judgment into question, I didn't have anything else to go on. And his steady electricity soothed me, a soft hum that tingled the back of my scalp where my nape met my skull.

"Now what?" I said.

"Hit 'track now.'"

I clicked the mouse and the screen cleared. A map began to load. It showed the familiar thumb-shape of the San Francisco peninsula, with a scattering of location pins across it. "What am I looking at?"

"This is your phone's ping data for the last eight hours," Sebastian said. "Each of these pins is a spot where your phone contacted a cell tower."

I squinted at the crosshatched maze of streets. "That one's near my house."

He leaned over my shoulder, his focus intent on the screen, his proximity filling my awareness. "It pinged there twice. Once around 5 pm and then again around 9:30 pm."

"And in between," I said, "it was here. In SOMA, off Howard Street. The club. But we didn't get back to my apartment until after ten."

"He had it by then," Sebastian said. "That must have been when he did his...artwork. And maybe where he sent that message to Danny. We can find that out, too, if you want."

"I don't care about that," I said, impatient. "We know he sent it. Where is he now?"

"Here." Sebastian reached for the screen, pinching his thumb and forefinger to zoom the map out. His forearm brushed the top of my wrist, and the live-wire sensation of his kether jolted through me. I jumped back from the contact.

He froze and dropped his hand to his side. "I'm sorry."

"No, no." I scooted the chair back to give him room. "It's just very distracting." And I couldn't afford distractions right now. Not when Danny needed me.

"I feel it too, you know," he said, voice soft. "I don't know if it's the same thing you feel, but it's unmistakable. Like a pull, a rush. Like looking down from a height."

"Um." I glanced up and met his steady gaze. It shook me to my core. "It's not quite the same, but similar."

"I like it," he said, simple as that, his half-smile like an invitation. Then he shifted his attention back to the screen, and his expression turned somber. "There. This was only fifteen minutes ago."

Focus, Lily. I frowned at the pin that had appeared. "Twin Peaks? What's out there?"

He had already pulled up a second window, tapping in search terms, his answer a sharp indrawn breath. I leaned in close again, forgetting to keep my distance.

"Indie Journalist Kaine Puts Up 2 Mil for Designer Home in Exclusive San Francisco Neighborhood," Sebastian read out loud. I scowled. "Where does a guy like Tobias get that kind of money?" The guy couldn't have made those millions selling silver stakes on the internet or publishing video blogs about demons and government conspiracies.

"It could be a coincidence." Sebastian didn't sound convinced.

"It's not a coincidence." I stood, shrugging my borrowed coat back on.

"Lily." He straightened. "What are you going to do?"

"What do you think?" I avoided his look of concern, already headed for the door. "I'm going after him. I'm getting my friend back. Are you coming or not?"

IN THE PALE MOONLIGHT

"THIS ISN'T PARTICULARLY LEGAL, YOU KNOW," SEBASTIAN SAID, AND LET OUT the clutch on the Batmobile.

"I don't particularly care." I stared out the windshield at the lights of the city flashing past us. The breeze off the sea had cleared out most of the fog tonight, and a near-full moon hung yellow and huge at the tip of the Transamerica Pyramid. "That bastard tried to shoot Ariel and kidnapped my best friend. We're way past the point of legality. Besides, he's not human, and neither am I. This is cambion's law now."

He laughed his short, surprised laugh. "Lily Knight, law unto herself. I like it."

I didn't know if I liked it or not but I didn't have much of a choice. Any other time, his laugh would have warmed me to the core, but not now. In this clear, cold early morning, no warmth could reach me. My thoughts ran cold, too, if not entirely clear. In fact, the more I thought, the more a fog of anxiety and confusion descended upon me.

One week ago today, I'd stumbled out of the Black Cat into a morning much like this one. One week ago today, I'd wrestled with Tobias in the street. One week ago today, someone had crept into the Presidential Suite at the Ritz and driven a stake into Nepenthe's heart.

Tobias must have gone straight from his confrontation with me on the street to the murder scene. But Sebastian and Nepenthe would have almost beat him there, unless he pulled some kind of spidery cambion trick to get onto that balcony. I realized I didn't know much about how his capabilities stacked up to mine, or to a full-fledged demon. Maybe he had even fed that night to increase his strength, despite his self-hating denials. That would explain how he'd managed to overpower Nepenthe.

Shit. Maybe he had even used my kether. We'd touched in the club when Nepenthe and I ran into him, and then again after Ariel had given me a refill, when we struggled on the street. I hadn't thought he'd taken that much. But thanks to Sebastian's deep well, I'd learned that it didn't take much to make a difference.

What if this was all my fault? What if Nepenthe had died because of me?

What if I never saw Danny alive again?

The light touch of Sebastian's hand on mine startled me. As always, it carried that unmistakable charge of electricity, a tiny bolt of kether passing from his body to mine. He briefly wrapped my chilled fingers in his before placing his hand back on the wheel. I glanced over at him, but he kept his eyes fixed on the road.

"What was that for?"

"I thought you could use a little pick-me-up," he said. "We're almost there."

"What about you? It's late. Aren't you tired?"

"I'll be fine. You worry too much, Lily."

I liked him, I had to admit to myself. I liked him a lot. And for whatever reason, even if just because I reminded him of the woman whose loss still rankled fresh and raw in his heart, he seemed to like me, too.

Don't go down that road, I wanted to tell him. *It's not healthy.* People who loved demons...people who loved me...got hurt.

But I didn't say it. Right now, he was my one ally, and he had the technology and the resources to help me find Danny. And besides, it was a little early to say the word 'love,' even to myself.

A little early? No, it was way too early. I'd only known the guy for a week and he certainly didn't love me. Wanted me, yes. But love? I didn't think so.

The GPS chimed, announcing that we'd arrived, and I jumped. I peered out the car window at the darkened street, looking for house numbers. "Is that it?"

"I think so. The big Spanish revival one. So sayeth Ritter Intelligence Services."

I frowned up at the shadowy bulk with its arched windows and jacaranda trees. No lights on inside. "And you're sure he's at home?"

"Hmm.... My creeper technology says yes."

"Excellent."

"Lily," Sebastian said. He'd pulled up to the curb, but hadn't switched the car off. Worry swirled in his desiderata. "What's your plan?"

"I don't have a plan so much as a goal." I opened the passenger door. "Get Danny back by any means necessary. I'll figure out the rest as I go."

"What are you going to do? March up to his front door and ask him to give her up?"

I shrugged. "That sounds like a good enough plan to me."

"Dear God." He leaned back in his seat, casting his gaze toward the ceiling. "At least take the gun."

I shook my head. "I don't want it. I wouldn't know what to do with it. If I don't come out in twenty minutes, you can use it to come rescue me."

"Why don't I just come with you? You're going to need backup."

"No," I said. "He's half-demon, Sebastian. He's strong, he's volatile, and he's dangerous. You could get hurt, and I don't want to have to worry about that. You're staying here."

"What if he has other weapons?" Sebastian looked unhappy.

"I dealt with the gun. I'll deal with whatever else he has."

He sighed. "Have I mentioned that I don't think this is the best idea?"

"I didn't ask for your opinion." I got out of the car and slammed the door, stomping up the driveway and the curving stairs leading to the front door. The motion detection lights flared on as I went. I didn't care. Let the bastard see me coming. Let him feel afraid.

I pounded on the door. "Tobias Kaine!" I shouted. When nothing happened after about fifteen seconds, I hammered the door again. "Open up! I know you're in there."

Only silence answered me, and I raised my fist to knock a third time. As I did, the door swung open.

A tall, statuesque woman stood in the dark opening, her disheveled ruddy hair tumbling over her shoulders in wild waves. Its bright color made a stark contrast to her shock-white skin under the harsh illumination of the security lighting. Her eyes glowed green, wide and staring and inhuman.

"Theo?" I goggled at her. "What the hell are you doing here?"

She stretched her hands toward me, palms out, and I recoiled from the weeping, suppurating wounds that marred them, a monstrous stigmata. Her flesh had burned away until the white of bone showed beneath, as if she had clutched a molten bar with both hands. Pain and fear twisted her lovely face.

"Please, come quickly!" Her voice rasped over the words, hoarse and broken. "It's Tobias. He's killed him."

"What? Killed who? Theo, what happened?"

She didn't answer, the light in her eyes fading out as she crumpled to the floor.

Behind me, a car door slammed, and I whipped my head around. "No, Sebastian. Stay back!"

He halted on the sidewalk. "What happened?"

"I don't know yet." I pressed my fingers over Theo's pulse at her neck. It beat thready and fast. I took a breath, closed my eyes, and *pushed* a small amount of the kether inside me to her.

For a moment, I didn't think it would work, but then her eyes blinked open halfway, slitted and golden-green. I jumped back, but she didn't lunge for me.

I leaned closer again. Her chest rose and fell with her shallow breaths. Something dark and wet stained the sleeves and chest of her scarlet dress. Blood. Whose blood? Her own? Or someone else's?

I couldn't leave her there, half-blocking the doorway. Especially not with Sebastian so close by, humming with kether, the first thing she'd see if she woke.

"Upstairs," she muttered. "Help me. My hands...the silver..."

"Silver did this?"

She pushed herself up onto her elbows. "I tried to save him."

"Save who? Who did Tobias kill?" I looped my arm under her shoulders, lifting her bodily to her feet. Her answer turned into a grunt of effort, and she shook her head.

I bore her up, half-carrying her to the darkened stairwell that led up to the second floor. There, she faltered again, sinking down onto the bottom step. "I need a moment. You go," she said, voice faint. "In the bedroom. Maybe it's not too late."

I looked from her stricken face to the shadowy landing. Although nothing moved in the darkness, dread squirmed in my stomach as I climbed.

At the top of the stairs, a door stood ajar. Moonlight streamed from a window opposite, a dim silver glow that washed all color out to black, white, and shades of gray. It hid as much as it illumined. But it showed enough.

A man's body lay on the bed, sprawled and motionless. At the center of a spreading black stain, the stake protruding from the figure's bare chest glinted cold and cruel in the pale glow of the moon.

I crept closer. The body on the bed was long-limbed and broad-shouldered. The head was tilted back, mouth agape, a rictus of agony.

"No." My heart stuttered and stalled. I rushed to his side.

Then I stopped short, hands over my mouth. It wasn't Ariel staked out there like an offering, eyes wide and glassy, face purple with fresh bruises, blood seeping from his parted lips.

It was Tobias Kaine. And that meant he wasn't the one hunting us. He was one of the hunted.

I reached for the stake protruding from his chest, and halted just in time with a sharp indrawn breath. Remembering the oozing wounds on Theo's hands, I dug in my pockets and pulled the bloodstained gloves on over my trembling fingers.

I'd beaten him with those gloves earlier in the evening. Now, maybe I could save his life with them.

Kneeling above him, I yanked hard on the silver stake. The gloves slid and stuck to the blood that coated it. It resisted, then came free with a sickening sucking sound. I flung it away from me, and it hit the wall before clattering to the floor.

His chest had already begun to cave in. The corrosive power of the silver had ravaged his flesh. I hovered over him, irresolute. I didn't want to touch him, but I wanted the answers that only he could give me. I wanted to know what he knew. I wanted to know if he'd seen the face of his killer.

"Let me," a soft voice said from the doorway.

I turned to find Theo standing there, leaning heavily on Sebastian's shoulder. In the moonlight, Sebastian looked as pale and ill as she did.

"I thought I told you to stay in the car." My voice shook, and I lifted my arm to wipe the sweat that stood out on my forehead despite the chill of the night air from the open window.

Sebastian ignored this, his gaze fixed on the bed. "Is he dead? He looks dead."

"We are not dead until we are dust." Theo patted his shoulder, taking an unsteady step forward. "Let me," she said again. "I felt him fall. I feel him still. This one is mine."

"What do you mean, yours?" I stood back from the bed, frowning.

"I told you of the Claim," she said, with a trace of the imperious impatience she'd shown in my office on Tuesday morning.

God, that seemed like forever ago. It was only Wednesday now. No, Thursday. Today was Thursday... I shook myself, the import of her words registering on a several-second delay. "You can Claim a cambion?"

Theo inclined her head. She climbed onto the bed, straddling Tobias's prone body. His blood smeared her dress and bare legs. I averted my eyes, focusing on the same blood blackening my jeans. This moment between them seemed private and I didn't need to watch.

Sebastian made a choking sound, and I jerked my attention back to the bed. Theo had taken Tobias's face in its rictus of death between her bare hands, pressing her mouth to his.

"What are you doing?" Sebastian asked, the words strangled and shot through with a horror I didn't quite comprehend.

Theo dropped Tobias's head back to the pillow. She lifted her head, panting like she'd run a race. Her eyes had darkened, their pupils blown to black, ringed with green fire. "The kether gift," she said, gasping. "The vital kiss. It will knit his flesh together. He still...lives..."

And then she toppled to the side, her limbs sprawled akimbo, arm swinging limp from the bed.

"You can do that?" Sebastian turned to me. "You can give *each other* life force?"

"Sometimes, if we have enough reserves." I examined Tobias's still face. It did seem that his face had relaxed a little, his mouth slackening. His wide eyes fluttered shut. Around the hole the stake had made, the charred, blackened, desiccated flesh began to pink up as I watched.

"Holy shit," I muttered. "It worked."

"What about her?" Sebastian said.

Rounding the bed, I lifted her wrist with my gloved hand, inspecting the wounds on her palms. She must have taken the stake between her bare hands and pulled as the flesh sloughed away, until she lost her grip. But she, too, had already begun to heal, the wounds shallower now, scabbing over. "I think she'll be okay," I said. "If I understand it right, contact with silver stops our healing abilities and drains our kether. But once the silver is removed, the body can rebuild and sustain itself if enough kether remains. Or," I glanced up at him, "if we have a source available."

Desolation washed through his desiderata, a wave of regret so strong it rocked me from across the room. "You're saying that if I'd removed the stake like you just did, Nepenthe would have lived?"

Oh. I wanted to lie to him, tell him he couldn't have saved her. Tell him I couldn't have.

I chose radical honesty. "Maybe," I said. "But maybe not. She wasn't a cambion. We're stronger, in a way. We make our own kether. Not like you humans do—we still run on a deficit if we use our demon abilities at all, and it's hard to control that. It's instinctive. But we don't die without a source the way a full demon would."

"And there's no chance that we could...that she could..." He struggled to find words, grappling with a possibility he couldn't quite wrap his mind around.

I shivered. "I don't know." *We're not dead until we are dust.* Astarte and then Nepenthe had crumbled into glittering dust on the slab in Danny's morgue, and I'd just stood there. Could we have saved them, if we had known how? Could I have pulled the silver from Nepenthe's flesh and breathed her back to life?

Could Sebastian have done the same? Could Ariel?

Why hadn't Ariel...?

"Hand me that gun, Sebastian," I said softly.

"What?"

"The gun. Now!"

He pressed its weight into my hand, his fingers folding briefly over mine. Caution or comfort? Right now, I didn't care. I bent again to Tobias, taking him by the shoulder and shaking him until his teeth rattled in his head. Beside him, Theo didn't stir.

"Lily!" Sebastian sounded shocked. "Be careful."

Unheeding, I shook Tobias again. "Wake up," I said through gritted teeth, my face close to his. "Wake the fuck up, you rat bastard, and tell me who did this to you."

His cheek twitched, his eyelids fluttering. His lips moved, soundless.

I pressed the muzzle of the pistol to his temple. "What? I can't hear you!"

"'M sorry."

"Don't tell me sorry! Who did it?"

His throat worked. "Demon," he mumbled.

"Yeah, yeah, you and me both, buddy. We've been through this. Who?"

His eyes sprang open, and for a moment he fixed me with a lucid, terrified stare. "You..."

"Yeah, be afraid, Tobias. It's me. Focus, will you? Did you see his face?"

"You...know..." He grimaced, pained. His eyes drifted shut again. "Who."

"No, no, no, no. *No.*" I shook him again. "You don't get to do this, Tobias. Tonight, you get to be useful for once in your useless life. *Tell me who it was.* Or I swear to God I'll finish the job myself."

For a moment, Tobias didn't answer. Had he passed out again? But then he reached up and grabbed my shoulder, dragging me down toward him with surprising strength.

I yelped, trying to pull back. But he didn't touch my bare skin, only whispered something close to my ear. A single word that froze me in place, making me hope I hadn't heard right.

As if he'd expended his last conscious effort with that word, his grip loosened and his hand dropped away. I leaped back from him, but he didn't move again. Only his chest rose and fell with his shallow breathing.

"What is it?" Sebastian's urgent question made me jump. "Lily, what did he say?"

"We have to get out of here." I turned, brushing past him. "We have to go, now."

Sebastian followed close at my heels. "Why?"

I took the stairs two at a time. "I know who did it," I said over my shoulder. "I know who killed Nepenthe. I think I knew already. I just didn't want to think about it, so I didn't. I didn't even consider it. I'm so *stupid*."

"Lily—"

I turned back to him at the foot of the stairs, and he reared back, startled. "I want you to teach me how to shoot a gun," I said, low and fierce. "I want you to teach me first thing in the morning."

"Done," he said. "But I don't understand…"

"Neither do I." I took a deep, shaky breath. "And I don't know if I ever will."

He didn't say anything this time, just looked at me. His compassion welled up around me, acceptance without the need to understand. It enclosed me in a fragile bubble of safety. It gave me strength enough to finally say the words.

"It was Ariel." My voice trembled and broke on the name. "It was always Ariel. Oh, God…"

28

SILVER AND COLD

To his credit, Sebastian didn't ask any more questions just then. He didn't ask me if I was sure. He didn't even look that shocked. Instead, he bundled me into the car, turned up the heated seats, and sped back toward Pacific Heights. I sat motionless, but my mind raced faster than the roadster.

Most of what I knew of Nepenthe, I had learned from Ariel. Hell, most of what I knew about myself, about demons, about my powers and their source, came from lessons Ariel had taught me. If he had killed the three succubi, taken Danny, written that terrible warning on my wall, and tried to kill Tobias, I knew even less than I thought I did. I didn't know anything for sure.

Nepenthe had tried to tell Sebastian. She hadn't said *tell Lily it's a…*

She'd wanted to say, *Tell Lily it's Ariel.*

But if he had done all that, if he had lied to my face, manipulated me, and led me down the proverbial garden path, I really only wanted to know the answer to one single question.

Why?

"How are you holding up, Lily?" Sebastian finally chose to cut into the thick silence with a soft query.

"Pretty freaked, to tell you the truth." I stirred in my seat, grateful for a distraction from my pointlessly circling thoughts. "I'm worried for Danny. I'm worried about Theo and even that asshole Tobias, damn him. And I'm scared. Ariel knows everything there is to know about me."

Sebastian frowned. "Do you think he would hurt your friend?"

"I don't know what to think," I said. "Four days ago, I would have said that I didn't trust him. But now...I may not have trusted him to do what I thought was right, and I didn't trust him to always tell the whole truth, but I certainly trusted that he was no murderer. Now...the truth is, I don't know what he's capable of. That scares me more than anything else."

"But he hasn't hurt any humans, just demons."

"And now one cambion," I pointed out. "He hasn't hurt any other humans *that we know of.* Ariel...is not fond of humanity, and he's a sneaky bastard. That's part of what makes this all so strange. He did this...if he did this...in a way that people would notice."

"He's putting on a show."

"It seems like it," I said. "But for who?"

Sebastian spared me a quick, grim glance. "At a guess? You."

A chill crept up on me, quick and enveloping as evening fog rolling over the Golden Gate Bridge. "Of course," I said, numb. "If Ariel took Danny, he did it to get my attention. It's me he really wants. He wouldn't have pushed me to get involved otherwise."

"What does he want from you?"

"I wish I knew," I said. "None of it makes any sense."

Sebastian glanced at me again, then away. "You two have a history, right? You said he was your mentor."

"He was a bit more than that," I mumbled. Lover, teacher, tempter, friend. Dear god, I'd let him take me on the balcony where she died, outside the room where he'd killed her. "I'm starting to think that everything I ever knew about him was a lie."

"And you think he might come after you next?"

Hysterical laughter bubbled in my chest. "I hope he does. I really hope he does."

"Lily..." Sebastian's desiderata roiled with concern and fear. "Don't talk like that."

"What? No! It's just...it's the best chance I have of finding him. If he's trying to lure me somewhere or send a message, he hasn't done a very good job." I only hoped that Danny's dead body wouldn't be the rest of the message. "But if I do know Ariel at all, he has a plan. He'll seek me out when he's ready to execute it. And then…"

"And then you'll execute him," Sebastian said. "Is that right?"

"No," I said, too quickly. "I don't know. That's not what I meant."

As I spoke, we pulled into Sebastian's winding driveway. Relief washed over me, followed by a new wave of apprehension as the sunken garage door closed behind us. What if Ariel had beaten us here? Based on what had happened this weekend, even Sebastian's bespoke security system couldn't keep the incubus out if he wanted in.

Sebastian must have had the same thought. Rather than getting out of the car, he studied his phone, swiping through camera feeds of each room in his gigantic home, and then through each exterior view.

"More creeperware," I said, peering over his shoulder at the screen.

"The best that money can buy."

He thumbed the display off. "It looks clear, but I don't have 100% visual coverage. Give me the gun."

I sat back with a quick intake of breath. Somehow I'd forgotten the weight of Tobias' pistol in my pocket. It lay against my hip, the cold promise of violence. "You're serious," I said. "You think he's in there?"

"Better safe than sorry." He took it from me and checked the chamber in his precise, methodical way, then re-seated it with a click that echoed in the small, enclosed cab. He'd gone through the same motions earlier, but the routine of double-checking seemed to center him. "Ready?" he said.

I nodded. His adrenaline shimmered in the air, colored by a hint of fear. Not for himself, but for me. He wanted to protect me. It warmed the frost in my veins, just a little.

A thorough sweep of the house revealed nothing except the obscene size and elegance of his bachelor pad.

"Looks clear." Sebastian finally relaxed a fraction and turned to face me on the landing. "I can't guarantee my security will stop him if he does come back, though this might." He patted the handgun tucked in his belt.

I eyed it, hyper-aware of its presence but even more hyper-aware of him. "Do you really think a bullet can stop an incubus? The silver's only good if it sticks. You saw how quickly Theo recovered tonight."

"Maybe not," Sebastian said. "But I bet one in each kneecap would slow him down a bit."

I shivered. "If he didn't see you first. Demons are fast."

"All other things being equal, I'd still rather be armed." His clipped tone softened. "What's your plan, Lily? If you don't think the silver will stop him, then what?"

I laughed. I had no more than the rough semblance of a plan, but he flattered me by assuming the best. "I'll learn to handle that thing well enough to look intimidating. I'll track Ariel down and point it at him until he tells me where Danny is. Then I'll do whatever I have to do to get her back."

"I see." Sebastian raised an eyebrow, but didn't prod me further.

I appreciated him for it. As plans went, mine didn't offer any stunning brilliance. It presumed I could find Ariel, to start with. If the phone tracking method proved itself a dead end, I didn't have the first idea where to look for him. Did he have an apartment here in the city, a hotel room? Why hadn't I bothered to ask him such a simple question?

I shivered, wrapping my arms around myself in Sebastian's too-big coat. A faint, woodsy scent teased my nose, a ghost of his cologne, and I drew it into me like it was his kether, on a long, unsteady breath.

If I did find Ariel, my half-assed plan depended on my ability to make him believe I would shoot him with a silver bullet. My Presence didn't work on the incubus, so I would have to mean it.

Finally, my plan took it on faith that Ariel didn't intend to kill Danny or torture her or worse. I clung to that faith, that he'd taken her as collateral to increase his hold over me. The alternative didn't bear thinking about. He had to have a motive beyond mere sadism or revenge for...what? Why would Ariel want to hurt me? It didn't make any sense.

Then again, why would he want to hurt Penelope? None of this made sense.

"The truth is..." I scrubbed my hands over my face, rubbing grit from my eyes. "Ariel's older than me. He's more powerful. He has my best friend, and I don't know how to stop him. I don't know the right thing to do."

Sebastian frowned, his desiderata muted and soft with worry. "You should try to get some sleep," he said. "There's nothing more you can do right now. It's not a good idea to shoot a gun for the first time when you're sleep deprived, let alone facing down a demon."

"You're right, I'm exhausted." I didn't know how I could sleep with Danny out there in Ariel's clutches, and I didn't trust Sebastian's extra proximity alarms and motion detectors to alert us if the incubus returned. But my steps dragged with fatigue as I headed to the guest room.

Then I remembered something, and stopped. "Sebastian?"

"Yeah?" he said, immediately.

I glanced back. He hadn't moved toward the master bedroom, but instead stood still, his intent gaze fixed on me. "I need your help," I muttered, blushing. "Again."

That quick half-smile flashed across his face, making my stomach quiver. "What do you need, Lily?"

My face heated further as I shed his coat and handed it to him, revealing the form-fitting golden corset I'd worn on stage. It seemed more like days than hours ago, now. I dipped my head, turning my back to him. "Will you unlace me, please?"

His sharp inhalation electrified me. I held my own as his footsteps drew near, his closeness flooding the exposed skin along my spine with the warmth of sunlight. Warmth, and yet I trembled.

"It would be my pleasure," he said, his voice soft and rough at once, like cut velvet.

Then he touched me, ever so lightly. The tips of his gentle, clever fingers brushed my skin as the corset laces came undone under his hands. I closed my eyes, his kether beating its sweet song into my veins, and tried not to moan out loud.

Then it was over, too fast. I breathed again and raised my hands to my chest so the corset-form wouldn't slip off and expose me completely.

He didn't move from behind me. His breath stirred my hair. Just a single step would close the gap between us but neither of us took it. Instead, I stepped away from him and all he offered me.

"Good night, Sebastian," I whispered, and fled the landing for the safety of my lonely room. His kether lent me speed beyond human ken, and I didn't give him a chance to answer me, or even to watch me go, this time.

✣

I DIDN'T DREAM of flight or halls of mirrors. I dreamed of fireflies sparking and dancing in the dark, hot, humid summer nights of my childhood, and a man's hand on my shoulder. He guided me forward the way my father would guide me, before he discovered my true nature.

"Don't fear the darkness, Lily," he said, and it wasn't my human father's voice at all. "There will always be a light."

I woke with a start and the sharp ache of loss in my throat. Early sunlight filtered through the curtained window of Sebastian's guest room. Delilah had left her refuge under the bed and curled up beside me, her warm weight pressed against my leg. Sebastian's kether gift lingered in my veins, waiting for an outlet, but none of that brought me comfort as cold reality flooded over me.

Last night, the whole world had crumbled beneath my feet. I had to find Danny before I lost her, too. I swallowed, the ache in my throat tightening into a hard lump. What if it was too late? What if I'd already waited too long? I should have done more, faster. I should have known Ariel was behind this. I should have—

A brisk rap on the door made me jump. Pulse racing, I sat up. "Hello?"

"Good, you're awake." Sebastian's brusque tone didn't do anything to ease my anxiety. "Are you decent?"

I glanced down at my long t-shirt and bare legs. No, I couldn't hang around Sebastian like that, or we wouldn't get anything done. "Give me a second." I dragged on the pair of jeans I'd shoved in my overnight bag and flung open the door.

His face grave, he barely gave my braless and bedheaded state a second glance. "Come with me. I need to show you something." He turned without another word, moving with long, swift strides toward the study.

I hurried after him, still buttoning my jeans. "What is it?"

"Look." In the study, he had the phone tracker application pulled up on his monitor. Now he pushed a button, and it reloaded to show the Western United States. A new pin marker had appeared there overnight. It located my phone somewhere in the Sierra range, hundreds of miles east of San Francisco.

I rubbed sleep out of my eyes and squinted at the screen. "I don't understand."

"The time stamp on this is 4:25 am," Sebastian said. "Why would he have gone that far? And how did he get there so fast? We know the phone pinged from Tobias's neighborhood at 12:30."

I squinted at the screen. "If he drove top speed and left right away, he might have gotten to the mountains in a few hours."

"No." Sebastian shook his head. "The math doesn't add up. That's over two hundred miles from here. He'd have to travel more than a hundred miles an hour without stopping and you can't drive like that over the summit." He hit a few keys to bring up a new map, this time with a series of little pins, and his face changed.

"What is it?" Foreboding curled in my stomach.

"It's your phone's location history over the last twelve hours," he said. "Interesting, don't you think?"

I leaned in close, my efforts to keep space between our bodies forgotten. The little pins told a story. The first few clustered around the city, as we'd observed the night before. But then, around 2:00 am, my phone had moved east at a startling pace. It had taken just over two hours to travel from San Francisco to the spot in the mountains where it had pinged its last known location, somewhere in the no-mans-land southeast of Reno.

"That makes zero sense."

"It is odd." Sebastian threw himself into his chair and began playing with the map, zooming it in over the city. He traced the first cluster of pins like breadcrumbs, then slid the map sideways. "So is this. Notice how straight this line is?"

That sinking sensation began again, like the ground had dipped beneath my feet. "He didn't follow the freeway, or any roads. He took the most direct route, as the crow flies."

Or as the demon flew, on black wings made of smoke and shadows...

"Maybe he got on a plane." Sebastian studied the pins. "But I've never gotten from downtown to SFO in less than an hour and a half and he didn't even go far enough south to hit the airport."

"Maybe he has his own private helicopter?" I ventured.

"Maybe." His arched eyebrow told me he knew I was stretching it, even if he couldn't guess why. "Where do you think he would go?"

"Back East somewhere. New York City, maybe?" But my spine crawled. Another location fell on a direct line from the trajectory of pins, closer and yet more frightening than what I'd voiced. Out there in the desert, beyond the Sierra Mountains, lay the site Ariel always spoke of with reverence, hatred, and near-obsession: Tonepah Valley.

You're far too young to understand what it means to survive like we did.

The things we did. The things we saw.

Sebastian shifted his attention back to me, a narrow, speculating gaze. "What are you thinking?"

"I'm thinking Ariel didn't go to New York." A surge of restless energy seized me, the need to move. I folded my arms over my chest, pacing the length of the room and back. "I'm thinking I know where he went, where he must have taken Danny." Pausing behind him, I leaned over his shoulder and jabbed my finger at the screen. "*There.*"

Sebastian's brow furrowed, though his energy jumped at my proximity like I'd given him an electric shock. "That's the Tonepah Exclusion Zone. There's nothing out there but miles of trackless desert. Why would he take her there?"

"Because," I said, grim, "he wants me to follow him."

"He's using her as bait." Sebastian's desiderata shifted, darkening. "And you're going to take it. Lily—"

"Don't." I set my jaw. "I have no choice. If I want her back, Sebastian, I have to play by his rules. That's how this works with him. That's how it always worked. He holds all the cards, and he cheats."

"That sounds like a losing game." Sebastian waited for me to answer, and when I didn't, he sighed. "You think he knew we would track him there?"

I shook my head. "No, I think he'll come back for me. Soon. Tonight. And when he does, I need to be ready." In the doorway, I faced him. "There's no time to waste. Teach me how to shoot that bastard down."

I didn't know Ariel like I thought I did. He made that much clear last night. But I knew him well enough to guess his next move, after all. And with that, the first inkling of a real plan began to form in the back of my mind.

My stomach quivered, nausea and anticipation fluttering like a flight of poisonous butterflies, and I turned away from Sebastian's questioning eyes.

To beat Ariel, I would have to do the one thing I swore I wouldn't do.

I would have to give in to the demon inside. I would have to become more like him.

29

NO ANGEL

"Give me the gun, Sebastian," I said.

He tucked the weapon in his belt and fixed me with a stern gaze. "No."

"What do you mean, no?" I considered taking it from him, just to show him that I could. Easy enough, since his lanky strength couldn't match me after a dose of his kether and a good night's sleep.

I had only one problem with that theory. I'd have to touch him again, and each successive touch we shared seemed to carry higher stakes and higher voltage than the last. I crossed my arms instead, imitating his stubborn posture. "I thought you were going to teach me how to shoot."

"I am." He sounded annoyed. "But before you handle a gun, you have to learn the first rule of gun safety."

"It's not 'don't talk about gun safety'?" I bounced on the balls of my feet. My body hummed with unused energy. I didn't want to talk. I wanted to run a marathon or go several rounds in a boxing ring. I needed to do something, anything, to take my mind off what Ariel might have done to Danny, what he wanted from me, and what I might have to do to get her back.

I looked Sebastian up and down, not bothering to keep it surreptitious. Even in his range gear, with ear and eye protectors, his desiderata rang out clear as a struck bell and belied the frown he gave me.

He sighed. "The first rule of gun safety is that your gun is always loaded. Even if you think it's not, you treat it like it is. Got it?"

"Got it. Now can I try?"

"Not yet. The second rule is something we call muzzle discipline."

"Sounds kinky."

"This is serious." He didn't even crack a smile. "Muzzle discipline means that you never point a gun at anything you don't want to destroy."

"Oh, okay." Less sexy, but pretty badass. "I'm listening."

"The third rule is what's called trigger discipline."

"Seems like gun people are really into discipline."

His eyebrow arched higher. "Trigger discipline means that you don't put your finger on the trigger until you're ready to fire."

"And destroy something."

"Yes. I'll show you." He drew the gun out with care, pointed toward the floor as he swung around to face the target. "Watch my hands."

I edged around to the side of him. He stood with his left foot slightly forward, knees bent, both hands gripping the weapon. His finger stretched along the slide of the gun, beside the trigger but not crooked over it, right up until he moved his finger to the trigger.

I expected it, but the gunshot still startled me, thunderous in the underground range despite my ear protection. The paper target shuddered, a small, precise hole cut through its center.

"You're a good shot," I said.

"I'm a passable shot." But he flushed slightly at the compliment as he laid the gun on the shelf built into the booth. "Now you try. I loaded it with regular rounds so you won't waste the silver. Go ahead, pick it up. And for the love of God, try not to point it at me."

I glared at him. "I won't. This isn't rocket science."

"You'd be surprised how many people forget, especially when it's their first time. Come on, post up."

I took his place at the front of the booth, trying to imitate his stance. "Like this?"

"Other foot forward. May I?"

I nodded, then stilled as he stepped up behind me. His hands closed over my hips with a firm but gentle grip, his breath warm on my neck as he adjusted my posture. His desiderata enveloped me, caressing me, inviting me. Heat pooled low in my belly. I licked my lips, fixing my eyes on the target. I couldn't let him distract me like this.

"No," he said. "Don't look at the target. Line up the sight and focus on that."

I lifted the pistol. It weighed more than I'd expected, heavy as death and cold as justice. "Okay."

"Now, breathe out as you squeeze the trigger. It will improve your aim." Sebastian dropped his hands, moving back to give me space.

Target. Sight. Breathe. Shoot. The gun jerked like a living thing in my hands. The target shuddered. The acrid scent of gunpowder filled my nostrils and coated the roof of my mouth, saltpeter and sulfur, like the stinking breath of hell. It dampened my awareness of Sebastian's desiderata and chilled me to my core.

I deposited the pistol gingerly on the shelf as if it had burned me, backing away.

"What's wrong?" Sebastian said. "That was a pretty good first try. A little low, but you hit the paper."

I shook my head. "I don't like it."

"We can try a different—"

"No!" My voice cracked, and I covered my face in my hands. But my fingers smelled of gunpowder, too. It choked me with its reek of death and justice. "Fuck! I can't do this."

"Whoa." He was at my side, his arm around my waist to steady me as he led me to a bench against the back wall. "Sit."

I sank down on the bench and swallowed hard, wiping my palms on the vest he'd lent me. "I'm sorry."

"It's okay." He sat down next to me, shoulder to shoulder. "We can take a break."

"No, I can't." I pulled away from him, hugged myself to stop from shaking. "He'll come for me, Sebastian. I have to face him. And then…"

"I know," he said. "It's not an easy thing."

"You don't know. You can't know." I ripped the headset off, tossing it to the ground. "I can't just practice to… It's *Ariel*. I can't just shoot him!"

"You're practicing so you can defend yourself," Sebastian said. "There's nothing wrong with that. I know he was your friend, but he's no angel, Lily."

My harsh laugh tore from me, half a sob. "You can say that again. But..."

"But you still feel guilty?"

"It's not that." I fiddled with my safety glasses, turning them over in restless fingers. "Not exactly. It's more, who am I to decide his fate? I never wanted this."

"You're a prosecutor," he said. "If anyone's qualified to make that call, it's you."

"Prosecutor, yes. But judge, jury, and executioner? I don't think so. I'm no moral authority among demons. I'm not without my own sins." *Chief among them, you.* "And it's not much of a case. Some biased testimony from an unreliable witness. Circumstantial evidence. I don't even know his motive in all this. Why would an incubus kill his own kind?" I broke off, Ariel's words floating into memory.

Why does anyone kill anyone, Lil? We're not so different from humans, you know.

Jealousy comes to mind...

"You believe he did it, though," Sebastian said.

"Yes," I said, quiet and cold. "I do."

"Well, then." Sebastian unfolded himself from the bench. "You said it yourself last night. Human law doesn't apply here. This is cambion's law."

"All that means is that there's no one else to do what must be done." But I stood, picked up my discarded headset, and donned my safety glasses. For the moment, the world held steady as Sebastian, waiting for my word. For the moment, that would have to be enough.

"Ready to try again?" he said softly.

"Let's do it," I said.

Stepping forward, I called on his kether to steady me. Then I took up the gun again in both my hands, squared my hips, and faced my target.

Target. Sight. Breathe. Shoot.

"Bang, you're dead." The whispered words rasped, dry as dust and ash in my mouth.

If only it were that simple.

REVELATIONS

"THERE'S SOMETHING YOU'RE STILL NOT TELLING ME," SEBASTIAN SAID.

I leaned my elbows on his balcony railing, swirling the half-full glass in my hand, and glanced sideways at him. Behind him, the western horizon blazed with the light of the sinking sun. In a few minutes the cresting wall of fog would roll in from the Pacific and swallow the last of the late afternoon light, and my time would run short.

After our extended shooting lesson, we had checked in with Berry, just in case I had misinterpreted everything and Danny had come home safe in the night. But she hadn't, and the medical examiner's office had heard nothing from her, either. Berry had made a police report. She cried tears of rage over their wait-and-see attitude, and Sebastian said all the right things while I stood by, unable to touch her or speak words of comfort that didn't choke me with their lies.

I'd called Detective Huang, too, and pleaded with him to track down Ariel's local address. But he seemed more interested in asking me about my whereabouts at the time of the murders and became increasingly skeptical when I tried to explain why I couldn't turn over my phone.

Sebastian had paid for an expensive dinner I could only pick at. Back at his house, he made me a fancy cocktail that, thanks to my demon nature, did nothing to lift the weight of dread in my chest.

"This is a stunning view." I kept my tone light, sipping my drink to cover my discomfort. "And an exceptional cocktail."

"Lily, I may be only human, but I'm no fool. I can tell you're buying time with flattery so you don't have to say what you're actually thinking."

"Damn," I muttered. "I must really be off my game."

"Seems so. You're not even succubusing me properly. You're just using plain old human-style deflection."

"Apparently not very well." I flashed him a winning smile. "So 'to succubus' is a verb now? I like it. Very modern. Like 'to impact.' I bet it'll catch on like wildfire."

"Well, you don't have to tell me if you don't want to." His energy had gone jagged, his guard snapping up.

"Look, I'm sorry," I said. "It's not that I don't want to tell you the truth. It's just that I think it might be hard for you to believe me."

He turned to face me, his expression even and challenging. "Try me."

I opened my mouth, then closed it again, my focus distracted by the sun dropping behind the fog bank and the swift twilight falling with it. "Maybe it's better if I show you. Come with me."

He frowned, but followed me back inside and down the hall to his study. I touched the monitor, waking it, and brought up the tracker that still showed the pings from my lost phone. The last one still showed a time stamp from twelve hours ago.

"What am I looking at?"

"It should—" I drew a sharp breath. "There."

The tracker app refreshed itself. A new ping appeared, just east of the Sierras. Out there, the sun would have dipped down below the peaks already, spreading a cloak of darkness in the mountains' shadow.

"That's current," Sebastian said. "He's on the move. How did you know?"

"The last thing I remember from Friday night, before I woke up here…" I stumbled over the words. "Ariel and I visited the crime scene."

He went still, his eyes widening. I pushed on. "We weren't exactly supposed to be there, and we were surprised by some cops. We panicked. He…he asked to take my kether, and when I said yes, he drained me dry."

"*Ariel* did that to you?"

"I let him do it! I said yes to the kether pull. I didn't expect him to take everything I had, and we were a little short on options."

"He took advantage," Sebastian said, his tone severe.

Funny how he said it like that, as if it were obvious. And yet I had consented to the pull. Hadn't I? "That's not the point." I searched again for words that didn't sound ridiculous. "The very last thing I remember, before I blacked out… We were trapped out on that balcony. Sebastian, I think he picked me up and just…flew away."

He stared. "What do you mean, flew?"

"I mean just that. I remember looking up and seeing his wings unfolding against the sky."

"Okay," Sebastian said, dubious. "Ariel's a big guy, but I don't know how he would hide a pair of giant wings, even under that big trench coat he wears."

"He doesn't have them all the time. He never did before…I told you it would be hard to believe."

"It's not that I don't believe you," he said. "I'm just trying to understand."

"I think the wings are more…ethereal might be the right word. Energetic? He had to do a kether-pull to manifest them, and he had to pull a lot. That's why he drained me like that."

"I see. It's more of a final form kind of deal."

I grimaced. "You're making fun of me. But yeah, that sounds right."

"I'm not making fun." Indeed, his face held no mockery. "You're saying that after Ariel kidnapped Danny, he flew east under his own power. Wouldn't he risk being spotted that way?"

"That's why he'd wait for nightfall to come back. At night, he'd hardly even need a glamour to turn away curious eyes. And he'd need all his kether reserves to make the return trip."

Sebastian said softly, "Do you think he took kether from Danny?"

"I sure as hell hope not." But his words hit like a punch in the gut. Despite all his pretty words to me, I knew now that Ariel wouldn't stop at dubious consent for a kether-pull. And while Danny exclusively dated women these days, she still identified as bi when the topic of sexual orientation came up.

The thought of Danny helpless and unconscious, maybe even brain-damaged and changed forever, hurt worse than the thought of losing her completely.

On the monitors, the tracking app refreshed again. The pin ticked closer, over the mountains now, marking Ariel's swift, inexorable flight.

I had two hours, maybe less, before he reached us.

I straightened and turned, meeting Sebastian's gaze. The blue eyes that just a week ago seemed cold and hard held the depth and warmth of twin lakes in sunshine, but the shadow of worry dappled his desiderata. "Sebastian." My voice shook, but I had to do this, for Danny, for Penelope, for Astrid…and for me. "I need to ask you something."

His energy shifted, deepened. "Then ask."

"I don't…" I struggled for the right words, guilt twisting in my belly. "You've done so much for me in these last few days." And this final thing was a hell of a favor to ask. Theo's words echoed in my mind.

Their souls become our own, at least in part.

If I believed Ariel, that process had already begun. But I didn't know what to believe anymore.

"I don't mind." He stepped toward me, close enough that his warmth radiated across my skin. "What is it, Lily?"

The steady beat of his desiderata strengthened, a slow counterpoint to my own pounding pulse. It drew me like a lodestone, anchored me. "If I'm going to face Ariel and survive," I said, "a silver bullet won't be enough."

"Ah." It shuddered out of him on a long exhalation. "You need a secret weapon. You need kether."

"Yes," I said, and then winced at the ripple that went through his energy. "I'm sorry. I didn't want it to be like this. I wanted—" I wanted something different, something I couldn't have, an exchange of pleasure that didn't include trading power. But I needed that power, now. Ariel had left me no choice. "I need your consent to do this. I need you to understand what it is I'm asking for." *It's your soul we're risking.*

But what did that mean? I couldn't wrap my mouth around the words any better than I could wrap my head around Theo's warnings.

"I've done this before, remember? If you're asking what I think you're asking, I understand well enough." His short laugh trembled out of him. "I find I want you very badly right now. Is that the glamour you warned me about? Are you succubusing me?"

I shook my head. "Not on purpose." How could I know? Could I really trust his consent in this moment?

But then he cupped my face in his hands, stroking the hair away from my cheek. That skin to skin connection snapped into place between us, his kether a soothing pulse of heat, a low-voltage current rather than a full strength charge.

"My answer is yes." His tone roughened, pupils dilated as his desiderata surged. "I'm not afraid of you, Lily."

"I know," I whispered. "But you should be."

"Maybe you should let me be the judge of that."

"You don't understand," I said. "What I've done, what I can do. I could hurt you, Sebastian. You wouldn't even be the first."

"The capacity to hurt one another is a feature of interpersonal relationships," he said. "It's a risk I'm willing to take."

"But *why*?" The question tore from my throat, hope and despair in equal measure.

"I know you think you're a monster." His voice dropped low and soft, caressing. "But I don't see that. I see a woman who tries so hard to do what is right. And I trust you, Lily. Understand that."

I shut my eyes. "I trust you, too," I whispered. "It's myself I can't trust."

"Then let me help with that," he said. "If you want me. Do you, Lily? Do you want this as much as I do?"

He left the second part of the question unspoken. Did I want him, or did I simply need what he could offer me? I opened my eyes again to find him standing before me, waiting for my answer, his intent gaze fixed on my face. His desiderata blazed around him, an afterimage that reached across the space that separated us.

"I..." My voice failed me, and I took a breath. "Yes, I want you, and I need this. But I'm afraid..."

"Don't be."

Don't fear the darkness, Lily. There will always be a light...

I drew a sharp breath, and he stepped toward me, took my face between his hands again, and kissed me.

The renewed force of his kether washed over me, pure and intoxicating, and I opened to him. He responded by deepening the kiss, his tongue sweeping my mouth as if tasting me. I shut my eyes, willing myself not to draw too much despite the connection firing between us. I wanted this to last.

If my plan didn't work, I might never get another chance. I might not survive the night. But I had to make sure Sebastian would.

When we broke apart, breathing hard, I put both hands on his chest to steady myself. He dropped his hands to my hips, light pressure holding me against him.

"I have one condition," I said, and his inhalation lifted his chest beneath my palms.

"What is it?"

"I need your control." My voice wavered as I struggled to maintain my own. "Bind me, Sebastian. Stop things if I pull too hard. Only touch me where you have to. Please…" And I remembered as I spoke the first time I had begged him, in a voice barely human, barely a person's voice at all. Just a demon, hungering.

But he looked at me like I was some kind of miracle, like an angel bending down from heaven. "You mean that?" he said. "That's your condition?"

"Is that a yes?" I ventured, tentatively.

"Yes, Lily, I can do those things. And gladly." His hands on my hips tightened, pulling me closer. "Condition accepted." His lips crashed into mine again, harder this time, aggressive, claiming, and I melted against him, letting the force of his kiss sweep me up and intoxicate me, crying out into his mouth with what was at once relief and deepening need.

"Sebastian," I said, pleading, when he drew back again.

"Shh. Come with me," he said, and offered me his hand.

WE BARELY MADE it to the bedroom. I would have gone for it on the landing, but Sebastian kept pulling me forward.

"I figured you'd take me to your dungeon," I teased him.

"Bold of you to assume that I have one."

"Are you denying it?"

He shook his head at me. "Sweet Lily, we haven't negotiated anything we could do in a room with hard points that I can't do with you in this one."

"Show me," I said, and surged against him. His hardness strained toward me through his jeans and he cursed under his breath, pushing me backwards until the back of my legs hit the bed. "That's what I intend to do." He shoved me lightly so that I fell onto the mattress. Then he leaned over to open a drawer in the bedside table and pulled out the padded leather restraints I'd worn once before.

"Hold out your wrists." His desiderata crackled with electricity strong enough to give me goosebumps.

I obeyed, and he fastened them, fingers sure and gentle. Each time the tips of them brushed my forearm, I trembled at the sweet shock of kether that leaped from his skin to mine. The connection strengthened with each touch. How could a bond between human and demon grow this fast? What did it mean for the future? And what if I couldn't hold back despite our precautions?

He used the restraints to draw my arms up above my head. The soft clink of chains made me shiver all over again, and I craned my neck to get a better view. His serious, focused expression and methodical movements stoked the heat building in my core.

"Test them," he said. "Make sure they're comfortable."

I experimented, lifting my arms and pulling the chains taut. He hadn't left me much slack and he'd fastened the cuffs tight enough that I couldn't slip out of them. "I'm good."

"Good." He stood over me, head tilted to the side, as if admiring his work.

My breath hitched and I didn't stop the soft whine rising in my throat. "Sebastian, please..."

He didn't move, but his lips quirked. "Please, what?"

"I need it," I whispered, face aflame. When he raised an eyebrow, I added in a rush, "I need you."

"Hmm," he said, and his tone shook me. "If you mean that, open your legs for me."

I bent my knees up and let them splay outward. My skirt rode up on my thighs, and I had no way of pulling it down again. His face changed then, his desiderata shifting to a swift, dark current. He knelt between my legs, gripped my hips, and locked his gaze on mine. After a long, dizzying moment, I had to turn my head to the side. I couldn't bear the intensity of his regard.

"You're not used to this, are you?" he said.

"Used to what?" My tongue stumbled over the words, half-drunk with his proximity.

"Being the focus," he said. "You're used to giving others what they want to get your needs met. You haven't had much opportunity to think about your desires."

I shook my head, mouth dry. He shifted forward, his weight half-pinning me, and dropped his lips for a brief moment to my collarbone, a feather-light touch that sparked through me like a fireworks display. His hands skimmed up my thighs, pushing the fabric of my skirt aside, and he bent to press his mouth to the seam of my panties, just above my hip. I dropped my head back onto the bed, a moan rising unbidden in my throat.

Then he halted his leisurely exploration and pulled back. I whimpered, head tossing from side to side, straining for the touch I wanted. I hadn't let myself have this in so long, and the pure physical pleasure of touch alternated with momentary sips of kether threatened to tip me over the precipice of my precariously held control. "You're torturing me."

"Patience, Lily. All in good time." He punctuated his teasing words with a long kiss pressed to my core. The warmth of him radiated through the thin fabric of my panties, and I moaned again. Pleasure without kether felt wholly unfamiliar, raw, both incomplete and exquisite.

He used the cloth as a barrier at first. Then he slipped one finger underneath and dipped into me, his touch agonizingly light, drawing back when my kether draw became too strong, returning before I started to weep in frustration. But this was good, this was enough. The slow inexorable sensation undid me. I floated on a kether-high the likes of which I'd never experienced.

But when he positioned himself over me, hard against my entrance, I froze.

He stilled too, looking down at me, breathing hard. His desiderata roared like the ocean, held back by a seawall of uncompromising control. "We don't have to do this, Lily," he said. "Do you want it? Tell me."

"I want it. I want you. But…"

"But what?"

I turned my face into his stroking hand. "With you inside me…it's all I want. It's everything, but I don't know if I could hold back. I can't protect you from the kether-drain."

His lips brushed mine as he spoke. "Remember, I am in control. Do you understand?"

"I understand," I said, shuddering. "I'm ready if you are."

He held my gaze. "I am."

In answer, I bucked up my hips against him. His breath caught on a ragged gasp at that, and he drove himself into me. The contact electrified me, our communion beyond words now, a connection throbbing through me from the point where our bodies met. His pace matched the rhythm of my need and his steady desiderata surged over all of it in an exquisite feedback loop, building until it crested in a wave that carried us both up and over the edge. We reached our peak in a wild, sweet unison that shook and echoed through our joined bodies like music.

I lost time. I lost myself. I didn't know how many minutes had passed when I came back to myself with a start, afloat on kether, full and sleek and sated. I wanted to move, to dance, to laugh out loud in joy. I stirred.

Sebastian's weight lay atop me, a dead weight pinning me to the mattress in his master bedroom, arms and legs limp and motionless.

Horror seized me, even through the kether-glow, a cold knife of dread sliding into my heart. *Please just let him be asleep.*

"Hey," I said, mouth at his ear. When he didn't respond, I called his name. "Sebastian!"

Nothing. No movement, not even a hint of his desiderata buzzed against me.

Then, through my panic, I felt his breath, warm and even, tickling me where my neck met my shoulder. The whisper of his kether still trickled into me where our skin touched. I hadn't killed him.

My arms still stretched above my head, the snug cuffs binding my wrists to the bedframe. I gave them an experimental tug, and the leather split with a soft tearing noise, easy as ripping paper. I was free.

"Damn," I muttered. "Sorry, Sebastian." I put one hand on each of his shoulders and shook him, once. This time, I took extra care not to use too much force. But when he still didn't move, I rolled his body off me with almost no effort at all, and sat up.

He lay on the bed in a state of half-undress, chest rising and falling, a faint half-smile curving his mouth. By all appearances, he was asleep. I might have believed it if I had any success at rousing him.

"Oh, no. This isn't happening. Not again..." Rising, I paced the bedroom floor, trying to think.

It could be okay. He'd done this before. Nepenthe had drained him unconscious last week, and he was walking and talking by the next day. He hadn't suffered brain damage then. But she'd woken him with a kether gift, and I didn't know how to do that. Ariel, in his infinite wisdom and fathomless lies, had never seen fit to teach me that trick. When I drew from humans under his tutelage, I maintained control by never getting too close, never letting a connection grow, and never, ever achieving climax. Only with Ariel did I allow myself a true release, trusting his experience to guide me and keep me safe.

Oof. That realization knocked the wind out of me. In hindsight, I couldn't have made a more disastrous choice.

But Sebastian told me he and Nepenthe always played hard. He'd known the effects and he'd survived them before. It probably went a long way toward why he hadn't feared me.

Well, the least I could do would be to tuck him into bed so he woke up comfortable, instead of half-on, half-off the bed with his pants around his knees. I turned back toward him and froze, staring.

But not at him. A mirror hung on the wall above the bed, and I'd glimpsed my reflection in it.

And my reflection had wings.

They rose from my shoulders like twin shadows, indigo shot through with tiny glimmering lights. The pinions shimmered and shifted with me, faintly translucent, skimming the floor like a queen's train. I could see the wall behind me through them as I gaped at the mirror.

I glanced over my shoulder. Viewed directly, they confused my eyes, a transparency of a night sky full of stars laid across my field of vision in the shape of trailing feathers. Curious, I shrugged my shoulders back. Silent, weightless, the wings flexed and unfurled, stirring a breeze that caressed my cheek. If they stirred the air, they could theoretically carry me.

Holy fuck.

Like a woman in a dream, I approached the bed, entranced by the play of those feathers in the mirror, the sparkle of their tiny starry lights. They twinkled like fireflies in the warm darkness of a summer evening.

I tore my eyes away from the mirror just long enough to wrestle Sebastian under the covers. His weight meant nothing to me now, but his long limbs sprawled everywhere and made his bulk unwieldy.

Finished with my self-appointed task, I straightened. Out of the corner of my eye, movement flickered in the mirror: another winged figure, silhouetted in the window. I whirled, pulse pounding loud in my ears, but there was no one there, only my own reflection.

My hand lingered at Sebastian's temple, brushing back a wayward lock of dark hair that had fallen into his face, careful not to touch his skin. I'd taken enough from him already.

"Sorry, Sebastian," I said again. "I warned you…"

"Well, well," purred a resonant, slightly accented voice behind me. "Isn't this a pretty scene. The demon tucking in her lover like a mother with her child. So very touching."

Heart in my throat, I leaped to my feet. Or rather, floated. My wings lifted me on their downdraft, pinions scraping the ceiling. I turned in the air to face the golden-haired, golden-eyed incubus who stood by the window, smirking at me.

"Ariel." My feet touched down lightly on the floor, and my wings settled and folded as if I'd always known what to do with them. "I've been waiting for you."

CHILD OF NIGHT

"Waiting for me, have you?" Ariel drew out the words, slow and sweet as poisoned honey. "I must say, it doesn't look like you've been waiting. In fact, it looks like you've been quite busy, haven't you?"

"What the hell do you care what I do?"

"Let's call it a professional interest, my dear. Always good to see a student earn her wings, so to speak."

"You wanted this," I whispered. Of course he had. He'd planned this, engineered it, whispered suggestive phrases in my ear, and when that didn't work, he'd laid me at Sebastian's feet in kether-draught. "Why?"

"Lily, darling, I was only looking after you. He's the only prey in which I've ever seen you take more than a passing interest. I must say, I was beginning to despair of you."

"Prey? He's not my prey." Was he? We were... the word *lover* didn't seem quite right, but then, neither did *friend*. But what we had just done hadn't felt like an interaction between hunter and quarry. Maybe Sebastian had it right when he called the Exchange a kind of symbiosis.

"If you say so, my dear. Whatever you call it, I believe thanks are in order."

"What, so you found him for me and dangled him until I took the bait, and now you're patting yourself on the back for it?"

"Oh, no." He sounded amused. "I wish I'd planned for this. But no, this was just a bonus prize."

His smugness infuriated me so much I almost forgot to fear him. That could be a deadly mistake. *He killed Nepenthe!* "Where's Danny, you bastard? What did you do to her?"

"Ah, I'm so glad to hear you got my message." He smiled upon me with beneficent pride. "She's safe, I assure you. Well, as safe as she can be, under the circumstances."

"What the hell does that mean?"

"Come with me," he said, "and you'll see."

"Come where?" I demanded. "What is this about, Ariel? Why did you kill them? What in heaven and earth do you want from me?"

"There are more things in heaven and earth, my child," he said, singsong. "I told you, I only want the best for you. I want you with me, my dear. Now that you have come into your full powers, I'd like to show you what you can do, what we can be. Leave your human life behind, Lilith, child of night, and come...with...me."

His voice carried a Presence, the strongest I'd ever experienced. It drew me toward him, viselike, inexorable. But the kether in my blood resisted it, as if along with Sebastian's soul I'd absorbed some of his ironclad control. Or some existential human power of free will.

"I'll come with you," I said, through gritted teeth. "On one condition. You must release Danny to me, unharmed and alive. And leave Sebastian alone."

Ariel cocked his head to one side. "Would that not be two conditions?"

"You heard me, you two-timing, murdering, lying excuse for a demon. Take me. Leave my friends alone."

"Done," he said, without hesitation. Then he turned, striding toward the closed window. When he reached it, he simply passed through it as if it were no more solid than smoke and walked onto the rooftop balcony beyond.

Spooky. So that was how he got in and out of places so easily. *A cat who walks through walls,* Sebastian had called him.

I pulled on my jeans and buttoned up my shirt with shaking fingers. Sebastian's abandoned jacket lay on the floor, and I snatched it up, wrapping it around myself. An unexpected weight in the right-hand pocket bumped against my hip. Sebastian's pistol. He'd loaded its clip earlier with the remaining silver bullets we'd salvaged from Tobias. It pulled down that side, but the coat was well-made. It would hold, I hoped. It comforted me, having the weapon there, even if I barely knew how to use it.

My wings didn't seem concerned with my shirt or the jacket, any more than Ariel's seemed concerned with his black trench coat. They didn't snag on it, but rather passed right through to rise triumphant above my head.

I spared one last long look at Sebastian's still form, then followed Ariel out into the night.

I didn't risk the demon's flashy window trick. No need to crash through Sebastian's glass as I had his life. There was a perfectly good door that led out of the master bedroom to the balcony. Ariel had probably chosen to step through the window just for theatrical effect.

He waited for me at the edge of the roof. His wings gathered and hunched around his shoulders, the way a hunting hawk would hunch on a wire, head swiveled to watch my progress. "Dawdling, Lilith?"

The kether suffusing my body insulated me from the worst of the cold. Barefoot, I stepped toward the dark figure of my old friend and new enemy. I had to stop myself from glancing back with longing at the square of yellow light behind me, the light of Sebastian's home, the warmth of the human world. "I'm here now, aren't I? And my name is still Lillian, you know."

"Is it?" His eyes glowed at me, twin lanterns in the dark. "Little fledgling, you know that's not your real name, don't you? Those human names will come and go as they do. But you, you have your wings now. You've earned a real name, just like the rest of us. Lilith, our oldest name, for our youngest fledge. Are you ready to fly, child of night?"

A sense of *deja vu* flooded through me. I'd stood with Ariel once before, looking down at the lights of San Francisco spreading like a jeweled blanket below us. With the dreamlike memory from that night at the Ritz came a twitch of fear. Good gods and little monsters, did we have to fly away from here? Why couldn't we just use the perfectly serviceable stairs, followed by the perfectly serviceable road?

But Danny was out there, somewhere, afraid and alone, or unconscious and defenseless. In fact, I had a suspicion of where Ariel might have taken her and I didn't like it one bit.

"I'm ready." I tucked my hands deep into the pockets of the leather jacket, where the heavy, cold, unyielding metal of Sebastian's pistol lent me small but tangible comfort.

"Good. Follow." With a single beat of his wings, silent as an owl, he leaped into the air.

Just like that, then? I spread my own wings, stretching them to their full span. As I did, the dream I'd had while kether-starved came back to me. I knew then in my bones what to do, as if a genetic memory had unfolded from my cells into full form.

I beat my wings once as my once-mentor had and leaped out onto the updraft, wheeling after Ariel, two shadows that climbed into the city sky like a pair of giant, noiseless raptors.

WE FLEW EAST. I'd expected that. We followed the same tack as the little pins had taken in Sebastian's tracking app. But the world below me now looked very different from the map. The Bay Bridge stretched from the Peninsula to Richmond, a single strand of pearls over dark water. Beyond it, the myriad cities of the Northern California mainland became much more difficult to differentiate: clusters of lights like barnacles, tangles of highways like phosphorescent kelp. We flew fast, our speed enough that moisture streamed from my eyes. Each slow beat of our great dark wings carried us for miles as we hurtled inland.

From time to time, I fell behind, caught in air currents that pulled me off course or sometimes breathtakingly downward through pockets of warm or cool air. When I did, Ariel would circle back around to me, and his words of soothing encouragement and instruction dropped down the wind to me. It made it less likely that he planned to lead me far from home and then lose me, or fly me around until I became exhausted and plummeted from the sky. Besides, exhaustion didn't seem to present much of a problem. With the kether-strength throbbing in my blood, I could probably fly all night.

What did he want from me? Why threaten me, misdirect me, and then compel me to follow him? And why in the hell was he being so kind, playing the mentor again? My anger propelled me forward, and I flew faster to catch up with him. Maybe he hadn't hurt Danny. Maybe this all had some purpose I couldn't guess at, more than one of his impenetrable games.

The freight train sound of the wind rushing past us made any back-and-forth conversation unreasonable beyond the occasional shouted word. As I started to figure the flying thing out and the novelty wore off, I had plenty of time to mull things over.

Ariel had never talked to me the way he had in Sebastian's bedroom. All that stuff about real names and showing me the true power of demonkind bore little resemblance to the tune he'd sung in my living room last week about all things in moderation and how I shouldn't think of it as a hunt.

Had I finally met the real Ariel? Or was his new story just more lies? And how did any of that explain why he would kill so many of our kind?

Ahead of me, Ariel flew on against the wind, a tireless shadow. We soared above the mountains now, the cold in the air intensifying as we began what felt like an endless climb in darkness toward a gap in the jagged peaks distinguishable only as black voids that blocked the stars.

How funny that Ariel had called me a child of night, yet I couldn't see in the dark. That seemed like a major oversight.

Experimenting, I focused my kether reserves on my vision. Within moments, my perception sharpened. The moon and stars now provided enough ambient light for me to see the darkened land spread out beneath us, forested slopes bounded at intervals by subtle ribbons of swift water. I wondered if my eyes glowed now, like Ariel's in the dark.

We gained the peak and suddenly, Reno glittered below us, the last outpost of humanity at the border of the desert. From our great height, the tiny flashing signs of the casinos took on a desperate rhythm, a hopeless canticle against the wild dark that lay beyond.

And then the city fell away behind us. A highway had led this way, long ago, but humans had abandoned it since they had surrendered the desert east of the Sierras to the wasteland. Drivers heading east towards the Rockies would go south to Interstate 15, which skirted the bad country, or they could go further south to Interstate 10 or far north to 84. Interstate 80 trailed away to dust a few miles out of Reno.

But we didn't go around. I felt surer than ever of our destination now, though I still didn't understand why. It filled me with a sick, inevitable dread.

Ariel was leading me straight into the heart of the Exclusion Zone.

Ariel was taking me to Tonepah.

NO MAN'S LAND

THE TRACKLESS DESERT STRETCHED BENEATH US AS FAR AS EVEN MY KETHER-enhanced eyes could see. The Exclusion Zone of the Tonepah disaster spanned a thousand square miles or more. It was dark and wild down there, but not as dark as I had expected. I glimpsed lights here and there, orange and flickering like campfires, or sometimes eerie and green, glowing like spots of phosphorescence on a nighttime ocean.

Life persevered in the wasteland after all, but what kind of life, I couldn't say. We began to drop in altitude, skimming just a few hundred feet off the ground. Faint sounds carried on the wind at times. The howls and screams lifted the hair on my neck, harsh voices without words. *It must be animal cries, coyotes or mountain lions.* Surely lands abandoned so utterly by human civilization would soon become a haven for natural creatures, even with a radiation load.

Still, I couldn't convince myself that every sound I heard had a natural explanation, especially when something huge swooped across our path on gigantic batlike wings. Another cubine? A huge, mutant bird? Some other kind of feral flying thing? Before I could make out anything more than its shadowy form, it had moved out of sight, swift and silent as a giant owl on the hunt.

Ariel's path turned south now, racing parallel to the uneven black wall of the Sierras on our right. After a few minutes, buildings began appearing below us, rearing out of the shadows like a giant's shattered teeth. Ruins, more accurately: burned out and blackened shells of civilization in grim rows and broken blocks.

We circled lower, over the remains of old tanks and military Humvees. Ariel had spoken of camps like these with such bitterness in the Ritz Carlton's Presidential Suite almost one week ago, against a background of comfort and privilege. That time and place seemed so far away now.

Ahead of us stood a structure less hollowed out and higher than the rest. Ariel's flight led us to this ruin, and we touched down on a roof that had only half-crumbled. My bare feet met the rough and dusty concrete, and once again, I had the kether-warmth to thank for shielding me from the sharp cold of night in the high desert.

Ariel stood still and silent mere feet from me, a winged silhouette against the stars. Only the flash of his golden eyes gave away his watchful gaze on me.

"Well?" My quiet challenge rang loud in that lonely place. "I've come as you asked. Where's Danny? What did you want to show me out here?"

His chuckle held no true mirth. "The truth," he said. "The history of demonkind…and its future. Welcome to Tonepah, child of night."

I glanced around us at the broken walls and decaying concrete. "If this is our future, it sure doesn't look like much."

"It's only the beginning of something, my dear. Reclaiming our power from the place of our destruction. Building a home that belongs to us and only us."

"Seems more like living in the radioactive past," I muttered. "Is that it? We had a deal, remember?"

"Tsh. So impatient, Lilith. That's your human blood speaking."

"And that's supposed to be an insult?" I edged closer, squinting to focus my night vision on his face in the shadows, not just the reflective amber glint of his eyes.

"It *is* an insult. Humanity is weak, ephemeral, short-lived, a flash in the pan. Demonkind is older, stronger, faster, more perfect. We were the first, you know."

"What do you mean, the first?" Despite myself, despite my distrust for him, I couldn't hold back my curiosity. "What is our real past, Ariel?"

"Oh, my child. Haven't you figured that out by now?" He unfurled his wings with a rush of displaced air, extending them to their full span. Unlike mine, his were black and opaque, a night without stars. "Little Lilith, we were angels once."

"Angels," I said, flat-voiced. "Seriously?"

I'd grown up in a household that believed in such things. The human whom I'd called my father had taught me of the Fall of Man and of angels, of bright beings cast from heaven. They were fairy tales I'd long abandoned. Yet... Once again, I remembered my dream in kether-drought, light sparkling on my shining wings, and uncertainty crept in with the memory.

"Not exactly," Ariel said. "But close enough."

"What the hell does that mean? Messengers of God? Is all that true?"

"No." Ariel closed his wings again with a snap. "If there ever was a true god, it was before the time of men or angels. I do not remember it."

A nihilist angel. That was a new one. I frowned at him, or at least at his outline. "Ariel, how old are you?"

"Old enough." He sighed. "Old enough that I watched humans rise from their knuckles to their feet, from caves into cities. Old enough to remember when we were called the Nephilim. Older than the oldest tongues of man. I've lived a thousand lifetimes, only to see our kind reduced to *this*."

He had lived a thousand lifetimes, only to become a murderer of his own kind. And that was if he was finally telling the truth, and not a whole new pack of lies. Had the atrocities he'd witnessed here driven him to this? Or had he rotted from his heart outward under the slow grind of time?

"I still don't understand," I said. "If you hate humankind so much, why kill other demons? Why Nepenthe? She meant something to you, I know she did."

"She refused me." He turned away, hunched again like a hunting raptor. His voice floated back to me harsh and clipped with fury. "She and her disciples chose humankind above their own. They loved their prey too much. They perverted the natural order. They exposed our secrets and for that, they had to be purged."

"Purged?" Everything he had told me about the dead succubi and his relationships with them had been a lie. "This is about ideological purity? That's fucking psycho, Ariel!"

"Ah," he said. "Resorting to an *ad daemonium* argument already. I expected better from you. You are my last hope, you know. Holding yourself apart from them even as you strove to mimic them."

I stared at him in horror. "So what, you killed them and tried to recruit me? Need I remind you, I'm half-human. I'm never going to meet your purity test."

"Every cambion has a choice," he said, without turning. "And every cambion must choose. It's your time to choose now. Predator or prey. Hunter or hunted. Power or weakness."

"What about Tobias?" I demanded. "Did you give him the same choice?"

"Tobias Kaine?" His tone danced between disgust and amusement. "He made his bed a long time ago. No, not him. He thought he had me. He thought he knew something, but he only got in my way."

"Then why me?"

"Stop stalling, Lilith. No more playing the middle. You don't get to take up with whichever side is most convenient in the moment. Time to grow up and join the real world."

"I think you're lying," I said. "I think you need me." He didn't answer, but the twitch and rustle of his wings as they resettled betrayed the nerve I'd struck. Emboldened, I circled closer. "That's it, isn't it? You know I can survive without feeding, the way you can't. I *am* independent. I generate my own kether. You need humanity to survive, Ariel, and I don't. But you can feed from me…"

The hunched wings shuddered again. He still didn't speak. He didn't even look at me.

My anger rose higher, the extra kether in my blood both a fuel and a leash for my rage. It held it taut as a notched bow. "Does that make you feel better, preying on your own kind? On your own blood? Does that make you feel pure?"

"You don't understand!" The words burst from him as he whirled on me. "We were free once. *They* used us for their pleasure and their wars. They tortured us like animals and bound our fates to theirs. Tonepah wasn't the first time, and it won't be the last, unless we stop them."

"I thought humans were weak, pathetic creatures," I said. "How could they possibly do all that?"

He ignored this. "You weren't alive during those dark ages, but I was. I lived through it all. I've tasted the terrible depths of their cruelty, their hatred, and their fear. I had no choice."

The bitter pain vibrating in his words chilled me to my core and gave me pause. He had tasted them. Had he fed on tainted kether so many times that it had twisted him and brought him low, brought on this deadly madness?

Then I shook my head. I couldn't excuse what he'd done. "Everyone has a choice," I said. "You chose hatred. You chose murder. You killed those succubi because they made a different choice. They chose to love. You said it yourself. Nepenthe went through the same thing you did, but it didn't make her a killer."

"What they did to us, to her..." His voice dropped low and flat. "We were both broken. What she chose wasn't love! She chose bondage."

I thought of Nepenthe's powerful Presence on stage in the Black Cat Club, her magnificence as she stepped into the light and held an entire room in thrall. If her spirit had been broken, she did not show it.

Then again, who knew what pain or anger she had held in her heart? Who knew what choices she made there and what compelled her? Not even Sebastian, whom she had cared for and perhaps even loved, had known that. Ariel, who knew her best, didn't seem to care. And I hadn't had a chance to ask her.

And now no one ever would.

"You fool," I said, calm and cold with fury. "You took her choice away."

And like an arrow from the bow of rage, I sprang at him.

SOME KIND OF SUPERHERO

MY KETHER-WINGS LENT ME UNEXPECTED SPEED AND FORCE AND I SLAMMED into Ariel with a bone-rattling crunch that knocked him sideways.

He made a noise like an eagle's wordless cry. The gusts from his wings raked my face in a desperate, uneven rhythm. "You're the fool!" Panting, he struck out at me. "You made the wrong choice, Lillian."

Silver gleamed in his black-gloved hand. I blocked his blow with a raised forearm and caught his arm, twisting it back.

He meant to kill me, just like he had the others.

His muscles bunched under my hand, straining to drive the stake toward my heart. We swayed together on the edge of the roof, a breathless, inelegant dance. Inches from mine, his face contorted, his snarl and burning amber eyes no longer anything like human.

"Not this time," I said, and flung him from me.

He fell from the roof for only a fraction of a second before his wings caught him and propelled him upwards. The wide span of his black pinions blotted out the stars above me for a moment, an angel in the negative. And then he disappeared.

I rose after him, searching the sky for any sign of my adversary. But even my kether-sharpened night vision could detect no trace of him.

I should never have let him out of arm's reach in the first place.

But no, Ariel wouldn't just flee. We hadn't finished this yet. I felt his presence in my bones, in my blood. Somewhere out there in the vast desert night, he watched me, waiting for me to drop my guard.

I hovered above the broken buildings, sharpening my hearing for the rush of air that would herald his return. "Ariel! Come out and face me. Don't tell me you're afraid of a lowly half-breed like me."

Nothing but stillness and silence answered me.

Then, from somewhere below in a block of half-crumbled barracks, came a faint, familiar voice. But it didn't belong to Ariel.

"Lily! Is that you?"

"Danny!" I dove toward her voice. Closer to the ground, her energy signature shimmered in the air, a diffused tangle of hope and fear and confusion. I'd know that desiderata anywhere: sea salt, cinnamon, and spice, sweet and bright as a beacon, like the light of home.

I followed her shining thread into the darkness of the ruins.

Rows upon rows of barred doors opened into tiny, barren compartments without bunks or commodes, just grates in the floor, like a kennel. Some of the bars on the doors looked twisted and torn, as if a giant's hand had pulled them asunder. A powerful explosion had long ago ripped through the outer walls, leaving half the rooms open to the air.

I shivered. The taint of silver hung heavy in the air, clogging my throat. Those bars weren't iron and the rooms weren't barracks. They were cells. No, they were cages, the kind made to hold people, and the cages had silver bars.

They'd kept demons here, torturing them like animals. Ariel hadn't lied about that after all.

In an intact cell about halfway down the shadowy corridor, movement caught my eye.

"Lily?"

"I'm here." I picked my way over fallen chunks of concrete and exposed scaffolding. My wings could have lofted me past the obstacles, but I kept them folded close to my body. I didn't want any part of me, ethereal or otherwise, to brush the poisonous bars on either side of me.

Danny came forward with halting, uneven steps. "Jesus, Lil. Is that really you?"

"It's me."

"Um, wow. Did you know that you're glowing?"

Taken aback, I glanced down at myself. My skin gave off a faint phosphorescence, like reflected starlight. "Never mind that. Are you hurt?"

"No." She gripped the bars that separated us, holding herself upright.

I winced before I remembered that the silver wouldn't hurt her. "Are you sure?"

"No," she said, with a small, shaky laugh. "I feel like utter shit and I have no idea what happened to me or how I got here. Or where here is, exactly."

"Well, I can answer that last one." And I could guess at the rest. "We're in the heart of the Tonepah Exclusion Zone."

"What?" Her voice rose, sharp with panic. "All the way in Nevada? You can't be serious."

"Dead serious." I held my breath as I examined the barred door, even though silver didn't work like that. I hoped. Still, my stomach roiled, uneasy at my proximity to the poisonous metal.

"But it's not safe here! The radiation from the accident..."

"It wasn't an accident." And it wasn't radiation that worried me. For myself, at least. But for her...

"Lily...What happened?"

"They blew us up," I said, half to myself.

"Huh?"

"Sorry." She hadn't meant then. She meant now. I refocused on her, hands buried deep in my jacket pockets. My bloodless fingers encountered the cold metal grip of Sebastian's pistol, wrapped in something soft and silky. I frowned. "Ariel happened. He brought you here."

Danny squinted at me, her desiderata swirling with confusion and alarm. "Ariel? Your incubus friend? But why?"

"Because he's a fucking psycho," I said. "And he's not my friend, not anymore. Probably not ever. He killed Penelope. He killed all of them."

"Oh, my God," Danny said. "You're kidding me."

"Not even a little. Stand back, ok? I'm getting you out of there."

"Lily, no! It's—"

"It's okay." I pulled on my gold gloves, a reverse burlesque. I'd forgotten about stowing them in Sebastian's jacket last night until I'd shoved my hands into my pockets and found them waiting there.

Danny backed away, wide-eyed. I inhaled, drawing on the eager kether waiting in my blood. Suppressing my aversion, I reached out with my gloved hands and tugged at the bars. Metal groaned as the door frame parted ways with the wall. The bars bent to my strength like low grade aluminum instead of silver-plated steel.

I tossed the broken door away from me. It clanged against the far wall and crashed to the concrete floor.

"Whoa," Danny said, staring. "You're like…some kind of superhero. I didn't know you could do that."

Her renewed shock and fear prickled through me again. But it held a subtle difference now that pierced me to my core. For the first time in our friendship, Danny was afraid of me.

"Neither did I." I forced lightness into my voice despite the heavy shadow on my heart. "Turns out there were a lot of things I didn't know about myself. There were a lot of things I didn't know about demons. But I'm still the same person I was, just…more so, I think."

"She doesn't believe you." The low, melodious voice came from behind me.

Danny gasped. "Lily, look out!"

I spun, backing away as Ariel strolled out of the shadows.

"You can feel it as well as I can, can't you?" he said. "She's terrified, Lillian, and with good reason."

"No, I'm not," Danny lied with stubborn loyalty. It was a kindness, but it was still a lie.

"She's right not to trust you." The weight of Ariel's presence pressed down on me. But he didn't mean it only for me. "After all, who's to say you didn't kill those succubi yourself?"

"You're lying." I clenched my gloved hands to keep them from shaking. "Why would I do that?"

"You've always feared discovery, Lily fair. Penelope and her ilk threatened your way of life, didn't they? She lived out loud, the way you never dared to live until now."

"Stop it," I said. "You're too late. I told Danny the truth."

"What truth?" His words washed over me, smooth, relentless, superior. "It's your word against mine, my dear. Come now, why would I hurt my own people? But you—you feared knowledge and you wanted your Sebastian. And Penelope stood in your way."

"That's not what you said a few minutes ago! You admitted it all, you—"

He cut me off. "You wanted him, so you took him, didn't you? After you got your rival out of the way, you had your way with him. Did you tell your friend all that, dear Lily? Did you tell her that's how you got your wings? Did you tell her how you suckled on that man's sweet immortal soul?"

"Shut up." Furious and afraid, I glanced over my shoulder at Danny. "I didn't—"

Her wide eyes didn't hold any comfort for me. "Lily?" she said. "Is that true? You and Sebastian...?"

"It wasn't like that. I—He—"

"He asked for it, is that it?" Ariel crooned. "Did he give his informed consent? Did he know the cost of the Exchange? Come on, Lily, admit it. You're no better than me. At least I'm honest about what I am."

"Don't do this." I faced him again. My hand slipped back into my pocket, my gloved fingers curling around the grip of Sebastian's gun.

"Don't do what?" Ariel stepped toward me, eyes aglow. "Don't rescue Danny here from her poor, deluded demon friend?"

I drew the gun from my pocket, flicked off the safety, and aimed it right between the demon's amber eyes. "Don't take another goddamn step."

In the dark, among the empty ruins of his haunted past, his harsh and mirthless laugh made a mockery of the genial, playful incubus I once thought I knew. That Ariel, quick to joke and slow to anger, full of youthful joy and mischief, had sloughed away over the past week. He had worn that face like a mask, and beneath it lay cold fury and glittering madness.

"You think that puny human weapon can stop me?" he said. "You really haven't learned anything about demons, then."

"I learned how to kill us, thanks to you." I cocked the pistol. "Silver bullets, asshole. Still think I can't stop you?"

Surprise and uncertainty flashed across his face before it hardened into arrogance again. Then he grinned, the mask coming down as his hands came up. "You wouldn't shoot me," he said. "You couldn't."

I bared my teeth at him in a return smile, and my answer burned acrid as silver on my tongue. "I spent all day practicing for this. Want to bet your life on it?"

"I know you, Lily." His tone had shifted, sweet as honey, cajoling and caressing. "And you know me. Come on, it's always been you and me. Remember? We had good times together, once. We could have those times again, if you just..."

"No," I said. "I don't know you at all. The person I knew wouldn't do what you did. The person I knew wouldn't have brought us here. No more games, Ariel. No more lies. I've had enough."

"I'm not lying to you." He sounded pleading now, repentant, desperate. "You're better than this. You're better than me, all right? You always have been. I admire you for that. You could make me better, too. You could save me. Don't be like me, Lily. Don't become me. Be better. Help me. Please..."

The words wrapped around me, almost tangible in their promise. My hand faltered, the pistol dipping. He hadn't turned out to be who I thought, true. But trauma and unimaginable pain had made him this creature in front of me now, this blacklight angel, the silhouette of something beautiful and terrible and broken.

I had loved him, once. Parts of him, at least. And in his way, maybe he had loved me too. He'd wanted me with him in his imagined future, us against the world. He had chosen me. He had...

He had fed from me.

He had *claimed* me.

And he had kidnapped Danny.

My head came up, and the gun came up with it, though the hand that held it trembled now. My vision swam. Dimly, I saw him move, like a shadow falling over me. "What did you do?" The words came out thick and toneless, my tongue stumbling over the syllables as though he'd struck me dumb. "What did you do to me?"

His voice when he spoke came close to my ear, his breath hot on my neck. "Nothing that you didn't ask for, Lily fair. You consented, remember? You said yes to all of it. Every time. You let me in. You knew what I was. You let me—"

Acid rose scalding in my throat, and I wheeled toward him. The gun pointed at the dark space between his stretching wings. They seemed to take up the whole world. "Get away from me," I said, choking. "*Get away!*"

But I still couldn't see right. I shook my head to clear it, wrapped in the shroud of his Presence.

"Careful, Lily," he murmured. "Or you might hurt someone you love."

As he said it, my vision cleared again. He stood before me with Danny held close to his chest, facing me. Her wide eyes fixed on me, filling with tears. His broad fingers splayed around her throat, not tight enough to stop her breath, but enough to tell me that he could.

"I'm sorry," she mouthed to me.

"Let her go," I whispered. "Or I'll shoot."

"Curious," he said. "Do you really trust your aim so much after one day of practice? Your thrall Sebastian must be a very good teacher."

"He's not—"

"Oh, give it up, Lillian. You and your high horse." He tightened his grip on Danny's windpipe. "I'll make you a counteroffer, how about that? Put down the gun, and I won't snap her neck. Even though it would be so easy. Humans are so very fragile, you know."

Danny shut her eyes. Her lips moved again. This time, the words weren't meant for me. She was praying.

"Santa Maria, *Madre de Dios*…"

Pray for us sinners, now and at the hour of our death.

I let out a breath, half a sob, and bent before him, laying the gun on the cement floor.

"Good girl," he said. "Kick it over this way, please."

Despair swamped me. I toed it toward him.

"Thank you," he said, and released Danny, leaning to pick up the weapon. "Ah, ah," he added, when I twitched. "Don't get any bright ideas. I wouldn't want to have to shoot you after all this. That would just be anticlimactic."

"What do you want?"

"You know what I want, Lillian." In one smooth movement, he grabbed Danny again, by the arm this time. She flinched, then froze as he trained the gun on her. "Now," he said. "Isn't this interesting? Silver bullets mean something deadly to us, but it's no different to her than the regular type. Either way it will kill her, won't it?"

I forced myself to remain calm despite the fear rolling off Danny's desiderata. "You promised me you'd let her go."

"Did I?" He grinned, teeth and eyes gleaming. "Let's talk about promises, shall we, my dear? You promised you would come with me in exchange for her safety."

"I did come with you! I followed you to this godforsaken place, didn't I?"

"Oh, Lilith fair. That's not what I meant, and you know it." He dug the barrel of the gun into Danny's side and smirked when she whimpered. "If you want to save her, you have to give her up. Give up that life and join my world without reserve. And when we strike, when our time comes, she and Sebastian will be safe. They'll be yours and yours alone. Your Claims."

"Danny doesn't belong to me," I said. "I never claimed her."

"Are you sure?" He tilted his head, considering her. "Because your mark is on her."

"Lily?" Danny didn't move, but her eyes slid sideways toward me. "What is he talking about? What claim? What mark?"

"He's lying," I said.

"Not this time, my dear," Ariel said. "I noticed it straight away. She's not susceptible to me. I can't feed from her and there's only one way that could happen."

I shook my head. "It's not true. I never touched her."

"It is true," he said, relentless. "The only way she could be immune to my considerable charms is if another cubine got to her first and staked her claim."

"You bastard! You're not even her type. She likes women, in case you missed that."

"I didn't," Ariel said, with his wide, shark's smile. "Did you, Lillian?"

"What the hell are you getting at?"

"Don't play dumb," he said. "It doesn't suit you."

Frozen like a rabbit in the high beams of his knowing gaze, I stared at him. I never touched her, except that one time, when she touched me. When she had tried to comfort me and gotten more than she bargained for. I made her promise never to touch me again. I hadn't staked any Claim.

I tried to catch Danny's gaze, but now she wouldn't look at me. "Ariel, stop talking in riddles and just say what you mean."

"I'll do you one better." His tone was pleasant, conversational even, but his eyes blazed. "Why don't we have a little demonstration? Come here, Lily fair, and give your friend a kiss."

"*What? No!*"

"Why not?" he drawled. "One kiss, Lillian. One little kiss to save a life."

"It's okay, Lily," Danny said in a small voice.

"No, Dan," I said, glaring at Ariel. "It's not. Not like this. You don't understand. He wants me to take your kether. He wants me to bind your soul and I won't do that. Not at gunpoint, not ever."

"Oh, for the love of your monstrous namesake." Ariel huffed, exasperated. "I just told you she's already bound. What can it hurt? Why the hell not?"

"I said no." I faced him, the beginning of a snarl twisting my mouth. "Not Danny. She's my best friend. I won't do it. You don't get to taint this with your sick power games. You don't get to take this from me, Ariel. You don't get to take everything."

"Don't I?" he said, still smiling that wide, cold smile.

And then he shot her.

FLY WELL

THE CRACK OF THE PISTOL ECHOED LIKE THE END OF THE WORLD, A DEAFENING, impossible sound that seemed to crash around us for an eternity. In that long drawn out moment, Danny crumpled with an agonized cry. Ariel watched her fall, his mouth curving, satisfied in victory.

"No!" Heedless of the loaded threat in Ariel's hand, I fell to my knees by my friend's side. She pressed her hand to her stomach, her face drawn with pain and shock. Dark blood oozed between her fingers.

"It's okay," she whispered. "I'll be okay."

I leaned over her, a sob catching in my throat. "What do I do? Tell me what I need to do."

"Pressure," she said, gasping. "Here."

I put my gloved hand over hers. She dropped it to her side, feeling for something under her bomber jacket. I frowned. "What…"

She shook her head, the barest fraction of a movement. I fell silent, her warning jangling along my frayed nerve endings. Metal glimmered as she withdrew her hand from her coat, and I had to control my instinct to pull back.

Not just any metal. Silver. A silver stake.

Where had that come from?

Ariel loomed over us. "She'll die if she doesn't get help," he said, his tone conversational. "And it won't be an easy death either. Bullet to the abdomen. That's a long, painful way to go."

"Shut up," I hissed over my shoulder.

He went on as if he hadn't heard me. "I can save her, Lillian. With your help."

My body shielded Danny's hands from his view. "What do you mean, save her? How?"

"You know how," he said. "The kether push. I can give her life force, even if I can't take it. But I need your strength."

I looked down at Danny. She pressed the stake into my hand, then put her other hand over mine, curving my fingers around it. Even that small motion made her flinch, her eyes squeezing shut.

"Danny..."

"Don't worry about me." Her voice shook, weakening with every word. "Don't let him..."

"I have to," I said. "I can't let you die!"

"Lily, no!"

I stood, ignoring her protest as I turned once again to face Ariel. My voice rang out clear and brittle as a winter's night. "What do I need to do?"

He stretched out his arms to me, welcoming me and damning me. "Kiss me," he said, and the note of command shivered through the words, drawing me into his embrace. "Come to me. Join me."

I stepped toward him deliberately and put my mouth to his.

He pulled me closer, holding me still, as kether flowed out of me into him. The sensation overwhelmed me. It made my head spin and my stomach sick, even as I surrendered to the kiss. He made a pleased, purring noise deep in his throat.

The stake slid out of my sleeve into my gloved hand without a sound. With the last of my strength, I drove it upwards between his ribs into his heart.

The sick, meaty thunk of it resonated down my arm, and his noise of triumph changed to a strangled scream against my lips. He staggered back, his face frozen in a ludicrous expression of outraged shock and pain.

I stood over him as he collapsed in slow motion, folding at the knees.

The glowing amber of his eyes dimmed as his long fingers scrabbled at the metal now protruding from his chest. He couldn't grasp it. His skin seared and curled where it touched the silver.

My own knees suddenly weak, I sank down beside him and pinned his arms above his head. The struggle had begun to ebb from him already with the blood from the wound and his fading kether. His wings, little more than shadows now, beat feebly against the ground, sweeping pebbles and chunks of decaying concrete aside.

"Lily fair," he said, hoarse and pleading. "Lily, please…"

I swallowed hard, but I did not release his arms. I had seen one of my kind die through Sebastian's eyes, but it wasn't like this. Not like watching him die with my own eyes, by my own hand. Despite myself, tears sprung to my eyes, splashing down to dilute the blood that bubbled from his mouth. I had to do this. If I didn't, he would never stop coming after me and everyone I cared about.

"I'm sorry," I said softly. I wasn't sorry for his death, just for whatever suffering had tainted and warped him like this, beyond saving.

His lips twisted. His wings shriveled away. He choked a little, turned his head and spit a flume of bloody foam, black against the concrete floor.

"I'm…not," he rasped. "Fly well…Lilith Knight."

His body convulsed, seizing under my hands. And then he went still, his eyes now fixed and lightless. I sank back on my heels, wiping my hands compulsively on my jeans. There was so much blood. Ariel's blood, and Danny's, human and demon, yet they both left the same stain.

I turned to look at her, and she met my gaze, her eyes wide in shock.

"Is it…done?" She propped herself up on her elbows. Her breathing rattled in the space between the words, ragged and labored. "Is he…?"

"Dead?" I rose, my legs unsteady and my voice harsh. "I think so." As I spoke, a strange sensation shivered over me: a wave of new strength, as if ghostly kether had flowed back into my body from…where? I jumped back, almost stumbling as I stared at the still form at my feet.

That had felt like…*Ariel.*

Theo's words echoed in my mind. *If we die, the kether becomes unbound, and their souls are released. The Claim is broken. They are freed.*

Ariel had put a Claim on me. He had more or less admitted as much.

Long ago, when we hunted together, and then again, on the balcony of the
Ritz. He had taken my essence, my kether, part of my soul. And now…

No, it couldn't be. Could it?

"What is it?" Danny's tone was reedy with panic.

"I don't know." I backed away from the fallen incubus and tried not to
shudder at the blood and dust that mixed half-slick and half-sticky under
my bare feet. I didn't want to put my back to the body, so I went around to
Danny's other side, crouching beside her. "Quick thinking with the stake.
Where did that come from?"

"Picked his pocket." Danny grinned, but it shifted into a grimace, her
face gray and her desiderata shot through with jagged pain. "Don't look
like that. Eighty percent of people who get shot somewhere other than the
heart or head survive it. I'll be fine."

Sure, eighty percent survived if they got to a hospital, if they didn't
bleed out first, and if they didn't get shot in the middle of no-man's land a
hundred miles from the nearest city. If they had transportation other than a
half-drained succubus to get them there. My wings had dissolved into
smoky shreds, their light dim and wavering, distant stars glimpsed
through a thickening fog. "I want to try something," I said. "I want to see if
I can stop the bleeding."

"That'd be…a good start." She laughed, winced, gasped. "How?"

I pulled off my golden glove, now stiff and tacky with blood. *Ruined.*
Oh well. I didn't foresee an encore on the burlesque stage. "This might be
weird. I'm going to have to touch you."

"Okay." .

"Not like he wanted me to." I spread my fingers out in front of me. My
hand shook slightly, my dark vision revealing smears of drying blood. I
shuddered again. *Murderer.* "I wouldn't do that to you. Not like this."

"It's okay," Danny said. "I trust you, Lily."

She did, too. It had never wavered, that trust, even under the beat of
Ariel's seductive lies. Now it shone out like a lighthouse in a storm, like
water in the desert.

Water would be a problem, wouldn't it? We had survived so far. But
even if I could save her now, what would happen when the sun rose? We
were stranded out here, where no humans dared to tread.

One problem at a time. I placed my hand on Danny's forehead. Closing my eyes, I said a silent prayer to anyone and anything that might be listening.

If this is Ariel's last gift, let it go to her. Let it heal where he hurt, fix what he destroyed.

My kether flowed into her, and I flowed with it. I felt it all. Her torn flesh, the bullet's awful wake. The bullet itself, a venomous seed nestled deep within her abdomen. I felt her fear, her pain, her love and trust.

My life for hers, if that's what it takes.

"Oh, my God." Danny sounded far away, but somehow less faint. "I don't know what the hell you're doing, but it's working. Lily, look!"

I opened my eyes, returning to myself with an effort. The taint of silver coated my tongue, metallic and corrosive, and I dropped my hand to my side. A numbing sensation traveled up my arm, creeping toward my heart.

I ignored it, squinting down at Danny's side in the non-light. Beneath the blackened hole the bullet had burned in her jacket and shirt, the wound had begun to close. Her body knit itself together as I watched, torn flesh replaced with smooth new skin. "Whoa. Did I do that?"

"You did that." She looked up at me, eyes wide. "What did you do?"

I sat back with a shaky laugh. The numbness had reached my shoulder now, spreading like cold fingers in my chest. "I'm not entirely sure. I've never tried that trick before."

"Hell of a trick," Danny said. She sat up, her movements slow, experimental. "Now what?"

"Now we get out of here." The words clustered thick and clumsy in my mouth. Everything still seemed very far away. A sudden headache throbbed in my left temple, heavy as a funeral march. "Can you walk?"

Could *I*? Shit. Had I given her too much? Or was it the silver after all?

"Maybe." She used the wall to lever herself up, her careful movements telling me she was still hurting. I had repaired her flesh, but that slug was still in there, getting cozy with her internal organs. I couldn't touch a silver bullet with my power. Instead, I had to work around it.

"Let me help you," I said, rising.

Too fast. Darkness swirled in my vision, the kind of darkness no cubine vision could penetrate. It wrapped me up like a promise, comforting somehow despite the acid taste in my mouth. I'd done what I had come to do and now it was over. I could rest.

My life for hers.

"Lily!" Danny's voice pulsed with alarm, vibrant with the life I'd given her. But she couldn't reach me now.

Willingly, I fell into the dark.

WITH YOU ALWAYS

IMAGES CAME TO ME IN FLASHES, SLOW AND SHUDDERING, MOMENTS THAT flared and faded into the dark.

Someone shouted in the distance. Harsh, staccato words rang out as a clattering wind descended from above.

Light washed over us, bright as day. Rough hands grasped me.

Danny's face hovered above me, gray with worry like a clouded moon. We rose into the air as if carried on great black wings, hurtling toward an unknown horizon. Was I dying, or only dreaming?

Far below me, a body writhed, wracked and seizing on a stretcher, restraints digging into its flesh. Dark veins traced a leonine brow.

"Will she be all right?"

"Don't touch her, ma'am. It's not safe."

"But she's my friend! She saved my life!"

"Stay back!"

That face—there was something wrong with it. It was so alien, inhuman, the face of a demon.

It was my face.

"No!"

More lights flashed. The stretcher rolled down a long, white, never-ending hall.

Then a door slammed, and silence fell.

SOMEWHERE—FAR away, it seemed—someone was holding my hand.

"Lily."

Kether flowed into my veins, gentle, warm, and steady. I swam up out of dreams of torment and death, horror and blood, into a flood of morning sunlight.

"She's awake." I knew that kether—intimately, now. "Sebastian?"

"Welcome back." He released my hand, and his relief washed over me, poignant as summer rain.

"Where...?" Heart pounding, I tried to sit up, but my putty-like limbs refused to obey. I sank back onto the thin pillow, breathing hard.

With a groan, I craned my neck to the side. The movement hurt. My whole body ached as it had the last time I'd come down from a kether drain. Only this time, I'd chosen it.

Sebastian grimaced. "Do I really look that bad?"

In jeans and a black t-shirt, he looked anything but bad. "You look good enough to eat," I told him, and his sharp, startled laugh warmed me to my core.

Danny made a gagging noise. "Sheesh, you two. At least wait until I'm out of the room."

"Danny!" Sudden tears blurred my vision. "You're okay."

"Of course I'm okay," she said. "You saved me."

"Anytime," I croaked. "But how..."

"Sebastian here called in the calvary." Wry, she added, "We weren't sure for a while if the calvary would give you back in one piece."

"What do you mean?"

A pause stretched between them as they exchanged glances. "It's okay," Sebastian said, voice soft. "You're safe now."

"You rest," Danny said. "We can talk about all that later."

"Good." I closed my eyes. Their curiosity and confusion tinged the joint concern that swirled around me. I didn't want to think, let alone talk. I didn't want to remember.

But I did remember. I remembered too much, remembered what I'd done. And I remembered things I hadn't done and hadn't seen.

Ariel waited on the balcony of the Ritz. He tilted his head, listening expressionless to the ecstasy of two heedless lovers, biding his time. His black-gloved hand fingered the silver in his pocket.

Nepenthe's eyes fixed on him in fear and recognition. She saw her death in his face.

Sickness rose in my throat. I swallowed and swallowed again.

"All right, Lil?" Danny asked.

His lips curved with triumph as he sent the autopsy pictures to Tobias, while I lay in kether-drought on the bed behind him. My bed. Days later, the same smile of cold satisfaction twisted his face as he painted those hateful words on my wall.

He'd slipped my phone into his pocket, tapping out just the right words to draw Danny to him and Sebastian to me.

He'd watched me with Sebastian, invisible on the other side of the glass.

"No," I rasped, dry-mouthed and stumble-tongued.

"What do you need?" Sebastian sounded far off now, his voice somehow garbled to my ears. "How can we help?"

Slipping, I was slipping again into the dark.

How could I remember what only Ariel had seen?

He had me fooled from the beginning. That devil's mask he'd shown me before he'd drained me had been nothing but a kether-trick of air and light and shadow, illusion and misdirection. And I bought it. I bought all of it right up until he wanted me to see the truth. I'd played right into his hands.

His whisper teased at my mind, clear as if he too sat beside me.

"I'll be with you always, now. So, who really won in the end, Lilith fair?"

"I did," I said, teeth clenched. "I won. I'm alive, and you're dead."

"Lily?" Danny's voice pulled at me, bringing me back. She hovered over me, forehead creased and her desiderata swirling with worry. "Who are you talking to?"

"Nobody. It doesn't matter." *He* didn't matter. "Not anymore."

I smiled up at her and pushed the darkness down.

LILY 2.0

TWO WEEKS LATER, THE AIR IN MY APARTMENT HUNG THICK AND PUNGENT WITH the scent of the fresh paint on the bedroom wall. I cracked the kitchen window, sat at my small table, and unpacked the box that held the contents of my old work desk. My coworker had brought it over, apologetic and nervous, in a hurry to leave again. I hadn't kept him. My firing came as a foregone conclusion, even a relief.

The box didn't have that much in it. I pulled out a framed photograph of my swearing-in before the court and my law school diploma. Beneath it, I found my nameplate, my Distinguished Young Lawyer award, a set of decorative scales, and a sad, scraggly plant with long drooping fronds that had languished among my stacks of pending case files for months.

I picked up the plant and placed it on my windowsill where it might catch a sliver of the late afternoon sunlight. After considering it for a moment, I filled a glass from the tap and watered it. I didn't like its chances with Delilah always on the prowl for something to chew on, but I could at least give it a fighting chance.

I'd spent the last six years at the DA's office, working twelve and fourteen hour days, trying to prove myself worthy, trying to atone for my own past crimes. But I'd made no lasting friends there. I'd kept everyone at arm's length, and in the end, my keepsakes amounted to nothing more than a cardboard box half-filled with accolades that didn't mean anything and a neglected houseplant that had seen better days.

I stacked the photographs and the framed diploma on the table to deal with later. Tomorrow, my job search would begin. But tonight, I had a party to go to.

Right on cue, my doorbell rang and sent a flight of agitated butterflies fluttering through my stomach. I checked myself out in the small mirror that hung over the stove. I had dressed in a work blouse and skirt at first, but at the last moment, I'd changed my mind. The blue silk blouse that Sebastian had given me on our first morning together complemented my eyes and brought a slight flush to my cheeks. The buttery-soft jeans hugged my curves and the black booties put a spring in my step.

"Hello, Lily 2.0," I whispered to my reflection. Then I pulled on my thin leather driving gloves, went to the door, and let Sebastian in.

He stood for a moment in the doorway, eyebrows raised and lips quirked in a half-smile, looking me over. "Nice outfit."

"Thank you. Someone with excellent taste picked it out for me." I gave him a once-over of my own. In a slim-cut navy-blue blazer, dark jeans, and white button-up, his dark hair slightly tousled, he looked downright delicious. "You clean up pretty well yourself. Thanks for agreeing to be my date to this shindig."

He laughed. "Thanks for inviting me. Are you ready to go?"

"Yes—no. Come in for a minute. I have something for you."

One eyebrow arched higher, but he stepped inside. I darted down the hall to my room and returned with his coat and a shoebox.

"I had it dry-cleaned," I said, holding the items out to him. The coat had needed it because it had soaked up a considerable amount of blood.

"What's this?" He frowned down at the shoebox and lifted the lid to peek inside. Then he glanced back at me. "Not the most secure storage procedure for firearms. Maybe you need another safety lesson."

"I'm sorry I didn't give it to you before," I said. "I've been...I needed time. This has all been a lot."

"I see," Sebastian said. He didn't say anything else. He didn't ask what was a lot. He just looked at me with eyes that shone blue as the autumn sky. Coat over his shoulder and box tucked under his arm, he withdrew the gun and released the magazine. His frown deepened.

"What?"

"There's a bullet missing. And—" With the barrel pointed at the floor, he racked the slide, once and then twice. The sound of metal hitting my hardwood floor rang loud in the silence. "One in the chamber."

I looked away. "It's a long story."

He didn't push for details. He put the disassembled weapon back into the shoebox and, to my surprise, held it out to me. "You should keep this."

"I don't want it. Besides, I don't even know how to put it back together."

"I'll teach you," he said. "I mean it, Lily. You might need it."

"Between the two of us, I'm not the one at risk of being eaten by a demon."

He didn't laugh. With a sigh, I gave in and took the box back from him, placing it on the table next to my work detritus. He followed me and picked up the photograph of my swearing-in.

"Hey! Give that back."

"You look different here."

"Well, yeah, I was six years younger and I had bangs." Ariel had liked my hair like that, bobbed and fringed. It took me years before I dared to grow it out.

"I like how you look now," he said mildly, stunning me into momentary silence. He set the framed picture down and his too-observant gaze traveled over the rest of my sad little collection.

"We should get going," I said, to forestall any questions I didn't want to answer. "We're going to be late."

He nodded, grave, and offered me his arm. After a moment, I took it, and we went out together, down the stairs into the late sunlight.

BY THE TIME we got to Ladybirds and found a parking spot that met Sebastian's fussy standards, the sun had dipped into the fog bank cresting offshore and the late fall chill had set in. But the backyard garden glowed with paper lanterns and hummed with voices and laughter.

Danny detached herself from the crowd and waylaid me as I stepped out onto the patio, her desiderata lit up like the lanterns strung across the courtyard. "Lily, you came!"

"Of course I came," I said, and hugged her—carefully, of course, so our skin didn't touch. In the desert, when I saved her, when I almost died, I'd given her back whatever I'd taken from her all those years ago, and I refused to mess that up. She was free, not bound to me anymore. "I wouldn't miss it for the world. Congratulations."

She stood stock still for a moment in surprise, then hugged me back tightly. "It doesn't seem real yet, but I'm so glad you're here." She released me and hugged Sebastian too, leaving him with a bemused expression. "Both of you," she added, and waggled her eyebrows at me.

I rolled my eyes. "Stop it."

"Never." She winked and headed inside to the bar.

"She likes you," I told Sebastian.

He chuckled. "She likes that I called in a favor and got a Marine helicopter to fly you both out of the wasteland."

About to respond, I started when my phone buzzed. I pulled it out of my purse and made a sour face at the caller I.D.. "Want to get drinks?" I hit the decline button and put the phone on silent, tucking into my back pocket.

"Sure," Sebastian said, but his brow creased. "Who was that?"

"Just Tobias Kaine." I sighed. "He still wants me to do that interview and come out as a cambion live on-air."

"Are you going to do it?"

"No!" I stared at him, taken aback. "If he wants someone to go public, he can do it himself."

He shrugged, hands half-raised. "Just asking."

Danny and Berry burst out of the bar's interior together and saved me from having to answer. Both women were flushed with excitement, and behind them came a smiling bartender carrying several champagne bottles and a stack of plastic flutes.

Danny seized a glass and spoon from a nearby table and struck them together. The conversations around us hushed, and everyone turned to look at her.

"We have an announcement." Danny's voice shook slightly. "As some of you may know, I had a smidgen of a brush with death a few weeks ago.

It made me realize that I didn't want to live without this woman right here." She turned to Berry and they joined hands. "I asked Berry to be my wife, and she said yes."

"That's right," Berry said, with her sparkling smile. "We're getting married!"

The crowd broke into wild cheers, and Danny's desiderata swelled around her, mingling with Berry's into a joy so bright I had to look away. I turned to Sebastian, and found his blue gaze fixed on me, his expression grave.

"May I kiss you, Lily Knight?"

I flushed, remembering the way those eyes locked with mine when I told him I needed his control. I wanted that again, wanted the full force of his kether rushing through me.

Sometime. Not now. Right now, he needed time to grieve Nepenthe, and I needed time to process. We'd agreed to take things slow, to date like normal humans. But that didn't mean I couldn't accept this small offering.

It didn't mean I couldn't taste him.

"Yes," I whispered, and he bent and covered my lips with his, gentle yet firm, like a promise.

I tipped my head up and savored what he gave me.

EPILOGUE

6 MONTHS LATER

ABOVE THE OLD-FASHIONED GABLED ROOF OF THE DELTA ALPHA MU fraternity house, a fading red stain spread across the overcast sky like blood slipping from an open vein. A late-season storm had come and gone just before sunset, and the wet pavement gleamed with reflections of warm yellow light from the open windows of the house. Masculine laughter and shouts echoed across the lawn as fraternity members milled about in the common room, setting up tables stacked with food and alcohol.

Tonight would be a night to remember, but not for the reason they thought.

The real reason stood hidden in the shadows under the trees outside, her muscles coiled, ready to spring. Her lips curved at the humans' restless exuberance, the undisciplined energy drifting out to her on the evening breeze. She ran a quick hand through her hair, tousling her honey-blond waves into an artful tumble past her bare shoulders, then tugged her black miniskirt up another inch and the neckline of her sparkly red top a little lower.

They had what she wanted in there, and they didn't stand a chance.

She shouldn't have come here, not again, not after what had happened last time, but she couldn't help herself. It was so easy, so simple, the way so little in her life seemed these days.

This, she was certain of. This, she was good at. She was born for it. She needed it.

Her nostrils flared as one of the young men stepped out onto the porch. This one had an edge to him, a subtle darkness that both repelled and drew her. He believed he was the predator on the hunt, the one who held the power.

It made him the easiest kind of prey. Her father had taught her that.

"We are gods among them," he'd told her. "But you must never let them see it. Humans have always killed their gods, and their hubris has always been their undoing. They can't stand knowing that they are less than us. Don't let them see, but always remember that you are more powerful than any of them." His amber eyes glowed with pride, and he had brushed back a lock of hair from her face that matched his own golden curls. "You're special, darling Evie. Don't ever forget how much."

She had never forgotten it, not yet. She tried her hardest not to. But now and then, doubt crept in.

If she was so special, why hadn't he stayed?

As the months stretched on since his disappearance, her hopes had dimmed for his return. He'd left her with only his destination, San Francisco, and the name of an old friend he'd gone to visit, a lawyer named Lily Knight who was a cubine just like them.

Surely he wouldn't have left her alone for that long without sending word unless something bad had happened to him. Maybe he had let a human see him for what he truly was, a god among men. Maybe they had killed him for it.

Whatever the reason, she had to make her own way now.

She would find Lily Knight. She would find out what happened to her father.

But first, she would hunt. She was hungry.

These days, she was always hungry.

***

Thank you for reading! Did you enjoy? Please add your review because nothing helps an author more and encourages readers to take a chance on a book than a review.

And don't miss more of the Cambion series coming soon, and discover
Erin Fulmer at www.erinfulmer.com

Until then, read more paranormal fun with <u>CATCHING HELL</u> by City Owl
Author, D. B. Sieders. Turn the page for a sneak peek!

You can also sign up for the City Owl Press newsletter to receive notice of
all book releases!

SNEAK PEEK OF CATCHING HELL

BY D. B. SIEDERS

Life goal number 666: Be the kind of woman that when your feet hit the floor each morning, the devil says, "Oh, crap. She's up!" — T-shirt worn by Jinx McGee, demon hunter.

I saw my first demon when I was five. I was looking in a mirror.

I'd been brushing my teeth when I glanced at my reflection and noticed I wasn't the only one there. A presence lurked behind my eyes. It wasn't nice. It was angry, and it wanted out. I don't know if the demon living inside me had always been there, but that was the first time I saw her. My scream almost burst my own eardrums—and my older sister's since she'd been standing beside me. She didn't see the demon. Neither did my mom. They both thought I was imagining things.

They were wrong.

Still, when life gave you lemons, you were supposed to make lemonade. Life gave me a demon, so I became a demon hunter. I never learned how to make demonade, let alone market it.

Since becoming a demon hunter, I'd seen six hundred and sixty-four demons…not that I was counting. Demon number six hundred and sixty-five targeted the man I was currently surveilling on my latest stakeout. The man and his demon stalker were my latest demon-hunting assignment in downtown Nashville, and shit was about to go down.

Like the fact that said demon stalker was currently speeding through the air on a collision course with a wagon full of drunk tourists who, being strictly human, couldn't see it.

"Look out," I yelled. Damn it, where was my partner? She'd texted to tell me she was stuck in traffic, but I could've really used some backup. While unseen, the freaking demon could do real, visible damage.

Crap, I couldn't wait for Lacey. I'd have to break protocol and go after the demon and its mark on my own.

The demon, who was a streak of black only I could see, whizzed past the man it was targeting and through one of those pedal taverns clogging up Broadway and Second Avenue. The damned demon knocked the penis headband right off one of the intoxicated bachelorettes. Bummer. I enjoyed phallic party favors almost as much as I enjoyed drunken revelry. It would've been fun to pick it up and crash the party. I could shove one of those drunk gals off her stool and take her spot, pretending to be a sixth cousin twice removed who no one really knew, but she endeared herself to the group anyway.

Jane McGee the jolly bridesmaid had a nice ring to it. It was what a gal my age should be doing.

Too bad I was working.

I was Jane "Jinx" McGee, demon hunter, and would be until I figured out how to get rid of the demon currently possessing me. Long-term relationships, marriage, white picket fences, and a whole lot of normal weren't possible for me at the moment. I'd have to settle for keeping drunken bridesmaids and the rest of humanity safe from unauthorized demon shenanigans.

"Oh! Sadie lost her wiener."

The shout came from another one of the rolling bar's occupants, who nearly fell out of her seat laughing, blissfully unaware she'd been dive-bombed by a demon. Damn it, tempters moved fast. I hoped this one was corporeal. They weren't necessarily easy pickings, but easier to catch than the immaterial variety. Corporeals were still fast as all get-out, even with a body, but at least they couldn't transform into ether and vanish into vents or gutters.

I needed to slow the demon down, but first I had to follow it to the more private location it had chosen to claim the human it was after.

One of the gals on the pedal tavern handed me a shot glass as they passed, and I downed the contents in a single gulp while they hooted and hollered, giving me high fives and shouting, "You go, girl." The bachelorettes had good taste in tequila, at least. Ah, to be an ordinary human, blessedly unaware of creatures that go bump in the night. With a nod of thanks, I returned the glass and set off at a light jog to catch up with the demon's target.

The oblivious human hadn't noticed the demon tracking him, of course. Poor sap. He just had the inexplicable compulsion to go wherever the demon had chosen. Demons had all kinds of nasty mind tricks they used to manipulate their prey. If they went around openly on the attack, people would soon become too afraid to leave their houses and hunting would be harder.

Demons were ambush predators.

I'd been watching the demon's target, a middle-aged father of two, for over a week. He'd been demon marked, and when one of our patrollers spotted the demon's mark—invisible to humans but a clear signal to other demons the bearer was already taken—she'd called us in. I'd been waiting for the demon, intent on siphoning his soul—or stealing his life-force for those who didn't believe in souls and such—to lure him to a secluded location so it could claim its next meal.

The poor guy looked more like Santa Claus than demon chow with his jolly round face, salt-and-pepper beard, and generous belly. The red Hawaiian shirt really tied the look together, but thankfully he wore khaki pants instead of red crushed velvet.

That would have been completely over the top.

I wondered what this guy had done to get a bull's-eye on his back. The case file was scant on details but flagged as urgent.

No matter. I'd find out soon enough based on the flavor of tempter demon he'd attracted. He ducked into a dark alley—how original—as his demonic stalker finally stopped zipping around and stepped out of the shadows. With my enhanced senses, I observed the demon stalker assume a form that halted the man dead in his tracks and turned him into a quivering mass of lust and longing.

Ah, a succubus had tagged him. My demon stirred within me, excited by the prospect of hunting.

She's hungry. So am I.

I shuddered as my demon's thoughts echoed in my mind along with her ravenous excitement. Fortunately for me and the rest of the planet, my demon was under my control and on a tight leash. She'd only taken over fully once when I was young, but once had been enough.

Nothing would ever be as bad as that, and the memory sent a shiver down my spine.

I couldn't afford that little trip down memory lane. I had work to do. And I needed my personal demon, who I called Hannah, to do it. When I summoned Hannah, she gave me the strength and demon magic to subdue and capture rogue demons. The fact that she was much more powerful than the tempter demons we hunted—and currently an unknown entity in the demon hierarchy—made us a winning team if a tad unstable. The obsidian mirror Hannah was bound to was supposed to prevent her from taking over and going off on any unauthorized side quests or killing sprees.

That made the two of us unsuited for normal careers like banking or public relations. Since it took a demon to find one, however, being demon possessed made me eminently qualified for my current job.

I reached the alley and took a closer look at its occupants. The corporeal shape-shifting succubus's appearance surprised me. Instead of going all hot, sexy, and ho-bag, she went for plain and unassuming. Her baggy skirt, oversize sweater, and mousy brown ponytail screamed librarian. Maybe her mark had a book fetish?

Nah.

I unsheathed my enchanted knife, crept down the alley, and prepared to kick some demon ass.

Don't stop now. Keep reading with your copy of <u>CATCHING HELL</u>.

And visit www.erinfulmer.com to keep up with the latest news where you can subscribe to the newsletter for contests, giveaways, new releases, and more.

Don't miss more of the Cambion series coming soon, and find more from Erin Fulmer at www.erinfulmer.com

Until then, find more paranormal fun with CATCHING HELL by City Owl Author, D. B. Sieders.

Jinx McGee saw her first demon when she was five...and looking in a mirror.

Never one to let life get her down, Jinx turns her unfortunate state of demonic possession into a lucrative career as a demon hunter. It takes a demon to find a demon, and Jinx's demon is very good at finding the others...when inclined to cooperate.

The hours suck, management's deadly, and her co-workers are almost as weird as her. Still, it beats retail. And once she's worked enough cases, she'll figure out how to separate from her demon and live happily—and normally—ever after.

But a rebellion is brewing in hell that threatens earth. The leader thinks Jinx and her personal demon hold the key to his victory. Jinx's boss believes it makes her a liability and puts her on a strict deadline to sort it out—or else.

And now the smoking hot demon who once broke her heart conveniently shows up to serve as a consultant on the case. But Jinx suspects he knows more about the rebellion than he's saying.

Trust her sexy demon ex with a second chance and her rag-tag band of fellow demon hunters, including a wolf-cursed Russian giant, a genius with a Wikipedia demon, and the twin demons of technology? Not likely. But it may be her only chance to save the world from Armageddon.

Please sign up for the City Owl Press newsletter for chances to win special subscriber-only contests and giveaways as well as receiving information on upcoming releases and special excerpts.

All reviews are **welcome** and **appreciated**. Please consider leaving one on your favorite social media and book buying sites.

For books in the world of romance and speculative fiction that embody Innovation, Creativity, and Affordability, check out City Owl Press at www.cityowlpress.com.

ACKNOWLEDGMENTS

To my editor, Heather McCorkle, thank you for believing in me and my book. Your edits made this book into the best possible version of itself. I think you understood Lily sometimes better than I did, but in the end, you made it clear that I was an equal partner in the editing process. I'm so grateful for your patience and hard work, not to mention your ongoing support as I hurtle toward my release date.

Thank you to the whole team at City Owl, especially Tina Moss for graciously answering a zillion and one questions (sometimes more than once) and Yelena Casele for her marketing expertise. To my copy editor and to the design team who produced a cover that took my breath away. And to the Owls author group, thanks for welcoming me with open wings and making me feel like one of the gang! It's been an honor getting to know you and learn from so many talented, amazing women writers.

To my Pitch Wars mentor, Ren Hutchings, who talked me through the highs and lows of this wild year while making me a better writer in the process—I'm so lucky to count you among my friends! Thank you so much for choosing me as your mentee, sharing your boundless energy and positivity, and helping me navigate the publishing world. And to the Chaos Bakery, my mentee crew, I love you all so much. Sorry this one doesn't have any time travel in it!

To my creative communities who nurtured me over the years: without you I would not have started writing as an adult, let alone still be doing this. A special shout-out goes to the Pirates of the Caribbean Livejournal community of the early aughts—especially those who stuck with me after I left the high seas behind. Dani, Victoria, Sharon, Alys: though our fandoms have diverged, your friendship remains a treasure of the highest water.

To the Twitter #WritingCommunity, you are a light in the wilderness of the internet, bursting with talent and joy—I learn from you every day. Especially to the Cool Kids Table, thanks for letting me sit with you! I'm so glad to know all of you. Your kindness and comraderie has meant the world to me. To the 2021 Debuts, thank you so much for showing me how it's done! And to the whole Pitch Wars community, particularly the class of 2020: we went through it together in a particularly hellish year and you are all absolute rock stars who are going to take the publishing world BY STORM. I'm so proud of us!

To the G-Spot Squad: you are my people. I am so grateful I found you. Jen, Jenny, Chey, Gabriella, Johan, all of you bring so much unique insight, knowledge of craft, and mutual encouragement. Gladys, I had no idea when I asked you for that invite it would change my life. Abby Jackson, my first real CP, I'm so honored and lucky to have you! Mel Grebing, I could never thank you enough for your unflagging support, your constant generosity, and your saintly patience with my lagging beta reads. Mia Tsai, I owe you so many drinks at the end of this apocalypse—thank you for your friendship, your wisdom, your humor, and the benefit of your red pen, which has absolutely leveled up my writing craft. Keir Alekseii, you are a goddamn delight—thanks for being trash for urban fantasy with me and sending such kind messages to my britches when they and I needed it. Adria Bailton, who read my first chapter right before I got my contract, sorry it took me so long to let you read the rest of it—your support has meant so much through this year!

I can hear the orchestra warming up to play me off, but I have to slip in a few more. To my mom, for sharing her love of stories and teaching me that I wanted to be a writer before I could even hold a pen. To my therapist, whose guidance shaped this journey to find out what it's like to live according to my values. To my furbabies—my volunteer editors, snuggle buddies, and crack social media team—who taught me how big I can love two small sweet souls and who keep me sane, grounded, and on task every day. To Debby and Jim, for embracing me as family. And to my found family and friends, you know who you are. You give me life.

And finally, to my husband, Jake, my best friend, my rock, and the finest alpha reader any woman could hope to marry. Thank you for always being in my corner, for loving me even when I am the loopiest of froots, and believing in me even when I can't. You were there when I wrote the last line of the first draft of this book, and you were the first person to read it in its entirety. You will shake your head at me for saying this, but I don't think I could have done any of this without you, because you make it safe for me to be my whole self and go after my dreams. I love you so much, Bear.

ABOUT THE AUTHOR

ERIN FULMER is a public benefits attorney by day, author of urban fantasy and science fiction by night. She lives in sunny Northern California with her husband and two spoiled cat daughters named after famous dragons. An elf at heart, she craves wild places, yearns for the sea, and put all her proficiency points in Nature with a specialty in bird facts.

Through her life's many unexpected twists and turns, words have always been her element and her escape. When she's not writing or working, she enjoys hatha yoga, taking pictures of the sky, playing board games with friends, and napping like it's an Olympic sport.

www.erinfulmer.com

facebook.com/ErinFulmerWrites
twitter.com/ErinFulmer
instagram.com/erinfulmerwrites
pinterest.com/Erin_Fulmer